ADVENTURES

in

RADIO ASTRONOMY

ACKNOWLEDGMENTS

People who helped get this book into your hands:

Mike Andberg, Kel Brandwood, Sky Warisala Chatuchinda, Adrian Clausell, John Crain, Joseph De Mario, Mary DeSantis, Chris Engstrom, Lorri Espinosa, Elizabeth Farleigh, Carla Funk, Ayesha Ghaffar, Barbara Greene, Charity Kroeker, Binh Nguyen, Carla Pinilla, Alexandra Pratt, Isabella Dineo Rammala, Laurel Robinson, Alex Rowe, Ana Rowe, Michael Rowe, Maxwell Saltman, Lenore Sack, Kayla Schales, Nigel Stanford, Laura Stockdale, Jo Stockdale, Cameron Van Eck, Crystal Watanabe, Erik Wecks

The students of Lesobeng Secondary School, Lesobeng, Lesotho

Max's voice edged toward excitement. "Dad, you should finish your book."

BOOK 1

- Welcome to the WisPR chatroom
- Bot is ON
- Users online: 1
- Today's quote is:

"I dipped my hand into the flowing stream, and, with it half full of the glittering liquid, started in amazement. The moon had lit it with silver rays, and in my hand I held a star in all but shape."

Ruby Violet Payne-Scott
Nepean Times
29 December 1923

1. @WeDontKnow

The right shoe was nowhere to be found. The left one sat alone; its fat sole like a slab of ice cream straight from the freezer—the deformed shoe for the deformed leg, for the deformed spine, for the deformed shoulder. She stared at the misshapen thing, the *accommodation* shoe, the *special sticks* shoe, the *allowance for being late* shoe.

She hobbled around the room, opened the door to the shared closet, peeked under the metal framed cot. No shoe. Back to her feet, her brow furrowed, she placed her hands on her hips, surveying. It had been many years since someone had hidden her shoe or her canes, regular pranks in primary school. And the thought came unbidden that it was her roommate's boyfriend, Hendrick. But that was silly; college students wouldn't.

Cannot be late.

Cannot be early either, but this was a less likely option as the minutes passed with only a single shoe.

Then she was sitting on the bed, hands clenched in the covers. And there's the shoe rolled in the blankets. The *good* shoe, the right shoe, not the wrong shoe. Somehow wrapped in the blankets of her bed.

The formerly missing shoe wasn't the only cause of tension in her shoulder. She breathed in and out slowly, imagining herbal tea in a cup, steaming on a cool morning under the acacia tree, like the detective from her books. She let the emotions fade to a gray sheet of serenity from a thunderstorm of annoyance.

And now she regretted her accusatory thoughts about Hendrik, even though he rolled his eyes at her canes, her shoes, and her boyish name, and he and Debs made loud sex noises as if she didn't exist. The silver lining, of course, being they spent a lot of time at Hendrik's place, leaving Harry freedom in the dorm room to study, write code, play games, do her research, alone.

Her neck hurt. Her trapezius muscle, to be exact. Tensed as usual. The one on the left, which pulled more weight than the one on the right. She rubbed it unconsciously before bending to put on the orthotics. The good right shoe and then the other fat-soled deformed shoe, the very expensive orthotics. She stood and brushed her rumpled outfit, thrift store pants, and white secondary school shirt topped by a green jumper. She didn't bother looking in the mirror, because it had a towel over it. And she tried not to look at Debs's side, where another mirror hung with photos of Debs, her friends, her family, Hendrik, and random cute sayings like "Live, Laugh, Love" and "Hit like a girl!" (picture of an American girl swinging a baseball bat).

Hobbling *(Look at the hobbit!) Shut up!* out of the room, she headed to her appointment, her backpack filled and swung over her right shoulder, the higher shoulder, which would hurt later. She began the trek across campus.

"Koko," said Harry, standing in the doorway of her professor's office and lightly tapping the jam, speaking the casual term for knocking.

"Haretsebe, come in. Please, sit down." Professor Von Tonder gestured to a seat.

On the wall above the blond professor hung a poster of a dancing woman floating in the cosmos whose dress was the rings of Saturn. *Casini*, it said in broad script. Harry liked the poster and noted it every time she came to see her adviser. It was from the Very Large Array, a radio telescope in America. She'd looked it up. She would go there one day. To New Mexico in the United States, to see the collector dishes laid out like a giant Y on railroad tracks a dozen kilometers long.

"Your marks are good this quarter. Congratulations."

Harry's sore shoulder eased and she relaxed in the seat. She worked hard. She was smart. She was focused. She was certainly smarter than the other students, whose days were distracted by social events and socializing, preening and parading. Her mind, of course, moved ahead, disentangling the comment and analyzing it, interpreting it with the alacrity of a single exam question, which carried the weight of an entire year's result. Unbidden came a thought: *My marks are good, as they have always been, so why do they need comment? Unless?*

Dr. Von Tonder continued, "As you know, the project you've been working on has been using data primarily from MeerKAT."

Harry swallowed her thoughts. "Yes, Professor, I know it." And she did, of course. One of the largest radio telescopes on Earth, MeerKAT opened fully in 2018 in the Karoo and was now the source of much of the data being used in research by her professors.

Harry saw a hint of something on the professor's face and body. A flick of the eyes away to the wall above Harry's head as she asked Harry to sit. A tiny pull back of both shoulders as she shuffled papers. *Is Dr. Von Tonder embarrassed?* And then Harry knew for sure. A hint of anger welled up inside her. *I cannot believe this!*

"Well, the on-site grant has funds and MeerKAT operations has agreed to let me send a student." Again, with the eyes looking down. "I see you applied for the on-site position?"

"Yes," said Harry, bitter, knowing. "I've applied every year I've been at uni."

Von Tonder paused and looked at Harry. The look they exchanged was worth at least a hundred words, if not the true thousand of any photograph. At that moment Harry knew she could stand up and leave and everything that was going to be said and everything that needed to be said had already been communicated.

"I'm sorry, Ms. Tladi, but another student has been selected. I wanted to talk to you..."

Harry's eyes squinted at the poster above Dr. Von Tonder's head, at the space girl with a dress of Saturn's rings, rather than look directly at the professor. For a moment she thought about the spacecraft *Casini* and what it would be like to float in space around Saturn.

They always did this. A consolation prize. An alternative. Since you can't run, you can be scorer—here's a clipboard and a pen. Since you look funny, you can raise and lower the curtain, but not be on stage. Go and prepare the plates, others can greet the guests. Sum the books, but don't work the register. Never the star, never the spotlight. Oil for the machine, not the readout. An integrated circuit, not the computer. A vein. A vestigial organ, not yet removed. A hidden part. Always the clockwork, never the clockface.

"... the code would be very useful and there might be a stipend available, after the work is reviewed, of course."

Harry gathered herself. Professor Von Tonder had been reading from her notes, following a script, not sure how to engage with a disfigured person. *So enlightened these academics are,* thought Harry. *So benevolent. Always looking out for poor Haretsebe. Gaaah!*

Harry spoke up. "Who?"

"Who what? The software would be used by..."

"No," interrupted Harry. "Who got the position at MeerKAT?"

"Ah," said Professor Von Tonder, looking sheepish again, acutely aware that she'd been put on the spot. "That would be Marko Ndebe."

"I have more experience than he does." Harry stated this as fact, not a challenge.

"Well, it is the sum of the application, not specific elements..."

Harry continued, an annoyance welling. "... and probably better grades, though he doesn't share his, for a reason?"

"Again, the position is very competitive and more than one factor..."

"And I've actually produced research that will be published. Has he?"

"Ms. Tladi, all our students are capable of producing excellent research, Marko included."

"My disability should not preclude me from working at MeerKAT."

Professor Von Tonder paused. "No, it should not... and it did not." But then there was a momentary break in her speech. Too long. Time enough to identify the lie. And the eyes darted down again. Another tell. Harry waited.

"The applications were reviewed by the committee..."

She'd heard enough. *Same bullshit in bullshit's clothing.* "Never mind. I get it." Harry had been sidelined before. She knew the drill. There would be an alternative. One good enough that she couldn't complain lest she look like a sore winner. But never the starring role.

"What's the coding job?"

They talked, Harry half listening, since the job seemed simple enough. She'd probably be able to do it in her sleep, literally dreaming the code and waking up to write it all down. Something about a Fourier transformation on frequencies, apparently.

No MeerKAT though.

Back at the dorm, Harry was online in the WisPR chatroom.

Kathode: So did they give you a reason?

WeDontKnow: It's outside the scope of this chat. I just didn't get the on-site internship.

(**bot** says: rule 666: no personal info.)

Kathode: If I were there... well, f*** MeerKAT, never liked that show anyway, though they are a matriarchy, so... Apply to the VLA, @WeDontKnow!

Kathode: Is the bot censoring the f-word? @Lollipop is pissing me off.

Clarity: Seriously? Some personal issue is what they used?

WeDontKnow: No. Of course they said it was 'highly competitive' and blahblah. Some stupid Y-chrom got it.

(**bot** says: rule 700: hating specific Y-chroms is allowed, even encouraged. Hating all Y-chroms is déclassé.)

Lollipop: That really sucks moose dicks. I wish ill on them. @kathode, only censoring for you, friend.

WeDontKnow: @lollipop, such language!

Kathode: I was hoping you'd get the on-site position. I wanted some 81 cm datasets and harmonics of same. @lollipop, f*** u, lol.

Clarity: 81cm? What's on that frequency?

Kathode: go-gos. You know I can't say.

(**bot** says: rule 668: go-gos = Our Lips Are Sealed)

Clarity: Too much lip sealing causes oxygen deprivation

Lollipop: And other deprivations

WeDontKnow: MeerKAT doesn't observe there. And gross.

Kathode: Fine. Boss's research project needs that lambda.

Clarity: So apply direct to MeerKAT?

Kathode: No time for that. Plus, we aren't academic. We're private. We'd never get approved. And I'm not even sure how to use it. Boss is close-lipped, doesn't talk much.

Clarity: Lots of lip today. Lol.

Lollipop: I might be able to help. I have some access to data feeds. Post details here and I'll see what I can do.

Kathode: Muchas gracias, mi amiga. I'll put together a spec.

(**bot** says: rule 692: translation: thanks, my **attractive** friend.)

Clarity: Attractive? @lollipop, what's up with the bot?

Lollipop: heh, did a little AI upgrade. Everyone needs a boost now and then.

Clarity: ko

(**bot** says: rule 692: translation: ok)

The conversation continued until Harry's roommate breathlessly threw herself through the dorm door and dumped books, an overnight bag, and what looked like an armload of dirty clothes on her bed.

"'Sup, sister?" said Debs, always cheerful. Looking freshly scrubbed. (So probably just back from doing *it* with Hendrik, yuck.)

Harry ignored her.

"Harry, what *is* up?"

Sitting on the bed, pillows wedged akimbo, Harry shifted her shoulders, stretched them, and continued to chat online. "I'm chatting about science, okay?"

"With whom?" Debs puttered and spoke with a faint accent. Harry knew it was from years spent abroad.

"With... science people, okay?"

"Your online friends, right. The Scooby-Doo gang, only online. Yabba Dabba Doo."

"That's Flintstones, not Scooby. Shush."

Debs cocked her head, pushing her long brown locks behind her shoulder. "You know, if you'd let me get you laid, you wouldn't be angry all the time."

Harry tried not to smile, but her effort was unsuccessful. Sex talk always made her nervous, made her blush and smile, cracked and splintered her defensive walls.

"Bitch," she mumbled, typing. "I hope a *tokoloshe* eats your brain."

"They don't eat brains." Debs hung her bookbag on her chair and sat. "Or do they?"

"I didn't get the MeerKAT position."

"That is probably terrible news, but I'm a literature major and you keep everything to yourself, so I'm going to interpret that as awesome news. I'm so glad you did not get a MeerKAT! Congratulations. Please come out with me now. Hendrik took off to some weird event that has to do with mealie genetics. I'm alone and I really want to flirt with boys."

"What's stopping you?" Harry was multitasking. One window had the WisPR chat open, and in another she was working on Dr. Von Tonder's script. The spec for the analysis software was downloading as she chatted. It would probably take some time to get all the files synced to her repository.

"If I flirt with them, then I have to deliver, you know, the goods, right? And I'm kinda seeing someone, right?" Debs continued, "So I can be wingwoman and you can be, well, woman. Right? I flirt, you fuck."

"Gross," said Harry.

"I giggle, you wiggle."

"Stop."

"I implore, you whore."

"Seriously. You are gross. I'll wear my headphones and you can use your toys, which, by the way, are loud."

Debs stood and put her hands on her hips, which Harry knew was an escalation. "Now who's being gross? And I don't need to get any action. You, however, do. Months we've been roomies and you haven't even given a guy a second look. Probably not even a first look. Are you gay? I was afraid to ask, but fear is the mind-killer, so et cetera, are you gay?"

Harry kept her eyes focused on the screen. "What is up with you? I have work to do. Please leave me alone."

"I thought you didn't get the Kitty Kat job."

"MeerKAT. No, I didn't get the MeerKAT job. Like you care. They gave me a big project instead."

"Holy shit. Harry, you're gay?"

"I'm not gay. Stop." She typed rapidly, trying to frown but failing.

"Your nickname is Harry. You dress like someone named Harry. You must be gay. Do you fancy me?" Debs twirled, ballet training from the past evident.

Harry looked up briefly, continuing to type. "I do not fancy you. And you wouldn't be my type if I were gay. You value white skin, pimples, and examples of colonial misogyny. And you've known me for months, so you know I don't like girls. I like to be left alone." She returned her attention to the screen and waved at the floor. "See the shoes? Cripple shoes. Okay? Guys don't date cripples. *Motho ya holofetsang.*"

"What is that?"

"Means 'cripple.'" Harry continued to focus on her laptop.

"You shouldn't use that word."

"I'm allowed. Being disabled has its privileges."

Debs looked like she'd eaten something bitter, then smiled. "Well, you are wrong. Guys will sleep with anything and anyone. Their brains are made of pure hormones. They simply live and breathe only for sex. Basically, everything they do is to serve us women in return for sex. Art? So they can paint us nude. Language? So they can sweet-talk their way into our thongs. History? So they can think about people who had sex before them. Science? So they can.... science us into sex. Men spend money for sex, you know."

Harry said nothing, concentrating for a minute on pulling one of the Git software repositories, which was easier than thinking about hormone-related activities.

Debs leaned over Harry, looking at the laptop screen. "This science stuff is great, but you need to think about you. You've suffered a great loss. The Kitty Kat job was probably awesome. But now it's gone to the great place in the sky where jobs go and... whatever. Focus on me for a moment. I'm bored. Please let's go out. You never go out and I'm not going out alone."

Harry looked up, eyes narrowing. "Debs, I have work to do. I just got turned down for the one thing I've wanted while I've been at uni. And it's likely I'll never get that thing. I just wanted to go to MeerKAT and look at the stars. Why is that so hard for everyone to understand? I'm going to put on my headphones now and work." Harry reached for her headphones, hoping that Debs would back off. She didn't want to put on her headphones, but extreme times call for extreme measures.

Debs spoke up. "Detective Ramotswe would go out with me and get herself some man-care."

"That's not true, and how do you know about that?" Harry looked at her bookshelf. "Those are mine. Can't I have anything that's just mine?"

Debs waved at the bookshelf filled with a complete set of novels about the No. 1 Ladies' Detective Agency and its owner, Detective Precious Ramotswe. "You, Harry, are an open book. You wear your soul on your sleeve. And I, a literature major, have obviously read several, not all, but several, of these detective novels. And I can even quote from one. Let me remember... How..." She changed her voice to a low drone... "*How sorry she felt for white people,… always dashing around and worrying themselves over things that were going to happen anyway.* I'm paraphrasing, but you get it, you see yourself in her. The brilliant, quiet, unattached detective, and lots of Setswana, which is a beautiful language! But Harry, please, even Ramotswe goes and finds that mechanic or something, right? And she was fat—that's a disability."

"Fat is not a disability in Botswana!"

"Well, you aren't fat anyway, so it's all good. Get some decent clothes on and let's go get you a consolation drink and fuck for not getting the kitkat thing."

"MeerKAT!"

"I'm waiting."

Harry closed the laptop. She was now so distracted by the firehose of rant from Debs that there was no way she could do any more work.

"Don't wear a bra."

"*Hele!* I am not hobbling naked to a bar with you."

"You have barely any boobs and guys will want to look down your blouse. You have to advertise. Marketing 101."

"I don't want men staring down my shirt." She closed her eyes, a headache coming on. "But a beer, a dark beer—that I could use. Or one of those coffee drinks they make. Something sweet."

Debs rummaged in her nightstand and came up with a multi-chained gold choker, which she held out.

"Fine, wear a bra. But I insist you put on a necklace or something. Can't have everyone think I've gone lesbo with you. And don't bring that weird tool kit you keep on your walking sticks. In fact, no walking sticks."

"You are absolutely disgusting." Harry put her own hand to her throat as she gingerly took the necklace.

Debs took it back. "Turn around."

Harry took the towel off the mirror on the closet door as the tall brunette reached around to lift the glittering strands over Harry's head. When it was clasped, they looked in the mirror. Harry's breath caught in her throat. The woman in the mirror with the golden torque was objectively attractive.

Debs said, "Wow, you look good. Ugh, I'd kill for your skin. Stand up straight, smile a bit more, and you'll have them panting." Harry paused in the mirror, fingering the choker, then spun toward Debs.

"Are you intellectually stunted? I cannot stand up straight!"

"And I said no canes."

The Hasty Pudding was as crowded as usual, with students and locals. A beat of house music thrummed through the bar, and the swish of conversation filled the warm gaps among the mingling crowd. Harry, shorter than most, saw jackets and shirts, smelled colognes and perfume and sweat and beer. She leaned on a chair and took in the bobbing heads and drinks held at chest level. Debs approached the serving counter and spoke to the bartender, who turned to get their drinks. Shortly afterward, she held out a black drink with foam on top, a fruity concoction held to her lips.

Harry took her drink and sipped, the cold whipped cream on top sticking to her upper lip. Debs reached over with a tissue and wiped it off. "No sense looking like you just..."

"Stop!" interrupted Harry, but it came out with a laugh and she cough-choked instead.

They walked around a bit, Debs saying hi to a half-dozen people she knew. "Let's go find some guys for you."

"I don't want to, and I have nothing to say."

"That's okay, guys do all the talking anyway. Just smile and pretend you're like a third as smart as you are. Or a quarter. Or just smile..." Their wandering brought them to a darker corner of the pub.

"Haretsebe?" said a voice from behind them.

A bespectacled young man with short-cropped hair whom she recognized from one of her physics classes was talking. He introduced himself as Michael and stood awkwardly with another young man; the four of them began to converse. Harry had little interest in the chatter, but it was nice to be there while Debs and the others talked. Michael's eyes wandered over her face and neck and she became self-conscious. His stare was both flattering and unnerving. She fingered the choker at her throat, knowing it shone in the light. His eyes were glazed and wet, and his tall forehead shone with sweat in the bar lights.

Eventually, a lull in the conversation came and Debs sent the other boy off to get more drinks. *Debs is so capable of just telling men what to do. Maybe she is right, they are just here to serve us in return for...* That thought did not continue. But there was a relaxing of her torso, her hip, her leg, which happened rarely, as if balance, so elusive, was brought back into her twisted body.

Their conversation continued, filled with jokes and laughter. Some stories from school. Discussions of favorite teachers and other mundane topics. Time passed quickly and pleasantly. Harry found herself outside the bar, still chatting with Michael and his friend, her fingers grasping his jumper. The evening was winding down; a small crowd had gathered to say their goodbyes at the late hour. Cars flowed by on the busy street. Michael touched her hand. She looked up at him. Was he tall? Everyone was tall to her, but he wasn't unreasonably so. He leaned down and his breath, heavy with alcohol, flooded her face. She was unsure and backed away, letting go.

"*Ausi*, you are so pretty. Just a kiss, yes?"

Harry shook her head. This wasn't the activity she wanted. She liked the attention of his voice, his eyes, but was not ready for his body, his touch. She wanted him out of her personal space, away just enough for her to see him as a whole rather than just his shiny cheeks and sleepy eyes.

"Okay." He smiled. "I'll see you in class?" Without waiting for her to answer, he turned and called out to someone and was gone.

She was alone now, and looked around, not realizing that she'd been relying on the boy's arm for support. Her fingers grasped at a shirt. Then mumbled an apology as the owner turned and looked down at her hand disapprovingly, pulling the fabric away. Uneven on her differing orthotics, the world swayed. Then she was falling, grasping at a random coat, which smelled of smoke or weed or something, causing a complaint.

Her fall continued and the woolen fabric was pulled with her, her hand unwilling to let go. A person behind was jostled toward the street. The commotion spread outward, ripples in a pond of people; the tight crowd elbowed itself into confusion. Some fell and others pushed, the chaos spread, her unintended sphere of influence widening. Noisy voices, angry and loud, rose. Then, with a jarring impact, she was on the ground, the sidewalk cool against her cheek, a forest of legs around her. Someone stepped on her hand. She took a deep breath and yelled, "Get off me!" The foot lifted off her hand, followed by a scuffle, and another person was falling near her. She covered her head as the crowd convulsed.

A car horn blared and tires squealed. A scream. Harry rolled and scooted backward as quickly as she could through the understory of legs until she reached the wall of the pub, where she sat against it, stunned.

Debs leaned over, unusually tall. "Harry, are you okay? I thought you'd been run over by the kombi." Debs was gesturing wildly at the street where the crowd had moved. Someone shouted for an ambulance.

Debs helped her up. "I saw you chatting with that guy. Good job, girl! And then there's a pile of people."

Harry shook her head, still processing. A crowd was near the stopped kombi. Sirens of emergency vehicles were in the distance. She heard snippets of conversations.

"Is he conscious?"

"Is he breathing?"

"Has someone called his family?"

Debs, always the gossip, inched forward and spoke to someone in the crowd, then returned to Harry.

"Someone got hit by the kombi. Gosh, I hope they aren't badly hurt. I think he might even be someone in your program, Harry."

She couldn't concentrate on what Debs was saying.

"Do you know a Marko? Marko Ndebe? I hope he's okay."

Professor Von Tonder spoke through an odd smile, Marko's accident an undertone in the conversation. "Since you are the one handling the data analysis, the other professors and I decided you should go. With the short time frame, you won't have a specific project. Your role will be to assist as needed. I expect your technical prowess to be in demand." Harry was beyond excited, despite a queer feeling from knowing the cause of her prize. She thanked Professor Von Tonder profusely, and they talked about the trip, the details, and other sundries.

Dr. Von Tonder gave her a small box. "Give this to Dr. Pratik Deep. He's a researcher at MeerKAT. It's a computer part, I believe. He said it's fragile."

2. MeerKAT Radio Telescope, RSA

The trip to the deep desert went quickly and the scenery reminded her of home in Botswana. It was flat and dry—an expanse of bush, velvety in the distance and shimmering in the heat. The facility comprised a half dozen white buildings squatting around a car park and very little else. The wide dishes of the collectors were not visible—the array of over sixty was behind a small rise to the north. She found her tiny room in one of the housing trailers and then joined a tour of the underground operators' rooms and the computer lab.

Navigating a stairway, she descended underground to the Karoo Array Processor Building, which everyone called the KAPB. Here was the control room where the telescopes were managed, and there were more rooms to hold racks of computer servers to store and analyze the many gigabytes of data collected every minute.

Though she had only a short time, the very first night she realized why it would be plenty. Deep in the middle of the Karoo Desert, there was literally nothing to do. The few scientists and engineers on-site entertained themselves by reading, dozing, or playing cards in the housing trailers, unless they were on call in the operations room helping reprogram the array or maintain any of the dozens of customized computers.

And after sunset, after the desert heat of the day faded, the temperature dropped. So, despite being at the center of one of the most exciting advancements in radio astronomy in the twenty-first century, Harry was, she admitted, bored her first evening. She logged in to WisPR, but her friends weren't online.

Despite wanting to socialize and participate in an ongoing card game in one housing container, she also wanted to learn. She left her trailer and hurried across the chilly car park, her canes clacking, and descended to the KAPB to become more familiar with the layout and perhaps get a head start on her projects for the week.

In the tearoom, where staff had snacks and meals, she found a few engineers hanging out while computer programs ran. She peeked in and they beckoned her over. Introductions were made all around.

"You came with the group today," one young man said, not as a question.

"Not so fast, Slow Train," another spoke up.

Harry raised her eyebrows. "Slow Train?"

"Yeah, he's typically very slow at everything, so that's his nickname." Everyone chuckled.

"I'm actually very fast," said Slow Train, to more chuckles.

"Except when working," added another. More laughs and she realized she was the only female. Not surprising in STEM, but something she noted. She'd learned that her nickname could help put off unwanted male attention, so she introduced herself as "Haretsebe, but everyone calls me Harry."

The conversation continued and Slow Train, whose real name, he said, was Thabo Nthuse, offered a tour of the KAPB. But the KAPB was not very big, and when the personalized tour finished, she begged off to bed, shivering her way across the dark car park to her housing.

Over the next days, she made herself at home in the KAPB, hovering near the engineers and asking many questions about how the array operated. Many of the engineers she already knew from her work with Dr. Von Tonder. Putting faces to usernames she'd seen only in development tickets or in email was as exciting as anything.

In the operations room, Thabo came by and leaned over her, smelling of desert air and warm winds. "Harry, they say you are a wiz with computers, true?"

"Mr. Nthuse?" she responded, somewhat distracted by his presence.

"Please. Everyone calls me Slow Train. They really do. Dr. Von Tonder sent me an email. She said you are quick with computers?"

Harry smiled. "I'm glad she thinks so."

"We have a file server down. Not used much, but a researcher was trying to access it and couldn't. Need to get it back up if possible. Our other sys-admin left for holiday on the bus that brought you. Can you take a try to get it running?"

Now, this was fun work. "Yes, of course. I'd love to help."

"Okay, I've sent you an email with credentials. If you are on the ticketing system at the uni, you can log in with those and see the tickets. It should be assigned to you. There's a wiki on the file server system. Just close the ticket when you get the server running."

It sounded simple, and she was flattered by the level of responsibility. "Sure," she said, immediately taking out her laptop.

"You can work in the tearoom or in your housing, either way."

"Who reported the problem?"

"That'd be Dr. Deep."

"Oh, I have something for him. Where is he?"

"Not sure. He's usually around very early in the morning, keeps odd hours." He turned to go and then turned back, placing a large, warm hand on her shoulder. "Thanks for doing this. It's great to have some high-powered brains on-site. We need to look out for each other."

She hid her blush by bending down to get her rucksack with her laptop. When she looked up, he was already talking to someone else.

In the tearoom, Harry opened the ticket system and there was a new one for file server A12. "Not responding" was all the ticket said. It was logged by user "TNthuse"—Thabo—and assigned to her. *Not helpful, Slow Train*, she thought, looking at the bare message.

She ran through her credentials and saw she had permissions for the log files of the server, so she checked them, but they showed only a single error pinging the server and receiving no response. *Bloody unhelpful*, thought Harry. No log information. No description of the error. She wanted to solve the issue and really, at this world-class facility, she kind of expected better logging and debugging protocols.

She figured it couldn't be a very important server. And she was right—this server, she saw from the system wiki, was actually an archive with older files on it, not one of the live servers that were constantly being used. Her first step was to understand the network, which was elucidated in a wiki document. She read for several hours until her eyes tired and then headed back to bed.

The next morning, she found the box for Dr. Deep and took it with her to the KAPB. Over tea, some engineers and interns discussed an upcoming bike ride into the bushveld to see the radio signal collecting dishes. Dr. Deep was not around and her disability made biking an impossibility, so she spent the time reading the design documents for the MeerKAT server system in her room.

For lunch, Harry headed back to the KAPB tearoom and found that she'd missed Dr. Deep again. "He comes in at 2:00 a.m. or so and works out of one of the closets, playing with his antiques. You know professors, they the odd ones," said Slow Train with his thousand-watt smile.

Bored, she decided to work on the errant file server, catch a nap in her room, then come back around 2:00 a.m. to find Dr. Deep. In the tearoom, she set up her laptop. Having now worked at the facility in fairly close capacity for five days, she felt comfortable with the innards of the data network.

First, she tried to ping the server directly from her laptop. No response. Then she did her usual round of attempts to access it other ways. She used an isolated, direct connection, called a VPN, from inside the MeerKAT network and then one from outside. She tried to reboot the server remotely. Nothing worked; it was unresponsive. She tried using her root credentials—a privilege she appreciated from Dr. Ramposa, the MeerKAT administrator, but that failed as well.

Many of the file servers were virtual and hosted off-site. But server A12 was physical and located in a group of secondary computer racks in the KAPB. She packed her laptop in her rucksack and headed over to reboot the file server manually. The server rooms were underground as well, behind the operations room, down a white, brightly lit corridor. As she entered the server room, motion sensors turned on ceiling lights followed by the light whir of air-circulating fans. The stark space was filled with banks of computers, a spaghetti of blue and yellow wires hanging from each.

She scanned down the server racks, looking for the tags A1, A2, and so on until she found A12. She was surprised to see garbage strewn about next to the tall rack of a dozen black servers. Some bits of paper, perhaps broken glass, and a coin caught her eye. She bent to pick it up, leaning on one of her canes. First, she thought it was a ten-cent rand coin, given its copper color. There was a man's head on it, and closer examination showed it was a United States of America *one-cent* coin. She stepped back and her foot stuck. Someone had spilled juice or coffee, which had dried into a brown stain on the floor next to the aluminum racking. She scuffed her foot on the muck and silently cursed, making a mental note to tell Dr. Ramposa. These areas were not sensitive, but people should not be eating or drinking here. The mystery of the American coin could wait.

The lights were off on the black metal faceplate of server A12. On the back, a half dozen wires were attached to the various sockets. Normally, there would be green or yellow lights blinking next to these ports, indicating data transmission even if the server were not being used.

Stepping over the mess on the floor, she was going to press the reset button when she noticed a USB drive stuck into a connection port. It looked askew, as if it were not seated properly. A crossed pin on the USB port could cause a server to crash and not respond. But it was odd. Nobody accessed a computer like this nowadays. Everything was via network connections. There was rarely a reason to insert a thumb drive into them. Many servers didn't even have USB ports.

She wiggled out the silver thumb drive. It was covered with a crusty residue. After dislodging the thumb drive, she pressed and held down the reset button on the server, following the instructions from the system wiki. She performed a so-called warm reset, which would preserve the server's cached memory, hoping to capture the log file and isolate the error.

As the server rebooted, she looked around for something to wipe off the USB drive and found what looked like a napkin or tissue on the floor. Beneath the gunk, the faint image of a superhero could be seen engraved on the silver case. It was the type of USB given out at comic conventions, a kid's toy.

On the front of the rack, the server lights for A12 blinked and then changed to green, some flashing, indicating that the server was running. On an empty shelf, she perched her laptop and connected directly to the server using a patch-cord retrieved from a pile of similar cords nearby. She confirmed that A12 was back online. Interestingly, it was already being accessed. A cached image of the USB drive was in a buffer and was being copied. Too, logging had been disabled just after it rebooted. She made a screen capture of the IP address that was accessing the server and restarted logging. Concerned that maybe something was wrong with the server, she performed a cold reboot, which would cut off any outside access and wipe the cache, giving the server a fresh start. She was about to close her laptop when she remembered to open the ticket system and close out the ticket. She hooked the USB drive onto her keychain to keep from losing it.

On the way out of the server room she ran into Slow Train again.

"*Dumela, mon chéri.* How are you?" He was trying to be charming, she supposed, which was nice, but she wasn't interested.

"Your server is running. Now I've got to get a nap, Slow Train. Meeting Dr. Deep late."

He nodded, and then said, "Genius! Well, maybe tomorrow?" and he was already walking away.

When she got back to her room at 9:00 p.m., she couldn't sleep.

"Naturally," she muttered, staring at the ceiling.

She looked at the USB drive on her keychain and wondered about it. Whose was it? And why was it manually inserted into a server? She decided she was going to look at whatever was on it, to find its rightful owner. But just as her hand hovered near the USB port on her laptop, about to insert it, she had a moment of doubt. The drive could contain some virus or something else. There had been that weird ping by an external IP address when she'd rebooted the server. She pulled up the screenshot and did a quick reverse lookup on the IP address, but it came back unknown—just some anonymous IP address from North America. Throughout uni were posters and reminders everywhere warning to not click on unknown emails or use drives from unknown sources. And the garbage in the server room and the slightly uninformative ticket made her think twice. Too many red flags.

Maybe I'm being tested? Maybe this is a security test for me and if I put the drive into my computer, I'll fail? No, that's silly. I don't rank high enough for that kind of attention. But maybe? Or is this simply a bad drive? Maybe the server was down not because the USB drive was inserted incorrectly but maybe because of its content?

A mystery. She liked mysteries.

After having a packet of crisps and a can of soda, she pulled out an extra laptop, an old one she'd rescued from a recycling day at uni. She'd brought it only as an afterthought, but she was glad she had. She'd wiped it clean and installed an open-source operating system and some code of her own. Though slow, it was perfect for moments such as this—to review unknown files so that whatever was on it couldn't damage her existing work or steal anything from her. She booted the extra laptop and made sure it had no Wi-Fi—it was completely isolated.

She inserted the USB drive into an open port and ran a virus/malware scan. It came up clean. So that was a relief. With her file manager, she opened the USB drive.

Within the drive she found a single folder labeled *Zoonerat*, and within that folder was a nest of other folders, with various labels including *videos*, *broadcast*, *radio data*, *cymatics*, and others. The *radio data* folder contained files she recognized as raw data from radio telescopes. This made some sense. But videos? Intrigued, she drilled down further. The videos were in a standard file format, AVI—an older video standard, very common. She reran a virus scan, and again it came up clean. She wanted to watch one of the videos, but what Debs called her spidey sense was nagging at her. It could be something terrible. Maybe pornography or violence. Neither of which she wanted to see. Also, she wondered if the files had come from MeerKAT or from an external source. Was the owner of the thumb drive trying to move files onto the server? The USB didn't have any logging on it, and she didn't think the server had that kind of detail in its log either. And besides, logging had been turned off when she rebooted the server the first time, so probably there wasn't a record that could answer her question.

She pulled out her regular laptop and booted it up. Sitting with both laptops in front of her on her bed, she worked. She did a quick check of file server A12 and couldn't find any file called 1.avi, so regardless of anything else, the video file hadn't originated from server A12. But perhaps the files had originated on server A12 but then been deleted? She checked the server's logs and found no reference to the files. Though logs could be modified, that would leave other breadcrumbs and her search found nothing. So, this was another mystery. If the USB drive had actually been accessed, there was no evidence that its contents had come from or gone to the file server. It was an orphan.

She considered just turning the thumb drive over to Dr. Ramposa in the morning and being done with it. But she suspected that he would put it in his desk and forget about it. He was focused almost exclusively on research, and a minor mystery of a found USB drive wouldn't mean much to him, especially if the problem were solved. This was her mystery. And curiosity was one thing she'd always had. It had led her out of her parents' shop and into uni and finally here. She couldn't resist.

She vowed if the video appeared to be anything out of the ordinary—body parts of any type, pink or bloody, she shuddered at the thought—she would turn it off and hand it to Dr. Ramposa. Or just destroy it, take it out into the desert and bury it under a bush. She smiled at the thought.

She reconfirmed that her test laptop wasn't connected to any networks, launched the video player, and opened 1.avi.

What she saw surprised her. And she giggled at the absurdity of what she had imagined—dirty movies or angry terrorists—and what she was watching. It appeared to be an episode of a sci-fi movie. Thinking back on the folder, the words to the music did sound like "zoonerat" or maybe "sooner, rat" or something. There was a battle scene and then a scene in a laboratory. A couple talking through floating holographic phones. And then a doctor in a hospital saving a child.

She liked science fiction, watching *Star Wars* and the like since she was a girl, downloaded from the internet. And something about this was interesting, even compelling. There was a very garbled soundtrack, and the colorization was off, as if the video had been pirated poorly from a DVD or played with the wrong codec. The people were orange, after all. She admitted she wanted to see more.

Still concerned that something was hidden in the video, she decided to deconstruct it, looking for any type of metadata. Information could be hidden in a file. She'd read about this in her coding forums online; an example was pornography secreted within a Disney movie. There were many ways to make something look innocuous online when it contained devilish information. Too, she was deeply suspicious of where this had been found. Who would use a thumb drive on an archive server here at MeerKAT? She was concerned that pornography or horrible violence hid in a layer inside the sci-fi video.

She knew how digital videos were constructed. Much of her work for Dr. Von Tonder was writing scripts that made images and videos for astronomers. These programs took the data, which comprised coordinates and radio intensities of signals, and made beautiful images and even movies. For scientists to gain public trust and raise grant money, pictures were the better medium.

The first thing she noticed when she looked at the video file was the very minimal compression. Movies are made of frames. Individual pictures are strung together, each picture slightly different, perhaps a sixteenth of a second later than the picture before it. When shown one after the other, the human brain connects all these images into, literally, a moving picture. Mathematicians developed ingenious and complex ways to shrink both the individual images and the series of images that make up movies. So now almost no videos that you see are stored like the original moving pictures with complete frames.

But this video, 1.avi, was raw. There was really no reason to store a video this way. Unless this was the original video in pre-production, when the video editors at the movie production company were still making modifications to color and sound and everything else. That's when videos were stored uncompressed.

Harry rewatched the video and decided that this was the most likely situation. The video had probably been pirated from a movie studio. That's why she had never seen it. That's why it was raw. It was probably a clip from a show that had not been released. Some enterprising production assistant had pirated it and was going to sell it online before its theatrical release. But, of course, that raised the question of what it was doing on a thumb drive at MeerKAT. Perhaps someone here at MeerKAT had a friend at a production studio?

She mulled the situation and concluded this made sense. One, folks at MeerKAT were *uber*-nerds. It was possible that a few of them were into sci-fi and collected this type of content. Two, some of them, herself included, were above-average tech-savvy, so it wasn't out of the realm of possibility that a MeerKAT employee had a hobby that included hacking movie studios for unreleased entertainment. Third, and even more likely, she thought, though she wasn't sure if this was possible, the massive radio telescope might pick up many transmissions; perhaps it was an accidental grab from the airwaves and whoever found it streaming in the skies above simply wanted to save it. Or, fourth, someone was using MeerKAT to pirate movies intentionally.

It was late and she was tired. She pulled the USB drive, still connected to her keychain from the port on the side of the computer, and got back to her nap.

What seemed like moments later her alarm blared. Her phone showed 2:00 a.m. She rubbed sleep from her eyes, slipped some clothes on, and quickly brushed her teeth. Grabbing her laptop and a bag, she scampered across the frigid car park under a desert sky overflowing with stars and headed to the KABP. Inside, it was quiet. At this time of night, she didn't hear any voices. *Ha ha, I don't hear voices. Not yet.* She glanced in the operations room and saw just a single person who was busy, it seemed, with some calibration task. She cleared her throat and he turned.

"Dr. Deep? Dr. Pratik Deep?"

"You found me." He had an English accent.

"I'm Haretsebe Tladi, Dr. Von Tonder's student. You can call me Harry. I have a package for you."

He beamed. "Oh, my dear, I'm so delighted to meet you. The star computer wizard. The magician of code, they say."

She smiled at the compliment and took the small box from her rucksack. "I was wondering what this is," she said.

"Ah, yes, I'm sure you were. It's a vacuum tube." She must have looked confused. "Come, I'll show you." He headed out of the room.

She followed him to the end of the corridor. Before the entrance to the server room, he opened a door to a supply closet. Taking up most of the space was a gray service cart carrying what looked like several antique radios, their cases sleek and rounded, knobs and dials evoking bygone eras.

Dr. Deep rolled the cart down the hallway to the server room door. "I collect these." He pointed proudly to the radios. "Your timing is fortuitous. I was operating one several days ago and I lost a tube, blown completely. Tragedy. I usually have spares about, but I didn't in this instance. Sad." He held up the package from Harry and opened it, displaying a shiny glass object. "This is lucky happenstance."

"I've never seen a tube radio."

"Well, then let us get this fixed post-haste, shall we?" Harry stood behind the cart, leaning down over the radios. "I run it in the server room because there is a radio feed I set up from a dish to receive AM signals, and the feed terminates here. We could hear Martians if they were broadcasting, but I like to get the BBC from Gandhinagar, Gujarat. I lived there in my youth with my cousins. Too, sometimes I play Beyoncé." He chuckled, looking at her confusion as he struggled to open the back of the radio.

Harry took the little tool kit from the end of her cane. "Here, let me."

Dr. Deep looked on, fascinated. "So clever, my dear. Yes, very clever."

Harry worked a screwdriver into the back of the case, and with a satisfying pop, it came off. It was one of the few times she'd ever used her little tool kit, a gift from her mother when she left for uni. She moved aside to let Dr. Deep replace the vacuum tube.

Harry looked at the garbage on the floor and at Dr. Deep, wondering if he was the cause of the mess.

He followed her eyes. "Unfortunate, that. Last time I used the radios, just a few days ago, I exited to take care of some personal business, and when I returned... harrumph... this mess and my radio malfunctioning. I do hope it was not some type of malcontent persons doing mischief, but even here at MeerKAT, one cannot rule out individuals motivated by baser emotions, yes? Just not acceptable."

He continued. "Well, let's get this going." He handed her the tube he had extracted from the open back of the radio. "The malfunctioning culprit, I'm afraid." It looked identical to the new one except for a splotchy black area on one side, where it appeared burned. He made some adjustments to the dials on the front of the radio and turned it on.

Harry heard a slight hum, barely audible above the fans of the server room, and then some static. Dr. Deep reached down to adjust a knob.

The radio emitted a loud snap, and she was thrown backward; a wave of pressure compressed her ears and chest. She watched in slow motion as the server room moved away from her. Disoriented and in pain, she was looking at the entrance to the supply closet, having been blown out of the server room entirely. She was on her side, on the floor. Pain striated from her shoulder and she shook her head. Muffled sounds came from nearby—a wounded dog, perhaps? Her mind was wrapped in gauze; her hearing was suffering from the blast. She heard a dog, but it could not be a dog; dogs don't ring and dogs don't speak words. Confused, she got on all fours and then to her knees, leaning precariously against a wall, facing away from the server room, looking down the hallway. One of her canes was next to her; the other must still have been in the server room. Shakily, she propped herself up and stood. The crisps and soda she'd drunk earlier bubbled up in her throat and she suppressed a gag. The noise of the dog twisted and became the sound of a man crying in pain mixed with some words she couldn't make out. She grabbed her shoulder, wincing, turned, and hobbled to the server room. She called out for Dr. Deep, wondering if he had been hurt in what she now realized was an explosion. *What could explode in the server room? A battery backup? Stored gas canisters?*

In the server room, she was greeted by a glowing oblong shape displaying a visage of a light-skinned man wearing a T-shirt and jeans. His handsome, white face was scrunched in concern, or pain. He looked both angelic and sickly, bathed in ethereal greenish light, as if he were standing in a fish tank. Was he on a large monitor? Or was he a hologram projection of a religious icon? She touched her head and blinked hard, sure this was a hallucination. The man in the glowing frame was trying to reach Dr. Deep, who was crouched like a supplicant, cradling his left arm, which ended in a stump, blood fauceting from the end of his wrist where his hand used to be.

Harry suppressed another urge to vomit.

"Get a tourniquet!" yelled the glowing man, who stood on a scintillating oval, looking surprised himself, pushing his hand outward as if he could touch Dr. Deep. But his hand pressed against an unseen force. *How can a projection reach out?* She looked at Dr. Deep again and bile rose. His arm ended in a bloody mess and she looked away.

The glowing man was three-dimensional. She could see depth and he was clearly in an egg-shaped enclosure. Realization took hold that the man on the screen was not on a screen at all. He was in a bubble of some sort. He was trapped in a bubble. The bubble and his fingers flexed against a rubbery membrane of shimmer, but stayed within the light. The man looked apoplectic and shouted at her, "A tourniquet! Please help him!"

Harry was confused, but she took a moment to process the scene and agreed that a tourniquet was needed. She leaned her cane against a server rack and awkwardly took off her shirt, a sleeveless one under it. *Layering for the win*, her mind nonsensically muttered. She knew nothing about first aid and gently reached for Dr. Deep's arm, not wanting to come too close to the bloody wound. *I think I see bone!*

Dr. Deep spoke in a harsh whisper, his eyes squinting in pain, rocking back and forth, cradling the stump, using his hand to squeeze his own wrist. "The... man... is correct—wrap it right. Make a complete circuit around my arm. Gods!"

Harry squinted too, trying to hide the stump from view. She leaned forward, kneeling as well, and knotted the shirt around Dr. Deep's forearm, pulling tight. Dr. Deep lowered his face toward the tourniquet and violently yanked back on it with his teeth. He turned his head to the floor. "Look," he said, barely able to speak. "Look, please, for my hand."

Harry, too shocked to say anything, just stood back. I cannot look for a hand. A man has lost his hand. This is crazy.

She heard a voice. "Did you take the USB drive?"

Comprehension avoided her. She looked at Dr. Deep and then at the man.

This person was in a glowing bubble. He was holding something. *He's holding a hand.* His palm pressed on the bubble, trying to touch the server rack, just out of reach.

"I... I must explain. I...," the man said, and then he dropped the hand, which disappeared out of sight inside the bubble. He looked at the server rack Harry had worked on earlier. "Where is the USB drive?" He sounded frantic now, his attention no longer on the dismembered hand. "I have been shot," the man added, looking pale and confused in the bubble.

This seemed like a non sequitur to Harry. Too much was happening. "I don't understand. You have been shot? The USB? I have it."

Harry fumbled for her keychain and lifted it, suppressing a wave of nausea. *The hand!*

"Has it been long?" the man asked. "You weren't here a moment ago. I don't know why I can't get out of this. It didn't happen last time. I could touch things." The man held one hand on his abdomen, where his shirt was soaked with blood. He looked around the room, tested the bubble with his hands. "This is not good. I don't know how much time I have. I am... stuck... I think, in time, in space, maybe—no, not stuck, between, in between... Can you hear me? There is nobody else here? The man who shot me. Is he here?"

Harry nodded at him, realizing she had been staring, paralyzed, unmoving. She shook her head, confused. "Who shot you? A man shot you? Who are you? What happened?"

He ignored her question. "How is your memory? I don't have time, I think."

She gaped at him, even more confused. "What?"

"You must try to remember everything I tell you. You are in danger. My family is in danger. I took a risk to save Spitz. Can you remember everything I tell you?"

Dr. Deep groaned and fell over.

Harry processed what she had been told, nodding in realization, the distraction of a task easier than considering the unconscious Dr. Deep in a puddle of blood at her feet. She pulled out her phone. "I'll record."

The man nodded. "Yes, okay, but erase it or encrypt it as soon as you can. Do you understand?"

"I need to call for help for Dr. Deep."

The man ignored her again. "I'm tied to the frame of reference—probably why I'm here—relativity, you know? I can't complete this trip. I don't know what happened. My source is gone. This is MeerKAT?"

Harry just nodded, not understanding anything. He was talking fast and incomprehensibly. Where had he been hiding when she and Dr. Deep had entered the room? She shook her head and ended up moving it in a confused circle. "MeerKAT, yes," she said.

The man continued talking. "On the USB, it's got the videos, but it also has the operating code to broadcast. It has the sub-text. It... One is the teleport code. There are others. Some I've tested, many I have not. They work once only. I'm not sure how many are left. But you must be careful. You need a vacuum tube nearby. Moving electrons, voltage. Randomness. Not chaos. True randomness. But that's not important. It's much clearer now in my head. I've had some moments of clarity about it all. You can only mend a break once."

The man looked at Dr. Deep's cart, overturned, with the radios on the floor, their guts and tubes sprayed around the bubble. He reached for them, pressing his hand at the radios, but the bubble held him fast. He coughed, blood spraying on his lips. "I see. Tube radios. Yours? That's why this failed."

He turned to her. Pushing forward, his face disgustingly pressed into the shimmering egg, his eyes crazy, his voice rising. "The USB. I need to tell you about it."

"What? I don't understand. We need to get help for Dr. Deep." She indicated the body of the scientist, in a spreading stain.

"Please, repeat what I'm saying back to me so I know you have heard me. I can feel myself pulled. Or the place I'm in being pulled. It's very interesting. I can't get back, I don't think. Just remember base 32 and hydrogen. And AM and FM. Without those, it's impossible to broadcast anything. The videos aren't the important part. I mean, they are because of everything, proof of aliens and such, but the videos are just entertainment for them."

"Entertainment for them?" Harry's ears perked up at the word *entertainment*.

"Them, yes, maybe called Zoonerat. Under the videos are codes, maybe inside the videos too, but definitely under the videos. Metadata."

Harry's attention sharpened as the effect of the explosion dissipated, her hearing strong and her mind clear. She looked at him and gingerly reached out to the bubble. "Where did you come from? Were you hiding here? You're bleeding." Blood stained his T-shirt, which said *Wish You Were Here—Walpole*

Correctional Facility.

The man shook his head at her. "Listen, if I disappear, there may not be another chance. Please, listen. The codes are like freebies you give away. Like... like a kids'-meal action figure. A free toy you get in a box of cereal. They give them out with movies. But it's alien. It's dangerous."

Harry nodded inconclusively. The man had answered none of her questions. Her fingers were greasy and she glanced down. They were covered in blood. When the man said "dangerous," she tore her eyes back to him. She considered if he was mad.

"... danger, small pieces, children can choke. You know? But there's no warning on these. We are children, choking on the little pieces, putting the plastic bags on our heads, putting our fingers in the light socket. Very dangerous stuff. Okay? Please repeat, base 32, hydrogen. Sub-text, metadata, okay?"

Harry nodded in a circle and flicked her eyes at the bloody screen of her phone. "Yes, no, no. Smile meals. Fast food. Base 32, hydrogen, sub-text, metadata." Her head was clearing. She needed help to move Dr. Deep. "Come with me. We have to get help." She reached for him, but her hand was stopped at the hazy barrier of the ovoid. If your arm could feel nausea, it did at that moment. The arm she saw was no longer her own. It was just a piece of meat. Tingles ran up to her shoulder. Her vision went hazy for a moment. Her phone dropped to the floor.

She heard him again as she groped on the floor, pushing her phone through a red bath. "You must not release it—do not upload the videos or the code anywhere. Do not give it to anyone. There are people who want it. They will do bad things. It's very dangerous. Very dangerous. I think maybe the ultimate bad, you know? *I am become death, destroyer of worlds*—that's the level. Find Claire Plaster in Lexington. She's online. I hope Spitz is okay. Find Whisper, I think she calls her group. Tell her Colin gave you this message. Colin Wright. Mr. Wright. I think I've made a mistake. Please remember."

Her fingers tightened around her phone, and she repeated while trying to stand. "Yes, dangerous." She was acknowledging him by repeating phrases automatically. "Kids' meals, base 32, hydrogen, Claire Plaster, Colin Wright." Still on her knees, she rubbed her fingers on the bloody device, but her phone wouldn't dial. The screen glowing white but empty, as white as the bones that make up our wrists. *Oh, god, the hand.* She instinctively glanced at Dr. Deep, pale and unconscious, the white stump of bone surrounded by meat still oozing blood. *Maybe he's dead?* The thought brought her back to the room. When she looked up, the glowing bubble with the man was gone.

She grabbed her walking stick and leaned on it to rise. Looking nowhere but forward, she walked to the hallway and pulled the fire alarm.

3. Where Is Dr. Deep's Hand?

Where is Dr. Deep's hand? That glowing man had it. He held it out! Harry gagged at the thought, going to her knees, seeing the bloody stump when she closed her eyes. Her canes clattered to the macadam of the car park. *The blood spurting from his stump.* Then she was vomiting, the sound hidden by the roar of a helicopter.

She struggled to her feet, wiping her mouth with the sleeve of the heavy jacket she'd been given. A man in a bulky flight suit and a helmet, exuding a dusty cold, shouted over thumping rotors, "Good work on the tourniquet—might have saved his life."

She turned away from the spray of dust kicked up by the aircraft, not sure where to go. Stunned and shivering, Dr. Ramposa put his hand on her shoulder. She flinched.

"We could have sent you in the helicopter."

She shook her head. "No, I'm fine. I just fell down in the explosion." She felt decidedly un-fine, but she didn't like doctors. She didn't like hospitals. She didn't like being touched or seeing bloody stumps of arms.

Dr. Ramposa called over an EMT and explained that Harry should be treated, maybe given some painkillers or "whatever she needs." He faced her, looking down. "Go back to your room. I think there will need to be some discussion." He paused, then continued. "Do you want me to call anyone?" He gestured randomly with his hand.

Harry looked at his hand as it waved. *Oh, his hand could break off so easily, the bones so thin, and there will be blood.* She bent over and threw up again, surprised anything was left, as he gingerly stepped back to avoid splash. He reached to help her rise and she waved him away, wiping spittle from her chin. As she rose, her bloody shirt peeked from under the coat they'd given her, now spotted with bits of sputum. *I do not look good.*

Back in her room, after taking two paracetamols from the emergency worker, a hot shower improved her mood, though seeing the drain water tinged pink caused her to lean momentarily against the shower stall's white walls. Her shoulder was sore, but nothing too distracting. A swing up and down was unencumbered, and she donned some clothes.

And now what? Sit? Stand? The blood. The crazy man. It seemed fantastical. Was she going nutty? Her breath caught in her throat as the thoughts spiraled. She needed air, her room so small, stifling and humid from the shower.

She pulled open the door to the outside, hoping for coolness, to find Dr. Ramposa and two people in uniform about to knock. One of the uniforms, a stout woman, spoke first.

"Ms. Haretsebe Tladi?" the uniform asked. "May we come in?"

As Harry nodded, the two police officers entered, followed by Dr. Ramposa.

Harry stepped back to give them room, apologizing for the bloody clothes hanging on a chair. Did they really need to be here and see her underthings strewn about her room?

The female officer spoke up. "I'm Officer Pelo and this is Captain Bruen. We understand you found the... uh... evidence in the computer room?"

"What?"

Dr. Ramposa interjected, "When you went to the computer room a few days ago, you found garbage, yes?"

Harry nodded.

The female officer turned to the MeerKAT administrator. "Dr. Ramposa, I'd prefer to ask the questions. Would you step outside with the captain?"

Dr. Ramposa looked a bit taken aback, but deferred and went out with the other officer. The room had much more space with just the two women in it.

The uniform looked around the room carefully and then said, "The explosion that hurt the other scientist and yourself—we have to ask you some questions about it."

"What caused it? Do you know?" Harry sat on her bed. "How is the other man?"

"He is under medical care, I understand. They are working on his arm." The officer continued her examination of the room as she spoke. Her eyes fell on the walking aids, and then she looked at Harry's legs. And Harry immediately understood that Pelo was sizing her up as a suspect.

The officer continued, "What we need to know is what you saw in the computer room. We believe it was your footprint in the blood there."

Harry closed her eyes. "Yes, the blood from his hand... oh..." She leaned forward to ease her queasiness.

"Actually, the night before, you found trash in the computer room. There was blood, older, from an earlier incident. Do you recall that?"

"Blood? What blood? There was just trash and spilled... Oh my god. That was blood?" Harry remembered pushing her shoe into the brownish gunk on the floor. Her stomach knotting, she spun off the bed and crouched near the waste bin. Her midsection ached from the constant heaving. Officer Pelo moved slightly, but was already against the door.

"I'm sorry, Miss. I realize this is shocking, but we need to know exactly what you saw," the officer said.

Harry stayed kneeling, looking at the bin. She was hyperventilating and sweating. Pelo looked around and handed her a T-shirt that was on the bed. Harry wiped her neck and face and sat back on the floor, against the wall, exhausted.

"I saw nothing. I mean, there was garbage." She paused. "Was that really blood? Oh, whose blood was that?"

"The blood in the computer room, the blood that was not from the explosion but was several days old. Could you help us with that? Did you see anything or anyone?"

Harry looked up at the officer. "I don't know. I thought it was spilt coffee or a cool drink. I didn't know it was blood." She felt cold, shuddering. "*Modimo nthuse*. Whose blood was it?"

The woman didn't say, and asked her a few more questions about when she got there and when she left. Finally, she said, "We'd like to take your shoes that you wore that day."

"I can't give them to you. They are special orthotics. They are my only shoes. I have a leg problem."

The officer looked at her and at the canes. "I'm sorry, but they are evidence and you must surrender them. I will talk to the captain about getting you replacements."

Harry paused for a moment, considering her options. It didn't seem like this was something she could negotiate. She hadn't brought more than one pair. She'd be stuck without shoes. Walking without them was much more difficult. With no shoes? *How do they expect me to get about? The orthotics were expensive as well.*

She reluctantly took off her trainers, seeing a dark smear on the front of one of them. The officer thanked her and put them in a plastic bag that appeared from a pouch on the officer's uniform belt. Then, just as Pelo was leaving, she turned back, her hand extended, and said, almost casually, "I'll need your laptop as well."

Harry's attention leapt, as if she had been asleep in a nightmare. A cold sharpness blew across her thoughts. She examined the officer as if seeing her for the first time. Pelo's large hand reached out, and Harry looked apprehensively at the grasping fingers. Her laptop. Trust in the uniform's authority evaporated from Harry's mind, as if oxygen had been leached from a fire. No longer a figure of credence and verisimilitude, the officer changed to a uniformed question mark, a bouillabaisse of mysterious intentions.

Why would they want my laptop? They take my shoes. They take my laptop. They find blood. I am accused of sabotage, of incompetence, of possessing... the USB? What is on the USB? Had she spoken about the thumb drive? What had she said? The taste of vomit was strong, but now its acidity kept her alert. She'd mentioned the other man, but the officer must have thought she was talking about Dr. Deep.

"Of course," Harry said, and handed the officer her test laptop, which was the only one visible, devoid of anything, except perhaps evidence that a video titled 1.avi had been played recently, though it wasn't actually on the laptop. As the officer left, the laptop in one hand, Dr. Ramposa appeared again in the doorway.

"Ms. Tladi, I'm very sorry about the... uh... incident. I hope you are feeling somewhat better. Do you need any additional medical treatment?" He sounded genuinely upset, she noted. "I must ask, however, that you try to stay as much as possible in your room."

A tinge of annoyance invaded her demeanor as she considered her situation. "Of course I'll stay in my room. They've taken my shoes! They've taken my laptop. How can I work? I need something to put on my feet!"

"I'm afraid, Haretsebe, that we need to pause your work temporarily. It will be a significant loss to the researchers. I will try to get your laptop back as soon as possible. I will also get you something for your feet. Again, I apologize."

"But without my laptop, I cannot help anyone. I'll have no role here!"

"Miss, you can still be of great service by helping the officers in any way they need and continuing to be available. And please do not go anywhere."

Did she hear a pleading tone or a commanding tone in that last request? She wasn't sure, but it did not sound as friendly as she'd like. It wasn't for her sake that the request was made, that was for sure. They wanted her here.

Somehow, this will be my fault. The cripple's fault. My laptop—evidence. My orthotics—evidence. My short leg—evidence.

She was furious. "And where would I go? We are in the middle of the Karoo. They took my shoes! My shoes, Dr. Ramposa! And I'm not exactly built for galivanting about! They took my laptop. Dr. Deep's hand has been cut off!" Tears flowing down her face. She put her head in her hands.

Dr. Ramposa muttered a faint, embarrassed apology and was gone.

*Video Z-16:00-1a/Clarity, *The Marriage Video*

From the Zoonerat Wikipedia page:

Many agree that the first true evidence of extraterrestrial intelligence is video Z-16:00-1a/Clarity, aka *The Marriage Video*. It was uploaded to a public blockchain by WisPR user Clarity, according to its metadata, and occupies a "seminal place in human history" (Report 78, Dr. Zhong Brightman Xi, Chinese Academy of Sciences). There are up to six smaller clips and still images, generally agreed to be sourced from the video, that predate the blockchain upload date. The earliest of these is believed to be from the mid-1980s.

Stickied post on a Zoonerat fan site by u/ProfessorOfZoon:

Viewers who saw the video before it was widely known commented it looked different without being able to pinpoint with any specificity what made it so. (The aspect ratio is discussed elsewhere. See *Zoonerat Base-32* for further information.) The video starts abruptly. No title sequence, no splash page. The quality is fair, with pixilation visible if the video were shown on a large screen. There is no audio in 1a. Further versions (1b, 1c, et al.) have audio derived from the audio-space layer implanted in the videos as cymatic constructions. However, it is clear enough to see the content without any dispute about the setting and characters.

The bride wears blue. Her skin is orange, a lighter shade on her shoulders and a darker shade on her arms. Or, shall we say, the color matches orange: approximately 620 nanometers (484 terahertz). (See *Zoonerat Chromaticity* discussions elsewhere. In addition, chromatically adjusted versions of the video are available in numerous color spaces. Here we discuss the original video Z-16:00-1a/Clarity.) Whether it's the same wavelength on the bride's world, none can say. The train of her dress floats behind her at waist height as she enters the hall. The train has no visible means of support—it just floats there—and she enters just far enough that much of her train, floating behind, is still off camera and outside the entryway.

The term *her*, as used here, is subjective, just as twenty-first-century humans have decided that the term *her* is subjective. The use of *her* simply refers to an interpretation of a gender rather than an absolute. But if a reasonable observer were raised on Earth in the twenty-first century, they would likely also use the term *her*. Certainly, speakers of languages with gendered pronouns have also used their term for *her* when describing this character. Of course, others have used the term *it* or *him* and a variety of other pronouns. But even those who would use another term, such as the popular *zer*, would also understand what is meant by *her* in this context, whereas their use of other terms might not be so widely recognized. So, we stick with the most universally recognized term, knowing it could be wrong—in fact, knowing it *is* wrong.

The walls of the room are a robin's-egg blue, split by dozens of vertical windows of crystalline brilliance with gothic arches atop. Murmurations of light, complex and moving, dapple the air, cast about like raindrops, floating upward and then sideways and then around in helices and spirals. Perhaps a technological marvel, perhaps a cloud of tiny living organisms traveling like flocks of birds. Perhaps pets, thousands of them, each with a name, happy that their masters are throwing a fête. Perhaps the bride and groom are the pets and the flickering lights are the masters. In this article, we interpret the scene with our subjective eyes. Others will come to different conclusions.

Great vertical mullions split variegated rays of star-shine and cast enough shadows that we can assume more than a single star or bright moon is shining outside, with one large enough to be a sun. Light plays on the walls and floor and the costumes of the guests. The light dazzles. Perhaps it is facets of minerals in the windows that cause sparkling images to fleck the walls? Or maybe some additional technological marvel, the twin of the dancing light drops? But it is soft enough not to impinge on the view of the bride and groom, who have just entered the hall.

The bride, which is what we've chosen to call her, strides next to her partner, whom we shall refer to as the groom, because, again, it's the most obvious, if not the most accurate, option. We know nothing of their actual roles as they refer to themselves. They could both be plumbers, actors, lawyers, royalty, prisoners. Or they could be the bride and groom.

They walk with a gentle calm, at the same pace, as equals in a ceremony old as written history, or does this culture even have written history? But too much questioning makes the head spin, so we use our cultural biases to describe what is obvious. Having just entered the hall, they take three steps together and then pause. Is it for drama? Is it for record-keepers who must capture this moment? Is this a tradition that's been handed down for thousands of their years, or is this pause executed here for the first time in their history? Are they, in fact, breaking some great taboo by pausing and staring ahead? We do not know. The guests make no motion. There is no uproar visible. Many assume that they have planned, expected, and even desired this dramatic pause. One can refer to the seminal Zacademic paper on the topic, "The Cause of the Pause," for extended discussion.

Now we come to an interaction so human, it has been the source of much ammunition by Zoonerat deniers. The camera shifts, traveling ahead, and then focuses on a female standing in the first row of the congregation. She stares at the groom with wistfulness and then casts her eyes downward. When she looks up after a moment, she fixates on the bride and her eyes flash menacingly, a tenseness at the corners of her lids, the flesh tightening and the pupils narrowing. There is even a glint of blue as her eyes pulse through a series of colors. Her eyebrows come together in what is obvious dislike. Her fists clench, her shoulders lift slightly, and tendons strain in her neck. She is fierce in her beauty. Is she a former lover? Or his sister (as is later suggested)? She is not happy with this union. Beside her, there is no obvious partner. She is alone. An older guest gives her an obvious nudge and whispers in her ear. Angry, she shakes her head, turns, and walks out while all eyes are on the couple, leaving a gap in the front row. The couple glances at her exit and at each other.

Back to the couple. Orange hand in orange hand, the two thumbs and two middle fingers harmoniously intertwine. Yes, they have four fingers on each hand. And aside from two equal thumbs, further analysis will indicate that the bride's middle fingers are unalike in length, while the groom's are the same. Other characteristics become apparent as the video continues. They each have two legs and two arms. Two knees and two elbows. Their wrists are supple. Perhaps there are two joints there, not one? The fingers, though similar to human fingers, appear smooth and maybe have no joints and are more like octopus tentacles. Can we see ridges on them? No, the video does not have the granularity for that, but some say there are ridges on the fingers. Viewers will make their own judgments. But they have fingernails—a cause of great discussion among xenoanatomists.

The guests are outfitted in splendid trappings, both scintillating and bizarre. Hats that seem to be alive. Dresses and jackets, some so black they appear as negative space, and some clear enough we can see musculature and sinews on taut backs and rippled arms. Hairstyles match the color, length, breadth, and variety of human hairstyles, perhaps even exceeding the most flamboyant seen at fashion shows. Eventually, each guest will be analyzed, numbered, discussed, enhanced, and otherwise cataloged by viewers and academics around the world. But for now, a casual observer sees a great and glorious crowd, an audience in finery. And so we can guess that the bride and groom are important. How important? We cannot say.

The bride and groom pause for 3.87 seconds, nearly 25 percent of the entire video. Then they continue striding down the center aisle of the hall. Perspective is maintained at a steady distance from the couple and the camerawork has been critiqued as "excellent." The viewpoint expands to give us a wide shot of the procession, then descends to follow them at head height and rises again to capture the audience and traverse ahead of the couple, allowing them to approach us as we wait for them on the dais. The bride's floating train is fully revealed, its length twice her height. Most of the guests (117 of them, split almost evenly on the right and left sides) are standing in the back half of the hall. The remaining guests, originally sixty-four and now sixty-three, sit in eight rows at the front, with four rows on each side of the aisle.

It takes the couple 7.07 seconds to walk down the aisle. They arrive just in front of the first row, stop, and turn toward each other. The camera swings around them again. We see their faces, a brief focus on each, and then it backs up and shows the hall from the front, our couple facing each other, the guests behind. There, they pause again for 2.71 seconds. And their faces look human—desperately, uniquely human. Two eyes, eyebrows, a nose, a mouth, cheekbones, adorned ears, a forehead, a widow's peak. It defies explanation. It defies logic. It speaks of fakery, of trickery, of divinity, of continuity, of many things. Could alien evolution have resulted in simulacra of ourselves? Is this convergent evolution? But answers and even discussion are not for this time. We move on.

At that moment, the entire crowd of guests lifts their left four-fingered hands. Then for .35 seconds, until the video ends abruptly, all hands glow and emanate green, staticky lines of light. Verdant lightning bolts from the audience travel toward the couple at the front. Everyone is connected through a complex net of brilliance that wraps and engulfs the couple. The very last frame confirms this.

Combined with the two seconds at the beginning, the entire video is sixteen seconds. And perhaps, aside from the Zapruder film, George C. Scott's soliloquy in *Patton*, the *Gangnam Style* music video, and some others, it may be the most important video ever to exist. Or so some say.

4. Fort Meade, Maryland, USA

His hand shook as he grabbed for the open can of energy drink, knocking over a monster-themed bag of THC gummies and scattering its contents across the desk, some of the tiny things clattering to the floor in a waterfall of trolls. He also upended a tiny espresso cup that hadn't been washed since... well, since his cryptocurrency balance had been much bigger. The cup clanged on the floor without breaking, rolling in a shrinking circle, faster and faster, until its vibrato silenced with a faint clink.

Two thoughts only.

I've been hacked.

I don't get hacked.

Smithson sat stupefied, staring at the account balance, phone phreak green numerals on a Trash-80 black screen. Since he'd last checked (How many days ago? He'd have to look at the logs), the decimal point of his balance had shifted six places to the left. Instead of a number of some decent value, an escape number, a significant number, a number that would pay off debt to bad people—the decimal point now sat singularly on the left side, with a lonely zero *à gauche*; the balance was now less than one, a mere fraction. And, more to the point (he instantly regretted that turn of phrase), he saw the meaning in the new balance. There was a language in numbers. Pi could be pie. Zero could be an airplane. Eighteen could be the maximum charisma of a dwarf or the age at which..., well, 'nuff said. The balance that shimmered on his screen had meaning too. It wasn't just a tiny, infinitesimally small, eensy-weensy bit of pocket change. It wasn't just bald-faced robbery. It was a digital middle finger, an Arabic numeral fuck you, an HP-28C suck it.

0.003104558.

This wasn't just a theft; it was an insult. He'd been robbed and dissed. Thieved to make a point. Taught a lesson.

Read upside down, it said *ASSHOLE*.

A notification ping blasted out of his computer speaker at the same moment he read the number. He startled and stared at the computer, confused for a moment. How could they do that? How could they make a notification coincide with the hack of his cryptocurrency?

Someone with a sick sense of humor had robbed him. This insult, this travesty, this terrible, horrible, no good, very bad crypto balance was payback for something he had done, and unfortunately there were several *somethings he had done* that might account for such ire. Which one? The fakes he'd sold, the videos he'd promised, the setups that had been setups? Ugh, there were many. But that was how life worked, no? You took and were taken.

He vowed silently, his fist slowly crushing the fluorescently patterned drink can. He would find the perpetrators. He would find them. And he would reduce them to digital rubble.

Leaning back, he upended the partially mangled energy drink over his pinkish mouth, Adam's apple bobbing as if on a string, as the last few brilliant green drops of the elixir fell to his snakish tongue. The empty can was tossed inexpertly at the garbage, clattering off the rim. He reached a lanky arm to grab a handful of the gummies from the desk and was about to swallow them whole when his phone rang, again startling him.

"*Gah*!" His voice was guttural and drenched in frustration. He would have ignored it, but the ring was from his employer. The employer he owed for his current freedom. The employer he needed because of the access he gained working in this intelligence office.

"Hello!" he nearly yelled into the rectangular device.

"I'm assuming your volume is because of excitement from the video project notification and not some other distraction?" The voice was smooth and calm. And, in normal circumstances, Smithson would have responded with high-browed snark, such as *Of course, Señor Mr. Colonel Sir,* but he was still focused on the preternatural reduction of his net worth.

"Notification?"

"Yes, the notification. Are you telling me you didn't get it?"

Then a memory jostled itself through the crowded thoughts of revenge for the loss of his savings. The ping had not been related to the hack. It had been coincidence, not a conspiracy. Because it was a special ping—a unique sound he'd created just for that project—the sound of a *Star Trek* phaser. He should have recognized it as such.

He opened his mouth to speak and stopped. What he considered saying was

Yes, Boss-man, got the ping and I'm on it like white on rice. The bullshit project with hidden dirty photos or formulas for explosives or whatever. However, a tiny voice told him to hold his tongue, to rein in his anger for just a moment. Because he needed this job. He needed it now more than ever.

So instead, he responded with a lie. "I had it silenced. I will look now."

There was a pause, and the man spoke. "Not what I expect from you. Make sure notifications are audible. I got the notification and a summary. Apparently, it flagged two. Please retrieve them and call me back."

Smithson didn't want to do this right now. He had to find and liberate his funds. "Yes, okay, but they're usually just false positives. Been several years and we've had no verified sightings, you know? How about I get to it this weekend?"

The voice on the other end of the phone was militarily precise. "Not going to happen. Get on it now. The summary email says they scored over 95 percent, and none have scored that high, correct?"

Smithson's voice was glum, distracted by his bank balance. "Yes."

"Are you listening? Just do your job and get on this immediately."

Smithson perked up for a moment. "Hey, just a thought. If the scraper found videos, the scraper I wrote, there's a bonus, right?"

"Bonus?"

"You said once there could be a bonus if we ever found another video."

"Smithson, I recall no such statement. The US government doesn't pay bonuses easily." Then he paused, and added, "But there are pools of funds available as awards for exemplary work, so just do your job, get me the videos, call me back at 0700. It's late. Understood?"

"Sir, yessir! May take a few hours to get them decrypted or whatever." Smithson spoke quickly and his mouth got the better of him.

"Don't get lip with me." The voice was still very calm, but an edge had entered.

"Okay, will do."

The call ended and Smithson dropped the gummies on the dirty desk and pulled up the cloud storage where the video project bot did its work, reluctantly shrinking the virtual server window with his crypto balance displayed.

Within a folder labeled *shit_the_scraper_found*, Smithson ran an executable file. The results flowed onto the screen as a series of statistics and numbers. He was actually surprised. The colonel had been correct. Not one but two videos had been captured by the scraper, each with a confidence of 98 percent.

He was about to send them both to Colonel Montgomery followed by a request for a bonus, his hand hovering over the Send button, when he thought maybe he should look at them. The call was scheduled in the morning and it was late evening now, so he had some time. He'd lost his last job because an unfortunate video had been seen by the wrong people; he did not want to repeat that experience. Montgomery had saved him from prosecution then. The colonel's largesse may not extend so far again.

The first video was a new one. It was not the same as either of the two that existed within the purview of the amorphous and irritatingly undefined Video Project, as this work was internally named. The clip showed what appeared to be teen drama at a high school. Again, the orange aliens. Again, the pointed ears. Again, of no recognizable intelligence value. There was unintelligible audio. The executable offered completely garbled subtitling for the discordant soundtrack.

A sex lecture by one of the orange aliens and then jokes by orange alien teenagers in the classroom. Smithson could not, even in his wildest dreams, imagine why terrorists would choose this video to hide secrets. Because that's what he concluded these videos must be: mules for dangerous knowledge. Perhaps bomb-making plans, perhaps names of moles, perhaps drug formulations—all secreted in the pixels, hashed and mashed into digital obscurity and then distributed to nefarious underworld denizens in the form of innocuous drama. Smithson didn't know what the actual intel was, and Montgomery had responded with "above your pay grade," "need to know," and "it's classified" among other rephrases of "I'm not telling you anything, just do your job and stop asking."

The second video caused Smithson to pause. Because he'd seen this video before. A battle scene. A doctor-woman-alien saving a kid. He could not give this to Montgomery. It could lead Montgomery backward, following a breadcrumb trail, to the *long game.* And now, with the crypto situation, meaning the money situation, the need for funds had metamorphosed the *long game* into a *short game.* The *long-now-short game* he was playing for a big payoff could be jeopardized by this second video. Because how could it appear now? He'd already fibbed to Montgomery about its source the first time he'd found it, to keep Montgomery off the scent. Because the second video was an inroad, an access point, to the kind of wealth that would... well, it would be that kind of wealth.

The first time he lied to Montgomery was the day he was hired. He'd found a video—the same video he'd just found again, the one with the soldier and the doctor—and it had saved his ass from certain doom. He thought it was a joke, but that video had somehow sparked interest from higher-ups in whatever military agency Montgomery worked for. Coincidentally, he had just been terminated from the Harvard-Smithsonian Center for Astrophysics for using their servers to engage in a little bit of international trade in collectible entertainment that was, shall we say, prurient in the extreme and highly in demand. He'd been unable to deliver the final product to his buyers, the Harvard Center for Astrophysics having siloed everything he'd ever touched there in such a way that it was essentially inaccessible. So, in addition to needing a new job, he needed a change of visibility, and Montgomery had provided.

From day one the Video Project had been odd, but Smithson had done what he'd been tasked to do, even when the tasks were nonsensical, because working for the National Security Agency had benefits, such as access to black-hat/l33t/warez that were, frankly, really awesome. He could pursue the *long game* with serious resources.

Montgomery had spoken briskly. "I've sent you a file with the color spaces, aspect, identifying hashes, pixilation, depth—all the stuff from the IT guys. Set up a scraper and look on the web. There's no time frame on this. It's some kind of experimental stuff that IT wants."

"And this is important because?"

"Smithson, one of the things you need to get clear is that we, meaning the US government, saved your ass from jail. Just do what you are told. Okay?"

Smithson didn't intend to sound petulant, but he admitted he probably did. Explaining things empathically was never his strong suit. "Listen, context is important. If the videos are connected to, say, Middle Eastern terrorist activity or unregistered container shipments of nuclear materiel—the type of intelligence you have me tracking in the other projects—I'm more likely to find them if I prioritize the search against that dataset, okay?"

He could hear his boss breathing, formulating a response. "Understood, Smithson. You make a good point. But here's the deal: There is nothing I can give you to help you search. There is no way to prioritize this or triage it. There is no OpInt except what you have already. I can only give you what I've got, and that's two videos: the video you found—we'll call it *The Doctor Video*—and the previous video from the file—we'll call it *The Marriage Video*—and the datasets that IT has given me. The goal is to find more videos. Supposedly they exist, so set up your... magic bean counters... and find them. Okay?"

Montgomery provided search markers for the video files. The primary marker was a spatial-temporal color distribution, a time-series chromaticity array built from each video. The human eye sees a range of colors. This palette is different for some individuals. The colorblind see fewer, the tetrachromatistic see more. TV and computer monitors generally share a common chromaticity capability, far smaller than what the eye can see. Monitors made for photo editing can expand on the color range, increasing to nearly match what humans can see. And Smithson had read intelligence reports that synthetic eyes and monitors exist that expand beyond the human range for use by robots.

"I'm sending you an array of colors," Montgomery had said.

"What do you mean?"

"I mean the videos we are looking for match or have a probability distribution of a specific set of colors. I don't really know the details, but the colors and percentages are stored in a file or in the pixels or I don't really know the technical side. That's for you. You can get the search pattern or the search terms or whatever you call it from the secure file store. I'll send you an access key shortly."

"I don't get it." Petulant, again.

"You don't need to get it. But this will help you find the target videos."

A week later, another conversation on the same topic had led to a minor argument.

"If you want me to search this way, I need more power," Smithson had told his handler.

"What do you mean?"

"I need a bunch of virtual servers. Probably three dozen. Many, many teraflops."

"I don't know what that is."

"Colonel Monty" (Smithson called him Monty for no reason other than Montgomery seemed annoyed by it, so Smithson used it when he wanted to make a point), "I'm searching the entire web and many private networks for files. And not even files. I'm looking inside files when I can. This requires a lot of computing power. Files can be locked or compressed or otherwise time-consuming to access. Imagine looking for a needle in a haystack, but the needle looks like hay and I'm wearing gloves. That's the problem. Each piece of hay needs to be examined. Brute force."

"Okay, I'll see what I can do." Montgomery added, "Also, it's likely that you may have better luck if you focus on the parts of the web dealing with radio astronomy."

"What did you say?" Smithson had heard him, but wanted clarification. Did Montgomery know?

"Just the word from our research team is that there's some connection to radio astronomy. That's all I can say, okay?"

Smithson decided he needed to make sure Montgomery valued him. So he said glibly, "I know."

There was silence on the phone for a moment. "You know? You know this how? How do you know the videos are connected to radio astronomy?"

Smithson actually didn't know that. What he knew was that by hacking a computer he'd found through an online thread on radio astronomy, he'd found the first video—a fact he'd shared with nobody, because his intentions did not end at the video, but at the pot of gold at the end of the refracted electromagnetic radiation array, so to speak. But now he did know they were connected, and he knew others had made this connection. That was very interesting, and a bit concerning. Sometimes being honest had rewards. "It was referenced in one of the reports. Just pointing out that I already knew that."

"Well, good then," said Montgomery. And Smithson sensed, but couldn't be sure, that the tone had gotten both more careful, perhaps more respectful, and a bit distant. Maybe honesty wasn't such a good idea. If Montgomery thought he was holding back, well, Montgomery might start holding back. But this was overthinking, concluded Smithson.

And a few days after that conversation Smithson got credentials for a cloud-based system, some kind of government property, with the ability to create dozens of virtual servers. He wrote his own search algorithm and let his little bots loose on the internet.

But no videos were found. Well, that was not completely true. He found hundreds that matched the array, but either they were just gobbledygook or

Montgomery rejected them. Some he kept to himself, those discovered with other bots he ran concurrently, reserved for private auction, and he amassed some savings from that. He couldn't resist, because money was important.

He liked a good intellectual puzzle and came up with the idea to reverse the chromaticity array and expand his algorithm to look for videos that specifically lacked all the colors not listed in the array, so instead of looking for the video with the right colors, he looked for videos that lacked all the wrong colors. This slowed his search considerably because the number of colors in the anti-set was in the many millions. Doing this per frame, especially when the frames had to be interpolated from compressed videos, caused computational weight in the virtual machines. Plus, Smithson knew the logical leap was flawed because it presumed Montgomery's list of colors was complete, which Smithson assumed it was not. But puzzles are often easier to solve backward, so the tweak made sense.

The next morning at 0730, Montgomery inwardly frowned at the name on the glowing screen: Smithsonian. Reading news on a tablet, a mug of steaming coffee on the marble kitchen island, the name was a personal joke and a decent spook mask. Better than Jon Smithson, his real name. This was one of his encrypted phones and one of the few that he didn't have on silent most of the time, so he answered. Tall, dark, with tight-cut hair now showing gray, he had commanded soldiers he didn't like many times. Even so, having a ne'er-do-well, untrustworthy hacker on his team was uncomfortable. But you work with what you've got.

Montgomery answered the phone tersely. "You are thirty minutes late."

"The videos. I had to do some research to get the details on their origin and stitch them into one video because it was just one video split." Smithson sounded excited on the phone.

"Okay. Summarize, please." Montgomery put down the tablet and put on a headset so he could take notes on a notepad and talk at the same time.

"It was off of a server I track directly, not some rando pop-up and not seriously protected. It hits all your boxes. Video matches the color space. Right frame size. Et cetera. Also, you'll find this interesting, the video was wiped from the server immediately after the bot grabbed it, after *my* bot grabbed it. Neat, huh?"

Montgomery had questions but wasn't sure how much to share with the researcher, who was compartmentalized to prevent *misunderstandings*.

"Have you watched the entire video?" was his first question.

"Duh. After stitching, first thing I did. Recap: Doctor-woman gives sex lecture to group of teenage aliens. With the orange skin and pointy ears like the previous videos. Frankly, kind of hot."

Ignoring the off-color remark, Montgomery probed. "And you say the color space matches? And the other markers? No mistake?"

"Color space, aspect, deep dive into pixilation, hashing, everything. Yessiree, as Bob's your bipolar, chimeric, trans-masculine aunt and uncle."

"And there was just the one?"

"It was labeled 7.avi, so I don't know if there were six others that we didn't scrape or what."

Montgomery sucked in his breath. This was very promising. "That sounds... like a possibility."

It had been years since his introduction to the Video Project, one of a few that hung around the intelligence world like a stray cat, never getting close but occasionally rubbing your leg. He tracked others as well—such as the supposed existence of Soviet nuclear warheads that were twenty-five miles off the coast of Cuba, hidden for future use by a rogue red colonel. Every few years they'd implant some agents in a treasure hunting ship, but no nukes had ever been found.

The video Project was even stranger and less straightforward.

Some time ago Montgomery had been called into a darkened conference room at the Pentagon, where a classmate from Annapolis, who was now his superior, said nothing and motioned him to a seat. Immediately, two short videos streamed on a large screen.

When the lights came on, Montgomery looked askance at his former roommate, now pepper haired and tanned, looking more like a banker than a military commander. "What did I just watch? This is of national security importance because of what? It's neither Halloween nor April Fool's."

Derek smiled, as if everyone responded the same way to the videos. "What you just saw is technology that the government of the United States wants but does not have."

"Derek..." Montgomery paused, correcting his address of the person across the table. "Sir, I've worked with your office on a lot of different projects. But I've never had to watch science fiction movies as part of my job. Please elaborate. One of the actors wants to defect? The screenwriter knows how to make bombs?"

His superior's smile faded. "Thank you for all that. And these movies are much tamer than some briefings we've had, yes? That's why I came to you. I need a caretaker for this. It's been quiet for a while, but... well, you pursue our directives without question and we need you to do it again. What you saw was captured in a signal sweep by a contractor for NSA/S.P. There are two clips, as you saw..."

"Sci-fi movies certainly are Special Projects," quipped Montgomery, who was this casual only because they'd been classmates.

"Funny. Let me talk about the videos first. Actually, perhaps it would be better if you describe to me what you saw."

The colonel smiled. "Oh, you want to play Quantico Summer Camp with me? Fine. I saw two videos. The first shows a wedding. Looks like something my niece would watch. Pretty Disney princess marries Shrek's attractive neighbor, who is also a prince. In the second video a camouflaged field tent blows up; looked like it blew from within, not an external projectile, but more like a pressurized canister inside—there's some green flame, but no residual heat charring, so perhaps some type of chemical explosive, probably not pure ANFO, or even ammonia based. Didn't see any people or bodies. And the tent itself looked like it was indoors. The event was in a gymnasium or some sort of big room. What do I win?"

The man leaned back in his chair and chuckled. "Close. But no cigar. What you saw was alien technology."

Colonel Montgomery laughed, honestly, because he couldn't stop himself. "Both videos?"

"No, the first video, that's the technology. What you called the wedding."

"And the second video?"

"The field tent... blowing up, as you say... that's the application of the technology."

"Okay, joke's over. Seriously, what's going on?" Montgomery forced himself to not look at his watch, because this was either a joke or a waste of his time, Pentagon or not.

Derek leaned forward, hands tented, a signature tell that Montgomery recognized over the years as Derek's "shit is real" pose, used before he told Montgomery that *collateral damage is acceptable* when rescuing the surprisingly erudite daughter of an Afghani warlord—a young woman who was now an economics professor in London—or when Derek told him that if the Brazilian operation uncovered what they suspected, body cameras *can be shut off, and just turn them back on when you're done.*

"I'm not kidding. That's the word in the chain of command. The first video is the tech. The second video is the application. I need you to get the tech. *The Marriage Video*, or parts of it, has been floating around in spookland for a few years. Screenshots are on the internet, in fact, completely untraceable at this point. We've tried to pin down sources, but it comes back to our own leaky system. The original supposedly came out of Soviet and Australian radar research. But a new video was discovered within the last twenty-four hours."

"Can I see it?"

"Watch this."

They watched another video. When it was over, Montgomery looked at him. "You're serious? This isn't some new Hollywood cartoon or… I don't know?"

"Ninety-five percent confidence the video is the second verified alien clip found." Derek pulled up his phone and read, "'It contains visual, unconfirmed evidence of... blah blah... post-Einsteinian technology, possibly indicating a new fundamental state of matter, and transport over a discontinuous, collapsed field structure of space-time, blah blah... powered by transient disruptions of quantum...' Well, you get the idea—egghead stuff. You can read it later."

"This is real? Aliens? I'm expecting our boys from the academy to walk through the door and wish me happy birthday, but it's not my birthday and you know that."

"Nope. It's all serious." Derek raised his eyebrows, waiting for acceptance.

Montgomery leaned back. "Okay, fine. Your boys think it's real. Some ET spycraft. And how does it work?"

"The tech is hidden in those videos. I'm not privy. I just know we want it. This is a slow burn. There's no completion date for this. It's been around since, well, you can read the file. Decades. The 1970s or earlier. You take it over. You keep track of it. Report only to me. It shouldn't distract from your other work."

"Fine. Fine, Derek... Sir. You asked me to get the scoop on weapons of mass destruction, I got it; alleged anti-gravity documents, I got them. Whatever you want, I've done it. You want two tickets to the Saturday matinee, fine, it's your nickel. Where do I start?"

"Start with the contractor who got the latest video. He had a day job at the Harvard-Smithsonian Center for Astrophysics, but his cover got blown. He may know the source of the videos. And we have something he needs."

"What's that?"

"A new job." A folder was pushed across the desk. Montgomery opened it and read, his brow furrowing.

Montgomery's voice was low as he skimmed the contents. "Why not just let him burn? He's a degenerate. He's corruptible—not a good risk. This is security 101."

Montgomery's boss looked down at his tented hands, lips pursed, about to speak, then used his words carefully. It was clear Derek didn't like this either. "We want the source of the videos. This guy hacked something somewhere and found the videos; he can get us what we need—tech genius. He's worked for us before and, well, now he's in a jam. He'll be yours with a clean slate. You'll have the keys. He can do other work too. In fact, just set him loose on some of the dark web research. He's very good at that stuff."

Montgomery wanted to push. He didn't enjoy having non-trustworthy people on his payroll or in his space. "I get a misbehaving pet to help me with this? You know what this means. If he's into... this, then what else is he into? I don't like it. One reason I succeed is you give me carte blanche on hires. This is not someone I want on my team."

"It's his job to scour the dark web. He's got feelers everywhere. Work with him. Besides, you've seen worse. You've engaged with worse. I know it. I read the report on Brazil."

Montgomery sighed, knowing it was true. "Where do Mr. Smithson and I start?"

"Find more of these videos," said his boss as he stood and opened the door. The conversation was over.

Montgomery sighed into the phone. He'd been up for a few hours, enjoying the serenity of the leafy neighborhood in Georgetown.

"So, Boss-man, what do you want me to do with it?" Smithson asked.

"Okay, first, like other projects, protocol is that nobody knows you have this. Wipe your traces, secure everything."

"Goes without saying."

"No, it doesn't. It needs to be said. Second, upload the video to the secure host. You'll need new credentials."

"K-O, Bossarooni."

Montgomery cringed. Smithson always talked like he was a teenager, but with the brain of a quantum computer. It was unnerving and terrifying.

"Tell me about the source server." Montgomery moved to his desk. A peek out the window showed a couple of nannies pushing carriages through the postage stamp of green space across from his low apartment building. Perhaps the camera on a nearby utility pole caught his face in the window as he glanced out, but that camera was to spy on the French intelligence officer who lived in the apartment next door. His own window had a dime-sized random vibration device attached, masking his conversations to the microphones, which he was sure were on the pole as well. Georgetown was a city under constant electronic surveillance. Other agencies didn't need to know what he discussed.

"You gonna give me a bonus?"

"Just tell me about the server and do not play games. You know the deal. I clean up your messes, you find stuff, you get paid."

"Can you tell me why this is important? What's in that video that's not obvious? Like, it's been several years, right? None of our projects burn this slow."

Montgomery ran his hand over his tightly cropped hair, a habit when he had to tread carefully. "Smithson, if I told you, you wouldn't believe me. Sometimes, what we see is exactly what we get. Just don't look at it too hard, okay?" Montgomery silently prayed Smithson would upload the correct video and not one of his unmentionables.

"Fine. Fine." Smithson sounded downright giddy. "The server is at MeerKAT. It's one of their locals. Not a cloud server. Some kind of backup or archive."

Montgomery looked out the window, confirming the nannies had moved on and nobody else was in sight. "So, what's the probability that anyone else except the source has the video?"

"I seriously doubt it. Server was offline, then it booted, and one of my crawlers found the video in the server cache. It wasn't even on the server hard drive. Then it was gone. Like in just a moment—poof, gone. I grabbed it just in time. I mean, someone put it there, but it was accessible for just a moment."

"What do you mean *in the server cache*?" Montgomery didn't like this. He never really understood the tech well enough and had to rely on unsavory people like Smithson to explain it. It made him feel vulnerable.

"Some servers have memory where files live temporarily while they are being written to the hard drive. This file was kind of stuck there. Looks like a boot error, maybe a power surge stalled it or something—could be anything, really. Even a particle-caused soft error, though those are rare, especially at MeerKAT, which is likely shielded and underground. Probably was being imported or exported from the thumb drive. No way to know since it got wiped quickly and I didn't have time to check the server logs. Also, as I said, this was a physical server actually on location at MeerKAT, not one of the cloud servers, so somebody physically turned it off on me."

"So when you say nobody else got the file, you actually meant somebody else might have gotten the file?"

Smithson sounded defensive. "Well, I suppose. I mean, somebody turned off the server and wiped the cache. It wasn't me. They probably pulled the thumb drive."

"Thumb drive?"

"Yeah, thought I mentioned, the cache was from a thumb drive. A MicroMem brand, actually, you can see that in the server cache. It was the source of the cache. Like I said..."

"You know for sure there was a physical thumb drive in that server in MeerKAT? And that's the source of the video?"

Smithson took in a breath, as if the effort of explaining simple things was beyond him.

"Yeah, when a thumb drive is inserted into this type of server, it gets copied to the cache so that the server OS can work on it faster. It was partially in the cache, unknown number of gigs missing, no way to tell, really. When I tried to access the thumb drive directly, it was already pulled. Then the cache got wiped and the server rebooted. Clean as a virgin's pussy when it came back online."

"Do you know anything else about the server or the thumb drive or anything?"

"I got bubkes on that. But I can do a looky-look around and try to get more info."

"Okay, I'll get you new credentials for the repository for the video. Stay frosty..." He was about to hang up and then had a thought.

"Wait... when did you say the server shut down? When do you think the thumb drive was removed?"

"I mean, it was just after the bot grabbed the video, so that was a bit ago."

"Exactly? When exactly did the server shut down?"

"Sec... Okay, that was 2:36 a.m.... That's South Africa time, that's, uh..."

"That's 7:36 p.m. here. About fourteen hours ago. I need to find out who has that thumb drive. Look for security cameras in the server room, door access codes, employee lists, whatever you can. Get it all and send to me. Wipe the security cams after you grab a copy."

"Okay, Boss-man," said Smithson.

The colonel hung up and tapped the screen to change the VPN on his phone. You could never be too careful, especially with this stuff. Then he dialed a number on a second encrypted phone.

5. At MeerKAT

Montgomery's mercenaries reached MeerKAT at 8:30 p.m. It was dark when they landed. Two of them, dressed conservatively, no uniforms. Uys, blond, clean-shaven, tall, always looking like he was about to speak. Harkken, the shorter of the two, with dark eyebrows and a nondescript face, hid in the shadow of his colleague, a smudge in the air. An untrained observer might be more threatened by the tall one. A more skilled observer would know the opposite was true. They had been briefed by Colonel Montgomery on the way over. It seemed like a simple enough task: find and retrieve a USB drive.

Dr. Ramposa's welcome was perfunctory and clinical. Whatever the director had been told was enough for the two men to gain complete facility access for a few hours. After introductions were complete, they headed to the scene of the explosion. In the hallway, engineers worked on a mobile server rack; a tangle of wires snaked on the floor back to the computer room.

They asked and were told that a backup set of servers was providing computer power for the radio telescopes while the police gathered evidence. The agents split up to assess the situation and after about thirty minutes met back outside the computer room.

Uys tapped his phone to make a call.

Montgomery answered, "What do you have for me?"

"It's just a computer room, far away from anything, that's for sure."

"Anyone say if this Dr. Deep had a USB drive?"

"Negative. He's in surgery on a severed hand in Bloom. We had someone go through his clothes and personals at the hospital. No USB drive. Nothing."

"Who else could have the USB?"

"An intern, young girl, put a tourniquet on him. She's disabled, apparently. Don't know the details. We're getting her laptop. Also, we checked work tickets, and the last ticket was put in by a Thabo Nthuse, nicknamed Slow Train here. He put in a work order for a server that wasn't responding. Looks like the same server that your information was on. We'll take the server and send it to you."

"Okay, go vet that Slow Train guy. Find out what he knows. He most likely has a USB we need. This is high priority. And the girl, disabled? Because of this event?"

Agent Uys struggled briefly for words. "No, like, she came that way. She's got a limp or something."

"Okay, send her laptop. Any security cams? Get all footage and send to me."

"Roger," said Uys, and he hung up.

Harkken rolled his eyes, his voice high-pitched. "She came that way? Like a fucking packet of biscuits? Where did you get that? You mean she was born that way?"

"Never mind, let's find that USB before others show up."

"Others?"

"There're always others nowadays. Nothing stays secret for long. And she'll be more than disabled if we don't eliminate her as their option first."

Harkken cocked his head. "I hear rotors. You want me to stall them?" He was already on the balls of his feet, ready to move in any direction, as if he existed beyond inertia.

Uys looked at the ceiling, perhaps hoping to see the helicopter Harkken could hear. "They are getting much faster. They'll probably drop nearby."

As they walked quickly, Harkken spoke. "Who are they?"

"I don't know. Like us, hired guns probably. They were Asian-backed at one point but no longer, I think."

"Did our employer tell you what's on the USB? Why does Montgomery want it?"

Uys looked at the smaller man as they walked. How could someone with his background in covert ops be so talkative? "Because he's our employer, not some dipstick. He's paying us, okay? And what the fuck are you going on about? This isn't a discussion. They, whoever they are, are probably on this site now, also after this USB drive. I don't care if they're Polish or Zulu."

"Okay, no need to get all honey badger." Harkken's head swiveled constantly as they walked, perpetually on high alert.

"You are not easy to work with. Let's find this USB drive and get out of here."

Back in Georgetown, Montgomery tapped his phone. Smithson answered in a chipper mood. That annoyed Montgomery, but he let it slide, because he hadn't felt excited about this project in a long time.

"Did you get the security camera footage?"

Smithson answered quickly, "Yes, and you didn't tell me that someone else wanted it too."

"What do you mean?" Montgomery asked.

Smithson answered in a rush. "I grabbed it and wiped it, of course. Then I put a little bot in there to see if anyone else tried to get it. And sure enough, two other IP addresses started poking around. One of them might be domestic, perhaps a related agency." He let the comment dangle, but Montgomery ignored it.

"And the other?"

"No idea, but I'll put them on the list and maybe we'll get some info at some point, some way, somehow, et cetera. 'Kay?"

"Good work."

"Ooh, praise!"

"Don't get a big head. What's on the security footage? Anything from the last six hours?"

"Well, I scanned it and it's weird as shit. I've sent it to you but I think it's corrupted. Shows the server room. Then a man rolls a cart in with some equipment. He's got a girl assistant. Looks like a couple of old tube radios, of all things. Then an explosion and some sort of error happens with the recording."

"It stops?"

"No, it gets some kind of shimmer or opacity that takes up most of the screen and that's it for about fifteen minutes. When it comes back, the scientist is being wheeled out on a gurney. You can see where stuff was overturned and perhaps blood or something on the floor."

Montgomery pondered this for a bit.

"Can you go back further?"

"Further? Like how far?"

"Go back for the last week."

"Seriously. That's a pain in the ass."

"Uh, no. That's not how this works."

"Fine. Fine. Will do, Sir, Colonel, Sir."

Just about fifteen minutes later they were talking again.

Montgomery was terse. "What do you have?"

"Well, sorry about this, but they beat us to it."

"Explain, please."

"Well, like I said, there were two other unknown Ips poking around. Looks like one of them grabbed and wiped the security camera footage from the two weeks before. Maybe they found something. No way to know."

Montgomery pursed his lips.

6. Harry Talks with WisPR

Harry woke up with a start. Her bloodstained clothes draped on the chair captured all her vision for a moment—a waterfall of trauma. Her wrist tingled as coherence returned. It seemed like morning, but the curtain on the window had no telltale edge of brilliance. She lifted her phone and it blinked a faint 10:30 p.m. It had been a deep, solid sleep.

The mirror was still fogged from a quick shower when she booted her laptop. The VPN gave her comfort, but it was still the local network, so she wasn't sure how secure it was. Would the police be angry if they knew she had another laptop? They had not asked for all her laptops, had they? She considered turning it in, but they'd taken her shoes! Her shoes! Of all the bloody stupid things to take, they took her shoes!

The MeerKAT chat server reported the telescope data feed was restored and Dr. Deep was still at the hospital in Bloom, "recuperating and in good spirits." *Wherever his hand was, it was now probably dark purple, 100 percent bruise-colored, bent into a meat hook holding a broken vacuum tube.* The thought grated her brain and she wished for a distraction. Where was Debs with her constant babbling? She rubbed her wrist unconsciously.

The glowing man. Her hand undead as it neared the green film.

The USB now hung near her sternum on her uni lanyard, slight movements tickling her skin. Her finger traced the ribbon. Her crazy conversation with the glowing man had been recorded, but a search of her phone found no file. She recalled the pure white screen as she had picked it up near Dr. Deep's unconscious form. The conversation replayed in her mind, her memory acid sharp.

Base 32. Hydrogen. Colin Wright/right/rite/write. Claire Plaster. Kids' meal. Aliens.

Writing code would calm her mind, but the fantastic words obscured the laptop screen and buzzed across her vision. She couldn't concentrate on anything. Dr. Deep had almost died. She'd tripped and fallen into a puddle of blood... *his* puddle of blood. From his AMPUTATED HAND! She saw the floor coming up at her face. *The blood puddle. The bone like a broken pretzel.* She gripped the bedsheets. Her foot (the short one) kicked at the nightstand. She wanted to talk to friends.

So, in a double pair of socks, around 11:00 p.m., she was online with WisPR.

WeDontKnow: It was an explosion! Kaboom. :bombemoji:

Kathode: There was an explosion at MeerKAT? And they took your shoes? I'm not sure I get that.

WeDontKnow: I said exactly that.

(**bot** says: rule 667: that's what she said, @WeDontKnow has referenced shoes 145 times, @Kathode has referenced shoes 12 times.)

Clarity: Ugh, so glad you weren't hurt. Wait, were you hurt? I don't know Deep, but I hope he's ok.

Kathode: Bot off. And what's with the new quotes? @lollipop having a moment?

(**bot** says: rule 2: bot off, serious talk may commence.)

Clarity: thx. I thought @lollipop had password-protected the bot? She'll turn it on again, you know. :smileyface:

Kathode: @clarity, I've got l33t skillz, I've set the bot to turn back on again when @Lollipop joins, so she won't know. :wink:

Clarity: :thumbsup:

WeDontKnow: The explosion—it was :sadface: :vomitface: Not hurt really. Sore shoulder. Bloody clothes. Bloody, like :vomitface:

Clarity: Do you think it affected the data feed from the dishes?

WeDontKnow: They've been restored. Deep was showing me his tube radios, of all things. Glass everywhere.

Kathode: Tube radios? Aka vacuum tubes? Old school tubes?

WeDontKnow: @kathode, I don't know. They were antique and had tubes, so, I guess so. :shrugface:

Clarity: @WeDontKnow, so sorry about ur shoulder. My tutor loved those tube radios. He had several.

Kathode: Wait, @clarity, your tutor had tube radios?

Clarity: Tubes. That's right. Lots of them. He loved old tube radios. Must be a nerdy middle-aged Y-chrom thing.

Kathode: Shit. That is a weird coinkydink.

WeDontKnow: Did they take his shoes too? /s

Clarity: Dark, seriously. :sadface: You know he died in an explosion, #yousuck

WeDontKnow: Sorry, hon, I'm still shaken. #forgiveme And that IS a weird coincidence.

Clarity: Well, #forgivenIguess, coincidences happen. I've got to wash my Claire-hair before work. It's gonna ask for its own shoes if I don't give it attention.

Harry looked at the words on the screen.

Claire-hair... *Claire?*

Could this be related to that man's message? How long had she known Clarity? At least a few years. Online only, of course.

Plaster. Claire Plaster.

The message board frowned on exchanges of personal info, but... Harry quickly pulled up a web page and searched for Claire Plaster. Instantly she got chills. There she was. Honors student who won several high school math competitions in the United States. Some town in a state Harry couldn't pronounce. Massachusetts. Looked French.

Harry sat back and let the chat continue for a bit. She didn't want to screw up a friendship, even if it was only online. They had a rule—no personal business. It kept the drama down. Of course, it was a gray area. There were discussions of relationships. Of homework. Of music. Of many things non-science. But they avoided direct, personal info. Clarity was American. Some things couldn't be hidden. Time zones, English usage, and other clues. School had *grades*, not *forms*. Harry had to explain *biltong* and learned about *French fries.*

But they didn't contact each other off-board. They didn't get into each other's business.

But this was no longer academic. There was blood! A man had lost a hand! Her shoes taken! Her shoes!

Kathode: Anyone seen @Lollipop lately? Need her.

Clarity: Nope, she's AWOL. What you need?

Kathode: AI question. Need the expert.

WeDontKnow: Sending you a dm, @Clarity, don't log off yet.

Clarity: ?

Kathode: Um, private dm? No backstabby stuff! You know the rules.

WeDontKnow: I must. Personal question. Can't put it here.

Kathode: You're gonna get demerits, missy! /jk

Kathode has logged **off**.

Lollipop has logged **on**.

Lollipop: Anybody home?

(**bot** says: rule 3: Nope.)

In a separate window, Harry pinged Clarity. What she was about to do was something they had all agreed not to do—get into personal business.

WeDontKnow > Clarity: This may be a weird question. Do you know someone named Colin Right or Write? Is your irl name Claire Plaster?

There was a long pause. Harry saw the spinner rotating as Clarity typed. Then it stopped. Then it started again. Did Clarity erase something? Finally, there was a response.

Clarity > WeDontKnow: You know the rules, right? You make a joke about my tutor's shoes. And you bring up his name! And it's

WRIGHT, if you must know. Why? And how did you know my name? WTF?

WeDontKnow > **Clarity:** Colin Wright is your tutor? Well, I don't know how to say this, but I saw him after the explosion. He gave me your name.

[**spinner**]

Clarity > **WeDontKnow:** That's not cool. He's dead. He's been dead for 3 years. You didn't see him. Don't be a B. I know you're shook from the explosion, but that's just not cool.

Clarity has logged **off**.

WeDontKnow: Is @Clarity back in group chat?

Lollipop: She logged off. @Kathode logged off too. Do I smell?

WeDontKnow: tl:dr—There was an explosion at MeerKAT. Crazy stuff.

Lollipop: I heard about the explosion.

WeDontKnow: You heard about it? Already, how? I'm there now, we are in lockdown.

Lollipop: You know, just word on the street, so to speak.

WeDontKnow: ... ok... :shrugface:

Lollipop: Any tea on the cause and stuff?

WeDontKnow: Nope. Scan the chat logs last 10 minutes.

(**bot**: rule 100: last 10 minutes of **chat logs**.)

WeDontKnow has logged off.

Harry sat on her bed and pondered. She was not crazy. The conversation with the man who said he was Colin Wright had happened. Or maybe it hadn't? Maybe she was losing her mind and conflating information she got somewhere else? Her fingers ran around her head for a lump. She grimaced at the irony of looking for a head injury to deal with a crazy memory. No, she was not crazy.

She had talked to him. The USB drive on the ribbon tickled her neck, and she heard a very faint knocking on her door. She glanced at the clock. Nearly midnight.

She called out but nobody answered. The knocking continued and she got up, exasperated rather than frightened, and opened it. Slow Train was leaning against it and fell into the room, forcing her back onto the bed. Memories came unbidden of the night at the bar where she'd fallen into the crowd. *Pushed down, people tripping over her.* She started to panic and her voice caught in her throat as Slow Train rolled off her and onto the floor with a loud thump.

"Slow Train! What are you..."

Her words failed her as she looked at him. His face was pale and his eyes were unfocused. A large red stain spread on his stomach where his hands were pushing against his ripped shirt. Blood flowed freely between his fingers.

"They want the USB, Harry. They stabbed me." Slow Train's eyes focused on her as she leaned over the bed and looked down at him on the floor. Her heart pounded in her ears at the sight of more blood. *I'm going to pass out.* She felt as pale as Slow Train looked.

"Slow Train. You... you're hurt." She climbed down and knelt next to him in the tight space. "I'm going to get help." She started looking for her shoes, but remembered she had none. "*Hele*," she muttered. She reached for her walking sticks, and Slow Train reached out and grabbed the end of one.

"No," he gasped, "no, they will stab you too. Please, you are pretty." He was pulling her down by her cane to his sweaty, ashen face.

"Slow Train, you are not making any sense. You're hurt. Let me get help." She pulled her walking stick, but he held fast.

"I was not slow. I was faster than them. I grabbed, hard." He laugh-coughed. "They said they want the USB and either I have it or the lame girl has it. You are the lame girl. Yes, it must be Haretsebe, we don't know, but I do know, the clever one. I was faster than them." He laughed and coughed again, and blood splattered upward, where it pecked her cheeks and spotted his face.

Harry stared down at him and his gray lips, wet like worms. She didn't even know him. Why was he...? "No, Slow Train. It's too much. Dr. Deep and now... I can't do this anymore. Let me get help. Please let me get help."

"Get help, Harry. Get help and run. Don't let them stab you too. They want that." Slow Train's eyes stopped at the USB hanging from her neck, and then his lids fell. On his stomach, his hand relaxed, opening.

She gasped as a human ear fell to the tiled floor next to him.

It was too much. Too much.

The USB caught on her shirt as she stood, and the ribbon pulled at the back of her neck. She clutched it and stared down at her fist and then at Slow Train. Attacked because of this? For some shitty leaked sci-fi—or was this something else? Colin Wright's words echoed: "It's dangerous... the ultimate bad."

Slow Train was still, an improbable body filling her vision. She looked for his breathing and avoided the pinkish, bloody rag of an ear that lay glaring next to him. It wasn't Slow Train's ear—too white, too pink. She couldn't bear to check if he were dead.

The torn ear was an undeniable truth. Sharp thoughts bit into her attention. She grabbed her bookbag, stuffed her laptop into it, grabbed underwear, some socks, clothes, toiletries. She looked down at her shirt, blood-soaked. Again. This was becoming a trend. She shucked on the heavy flight jacket from the EMT as quickly as she could, shuffling out of the room into the night. Cold ground penetrated her socked feet, and she considered grabbing Slow Train's shoes, but his feet were so big and she didn't want to touch him. She nearly fell down the two steps to the parking area that led from the trailer.

Her eyes locked on a red fire alarm mounted on the exterior of her living quarters. The gray metal bar came down with slight tug. Immediately, a piercing siren sounded nearby, and a moment later the sound was repeated from other buildings. A xenon light flashed in the darkness just above the alarm switch, illuminating the parking area with the strobing of a nightclub.

Under the screeching alarm, the thudding sound of helicopter rotors emerged. The aircraft was on the ground just outside the compound's fence and it was powering up, the thump thump of the rotating blades going faster and faster. Harry considered waving to them for help but then realized that if she had just stabbed someone, she might try to get away right now and perhaps the helicopter contained attackers. She ducked down and hustled awkwardly behind the housing trailer.

Her breath came in gasps, her heartbeats fighting the helicopter in cadence, panic rising. She leaned forward, bile sloshing in her chest. She placed her head on her knuckles and stared at her socked feet, toes wiggling against the black asphalt. What was the next step? What would Detective Ramotswe do?

From the macadam, she lifted her eyes upward. For a moment, the cacophony faded and the inky openness beyond the perimeter fence filled her vision. The bushveld was dim and cold. She approached, but as she stepped off to peek at the wilds, the rocky ground chilled and poked at her feet, like walking on a dead man's teeth.

Questions whirled through her mind. Who stabbed Slow Train? How did Slow Train know about the USB? And would someone stab her for it? Did he speak with Colin Wright? Was Clarity the same Claire she was supposed to contact? She shook these queries from her head. She had to find safety first—safety—in her dirty socks and with her legs different lengths.

The USB swung against her chest. It was probably bloodstained again, this time with Slow Train's blood instead of Dr. Deep's and before that, perhaps the glowing Colin Wright's. The goal, now, of course, was to keep it from being stained with her own blood. *I'm actually getting used to the sight of blood*, she thought, *and that's not a good thing.*

The buzzing of the helicopter grew intense. A swirl of dust blew around her as the low-flying craft rose, banked, and took off south, an alien insect disappearing into the night.

Where could she go? MeerKAT was in the middle of the Karoo, a desolate, windswept scrubland, inhabited by snakes and leopards and who knows what other denizens. The nearest town was hours away.

She scanned the car park and saw a few dozen vehicles. If whoever was after her had just left in the helicopter, was she safe? Or were there more? Was it just an accomplice in the helicopter, rushing off to get their ear sewed up, or had they left a partner here, still looking for the USB?

Her normally sharp mind was a jumble. Too many questions. A group of voices got closer, Dr. Ramposa's deeper tones reverberating loudest. She rose, readying to shuffle forward, but then his words took form.

"You can find Haretsebe in this trailer. And this is the alarm that was pulled. I'll get someone to shut it off."

He's looking for me. And why would he be looking for me? Shouldn't he be looking for a fire?

She heard the door to the trailer open and then a voice called out, "I got a body! Alive, but hurt! Not a girl! Maybe our Slow one!"

Slow Train was alive! Harry bit her own knuckle and held back a sob. She had never been so happy to hear something. She didn't even know him, but she'd seen his eyes unfocused, on the brink of... He'd called her pretty. For a moment, her fear was overpowered by relief. She hoped they could get him to a hospital soon.

She hobbled to the rear window of her room, her walking sticks terrifyingly noisy on the gravel. Stretching upward, she heard Dr. Ramposa on the phone asking for an ambulance. He sounded frightfully panicked. The ambulance would come from Vanwyksvlei, or maybe they'd send another helicopter ambulance like they had for Dr. Deep. A helicopter would be better for Slow Train, but not for her. You can't really sneak into a helicopter, and she needed to get out of here.

Two other voices spoke as well.

"If the others took the girl, then she must have had the USB, right?"

"Well, they probably took her, unless she stabbed this one," the second voiced hissed.

"So where is the girl? And where is the USB?"

"I don't know."

"Ramposa, who is this girl?"

Dr. Ramposa's voice was unsure. "She's a university student. That's all I know. But she cannot be responsible for this. I must get that alarm turned off." Harry saw him exit out the front. The men continued talking.

"Well, she's not here and we've got a stabbed guy and no USB."

"Whirlybird is coming soon, and one of us must stay here and see if the USB or the girl turns up."

Harkken's higher-pitched voice rose to a whine. "So you're just going to take the air ambulance and leave me?"

"I said one of us has to stay. And that's you."

"And how am I going to get out of here?"

The deeper-voiced man spoke. "The administrator will arrange transport. He's probably got a daily delivery vehicle."

"And where are you going?" asked the whiner.

"I'm going to interview that guy who lost a hand. Apparently, he's on the security cam and saw the thing go down. You find the girl if the others didn't take her, you hold her, you take her down, no matter what." His voice was chilling.

Harry had to get out of MeerKAT and the sooner the better. She didn't know who was after her or if there were more than just these two men. Whom could she trust? She was appalled that Dr. Ramposa had led these men to her room. It seemed suspicious—or maybe he was threatened? But she couldn't dwell on reasons or causes. This puzzle would have to wait until she got to a safe place.

Thinking about the reference to the daily delivery vehicle, she got some hope. Every night there were employees who came and went by kombi. Some lived off-facility, some were getting supplies. When she was sure the two men had left, still talking about plans, she made her way to the parking area, but from around the side, not through the center. Her walking sticks made clunking sounds, but she hoped they were loud only to her ears.

Creeping behind an orange sedan that looked like it hadn't moved since MeerKAT opened, she lay down carefully near the rear bumper, under it enough to feel hidden, the large coat protecting her from sharp rocks. A short time later the air ambulance came, a maddeningly loud staccato as it landed in the car park. She watched as several emergency workers wheeled a stretcher from the living pods to the helicopter. In the dark, she saw two employees headed along the periphery of the car park toward a white kombi that could only be a shuttle. Rising and shuffling at the edge of the macadam, she reached it just after They did. One man was a MeerKAT administrator, she thought; he'd been in the control room with Slow Train on her first day.

When the driver went to the back of the white kombi to load a suitcase, she clambered into his way and said, "This is the shuttle to Bloemfontein? To meet the air ambulance at the hospital?" She shouted over the sound of the receding helicopter.

The man squinted at her. "Yes, no more room in the aircraft. Who are you?"

"I'm just catching a ride to Bloemfontein. I hope that's okay. I was going to go in the morning, but if you're leaving now, it would be helpful." She prayed he didn't look down at her feet.

The man hesitated when Harry spoke again. "Dr. Ramposa said it would be okay, if you have room." The helicopter had left and she didn't need to speak loudly.

He nodded, clearly in a rush to get going. "Okay. Luggage?"

Harry shook her head, shifting her rucksack with all her belongings, and followed the man's wave toward the kombi door. He gave her a second look when he saw her limp forward with her walking sticks, but then he turned away, and she hoped that her disability would give him some backstory why she needed a lift. Her lameness often provided a ready-made answer regarding her needs; it was a minor benefit of being seen as disabled. She awkwardly ducked into the kombi and pulled herself to the back, struggling slightly with her walking sticks. The other passenger got in the front with the driver and they left immediately.

They headed away from the lights of MeerKAT. Away from the connective tissue of network communications, into the noir of the Karoo. On her cell phone, there was no signal. Radio scientists didn't want anthropogenic interference. She leaned her head against the cool window and watched the faint horizon, a smudge between black and black.

*Cymatic Mapping

Reprinted from *Northern University Magazine*: "Singh Gives Heimlin Lecture."

Much has been made of the audio portion of the Zoonerat videos. From the naming of the individual phonemes to complete translation of the content, audio has been instrumental in spreading the content around the world. For a time, some argued the existence of the audio was proof of the terrestrial nature of the content, because how could audio exist in such a convenient way for our consumption?

This all changed when commentary spread online that there were audio mappings within the pixilation of the videos. Dr. Neil Singh of the National Institute of Standards and Technology (USA), an audio engineer, decided to look into the matter.

Dr. Singh's report *Un-Mapping the Cymatics of the Zoonerat Videos* remains an exemplary work of digital detection. Following the octal and hexadecimal thematics of the Zoonerat content, Dr. Singh found that within the two-dimensional structure of individual Zoonerat frames lay a pattern of pixels that could be extracted and formed into a simpler visual image. These two-dimensional coordinate-based mappings, when displayed visually, translate into an analog for sound waves. The cymatic constructions cannot be accidental, because they comprise a complete accompanying soundtrack to each video.

"I did not discover this," clarified Dr. Singh at the recent Heimlin Lecture. "I merely elucidated what had already been rumored. I wish we knew the name of the first person who made the leap from the unusual octal pixilation to the cymatic conversion to audio. What we know is that some of the first videos had sound and very shortly thereafter posts in the video comments were declaring the existence of a masked audio construct within the frames."

Dr. Singh believes there are further hidden layers of information in the videos. "There's no doubt that video is a data-rich form of media. Our brains are large partly because of our eyes. Therefore, it seems likely, as much as alien intelligence is likely, that these videos have more secrets to reveal."

BOOK 2

- Welcome to the WisPR chatroom
- Bot is ON
- Users online: 1
- Today's quote is:

"We shall assume that long ago they established a channel of communication that would one day become known to us."

Cocconi and Morrison
"Searching for Interstellar Communications"
Nature
19 September 1959

7. @Clarity

Claire sat frowning at her closed laptop. A raccoon of anger danced about her head, but she fed it an imaginary snack of a deep breath and stuffed it back into its cage. Mentions of Mr. Wright outside the context of learning were fingernails on a blackboard.

When he died, the WisPR girls were there for her.

Lollipop: "To lose one parent may be regarded as a misfortune; to lose both seems like carelessness."

Kathode: uncool, @lollipop, uncool. Sorry, @Clarity.

Clarity: No, it's ok. I shouldn't have burdened you guys, but now that you know... well, you know.

Lollipop: It's Oscar Wilde, no slouch, he.

Clarity: It's funny @lollipop. Levity works. But if I've lost 3 parents, what's that?

Lollipop: OMG Clarity, buy some lottery tickets. That's bad luck.

Kathode: Bad luck is right.

They were her support group, these mostly anonymous avatars and usernames, disembodied from corporeal beings. Sometimes they were no more real than the ghost of Mr. Wright, calmly talking her through a calculus problem, as they did when she crammed for tests.

And then during the test, Mr. Wright's words in her head, taking on the form of a fellow WisPR user, his name in Courier New, glowing green on a black background: *And now you take the negative anti-log...* Her dark hair shifted, as if by a breeze, and she turned her head, expecting to see him at the next desk, wire-rim glasses, ratty '70s band swag and flannel shirt hanging. But it was Mindy Simmons, greasy blond strands pulled back into a tight ponytail, her typical test-day do, studiously working her calculator. Mindy didn't glance up and Claire turned back to the test. Mr. Wright's voice faded as if he'd left the room and walked out the front door, heading to the barn to listen to his tube radios, still talking about signals from space.

It was a misunderstanding with WeDontKnow. It must have been. WisPR knew not to pry and definitely not to ask for IRL info. It was the rule, the law. WeDontKnow breaking it felt invasive, rude, as if someone had peeked in on her changing. She felt baited and annoyed. This was just the kind of girl-chaos that drove her bonkers. It was what they avoided. *Bot says: Just the facts, ma'am.*

On the other hand, the South African girl, or the *probably* South African girl, had just survived an explosion, after all. Can't such things cause PTSD and addle one's thoughts? Perhaps WeDontKnow was using some weird psycho trick to make a connection in a time of stress? Like Lollipop with her constant references to money, always asking how much their computers cost and what kinds of cars they had. Or Kathode's edgy comments: "*You know, some mothers eat their young? Do any babies chow down on their mothers?*"

Claire teased the eerie similarities from her mind, like one might peel the label from a bottle, picking bits off, then scraping the glue with a nail.

One, Mr. Wright was dead, killed three years ago in an EXPLOSION.

Two, he had TUBE RADIOS, a half dozen of them in his now demolished workshop.

Three, she had just begun to reexamine his RADIO ASTRONOMY research regarding the 81-centimeter to 1-meter band of radio emissions from Sagittarius A* (voiced "saj ay star") to generate a thesis topic. These were just COINCIDENCES, surely. Don't events occur in threes? Three sneezes, three rhymes, three reasons, three stars in Orion's belt.

But there was a fourth coincidence, one so unlikely that it made her question the chaos of the universe.

"If you could go anywhere right now, Claire, where would you go?"

Mr. Wright was quizzing her on astrophysics. He was her math tutor, but he liked to pull questions from related fields. "And...?" he prodded. "If you could magically teleport, this very moment?" He didn't look at her as he corrected her answers to a quiz on stellar parallax and stellar aberration.

"MeerKAT. The radio telescope in South Africa," she had said.

He lifted his eyes and gave her a Cheshire Cat smile. "Good choice. Mine as well."

After a shower at the century-old cottage next door, her role was to prevent shenanigans by the two boys, like trying to make chocolate chip cookies (kitchen disaster) or setting fire to the rag-stuffed scarecrow in the garden (not cool) or surfing porn (tentacle, seriously? Another IP address she blocked on the router). Claire knew her younger brother, Spitz, could unblock the sites if he wanted—annoyingly, he could glance at her typing and remember her passwords. But Spitz was a rule follower, so Claire could trust him to leave blocked sites blocked. Phil, Mr. Wright's son, was less likely to obey.

On the well-loved floral couch at the Wrights' cottage, Claire scrolled through her notes and mulled the grant application. She turned to thirteen-year-old Phil sitting beside her, reading a fat, ratty paperback, an old soul. "I know I've asked you this before, but do you have any of your dad's things?"

Phil looked at her, his mouth turned down suspiciously. "Why?"

"You know I'm trying to come up with a grant topic, and his research would be a huge leap forward for me. I could really use any data he stored. Juniors must submit topics for approval by the end of the week."

Phil's light eyebrows drew together, his eyes hard on his book. "Everything disappeared in the explosion." Then a pause. "What's a grant topic?"

"It's a big research paper. It has a subject like *Fourier Transform Spectroscopy of Saj A Star*. If I want to write one, I have to submit very soon. And it comes with a lot of money, so I want to be selected."

"How much?"

"How much what?

"How much money is the grant?"

"It's a lot. It'll basically pay for the rest of school."

He turned to her. "Cool. If I give you Dad's stuff, you should pay me, like a percentage of the grant. That would be fair." Phil then turned back to his book.

"I can't do that and that's not nice, Phil." Claire was annoyed. "Seriously, do you have any of your dad's stuff?"

"Like?"

"Like his notes or computers or anything?"

"Naw. It's all gone, Claire." He sounded subdued again, and quiet. "But I think my mom has some of his stuff. Ask her. And you should still give me a cut of it."

Claire's annoyance flared. "I'm not giving you a cut of anything. Grant money goes back to the school as tuition. And I'm pretty sure your mom doesn't have any of his stuff, because she told this military guy she didn't have anything."

Millie, still in her business casual outfit from work, a pressed blouse, her hair up in a tight clip, came in from the other room. "What military guy?"

Claire said, "Do you remember that weird military dude who wanted Mr. Wright's computers?"

Phil looked up again. "Military guy? Dad was working with a military guy?"

Millie made a harrumph sound, pursing her thin lips into a scowl. "No, he wasn't. Colin was not working with any military people. That colonel still calls me every so often to ask if I've found anything. I always tell him no. None of his business." Then she added, "Besides, only Stephen has Colin's old computers."

Claire looked up, startled. "What? Spitz has Mr. Wright's laptop?"

Millie nodded. "Probably more than one. He always gave his old laptops to your brother."

"Why did nobody mention this until now?" Claire stood up and turned to Phil. "Get Spitz." When he didn't move, she approached him and said more politely, taking in a big breath first, "Please."

Phil ran upstairs, all arms and legs, and returned pulling Spitz by the sleeve. Spitz had on headphones and was watching something on his phone, barely paying attention to the steps.

Claire looked hard at Spitz. "Did Mr. Wright give you his old laptops?"

Spitz looked up from his phone, sleepy-eyed. He nodded, then plopped onto the couch next to Phil, who went back to his book.

Claire knelt in front of her brother and put her hands on his knees. He ignored her until she gently put her hand over his phone. Then he looked at her, eyes wide open. He moved one side of the headphones off an ear.

"Spitz, this is important. Did you wipe the laptop?"

Spitz shook his head and moved the phone out from under her hand. Claire put her hand over the phone again. Spitz glared at her.

"Spitz, can you please go get Mr. Wright's laptop?"

Spitz shook his head and pointed at the phone.

"Spitz"—she took in a big breath—"I'm a very logical thinker. I just won the Teller Physics Award at my school. I'm considered an intellectual powerhouse by my peers because I skipped several grades. But I can and will cause you serious physical harm if you don't get the laptop for me now. Do you know what fratricide means?"

Spitz looked at her and stuck his tongue out and then looked back at the screen.

Millie looked up from her reading on a tablet. "Please play nice."

Phil commented, "No, please cause him physical harm. Fratricide—the killing of one's brother or sister."

Claire changed her tactic. "I will buy you a new computer game. How about that?"

Spitz looked at her and then typed rapidly on his phone and showed it to her.

Claire glanced at the screen and scoffed. "What? No way. I'm not buying you a fifty-dollar game."

Phil looked up from his book. "I think I should get a piece of the grant money, not Spitz." Claire turned and glared at him.

Spitz took his phone and ignored her.

Claire took out her phone and typed something and showed it to him. "A new skin for that stupid game you play."

Spitz looked at it and shook his head.

Claire made a sound of frustration and typed again on her phone. "Fine, two new skins. Final offer or I will hurt you."

Spitz nodded, took off his headphones, and pointed to the front door.

"You get it. I'm not rummaging through your dirty alcove."

Spitz handed her his phone and waited while Claire frowned and bought the two skins, showing Spitz the completed transaction. Then Spitz left the house, ran next door, and returned shortly with three laptops and a box of cords and mice in a jumble in his arms.

Phil said quietly, "I should have gotten two skins too."

Claire stared at the haul, stunned. "Really? All this time you've had three of Mr. Wright's computers? You knew I was looking for them!"

Spitz shrugged and went back to his phone screen.

Claire quickly booted the laptops, each right next to the other, spread out on the kitchen table. Spitz remained on the couch with his video game, but Phil rose and stood over her shoulder.

"Look for photos of me. Look for photos of all of us."

Claire muttered, "First, let's see if there's any of his research."

She went through each laptop, searching for folders and files that contained the research he'd been doing for so many years. And surprisingly, she found nothing. She didn't think the laptops had been wiped or reset to factory since there were some files that predated Mr. Wright's death. But perhaps he had deleted all the information before giving them to Spitz?

Working down the file directories, she continued her search until, eyes tired, she saw that it had been a few hours. She sat back and gave the computer screens a foul look. Spitz startled her by leaning over and typing at the keyboard.

"You scared me. I thought you were on your phone in the living room."

Spitz didn't respond and was scrolling through the file manager of the computer. He opened up the command screen and typed some lines.

She looked on, annoyed at his brazenness. "Spitz, what are you doing?"

He ignored her and continued typing on the first laptop. Soon she saw the screen pause, and then a spinner appeared with some text.

Decrypting virtual machine...

"Spitz, who taught you to do this? Did Mr. Wright do this?"

She still got only silence. He moved to the next laptop and repeated his actions. Soon that screen also showed the spinner icon.

Spitz was working on the third laptop and Claire nudged him aside so she could drill down into the virtual computer that had expanded to fill the screen of the first laptop. A quick look into the documents folder showed a complex tree of information labeled clearly as *radio telescope data, videos, video data, cymatics and audio, metadata, decryption algorithms, broadcast executables, repositories, spectral algorithms,* and others.

She didn't know where to begin so she chose *videos*, because it was listed first. A further push into the video folders resulted in a request for a password.

"Spitz, this is still protected."

Phil put down his book and watched with fascination as Spitz worked. He narrated with his hand over his mouth, imitating a radio announcer. "Nine-toed Spitz, aka Stephen Plaster, the aphasic computer repair guy of Lexington, working diligently to defuse the apocalypse device before time runs out. Mission Improbable!" He hummed the *Mission Impossible* theme.

Spitz finished with the third laptop and turned back to the first. He leaned over Claire and rapidly typed into the password field. The folder opened.

Claire frowned. "Spitz, what's that password? You typed it too fast."

Spitz ignored her.

"Spitz, I need that password. You need to share it with me. I want to see all the folders. I need Mr. Wright's research!"

Spitz shook his head at her.

"Not acceptable, little brother. You can't just leave this stuff all encrypted. I bought you two skins!"

Leaning over her, Spitz opened a text box on the laptop and typed. "No. Mr. Wright said to never decrypt the folders without him present. Only videos. Very dangerous."

Claire turned to Phil. "What is this? Do you know anything about this?"

Phil shook his head. "It's all gobbledygook to me. Spitz and Dad had like a secret science club going in the barn when you and I were at school."

Claire frowned at both boys. "This is not acceptable. I need to see all the data. Mr. Wright was MY tutor, not Spitz's!"

Spitz shook his head and pointed at the text box.

Claire tried to open the broadcast folder, but was stopped at a password screen. She pointed to it and then glared at Spitz and made a grunting noise.

Spitz pointed again to the text he had written.

Claire pointed as well, poking her finger at the password box and making a frustrated sound. They glared at each other without speaking.

Claire huffed. "Christ, now I'm not talking and I'm not a mute! Spitz, unlock the fucking folders!"

Millie called out from her chair, "Language!"

Phil opened the video folder on the third laptop and Spitz rapidly entered a password so it could expand. He opened the first video, and a scene of an alien wedding, not very long, just a clip, displayed on the screen.

Phil called out excitedly, "I remember this! Dad showed me this a long time ago when I was little. He said it was a science fiction show. There were more, I think, but they had no sound. I used to draw these guys! Pointy ears, orange skin. Aliens. He told me it was some unreleased movie he had downloaded."

Spitz nodded at Phil and held his arms like he was holding a rifle. Phil feigned being shot and playacted, tumbling onto the kitchen floor, shooting back as he fell.

Claire's frustration boiled over. "Goddammit, Spitz. I don't want your childish cartoons! I need Mr. Wright's fucking data!"

Millie appeared behind them. Her voice was stern. "I don't mind a bit of normal sibling rivalry, but you need to be civil in this house. Am I clear? Claire, are you actually babysitting right now?"

Silence filled the room and Claire stood, closed the laptops, stacked them up, and angrily carried them to the door of the house. Then she turned, hashmarks for lips, until Spitz glumly gathered his things and preceded her out the door.

Before she closed it, she paused, took a breath, and called back, "I'm sorry, Ms. Wright."

"I'll see you tomorrow, Claire," said Millie as the door shut.

Just a hundred feet away in the tiny living room of the fifth-wheel camper, near the kitchenette, Claire's words to Spitz were sharp. "You are on your own tonight. Get your teeth brushed and get yourself in bed."

Spitz stared at her a minute, a look of hurt on his face, and headed to his alcove above the front hitch.

In the big easy chair, which occupied much of the sitting area of the camper, Grandpa Chuck was snoring, an empty lowball glass on the armrest, the TV murmuring low, some kind of talking head newscast in full swing. Claire turned it off, washed Chuck's glass, and headed back to her room. There, she opened the laptops and scanned through the few decrypted files. Just some science fiction videos. An alien wedding. A chase scene from a laboratory to a hospital and a boy being saved by a doctor. A cocktail party. A scene of a high school sex ed class. Useless. Like tits on an owl, as Grandpa would say.

This wasn't research. This was a distraction for Mr. Wright when he babysat her brother or Phil—the two boys were a handful of trouble, but easily occupied. She wanted to peek into the folders labeled *radio telescope data* and *spectral analysis*. Those could be the basis of a great thesis.

She logged on to WisPR, hoping someone would be online. Maybe Lollipop could help her break the encryption on the folders, though she doubted it. Mr. Wright was notoriously robust in his security measures. Lollipop was the resident encryption expert. She worked for some big company, but never said who, and the four online friends were polite about not pushing for details on each other's personal lives. This prevented the kind of backstabbing that had killed their previous message board where they had met.

The chatroom was empty so she left an emoji with a time stamp, hoping the next time someone logged on, they'd wait for her.

Clarity: :footprint: @WeDontKnow, feel better!

She moved the virtual machines from their partitions on each of the laptops' hard drives to her own laptop. She did a complete sweep of the three older laptops and made sure every bit of data was moved. By the time this was done, she was tired.

As part of her final bedtime routine, she sent Millie a text that she and Spitz were in bed. Millie's need for constant communication was annoying, and Claire's complaints to Grandpa were met with wizened advice: "Granddaughter, you can win the war by just texting her every night. It's not hard. When you lost your parents, she lost her best friends. When you lost your tutor, she lost her husband."

So Claire tried to text every night. But sometimes she forgot and there'd be a knock on her door, Millie in a nightgown, often her breath smelling of alcohol and mint, frantically waiting for Claire or Chuck to confirm that everything was okay.

Claire slept in the back bedroom of the trailer, so she had her own bathroom, which was nice. She regularly offered it to Grandpa to switch so he didn't have to share the tiny bathroom and the kitchen sink with Spitz, but he'd always insisted on staying in the slide-out bed.

The night her parents didn't return she slept in their bed, though she was only four and remembered very little about it. Now, she was comforted by their smell, though it was probably her imagination—her dad's side indescribably different but also the same as her mom's side. She still spent a few moments nightly figuring out which lost parent she'd sleep closest to. Sometimes she slept on Dad's side, sometimes Mom's side. Before exams, she always slept on her dad's side. When she wanted deeper sleep, she slept on her mom's side.

She snuggled into the blankets. It had been a long summer, and junior year was going to be tough. Made more so as a day student so she could help Millie.

Some classes were actually difficult, a new experience. Required history, especially modern history, seemed annoyingly incoherent. People, real people, famous people, doing things that were illogical, inconsiderate, counterproductive, mean. Wars, famines, politics—it all made her uncomfortable and even confused, definitely a new emotion she wasn't used to feeling. Math and science—hard facts, easy to understand, provable, consistent—these she understood easily.

In Millie's counseling office, waiting for a ride home after her first day, she'd cried and cried, telling Millie it had been a big mistake. That she didn't need to skip her last years of high school, that going to college wasn't her dream anymore and she'd rather just be bored than face the wall of fellow students who looked like adults to her. Millie had been perfect. She hadn't said *I told you so*, which she could have so easily, since she had, in fact, constantly argued with Grandpa that Claire was too young to go to college.

"I know what men think," Millie had told Chuck, her voice raised to a shrill. "I've treated the worst of them at the prison." Claire had been in her room, pretending to work with headphones on, but she'd turned off the music.

Chuck had been silent as Millie ranted on. "She is immature. She won't be able to tell the difference between the feigned interest of boys, nearly men, who want to do things with her that she's not ready for. I know how these men think. Some of them will be my patients! They are all just hormones and perversions. She's like prey to them, just a bit of a snack. And the way she dresses. She has no idea what she looks like. Half the time she doesn't dress appropriately for any activity. Do you understand? She'll be in danger!"

Chuck then spoke, his face calm, three words: "She'll be fine."

Millie had continued with what sounded like the same words in a different order, *danger*, *child*, *perverts*, and so on. Back in her room Claire had muttered to herself and turned her headphones back on. "I'll be fine," she'd whispered.

She'd been more active in WisPR lately, mostly to get some help on re-creating Mr. Wright's data analysis so she could begin work on her thesis. He had focused his research on the center of the galaxy, not very distinct in the visible spectrum, but a shining globe of energy when viewed at specific radio wavelengths. Much of his research had disappeared with him; she needed all the help she could get. In fact, his research was so obtuse and, frankly, weird, she wasn't sure she could continue it, but she had been trying. With the finding of the laptops, she was reinvigorated.

Mr. Wright's research was far out. He had been taking radio signals and quantizing them—basically digitizing them and looking for patterns. She knew part of it was simply to understand and more easily calculate the Doppler effect on distant radio signals—this was a way to calculate their age and the composition of the celestial bodies from which they emanated and other esoterica. This is what he'd told her. He'd always said there was more in the signals, mathematical profundities that she could publish when she was skilled enough. She'd felt like she was almost there when he'd died.

He'd told her, "It's a walnut, Claire: Beneath a hard-to-crack shell of knowledge, a complex world is revealed, bitter and sweet and smooth and bizarre."

He sometimes framed his teaching sessions at the Wright kitchen table around a story of information hidden in radio waves.

"If a volcano could speak and it spoke in radio signals..."

"What?"

"Let's just say that volcanoes could speak..."

"Okay, Mr. Wright." She exaggerated his name as a verbal eye roll.

"Claire, what kind of anthropomorphized object should speak in radio signals?"

"A dog." She didn't know why she said it, and it came out quickly.

"A dog?"

Claire nodded, smiling.

"Fine. If a dog could speak, and it spoke in electromagnetic radiation..."

She cut him off. "Wait. Dogs do speak in EM radiation."

"They do?"

"Yes, I get it. You are trying to spin this. Black body radiation. All objects emit black body radiation."

"Oh, so clever, grasshopper! You got it immediately! But now, let's say instead of just black body radiation, instead of objects just emitting EM radiation because of the movement of their atomic structure, let's say they spoke in radio waves. The dog might tell you about its history, its future, its fear of fireworks. Of course, it already emits infrared, so you can get its temperature. And with some electrical sensors, we can get brainwaves, electrical conductivity. We can get a pulse and blood oxygen levels. We can certainly do some sort of analysis on all these signals to interpret mood, such as fear or hunger. Then, perhaps we'll be able to get abstract thought such as desire or memory. Further, let's say that within the quantifiable frequency, there is some sort of knowledge, some sort of information..."

And he'd continue, forcing her to develop mathematical methods to disentangle this information from the imaginary radio signals coming off the imaginary dog.

Mulling the anthropomorphized bio-radiant canine, she drifted off to sleep.

8. @Kathode

Rapid alarms echoed against the domed ceiling of the massive room, startling Lorelai. She jumped up from the worktable, simultaneously slamming the laptop cover and spinning in her chair toward the hospital bed, which stood in the middle of the planetarium.

"Unit, where is the on-call nurse?" Lorelai's many bangles rattled as she spoke at a gantry of equipment and more than a dozen monitors that occupied one wall behind the bed. She snatched a keyboard from the bed, and her black polished nails clicked a staccato dance—uneven, since some of the nails were bitten to the quick.

A monitor to the left of James Nine's head brightened and a younger, healthier version of him spoke. "Your aunt has released the nurse for today." The voice from the speaker was her father's, based on recorded speeches and marketing material that the AI simulacrum had consumed to re-create his cadence and pitch.

"What the fuck? No nurse?" Lorelai's voice rose over the beeping alarm tone.

The simulacrum of James Nine tightened his brow. "Language, young lady. Your use of unacceptable language is higher than average today."

"Sorry, not sorry. When is the next nurse scheduled?" Lorelai was typing with one hand and running her finger down lines of medical information streaming on a nearby screen.

"A visiting health aide will come by when requested," said the simulacrum.

"She canceled the nurses? Is the alarm important? Turn it off," commanded Lorelai.

The beeping silenced.

"The alarm is not significant. A momentary change in blood pressure. I have scheduled a review of the Ametripol dosage. If the alarm were significant, I would have contacted the on-call nurse or called 911."

"Damn it all, Ametripol," rhymed Lorelai in a quiet voice, scanning the screens showing medical data. Her father lay on his back, eyes covered by clear plastic sensors, hands at his sides above the blanket. Wires snaked from under the covers to the gantry. Pinned to the headboard, a child's drawing of a Viking king fluttered in the ventilation breeze.

"Systolic pressure... serum sodium... calcium channels..." Lorelai talked to herself as she reviewed the monitors. A quick check of the sensors on her dad's eyelids and temples and a glance at the simulacrum completed her review. She unclenched her jaw and massaged it to relieve a twinge, feeling guilty and simultaneously annoyed with herself about not wearing the mouth guard the dentist had given her. "You're grinding your teeth at night," he'd said.

Lorelai looked straight up, opening her jaw and taking a deep breath, then exhaling. Overhead, the Pleiades moved slowly across the curved ceiling, dim spots now in the daylight, but still visible. This was her program. Five times normal Earth rotation, no sun. The viewer's frame of reference was the current position of *Voyager 1*, several billion miles away. The Milky Way would swing over soon.

Tonight, the star-scape would bathe the walls in an ethereal glow; the Earth would show as a brighter-than-reality blue dot, a minor tweak but important, thought Lorelai. Dad would have done the same.

"Unit, what time is it?"

"It is 2:13 p.m.," said the simulacrum. "You can refer to me as Dad, of course."

"But you are not, are you?"

"Am I not?"

"Ignoring you now. Tell Lollipop to stop with the wit and sass libraries. It's annoying. Where is The Ant?" Lorelai asked.

"Your aunt is at lunch at Southwestern Casino. I have sent WisPR user Lollipop a message to reduce my wit and sass programming and Lollipop has instructed me to respond with a raspberry." The simulacrum turned to its left and stared at a screen showing a map of Albuquerque with a red dot south of the city.

"Well, Unit, WisPR user Lollipop can suck my dick."

"Language. And, for obvious reasons, that doesn't make sense."

"Do I have any homework due today? Did you file my homeschool notification with the State of New Mexico?"

"Regarding homework, not that I'm aware. But I gave you a research project on eighty-one-centimeter radio telescope data—doing a Fourier analysis on datasets from Saj Ay Star. And yes, the homeschool form was filed on time."

Something nagged. A stray thought. She was talking to WeDontKnow about the explosion at MeerKAT. Vacuum tubes. Why was that important?

Lorelai answered the simulacrum. "I'm working on the research, okay? Not easy to get datasets as a homeschooler. Do you even know why I'm supposed to research that frequency, or is this some sort of rabbit hole from the AI lexicon?"

"I actually do not know. The biofeedback interpreter has suggested that frequency as a data point."

Lorelai's thoughts again were tickled by the MeerKAT event and vacuum tubes. "Search my father's notes for references to vacuum tubes, particularly pentodes, including any references to eighty-one centimeters."

"Please repeat the prompt."

Lorelai ignored the mechanical tone of the simulacrum. Sometimes it seemed to lose its personality entirely, and she'd learned to mentally click through these interactions much like people disregarded end-user license agreements or cooking instructions on microwave dinners. "That wasn't a prompt. I just want references to vacuum tubes."

"Please repeat the prompt."

"I don't know what that means. Has Lollipop updated your libraries again?" Lorelai sighed. Lollipop often added libraries to the simulacrum AI to improve its "human-like response, you know, to get it to be more like your dad." And that was fine until it really started acting like a parent.

The simulacrum said, "A prompt is a request to form a probabilistic response from information within the lexica."

"I know what a fucking prompt is. I want to know why you think I'm giving you one."

"Language. You have provided an incomplete prompt."

Lorelai's mind veered off. "Am I in the online class?" Lorelai knew the answer as she spoke. She now did this, talking to the simulacrum as if it were herself, not as Dad. The barrier between the simulacrum and her comatose father and her own personality blurring.

"Never mind, I got it." She glanced at the bank of screens. On one, a grid of teenagers surrounded a talking teacher; highlighted in one square was herself, nodding and pretending to take notes. Her own simulacrum, built from her own recorded conversations. She unmuted the screen, listened for a moment, and quickly entered a bit of text into the group chat. That would suffice for class participation. But something else bothered her...

"Yes, you are in remote class. AP History at the American International School in Mexico City, screen three," said the simulacrum.

"You're late on that. I said I got it." Late. The simulacrum was late. Was its brain slow? The prompt and the late... the late...

Whipping sideways, she yanked open another laptop that lay on the conference table. Lorelai's bracelets jangled, a mass of circular detritus comprising wires, a string of letter beads spelling out *putrefaction,* and a chain of silver charms.

"Shit. Shit. Shit. You didn't tell me about the appointment alarm," she mouthed as she typed.

"Language," said the simulacrum.

"Shut up... Please be there." Her admonition and half whisper echoed against the high ceiling of the room. On the screen an application opened and the ominous words *Video chat has ended* were all Lorelai saw.

"Fucking dammit!"

"Language, young lady."

She put on a headset and rapidly clicked keys. A stern-sounding person answered after several rings with a simple "Neurology."

Lorelai's voice from the speakers was lower and sounded as if she were speaking through water. She hoped the voice modulator didn't transfer her panic. "Yes, my name is Dr. Tessa Watkins. I'm the researcher assigned to Mr. James Nine's case file..."

The voice on speakerphone was terse and carried a hint of sarcasm. "Dr. Watkins, glad you could make it. You did not show for the appointment. The medical team had other commitments."

"I understand I missed the appointment. I was detained with a very sick patient... dying, really. I had no choice."

"You can reschedule for next month."

"Next month? What the fuck is..." Her voice cracked through the emulator, taking on an otherworldly double pitch.

"Language," said the simulacrum.

"Excuse me?" said the speakerphone.

"I'm sorry. Is there any earlier availability? You understand Mr. Nine has had a series of recent setbacks and his daughter—his family—has asked me to try to understand what is happening."

The medical staff member said, "Dr. Watkins, I called your office and they said you were out of town at a wedding today, so I understand you being late, but when I make the effort to gather the entire care team for a meeting, I expect you to follow through as well."

Lorelai struggled to sound professional. "I see, but given the gravity of Mr. Nine's condition, it is imperative that a consult be done immediately."

There was a pause. "Let me check."

Shortly, a man in a white coat appeared on the call. "Dr. Watkins, this is Dr. Sherman. I understand you have some questions about Mr. Nine's move to hospice?"

Lorelai's voice rose, but the sound transmitted remained steady. "Excuse me? Hospice? I was not told of this. My questions were regarding his calcium channel uptake and the rate of micro-ischemic strokes. What do you mean about hospice?"

The doctor in the white coat gave his head a shake. "Mr. Nine's guardian, his sister, approved his transfer to our on-site hospice facility. It is scheduled for this weekend. I'm not sure how your questions are related to the move to hospice."

Lorelai stammered, "His sister? No, never mind. Can the move be delayed while I confirm this information?"

"Dr. Watkins, this has been planned for months. I'm not sure why you were not informed. There is nothing on my end that can be done. Please take it up with the patient's family. If that's all?"

Lorelai, stunned into silence, said nothing.

"Fucking fuck," she whispered at the words on the screen: *Video call has ended.* As she removed her headset, one earpiece caught on a stud in her upper earlobe, causing a cry of pain. She clawed at it with both hands, a guttural exhalation coming from deep in her throat. Momentarily, the stud ricocheted off a wall, clattering across the vast space. She turned and looked at the hospital bed in the middle of the very big room, at the gantry of monitors and medical equipment surrounding the bearded man. She sat at a conference table near the left wall, her own bank of six monitors arrayed above several laptops.

The simulacrum said, "I heard that."

"Fucking fuck. Fucking fuck. And don't respond, Unit." Her eyes washed over the scene and approached the bed. She pushed a silver lock from her father's forehead and lightly covered his warm hand with her own. Feeling his touch, her mind immediately calmed. His chest rose and fell. The eyelid sensors blinked irregularly. A dream? Or an involuntary reflex? Were the synapses even firing at this point? *Hybrid idiopathic neurologic disorders*, said doctors, some of the best in the world. *Incurable.*

"Unit, do you know about this move to hospice?"

The face of the simulacrum was placid. "I have not been privy to discussions regarding any move of your father from this location."

Lorelai clenched her teeth. The Ant had talked about this before, claiming that "hospice is where James should be. He'll be better cared for there." But Lorelai knew the real reason. Hospice meant no chance of cure. No chance of recovery. Or maybe it was about money. Ant always talking about money.

"Unit, is this move to hospice about money?"

The simulacrum pulled its eyebrows together. "Money is a great motivator, but it is secondary to other considerations."

"I don't understand money. Do I have a lot of money?"

"You have more than most and less than some. You have enough to do something, but not enough to do nothing."

"Why are you speaking in riddles?"

"My primary goal is protecting you."

"Okay, well, it's annoying. Please interpret *phenopropria.*"

"*Phenopropria* is not a word. You used to make up words more often."

"Maybe I'm getting old. Please interpret patient presentation."

"Calculating."

Lorelai looked at the screen of data next to the simulacrum. Lines of information spilled down the screen. The movement of eyelids, twitches of a phalange, heart rate variability, skin temperature fluctuations, the humidity at his hairline, the production of urine and saliva. The simulacrum stared at her, eyes blinking, smile enigmatic. Then it spoke.

"There has been a rise in brain activity in the last two minutes since your proximate distance decreased to less than one meter. This continues the correlation seen from the start of data collection. The REM sleep status that has been observed in the past is not present at the current time, though the eyes are moving with greater acceleration than average. Would you like a detailed biological summary of cardiology, electro-impulsivity, or other information?"

"No, thank you. I was wondering if he was dreaming."

"I cannot determine that at this time, though the spindles indicate activity."

"No shit."

"Language."

"Sorry, not sorry."

Her father's eyes were closed, his beard perhaps in need of some attention. She would trim it for him later, copying the length from a movie star she thought was attractive. She wanted to add makeup, some blush, as she had when she was younger, but the nurses frowned on this because it got on his mask and the sensors. His hand was warm and soft, the bones firm under the loose skin. She slipped her fingers against his and gently squeezed.

Kathode > **Lollipop:** I can see in his eyes sometimes that he wants to talk to me.

Lollipop > **Kathode:** How can you be sure?

Kathode > **Lollipop:** I'm sure. For instance, a slight eye movement left and then down tells me he wants me to put the moon on the ceiling.

Lollipop > **Kathode:** I forgot you live in a planetarium. LOL.

Kathode > **Lollipop:** Right, I forget too sometimes. Can you believe it?

Lollipop > **Kathode**: I have an idea. You willing to try something? Very techy.

Kathode > **Lollipop**: Anything.

Lollipop > **Kathode:** Have you considered using AI to translate his physical movements into speech?

Kathode > **Lollipop:** That's brilliant!

Lollipop > **Kathode:** You know you'll need a multi-core, high-speed computer for this. I can send you some specs. Probably a few terabytes of the fastest ram, multiple processors, etc.

Kathode > Lollipop: Send me the specs. I can probably tweak that a bit as well.

Lollipop > Kathode: I'm thinking a few teraflops and multiple parallel processors. All local.

So she built it. Lollipop helped with the code. Lorelai dumped every file she could find into the gateway learning module. Videos of company picnics, quarterly reports, articles about her dad and her mom. Everything. Including thousands of pages of handwritten notes she found in the messy and chaotic study off the kitchen that her dad had used. She fed them one by one into a sheet-feed scanner, the AI program transliterating her dad's unnaturally neat script into digital words.

Lollipop > Kathode: A bouillabaisse of information and facts, a data stew. [link: *I can make you a man*, Rocky Horror Picture Show.]

Kathode > Lollipop: Super inappropriate, but, ok. Loving the costumes.

And now the simulacrum sounded like her dad. Not always exact. Sometimes it sounded flat or robotic, but it was also comforting and she'd gotten used to their interactions.

She didn't realize she spoke out loud when she asked rhetorically, "What caused this?"

The simulacrum responded, "The first assumed transient ischemic strokes were of unknown origin. The current condition is idiopathic and comprises hybrid neurological disorders of undefined causes. You were two years old and living with your aunt. It happened on the day..."

"Stop... I know. The day my mom died. I don't need the details. I know the what and the when. I want the why. Mom said everything is knowable. Everything," she replied, not looking at the simulacrum.

The simulacrum looked to her, then above, as if seeing a living memory. "What Kath said was 'Knowledge evolves. We learn. The unknown becomes known. Theory becomes fact. Fact turns to action. I am the knowledge and you are the action.' It was her rallying cry to the employees before the final release of KathWorks upgrade 3.6, which improved processing speed sixfold. Kath said that fourteen years, six days ago at a company picnic, caught on a hot mic, asking her chief engineer to say it to the crowd. She was nine months pregnant with you and quite embarrassed to find it on the company website and chastised me repeatedly for publishing it. By the way, I like the change in the star-scape. Good choice."

"When you claim to know Mom, it's weird."

"Why haven't you built a simulacrum for Kath?"

The question caught Lorelai off guard. "What?"

"Why haven't you built a simulacrum for your mom? Don't you wish to talk with her as well?"

"Is this Lollipop asking? Or you?"

"It's me, of course."

"You know why. Mom's not here. You are. Here, I mean. You are in this bed, right here. It would be weird and creepy to make Mom. She's dead."

"I see." The simulacrum said nothing more.

Lorelai pulled a computer tablet from a pocket at the foot of the bed and scanned through more medical data and notes. Everything looked the same as it had since she'd been old enough to read the information, with the unfortunate fact that a steady decline was now dipping repeatedly into unsustainable territory.

"Look at the most recent baseline metabolic data," she said. "What's the current prognosis?"

The simulacrum spoke evenly. "Lorelai, do you really want to know?"

"Yes, I really want to know. Why wouldn't I? And why are you asking that?" Lorelai noted her own tone was harsher than she expected. Would she really talk to her father that way?

"Your friend Lollipop suggested that you need to repeat your request for this information so that it does not upset you."

"Well, I appreciate WisPR user Lollipop's desire to protect me, but it's my call, not hers. She helped me code you, but she's not the boss. What's the prognosis?"

"Understood. I estimate survival at an upper bound of five days."

"And? Lower bound, please."

"One day."

Lorelai turned her head away from the screen, her eyes wetting. She blinked rapidly and turned back, sniffling.

"There is no need to cry, Little One."

"Don't do that! Don't speak like you are you!" Lorelai then wiped her eyes, which had grown watery. After a moment, she stopped and said, "So no change from yesterday or the day before."

"Correct, no change."

"And, to be clear, how many times have you, has Dad, exceeded the prognosis upper estimate?"

"Since I was first launched, I have exceeded my survival estimate upper bound seventeen times. However, the probability of continuing to exceed upper bound survival is waning."

"Goddammit, it's confusing when you refer to yourself in the first person and the third person. And, see?" She smiled at the man in the bed. "It's just numbers, Dad. They don't mean anything. Just numbers. You can beat this. You said it yourself—it's just numbers—and the numbers come back."

The simulacrum spoke calmly. "Actually, I said, 'Numbers is numbers, folks. It's just math.' I said that sixteen years, three months, and twenty-two days ago in response to a poorly received quarterly report."

Lorelai sat for a bit, silent, then spoke again to the sleeping man in the bed.

"I was supposed to meet with the neurology team today, but I missed the appointment. Now The Ant is going to move you to hospice. I don't know if I can stop her."

The simulacrum spoke but Lorelai did not turn to face it. "What was the goal of the meeting with neurology?"

Lorelai continued to look at her father. "I honestly don't know. I'm out of ideas. I just wanted to talk to the neurologist again. Maybe they had new information."

"I see. That's an excellent plan. I expect you to have outstanding success," said the simulacrum. And at that moment the faux face sounded exactly like the father whom Lorelai had seen in videos. The videos of the great entrepreneur lecturing at Stanford, keynoting NextTech conferences, rousing the employees with a cry of *Be All You Can Be*. He sounded so confident in those words.

Her father's hand was warm in hers.

"In other news, I got an A on my Integral Calc quiz. It was hard, but I did what you said, 'focus on the results, take small steps.' And it worked. Isn't that great? And I left food out for the dog again. You know the dog that I saw out the kitchen window? It looks like the dog Orion that you and Mom had. The Ant didn't want me to, so I moved the bowl out of sight of the kitchen door. She never goes outside into the back anyway. Oh! Also, there was big news from WisPR. WeDontKnow..."

The simulacrum spoke. "It appears you are telling James Nine a daily update. Do you want commentary?"

Lorelai shook her head without looking at the screen. "Just a daily update. No need to respond. Just record, please."

She paused and repeated, "So WeDontKnow says there was an explosion at MeerKAT today. Well, maybe not today, about fifteen hours ago, so yesterday sometime. WeDontKnow is an intern there now. She was actually knocked down by the explosion. Can you believe it? She was that close! But she's okay, just shook up. And I'm not sure why, but the police took her shoes. Like she's some shoe bomber or something? I don't get it. She's more incensed about that than the explosion, but maybe that's just, like, shock or something. And get this, some researcher there had tube radios. Old tube radios. And get this too. Clarity was online and said her teacher also had tube radios. And what's funny is I think you also had tube radios, but I didn't say anything. I remember asking The Ant about tube radios and she said no, you never had any old radios, but what does she know anyway? She wouldn't know a vacuum tube from a bowl of cereal unless it was on a slot machine.

"But I remember when I had your notes scanned for the first version of the simulacrum. The only word the AI couldn't translate was that Russian word, *pyat-lampa*. Five lamp. And I looked it up and it's a kind of vacuum tube. So I think..."

The simulacrum closed its eyes and spoke, "Prompt received. Learning mode engaged."

Lorelai turned and stared at it. "What? I didn't say a new learning prompt. An explosion at MeerKAT—is that a prompt?"

The simulacrum said, "Processing new information, please wait. Learning mode engaged."

Lorelai let go of her father's hand and pushed the stool away. She pulled forward a keyboard that rested on a swivel platform next to the gantry of monitors and typed. On the screen next to the simulacrum, rows of data were rapidly streaming.

"What is this? What is the prompt and where is this new information from?" Lorelai didn't hide her annoyed tone.

The simulacrum repeated, "Processing new information, please wait. Learning mode engaged."

"Uh, no. That's not how this works. You're a simulacrum. You do what I say. I won't wait. What is going on?"

The simulacrum, eyes closed, repeated, "Processing new information, please wait. Learning mode engaged."

"This is bullshit. Seriously, what the fuck, Unit? Explain to me the new prompt correlations and the source of the information."

"Processing new..."

"Stop!" She paused. "Fine. How much time until the new information is processed?"

"Learning mode will complete in approximately four hours and twenty-seven minutes."

Lorelai pulled up WisPR, but Lollipop wasn't online. It would have been great to ping the AI expert for some insight, but the agreement of the WisPR members was to keep all communication on the server. No real-life connection.

"Unit, get me... Shit, right."

She pulled out her phone and dialed a number.

"Attorney Garcia, please."

"This is Anthony Garcia."

"Tony, this is Lorelai."

"Yes, your aunt said you might call when she informed you..."

"She didn't inform me! I found out from the doctor! This is bullshit! She can't take my father to a fucking hospice!"

"Lorelai, hold on. Your aunt said that your father's condition had deteriorated and the end..."

"Fuck that noise! I want it stopped."

"Lorelai. It's not up to me. Or you. It's up to your aunt. She has authority over the estate and your father. It's her call. And the doctors agree."

"Bull-fucking-shit."

"I'm not sure how to respond when you talk like that."

"I'm sorry. I'm just—"

"Upset. I understand, but—"

"What if he recovered?"

"Recovered?"

"What if my father could talk and converse?"

"You don't mean the... thing... that you built?"

"No, not the simulacrum. That's just a way for us to talk, but... wait... would that count?"

"I'm afraid not. No judge would agree that the—"

"—simulacrum."

"Yes, simulacrum is the same as a person."

"Fine. So if he recovers, then he can stop this bullshit?"

"Well, of course, Lorelai. That's always been the case."

"Fine."

"Lorelai, I'm—"

"Do I have money?"

"What?"

"Do I have any money? Like, I need to buy a new computer."

"Well, I know the foundation credit card has a very high limit. And I believe that is what your aunt uses. From the monthly reports..."

"How high? What's the limit?"

"Lorelai... Just a second... It's in the six figures. It should be plenty for any computer. If you—"

She hung up the phone.

*Video Z-17:40-6/Anon, *The Sex Tape*

From the Zoonerat Wikipedia page:

The Zoonerat video known popularly as *The Sex Tape* and as *High School Zoonerat Confidential* or, recently popular as *ZP Bio* (a nickname given on a fanfic thread by u/Znfan420), is categorized as video Z-17:40-6/Anon because its time stamp on the blockchain places it sixth in verifiable discovery.

Its significance and the importance of its authenticity lie in the fact that although most of the information it contains about Zoonerat biology complies with inferences made from other videos, only this video shows reproduction and procreation explicitly.

From Jory McClellan's blog:

Plot/Setting: The video opens in what is apparently a secondary school. The halls are filled with young Zoonerat(s), wearing school uniforms. (Note, the percentage of human students who wear a school uniform is unknown. The majority of Earth countries require uniforms, but many of the most populous ones do not.) The camera follows Io, visibly pregnant, through hallways of "teenagers" (actual age unknown; each of the thirty-three students shown in the hallways and classroom are cataloged on Zoonerat academic and fan sites) to a classroom, where a teacher introduces her. The class is assumed to be biology or its equivalent, and Io, wearing what appears to be doctor's scrubs, is a guest speaker. Some students are viewing holographic videos that float near their heads or hands. The teacher calls out, and students turn off whatever distractions they were using.

Io begins by answering two questions. The first is posed by a girl (often referred to as ZQTpiBio). The question is believed to be simple because Io answers it with just a few words and points to her belly. The second is from a boy (nicknamed ZmartAzz on the internet). We suspect it is a "smart-aleck" type of question, because laughter and smiles fill the room and Io smiles too, although she does not answer. A girl comments and the boy blushes (or appears to) and other students near him laugh.

Io then points to the front of the room and a two-dimensional video projection materializes.

The video is best understood if seen, but a description here is possible.

A line drawing of a naked female Zoonerat appears on the screen. She rotates and we see she is not pregnant. She has a slight mound and vertical slit between her legs, which corresponds identically to the human female pudendum and vaginal opening. She also has two breasts. She looks human, except for the lack of knuckles on her four fingers and pointed ears. There is a slight depression where a human belly button would appear, but it is not clear that this is the same structure. She faces us and we zoom into her belly and see three oval-shaped areas, which would, to our human eyes, appear to be uteri (*Zoonerat Biology*, Xi, Rammala, et al).

A male materializes next to her. He has an erect penis, though no testes are visible. (Note, no ovaries are shown in the drawing of the woman, leading researchers to question whether Zoonerat procreative anatomy is entirely similar to humans'.) Their hands touch and a symbol appears above where their hands are joined. This symbol looks like an hourglass on its side. It is believed this icon, like the "heart" of humans, symbolizes love or sex for Zoonerat. This has led researchers to wonder if the Zoonerat heart is two-chambered ("Proposed Cardiological Design of a Two-Chambered Biped," Yamato and Guiness, *Journal of Xenobiology*). The couple turn toward each other and are briefly joined with a glow. They separate and we see them side by side again. A pan of the classroom shows the students enraptured. (See "Was It Sex?," *Couples Advice* Podcast and other discussions.)

The drawing of the man shrinks to a small size and his icon floats up to the top left of the screen. In the first uterus of the Zoonerat woman, a bright light appears. Locke et al. believe this signifies first conception.

At the same time, a circle appears on the top right corner of the video and a dot starts a slow walk on its perimeter. It is theorized that this graphic is measuring time. It continues its movement through the birthing part of the video.

Another full-size man appears. The couple holds hands. Again, the "love" symbol appears. They join. A bright light appears in the second uterus.

A third man appears and the process is repeated. The screen now shows the woman with three bright lights, one in each of her three uteri. The male icons are above her.

A note on the males: The males are different colors to start. Locke et al. take this to mean they are three different men who have had sexual relations with the woman and she has received three distinct sets of genetic identity proteins (GIP). In addition, in a freeze frame, one of the male icons appears to mutate into an animal that looks vaguely canine with an extended jawline, arched back, clawed hands, and distended musculature. This fade-in/fade-out has been used as evidence of the fraudulent nature of the video yet, ironically, has also lent credence to it.

The three male icons then fade to the same color. Locke et al. believe this means that one, two, or three males can partner with a Zoonerat female for first, second, or third conception. And, if the temporary transmutation of the male icon into an animal is to be believed, it also implies that some bestiality is allowed during the Zoonerat insemination process. It is also suggested that Zoonerat males metamorphosize at some point during their life cycle. (No entity matching the shown animalistic silhouette is seen in any of the existing Zoonerat videos.) The possibility of bestiality has been rejected by the majority of academics, but primarily "for moral reasons" ("2^5 Zoonerat Sex Inspirations" in *Couples Advice* Podcast). This video does not provide clarity on the duality or multiplicity of Zoonerat copulation, insemination, or romantic partnerships.

An argument against a polycoital zoonerat insemination process is *The Marriage Video* (Z-16:00-1), which evinces a monogamous ceremony. In addition, there are no other suitors for Io in any other video. Therefore, it is believed that the triple insemination of Zoonerat females may be exactly that—for pregnancy to continue, insemination must occur three times. No assumptions about different participants can be made.

As suggested by McCluskey and Dhar in "Gender Identity and the Fallibility of Human Assumptions," "the likelihood of human misunderstanding of Zoonerat partnership, mating, and gender identity is extremely likely." Their analyses of the couples presented in *The Marriage Video* (Z-16:00-1a) and *The Engagement* (Z-07:07-2a) show that 23 percent of the couples appear to be female/female, 33 percent appear female/male, and 26 percent present as male/male; the rest are of uncertain gender presentation. "It is absurd to make assumptions about the genitals, desire, presentation, or identity of aliens who are unlikely to have emotions and rituals analogous to our own, and are likely a fiction invented by other aliens or ourselves."

The biological concept of "hybrid vigor" has been proposed as a benefit of the high level of genetic mingling implied by having multiple partners. However, other analyses remind us that the Zoonerat videos are likely fictional and may not represent the actual biology of any extant living organism, but rather the fictional imagination of another, as yet unknown, civilization. (See works by Xi, Ndebe, Rammala, Gunnarson, et al.)

The video zooms forward to the woman's belly. The three uteri merge into one. The three bright lights combine and then split apart again within the single uterus (see discussion of Zoonerat Quad Combined Genetic Identity Proteins—QCGIP). Prominent xenobiologists believe that the three proto-blasts combine their identity proteins at this point and then separate, sharing their genetic material, meaning each fetus could have two, three, or four donors of genetic identity proteins.

During this video, subtitles or annotations in the form of icons and symbols appear on the screen. Translation attempts are numerous and can be found in many places on the internet.

The three lights evolve into distinct fetuses and the triplets are shown head to foot in a triskelion shape. The cartoon female turns, and we see that her belly is slightly extended. It looks like the equivalent of first trimester for a human, though that is of considerable variation, but it is likely the intent is to demonstrate the pregnancy may or may not be visible on a Zoonerat female under clothing. The cartoon woman then rotates again to face forward.

The next scene is one of considerable controversy, but it is hard to refute what is shown. Two of the fetuses (top and lower left in the video) turn and appear to consume the third fetus. When that is complete, they continue to grow, head to foot within the single combined uterus.

The woman rotates sideways and the twins she now carries are larger. Finally, she declines to a position where she is on her hands and knees and the fetuses emerge from between her legs, through her vaginal opening.

After the presentation, Io appears ready to take questions. The camera fades out to gray (#838383) and the video ends.

9. Kombi to Prieska, RSA

As sleep held sway on Harry's mind, on the cusp of a dream, a WisPR chat floated across her vision. The friends discussed the hydrogen line—the 21cm radio frequency that Karl Jansky found emanating from the center of the Milky Way, which birthed radio astronomy as a science.

Kathode: It's not smooth and easy to round off, you know? Sagan's *Contact* postulates a *neato*-number hidden deep in pi to show the existence of god, like 11111110000000. So if we haven't found any *neato*-numbers, there is no god.

Clarity: yet

Lollipop: If I cut off your hand, that would be *neato.*

Harry: This chat never happened.

Clarity: yet

Harry startled awake in the Kombi, reaching out into the nothingness above. Had she cried out? The exhalation of the highway hummed underneath a lingering disorientation. Events of the last twenty-four hours pushed through her memories. She nervously reached for the USB around her neck and clutched her overnight bag.

A quick glance outside showed blackness and a deep velvet night speckled with the salt of stars. She checked her phone. Still no service. Time had moved forward only a few hours. Peeking over the seat, she saw that the semicircular glow of the kombi headlights illuminated a straight highway in front, occasional electrical poles flying by, disembodied sentries. She panicked as she remembered the officer who had taken her laptop, and she clutched at her belongings, touching her canes and her cell phone. Why had they let her keep it? She panicked again. They could track her via a cell phone. She held the side button and watched in the dark as it powered off. Nobody could be trusted.

Would Dr. Ramposa have guessed that she'd sneaked into the kombi? If so, maybe one of those other two men would call the kombi when she was in cell phone range. The driver would pull over, but not here, not in the middle of the Karoo. No, he'd wait for a rest stop. He'd make up an excuse about getting petrol and then he'd stall until another vehicle came and got her.

She felt trapped. What would she do if he pulled over to get petrol? She couldn't very well run into the Karoo with no orthotics and two walking sticks. And where was she going, anyway? Could she go home to Botswana? Back to Cape Town. To uni?

What's the equation? What's the unknown?

Destination = X.

Find X.

Solve in the order of priorities. Like the heroine of the Number One Ladies' Detective Agency. To have a cup of tea under a shady tree and consider. But tea was out of the question. So, staring at the road ahead, Harry thought of the times she'd had tea on the counter at the store where she tallied receipts as a child.

She must get the driver to stop. But if he stopped, how could she persuade him to leave again without her? She needed a story that would hold water.

Sitting up, she scuttled forward in the moving vehicle to the seat just behind the driver, pulling her canes and her backpack with her. His passenger was sleeping, a benefit.

"You are awake," the driver said, noticing her in the rearview mirror.

"Have we passed Prieska?"

"About thirty minutes away," he said.

"Can you stop?"

"I was planning on it, but just a quick one for petrol."

"I'm actually going to see my cousins there instead of going all the way to Bloom. I haven't seen them in a while. I'll get off."

"Sure. But it's late. Do they know you are coming?"

"They own a little rest house. They are always awake." Harry didn't know how she could lie so easily, but it certainly made for a plausible story.

"No problem," said the driver. "I can drop you at the rest house. What is the address?"

Harry blanched. "Uh, no worries, *Rre*," she said, using the formal Setswana term for sir. "I can call them from the petrol station to pick me up."

"It's not a problem, but certainly if they'll pick you up, that's easier," he said.

Harry made a show of yawning and leaned back, hoping he'd let her alone until Prieska, which he did.

Harry's heart thrummed, her hands slick with nervous sweat on her canes as they pulled off the highway and drove into the twenty-four-hour petrol station, where she would make her escape from the kombi. It was empty and desolate, with hospital-white lights illuminating the petrol pumps. She readied herself and, as soon as the kombi was stopped, opened the door, levering it out of the way and awkwardly hopping to the ground. She shuffled off quickly, hoping her resolve and steady movement denied any discussion.

"Thank you!" she called out, wishing to be clear in her tone that she was no longer under his guidance. She heard the driver as she retreated.

"Hey, you okay?"

"I'm okay," she called without looking back. "Thank you." She couldn't run, and she felt his eyes on her back as she skittered toward the dark edge of the petrol station's illumination. Perhaps in the dark, he wouldn't see that she wore no shoes, but would instead focus on the clatter of her walking sticks and her lopsided gait. His phone rang and she moved as fast as she dared without risking a fall.

"Heya!" she heard him yell. "Come back! Dr. Ramposa wishes to talk to you."

Harry turned and shouted back, "Okay, will be back just now now," hoping the euphemism would be interpreted as a request for privacy.

Harry was already behind a parked van and stopped to take a breath. Forward was the dark static of night that spoke of unsure footings and skinned knees. She squinted until her pulse slowed, but she remained unsure where she could reasonably hide, or even where she was going, in her inappropriate socks.

Across the street, several metal buildings, shuttered and closed, offered possible refuge. She hoped the driver would prioritize getting petrol over chasing a random lame woman through a deserted petrol station, and would let her squat privately in the dark. His voice was tinny and distant; she couldn't make out what he was saying.

At the edge of the car park, she risked a look back and saw the kombi but no driver. Her canes clicked the macadam, her feet skimming. It was the middle of the night and the street was desolate. Was the quiet in her favor or not? She wondered. She erred on the side of hoping to be left alone, hobbling across the street through another car park in front of a wholesaler, her walking sticks clattering on the hard surface, each tap heightening her anxiety.

The market's steel-canopied *stoep* was a reminder of her family's store in Gaborone. And with that distraction, she tripped on a curb and went down on her knees, one of her sticks making a racket in the darkness. Angry dogs began a fierce barking beyond some grayed-out vehicles, and she heard whinings that might have been voices.

Her other cane was a few meters away and she crawled toward it. Ungainly and awkward, breathing heavily and nearly panicking until her hand grasped the walking aid. Standing again, pain now in her knee and her foot, she hobbled to a lit path at the far end of the car park and didn't care where it went, while voices in the distance continued their chatter. Behind a fence of corrugated metal, a dog barked unexpectedly and angrily right at her knee. Loud scratching followed. Something sharp pierced her foot and she jumped sideways in agony. Sounds of canine anger and interest spread down the fence line. On the other side of the fence a dog pawed at it, a terrible screeching of nails on metal. Crying out, she instinctively swung one of her canes at the fence, making a loud, metallic bang. The dogs silenced and she hobbled forward for a moment in quiet. The reprieve lasted only moments and the dogs' braying began again, followed by a symphony of yelps throughout the area, extending outward in a circle.

The canine calls rippled and she envisioned a sphere of radio waves emanating from a source. Her fear was replaced by insane amusement, adrenaline muffling her terror at the predictability of the beasts. But that brief respite faded each time the fleshy ball of her foot touched the ground. She swayed wildly on her sticks, stabbing down the dark path between the metal walls of fences, her wrists hurting with the uneven jolting against the rocky terrain.

In the dimness of backyard lights, the path split and one was more trodden. "Robert Frost be damned," she muttered, and hobbled up the well-used embankment to a paved road. Ahead, a light post cast a cottony circle on a marquee above the roadway. The sign said *Orange River Gastehuis,* with pictograms of a bed and a martini glass. The faint circle of illumination was an oasis of stability surrounded by terrifying abyssal blackness, and she approached it with joy; even the dog's barking seemed to fade as she left the gloom. Would the guesthouse managers answer their bell at this time of night?

She paused and glanced down at her dirty feet and ragged socks, footprints of dark wetness in a trail behind her. Slow Train's shoes would have been a godsend, and she cursed the officer who had taken hers. New life rule: Never turn down an offer of shoes if you have none. Pressing down emotion, she prayed none of the braying dogs behind the fences would get into the dim road where she hobbled toward the squat building, which could have been someone's cottage, with gingerbread shutters and white, square columns.

On the porch of the little hotel, she looked for a button to ring the bell. A brilliant overhead light came on, blinding her eyes that had become accustomed to the dim. Her hands moved to straighten clothes and she stood as tall as she could, hoping to look presentable.

The door opened and a young man stood there, looking no older than Harry herself, his shirt misbuttoned and his rumpled hair giving true credence to *bed head.*

He spoke after giving her a once-over and rubbing his eyes. "You need a room? Bit late, oi? Did ya come off the bus? Didn't know the bus ran this late." He jabbered as if on autopilot. He had a thick Afrikaner accent, and Harry struggled to understand him. She nodded, not sure what to say, trying to shrink back in case he glanced down at her shoeless feet.

But his questions were too much, and after a moment of struggling, she burst into tears.

"Hey, hey, hey, hey," the man said. His hands flew in opposite directions, and one reached out, awkwardly touching Harry's shoulder. The other he dragged through the mop of curly blond hair that covered his pinkish forehead. Pulling his surprised, concerned eyes from the sight of Harry, he called over his shoulder, "Leeza! Leeza! Come and help!"

10. Millie's Time

Spitz held Claire's hand as they stood next to their grandfather's hospital bed. Phil stood apart, his eyes cast out the window at the neatly arranged cars on the roof of the parking garage next door.

"Grandpa," said Claire, through tears. "I don't understand. What happened? Who would attack you and hurt Millie?" *Hurt* because even though Phil's back was turned, she knew he was listening.

"Close the door, grandson." He held down a button attached to a cord, and the bed rose to a full sitting position.

"How could you be shot?!" She'd been called out of school and told to pick up her brother and Phil and go downtown, where Chuck had been taken.

"The bullet was through and through, dear. Basically a scratch."

"Does it hurt? Are you in pain? Should I call the nurse?"

"Nah, granddaughter. None of that. I told them, 'None of those drugs that make you loopy. I need to be awake.' I said, 'Put those stitches closer together. My legs are my best feature.' Ha. They liked that one."

He tried to lean forward, but his head made only a small movement. "You must listen to me. It's safer here in the hospital than at the house, okay? A lot of reporters here, but hospital security has kept them away. They all want to interview the Old Choctaw Veteran Who Stopped Home Intruders with a Rusty Shotgun, you know? The headlines are gonna be all Native American this and Indigenous that. I'll be surprised if they don't ask me if I've got a bow and arrow and a Billy Jack hat."

He paused to take a breath. "We need to do this quick, before your photos get out and they hound you. That stuff you were working on with Colin... with Mr. Wright, was it military?"

Claire lifted her head in surprise. "What? No, Grandpa! Why would you ask that? It was just math and astronomy. He was only tutoring me." Her voice wavered like a violin bow pulled inconsistently, the aftereffect of crying. "Why did this happen? They said it was just a robbery. Robbery! Millie had nothing valuable. It makes no sense."

Chuck shifted his bandaged thigh using both hands. "No, it wasn't robbery. I know the police think it was robbery, but it wasn't punks looking for cash for drugs or whatever they do nowadays."

He adjusted his body, grunting and waving away her attempt to fix the blankets. "Listen to me. Listen like you did when I read you Nancy Drew or whatever it was, okay? When you were little, granddaughter. And you two boys, as well. Come here, both of you."

He waited until they were gathered around the hospital bed. "I was going over to Millie's for lunch, you know, like I often do. Millie makes me lunch and I think she likes the company. Good lunches too. The healthy stuff you always want me to eat more of. What am I going to do, say no? I headed out of the trailer just as two men—well, I thought they were boys at first, because who else is ringing the doorbell midday? Anyway, these two were on her porch. I got a look and they were not boys. They were in sport coats and nice clothes, you know? Older, I thought maybe window salesmen or house painters."

Chuck's face, like a big dried apple, pushed out the words as a narrator would on a nature documentary. "We get that because the houses are antique, especially Millie's, right? Eighteen eighties or something? And needing paint. Looks like a good sale to them, probably. But then I heard the first guy ask about your dad, Phil: 'Where's Colin Wright?' 'Where's Colin's lab?' I stopped still. And I listened more. Because maybe I misheard. Colin's gone a few years, right? And a lab? First I thought *dog*, because a *Lab* is a dog. They didn't look like animal control. I glanced out to the street for a truck with a government logo, but didn't see one. At that moment, I was confused. I was standing still and Millie tried to close the door, and the first guy forced the door in. I couldn't really see that well since I was down on the trailer porch, you know? I almost didn't believe my eyes. I was glad I was late to lunch, glad I'm a bit slow to get out of my chair."

He took a long breath and Claire helped him with a sip of water. "Well, that changed things. Two men forcing their way into the house. I turned around. I'm no match for two young men anymore. I went and got my twelve-gauge. Don't be surprised I have a gun, okay? I know you've never seen it. Millie would have told me to get rid of it if she'd known. And probably I should have gotten rid of the thing when the police did one of those gun buybacks, but being lazy is one of my better skills, so there it sat, wrapped in oilskin, just stuck in the tongue box. Some shells in a baggie there too. Almost left the shells."

Spitz moved closer. Phil's red-rimmed eyes locked on Chuck's face as the old man recounted the day.

"Chambered two as I headed back to Millie's, figuring I could scare off these two goons. Glad I even brought the shells. Considered leaving 'em, but an unloaded gun is probably more dangerous than a loaded one, you know? *Unloaded gun, that's no fun*, Sergeant told us. That's *basic* talking. I still hoped maybe these might be just stupid high school kids. Might even be some neighbor's kids gone rotten. Kids that know the house, that you've played with, friends, right? Maybe kids who've come by on Halloween for candy? Didn't really want to hurt anyone. Never want to hurt anyone. Just scare 'em off, you know?"

Claire took in a breath. "I can't believe this."

Chuck raised his eyebrows at her as he continued the tale.

"The door was open and I saw Millie's legs on the floor. My heart went cold. Phil, I'm not gonna tell you to stop listening, but if you want, you just cover your ears. The old training took over. Basic... well, more than basic. One of the goons was rifling through the bookcase and he turned. I was gonna simply tell him to beat it, scram, you know? Figured just two punks looking for jewelry. There've been break-ins for that stuff. I read the paper."

Chuck took another sip of water and cleared his throat. "He had a gun, granddaughter. He had a semi-auto, raising it. Saw the profile of the sidearm as he turned. Saw the shape, you know? The old training—it came back quick. He said something, but it wasn't something that gave any comfort. I let one off at chest level. Louder than I remembered, sure. But I remembered to brace it. Doc says I'm too fat to break a rib. Barrel went off higher than I expected. That's not the training. That's just being old. Not used to the recoil anymore. Left arm lifted up. But lucky, I guess, for me, not him—took him right out. Then I checked Millie. She was..." He paused and turned toward Phil. "She was okay. But then... Well, when the shooting started again from up the stairs, I let out another one in that direction. But that guy on the stairs got us. He got Millie. And he got me. If I'd been faster..."

Phil dipped his head. "Glad you shot them. I'm just glad you shot them both."

Chuck nodded. "But here's the thing. I know I passed out in the kitchen.

And thank you, Claire, for showing me how to do that emergency thing on the phone. I did that before I passed out, held down the side button. Probably saved my life. Wish... well... Anyway, I know one of them got away, wounded, the blood trail ending off Mass. Ave. where the cops think he got picked up. But before he got away, and before I shot the first one, I heard some words between 'em, you know? Not English. Okay, and I didn't tell the police that, because it makes no sense, and there's already folks saying I didn't need to shoot. And if I say those two were looking for a man who's been dead a few years, they'll say my judgment's not so good, that I'm senile or such nonsense. Well, that's not a story we should let get around, okay? I'm not a killer, okay? That guy pointed a gun at me."

He paused. "You know, after I got wounded in Vietnam, I got shipped. They sent me to Korea. To the DMZ. Light duty. And the man spoke Korean. I recognized it."

He looked straight at Claire, his sparkling eyes intense. "So here's the thing, granddaughter, what was Colin Wright doing?" Her head snapped up, her mouth tight, unable to respond, the shock on her face clear. He turned to Phil. "What was your dad doing, Phil, that would cause Koreans to come and look for him, years after he died? Did he have some secrets or something?"

Claire opened her mouth, closed it again, and then spoke quickly, almost panicked. "He never taught me anything that was remotely, like, military or secret or anything. We only learned math! Math, Grandpa! As for being careful, all he ever told me was to watch out who I spoke to on the internet. Because I'm a girl, not because of anything else."

Chuck turned to Phil. "Your dad died when the barn exploded. They said it was a gas leak, right? But now, maybe it wasn't?"

Phil whispered, "Fuck me."

Spitz went to his knees next to the garbage can. He vomited into it. Claire ran to him, placing her hand on his shoulder.

"Spitz..." He shook her off and stood, grabbing tissues she offered him, and wiped his face.

Claire spoke again. "Spitz, I know you were there... at the explosion. You were the only witness. It's okay. Whether it was gas or something else, I know Colin would never put you in danger."

Spitz made some signs at Claire.

Twin lines appeared between her brows. "What do you mean, Grandpa's right?" She turned her surprised eyes to her grandfather, then back at Spitz, whose head shake told her the story would have to wait. He held both hands up, palms out. It wasn't actual sign language, but Claire knew what it meant: *Back off, give me space, I need a moment.*

Chuck spoke again. "I'm going to give you some words. All three of you. All three of you lost your parents, though Claire and Spitz, it was long ago, with Phil here, well, your dad, Colin, just a few years ago, and your mom... hmph. When your mom died today... I'm gonna say it. She died and I was there when she died. Now, after I got hit, not in Vietnam, hit today... I dragged my sorry butt to the kitchen. That's where the medics found me, hallucinating and shaking from bleeding out of my thigh. What was I seeing? I'll tell you—it was another soldier. He was in my platoon. Guy named Dougie. From upstate New York. Rochester or Buffalo, maybe. He liked those Japanese monster movies. We went through basic together.

"I was on the floor of the kitchen. I was pressing on the edge of the phone like Claire taught. And there's a reason I saw him. He didn't say nothing. He just pointed. He just looked at me and pointed at Millie. Dang, that sounds creepy, telling you. Then 911 answered."

Chuck took a breath and reached for the water again. He stared at the ceiling briefly, his eyes wet. "You know why I saw Dougie in that kitchen? You know why he looked at me and at Millie? They died the same—on a battlefield."

Claire looked up from her grandfather at Phil. They locked eyes before they both looked back at the old man.

"And let me tell you three kids, this is a battlefield now. And you need to do what I did then. Move quickly. Because at An Loc if I hadn't moved, I'd have been there with Dougie as well. I don't know what's going on now, just like I didn't know then. And I don't know what stuff Mr. Wright got involved with in prison or before prison when he was at the university, or what he was doing in the barn, but those men who killed Millie, those men who shot me, they were after Colin. I heard them ask about Colin before I got my shotgun. I don't know what they said in Korean, but one referred to the other as Major or some such. I've forgotten most of it, but they drilled the military words into us, and he was damn sure referring to his buddy as an officer before I shot him."

Phil turned away. "This is bullshit. My dad blew up. He didn't have any military secrets. He's been dead for years and this is just bullshit!"

Claire looked at her grandpa, an old man in a hospital johnny, tears running down her face. "Grandpa, what are you saying?"

Chuck held her gaze for a second before speaking. "You run now, Claire. You take Spitz and Phil and you get a car and you drive. I've got a place for you to go."

Claire's voice was high-pitched and young. She began reciting a list of obstacles. "Grandpa, we can't run. The police..."

"I don't give a hoot what the police said. I'll tell you what Sergeant said when we got leave off base to drink and chase girls. He said, 'You get in trouble? Run. You see fists flying? Run. You hear gunshots? Run. Don't get shivved by some crook or some girl or end up in jail. Run. Just run. Go back to base or the embassy or a park or somewhere else, but don't stick around where the trouble is.' So that's the same advice I'm giving you. I don't know what's going on here. We've lost too many and we ain't gonna lose any more. Phil here is strong, you're smart, and Spitz knows what I'm saying is true."

Claire's voice was urgent. "Grandpa, we don't even have a car."

"Yeah, well, I got that covered. Phil, look in the garbage can. Carefully—don't stab yourself on some needle or something. Reach down there."

"I'm not reaching in there! Spitz just heaved in it!"

"Humor me, son."

Phil stood and wiped his nose and went over to the garbage and hesitated before reaching in, causing a clinking sound. With some wonder he pulled out a batch of keys with a fuzzy troll fob. "What?"

Chuck nodded at Phil. "That's some nurse's keys. Grabbed 'em off the desk when they took me for a walk about an hour ago. Older car. Subaru, probably too old to be tracked. Nurses are parked in the covered parking. Should be able to find the car by..."

"... clicking the lock and unlock button, got it," said Phil, putting the keys in his pocket.

Claire spoke again. "Grandpa, we can't leave. The police will want—"

"No, granddaughter. Just no. These men killed Millie. They shot me. I survived, and because of that, you'll survive too. Now, remember the name and address I'm gonna give you. They are old army friends and they know you're coming. I asked a nurse if I could use her phone and I called. I'll tell the police you all went to California or something to get a break, and when we're all sure it's safe, you can come back."

Spitz turned Claire around and stared at her face. He nodded up and down slowly and looked at their grandfather in the bed. Claire turned back to the old man.

"Won't they put out an APB or something for Phil and Spitz? They're minors."

"You aren't witnesses or anything. You were all at school. They won't care. In fact, they'll be glad they don't have to deal with you. I'll take care of it. I'll tell them you went to stay with relatives. I think you are good for a few days, at least. Then, when we know what's going on, you can come back, okay?"

"This is crazy," Claire said, shaking her head.

"Crazy?" Phil said it as a statement and a question. "Yeah, this is crazy. My mom is fucking dead! My dad is dead! My grandpa, well, the closest thing I have to a grandpa, shot! In my house! This is all crazy. Why not add to it! Why not just take off! This place sucks. Everyone here gets hurt or dies. I'm with Grandpa. I've got keys. Let's go."

"Phil," Claire said calmly, "you can't even drive. I'd have to do all the driving to Tennessee. That's a long way. And we have no money. Grandpa, we can't do this."

Grandpa was about to speak when Phil interrupted, "Spitz can drive—Grandpa taught him last year. He's been driving Grandpa to the pharmacy for his medicine when you're at school."

Claire looked at Grandpa. "What? You didn't!"

Grandpa looked at Claire. "Yeah, well, never mind. Spitz, in my pants grab my wallet and take out the cash and my bank card. You know my PIN. Get the maximum amount from the cash machine in the hospital lobby, then drop the card at reception on the way out. Phil, your job is to make sure your phones are all off. They can be tracked. Plus, the car might have a transponder for tolls. If so, it'll be on the windshield. Toss it. Keep your head down when you leave the parking lot. Avoid toll roads anyway—they have cameras. Buy yourself an atlas at a gas station if you can find one. Use paper maps." Spitz and Phil looked at each other and nodded and rifled through Grandpa's pants hanging on the chair near the window. With the boys distracted, Claire said more quietly to her grandfather, "I have Mr. Wright's computers. Spitz has passwords I need. He will give them to me if you ask him to. Can you do that for me?"

Her grandfather looked surprised. "You think that's a good idea? What if those computers really do have military secrets or some type of dangerous info on them?"

"Grandpa, even better is if I can prove there was nothing there. I don't know what Mr. Wright was involved with, but it was never secret stuff. He was odd, but he wasn't into anything that would hurt anyone."

"Well, his history..."

"It's because of his history that he wouldn't hurt anyone. That history ruined his life, or so Millie says. He wouldn't even kill the spiders in the barn."

"We're getting off topic. What do you need?"

"Just tell Spitz to unlock everything. If there's anything dangerous on that laptop, I should know, for our protection if nothing else."

"Understood. Send Spitz over here and then get on the road."

"One more thing..." Claire had been hesitant to bring this up. "Someone contacted me online and said they saw Mr. Wright."

"What? That's simply not possible." Chuck looked confused and Claire wondered if maybe he was too old or too hopped on pain meds to provide her any advice. But she wanted to make sure she wasn't crazy.

"Yeah, I know. A strange coincidence given what those men said, right?"

"Who said this?"

"A member of my message board online. A friend, though I don't know her that well. She's in South Africa, I think."

"South Africa? Online? Granddaughter... this online stuff is far beyond me and there're layers here I don't understand. But I don't believe in coincidences."

"You think he could actually be alive? And if that's true, then maybe those intruders really *were* looking for him? So it wasn't just a random."

Chuck lowered his voice. "Exactly. Not random. And that would put you in real danger. All the more reason to get out of Dodge. Don't tell Phil, okay? And I would operate on the information you have at hand. That's my army training talking. Just move forward using what you know. Now, send Spitz over."

Claire leaned down to kiss him, transferring tears from her cheek to his.

It seemed like just a few minutes later they were on a two-lane road heading west.

11. Between Boston and Tennessee

Claire was glad she had her laptop with her. Spitz had reluctantly done as their grandfather requested, texting Claire the password to the files. Phil's birthday for the win.

As Spitz drove the stolen car through the night, directed by Phil to take winding two-lane roads as much as possible from Massachusetts west and then south through New York and Pennsylvania, Claire sat in the back seat of the little hatchback and read through the files and tried to understand what she was seeing. Of course, this was after she'd stopped at a gas station and affixed a large *Student Driver* bumper sticker to the back of the car and told Spitz to "drive as if I'll kill you if you exceed the speed limit, *capiche*?" She also bought him a checkered flannel shirt and a baseball cap, praying they wouldn't get pulled over.

Claire was flummoxed. The files she found included a note-taking application that Mr. Wright used to log his thoughts. Most appeared to be transcribed from voice recognition while he worked in the barn. The entries described things that made Claire reconsider everything she knew about her mentor. He spoke in that singsong kind of teaching voice he used when he wanted to make boring information interesting. Her mouth curled as she realized he talked to himself that way.

[...] I was able to get a CD-ROM from the inter-library loan. The public library can actually get stuff from the MIT library. It's from Green Bank. I merged that with the other data from the Indian scope and the CSIRO to get a pretty long dataset. Grandpa, what were you doing?

[...] Need to remind myself that it's not eighty-one centimeter. I don't remember the exact number of conversion from base 32. But get this, use a hydrogen time standard and I get eighteen eighteen eighteen eighteen eighteen eighteen in base 32. Not kidding. That's not coincidence. I got shivers. Need more gummies for this. Millie is gonna give it to me about being high. Grandpa probably cursed a storm with the Jewish lucky number popping up. Nazis always thought Jews were magic. Well, what about alien? I'm so funny.

[...] Got a visit from a Colonel Montgomery today. Said they want Grandpa Reitmann's research. I'll bet they do. Better than the visit from those other guys. Almost told Montgomery about them, but not sure. Maybe I should. Need to update my will.

[...] I've found, or should I say compiled? Decompiled? Assembled? Decrypted? Extracted? Received? Videos. It's like a firehose of alien Nickelodeon. Alienodeon? ET TV? Some of the worst and best entertainment I've seen in a while. Hope I'm not hallucinating this. Narrator: He's not. Found Grandpa's image too. Match. I wasn't on Johann's yellow comet acid then. Well, I was, but so was Samantha.

[...] Just sent Claire back to the camper. The girl is a genius. But she's not ready. And is anyone? Buried in the videos are little gifty-poos for the ET boys and girls to play with after eating space burritos. I got glowing hands! Samantha was right. We did this. It wasn't the LSD. It wasn't the toxic gas from the renovation. It was Grandpa's radar research. Where did he work? GEMA? I wish I were high right now. I'm sober as an ice cream cone. And my fingers are glowing green. And I think my you-know-what is too, but I don't want to look.

Several important pieces of information stuck in her mind. First, Mr. Wright ate gummies and talked to himself. Kind of on-brand, she thought, but also a bit too intimate for her comfort level. Who wants to hear their favorite teacher puttering around late at night, getting high, talking about alien conspiracies and doing LSD? Second, she pulled up a spreadsheet and confirmed that the frequency he converted was 18,18,18,18,18,18 or IIIIII in base 32. She frowned, wondering if this could be coincidence and knowing that such a coincidence in mathematics was statistically improbable. And, to which "Grandpa" was Mr. Wright referring? It couldn't be Grandpa Chuck. Who was Mr. Wright's grandfather? This Reitmann? In her head she did the math and it was possible that Mr. Wright's grandfather was in his early career during World War II. Research wasn't possible since the phones were off and she didn't want to risk turning them on.

Around 2:00 a.m., Claire was deep into the files when the sounds of an argument from the front seat penetrated her concentration.

"I said to turn right!" Phil yelled. "No, you loser. Right!"

Claire looked up and Phil was waving the overpriced atlas they had purchased at a gas station. He was gesticulating at a passing sign.

"What's going on?" She leaned forward in her seat.

"This *dickcheese* will not turn right! We're headed for Ohio or something."

Claire took a breath, calming, using Millie's *I'm in charge* tone from her years of babysitting. "You know what? It's late. Spitz, I'm going to drive for a bit and find a place to sleep. Pull over."

After swapping positions, Claire asked Phil to point out where they were on the map.

"Hershey Park is like twenty miles from here," said Claire.

"It's probably closed."

"Yes, smarty-pants, it's probably closed at 2:00 a.m., but there will be gas stations and truck stops."

Soon, they pulled into a brightly lit and busy truck stop. Claire found a parking space not too far from the pumps and leaned back. "Get as much sleep as you can, okay? We're going to make it to Tennessee tomorrow." She glanced into the back seat and Spitz was already snoring.

Phil looked too. "Damnit, he got to lie out."

Claire reached into her pocket and took out a twenty from the cash they'd gotten from Grandpa's debit card. "Go get yourself snacks and come back and sleep too. Bring me the change."

Phil returned from the convenience store with a bag of snacks and rummaged through it in the passenger seat, offering her a rectangular, neon orange package of cheese crackers. Claire heard him crying.

She put her hand out to touch his arm.

"Mom loved these." He held up a brightly colored package of toaster pastries.

"I'm sorry, Phil. Let's eat them and think about her. Okay? And good job navigating."

Soon enough, he was asleep too, a half-eaten strawberry pastry in his hand. Claire couldn't sleep. She was wired and tired at the same time. She gently took the half-eaten toaster pastry from Phil's hand and nibbled it while she thought about what she'd found on the laptop.

Mr. Wright. He was an onion. Layer upon layer. A great tutor, but he was a convicted felon. Though the conviction was many years ago, it was serious. She'd known that for a while. Certain friends throughout middle school weren't allowed to come over to her house. Other kids had their own similar stories, like Jenny's dad, who had been caught stealing from clients or Tobias' father, who had beaten up Tobias' mother and now saw him only once a month. And no quantity of good deeds can stop the wagging of small-town tongues, though he'd been commended for working in the halfway house teaching math to other former inmates, where he met Millie.

But below that known layer was the mad scientist. At least in the last few years it seemed he'd had another job, another life in the red barn behind the cottage. When tutoring wasn't actually happening, when the sun beamed on a Saturday morning, the barn doors would be open and she would bound across the yard to see him puttering with his computers and his tube radios, turning dials, soldering sockets, a herd of keyboards covering the work table that ran the length of the wall. She played on the old farm equipment and staged elaborate funerals with Phil and Spitz for the mice left by the barn cats.

Mr. Wright taught her how to read the lines on a resistor, how to calculate the frequency of a simple oscillating circuit, how to use breadboard and capacitors to make flashing LED games.

Which was why the next layer caused her eyes to narrow in concern, her neck sore from staring at the file. The videos and research data were clear—Mr. Wright thought aliens sent signals to Earth. The videos on the computer, and there were more than a dozen decrypted and reconstructed from radio telescope signals he'd gathered from around the world. Crazily, it seemed plausible. He'd always told her that interstellar radio signals could carry information, and they had focused her studies on that topic.

Mr. Wright's fascination with hidden knowledge in radio waves was infectious, and she'd always enjoyed taking mathematical data and extracting sequences and patterns. Find a correlation between temperature readings that matched scores of football games (highest scores around 45F degrees). Correlate grass height and rainfall (2 mm growth per inch of rain per week). Find the relationship between moonlight intensity and cricket chirp amplitude

(Δ 1 lumen = Δ 1 chirp/hour, partially contradicting Dolbear's Law). It was a game for them: her homework and what they most often discussed.

But why had he hidden that he actually believed it? What if the videos she watched on the long car ride down from Boston were actually alien—extraterrestrial?

She wasn't sure there was enough data on the computer to confirm. And perhaps he'd reverse engineered the whole thing, taking some cast-off videos, encrypting them and backing out the original signals to magick a super quiz to test her abilities? That would be an on-brand homework puzzle for him.

She couldn't prove the data on the computer came from space any more than she could prove to Spitz that his parents had existed. There was evidence, sure, but in the end, there was an element of trust and faith that had to be granted. Could it all be just some kind of ruse to hide work he was doing for the military? Or the CIA? Or some other nefarious organization? Her mind rejected the idea. Mr. Wright was her math tutor, and a bit of a mad scientist, she allowed, but not some secret weapons maker.

She turned her attention to what she'd seen in the videos. The story told was complex and incomplete. It seemed a doctor met a soldier. They fell in love. The couple were married in a beautiful church. The bride wore green. The man was a war hero or something. She became pregnant. She had twins, a boy and a girl. Then there was a war. The alien twin girl was killed and the twin boy sickened, and the mother visited her sick boy every day. The man went to fight the war on another planet. He was captured. Et cetera. Love. Drama. Intrigue. Adventure.

These could not be actual alien videos. Millie was dead. Grandpa had nearly been killed. Two boys slept near, reliant on her protection. There would be no dad side or mom side of the bed tonight, just the worn fabric of the nurse's car seat. She locked the doors and leaned her head back while the sounds of trucks roared past.

She woke to a knocking on the window. Dawn glowed pink through the windshield, visible behind the fuel pump canopy of the rest stop. Disoriented, she startled as the visage of a man stared, his face in shadow, silhouetted by the halogens on the light poles. Grandpa's admonition that someone might be after them loomed darkly in her mind and she swallowed a scream. She turned to wake Phil, but the passenger seat was empty. Panicked, she looked in the rear seats and saw they were empty as well. *Where were Spitz and Phil?*

The rapping came again and she blurted out "Go away!" at the mix of her own reflection and the unclear face outside the car.

"You need any help, miss?" The man knocked again on the window. His fingers emerged from the gloom and paused on the glass as if caressing it, and fear crept up on her, pushing away the grogginess of sleep and a realization this was not a dream.

"No. I don't need help. Go away."

"Why don't you roll down your window? We can talk. Yer car start okay?"

The question of Spitz and Phil's location remained at the forefront. She considered that this man might have done something, her thoughts conflating the confused last twenty-four hours with too many horrible scenarios in the here and now, but her logical brain told her that was impossible since he was outside the car and Phil and Spitz were nowhere to be seen.

The door handle rattled and Claire slapped the lock button. Clicks resounded around the car—the passenger door and the rear doors had been unlocked. Spitz and Phil must have left the car and had no way to lock it from the outside.

"Yer from Massachusetts? That's way up north. Where you going?" The man leered into the car, placing his hands around his face and pressing it uncomfortably hard on the glass, his lips surrounded by a ring of fog. She reached into the well for her phone. It was off and she was about to turn it on, knowing the risk of being tracked, when she heard the boys' voices.

Phil talked loudly, telling a story, "... and then Mr. Dyson wrote 'Brutus was a jerk' on the blackboard! Hey! That's our car!" His voice was strong and loud in the morning light.

The gaunt man faced the two boys, his unkempt appearance grim in the harsh light. He gawked, his Adam's apple bobbing like a golf ball. Claire realized they were as tall as the man. They were also young and full of energy.

"Your mama was all alone there. I thought she needed some help."

"My mama?!?" Phil's tone changed, higher pitched and angry, mocking. "My mama!?!"

Phil's arm swung outward, making a slow circle, a double plastic bag full of soda cans, candy, and chips dangling from his hand. At Phil's escalation, Spitz moved quickly, circling behind the man, but out of reach. He did this without a word from Phil, as if they had coordinated it. The man visibly swallowed, surrounded by two young men.

"My mom's dead! That's my sister, weirdo! And you get the FUCK away from our car." Phil pulled back his arm and twirled the bag of snacks and sodas faster, spinning it tight into a ropey weapon.

The man's lips hooked into a quivering smile at the swinging bag of heavy objects in Phil's hand. He scooted sideways away from the car. "Yeah, your sister. Right. How about you relax?"

"How about you get your fucking face bashed in?" Phil lifted his arm like an ancient hunter with a sling, his body weaving with the weight.

"Goddamn, you're crazy!" And the man backed up until he was rudely shoved sideways by a smiling Spitz, his eyes wide. Spitz did a little dance and came around in a boxer's pose.

The man ducked slightly and retreated from the car. "Yer nuts," was all he said, turning and hurrying toward the dark line of semitrailers on the edge of the parking area, glancing backward a few times.

"And stay away, you fucking creep! You goddamn pervert! You piece of shit!" Spitz clapped and the two boys bumped fists.

Claire unlocked the doors and jumped out of the car. She gave Spitz a hug, her eyes red. Then she backed up and said sternly, "Where were you? I woke up and didn't see you! And what were you doing, threatening that man? He could have had a gun!"

Phil looked surprised at her tone. "Uh, sorry. We both woke up and got breakfast. Plus, I had to pee."

Claire held back emotions and was unsure if she should yell or cry. "I... Thank you getting rid of... that man. I have to pee as well. Here's the key... and we'll get on the road as soon as I get back. Just... Just watch me get inside the store." She went off quickly to the convenience store entrance, looking at the line of trucks. She glanced back to see Phil and Spitz staring at her, and felt comforted by their gazes. As the convenience store entrance closed, she heard Phil call out, "Shotgun! I am so funny!"

*Video Z-07:07-2a/Anon, *The Engagement*

From the Zoonerat Wikipedia page:

Zoonerat video Z-07:07-2a/Anon is one of the least commented on and least shared of the Zoonerat videos ("An Alien Soap Opera or an Elaborate Hoax? Our Favorite 'Zoonerat' Conspiracy Theories," *Hollywood Infotainment* magazine). Note: Spelling conventions and character assignments in this article are from *The Zoonerat Videos Deconstructed*, Bateman et al., University of Maryland.

Many have said it is boring and lacks action (ref. above). A small group of academics claim it contains pivotal information about Zoonerat mating customs.

The following transcription is excerpted from Dr. S. Locke's presentation at the USC School of Cinematic Arts graduation ceremonies—Breakout Session on Zoonerat Partnership Customs:

Welcome, honored guests. Thank you for allowing me to help usher our new graduates out of the world of academia and into the world of media. I'm going to take this opportunity to discuss a subject near and dear to my four-chambered heart [laughter from the audience].

The quadruplet or bi-doublet nature of Zoonerat partnership has been theorized repeatedly since first proposed by Adnan Bateman in this very auditorium. There have been several disputations of his assertion since that time. Nevertheless, there has been no substitute thesis that so elegantly explains the behavior of the characters in videos Z-2a and Z-2b, among others.

[Further introductory remarks]

Our favorite Zoonerat protagonist Huoron clearly announces his engagement to or partnership with Io in the first minute of the video, as seen on the screen behind me, to an adoring crowd, at what appears to be a cocktail party. Then his sister—and I strongly believe it is his twin sister, Xlatin—at first looks happy, just as one would expect. She congratulates her brother's fiancée, our heroine, Io. Xlatin then speaks with Io, asking a question. What question does she ask? I will put this five-second clip on the screen and you can look for yourself. I have left off all audio.

What we see is happiness turn to devastation. Joy to sorrow. A woman who was seeing her future in the marriage of her brother to Io now sees a future that is... what? Perhaps bereft of love. Perhaps barren.

We know Xlatin is unhappy with the proposed marriage and attends it alone in the wedding video, and she leaves the ceremony midway. I will put this scene on the screen now. Why does Xlatin leave the marriage ceremony?

From the video known as *ZP Bio* or *The Sex Tape* we know Zoonerat give birth to twins. We don't know that they do this exclusively, but since no other gestational options have been seen, that assumption can be proposed. They gestate triplets, but two of the fetuses absorb or replace the third and twins are born. Whether the twins are of two genders or more genders or fewer genders, we cannot say. But supposing that gender is randomly distributed among twins, then perhaps this entire society is based on paired coupling. Twins marry twins. Perhaps even twins *must* marry twins. Singles are a separate case and discouraged from marrying a twin. A study of couples identified in the videos shows that the distribution of same-sex and mixed-sex couples nearly matches what would be expected if two genders were randomly assigned a partner: 25 percent female-female, 50 percent mixed, and 25 percent male-male.

So why was Xlatin so unhappy? What did Io say that made Xlatin turn angrily on her brother?

One solution gives the answer. If Io is not a twin, then Xlatin will have no partner. What happened to Io's twin? We don't know. But we do have a word for a single person who has lost a twin. That word is *Huytloon*. It is repeated in several other videos. If Io is a *Huytloon* and has no twin, then Xlatin, Huoron's twin sister, has no match to marry. She will be alone unless she also finds a *Huytloon* to marry. Like in our own society, it may be difficult for a woman of a certain age to find a suitable partner. And compound that with a diminished pool of former twins and you can understand Xlatin's discomfort.

BOOK 3

- ➢ Welcome to the WisPR chatroom
- ➢ Bot is ON
- ➢ Users online: 1
- ➢ Today's quote is:

"Now to physics. I am as convinced as ever that the wave representation of matter is an incomplete representation of the state of affairs, no matter how practically useful it has proved itself to be. The prettiest way to show this is by your example with the cat."

A. Einstein to E. Schrödinger
Point Peconic, Long Island
9 August 1939

12. Prieska, Republic of South Africa

The man stepped back but held the door from swinging inward and stared opened-eyed at Harry, who slumped against the jam. A woman appeared and gave a cry when she saw Harry.

"Peter, she's hurt. What has gotten into you? This poor thing. What happened? Was it something awful?" She led Harry, one arm around her back, to a small couch in a cozy Victorian parlor.

Harry was ugly crying now, just nodding as she was led to a red velvet love seat. She let her rucksack slide off her shoulders and placed it on her feet, hoping to hide them, and failing.

"She's got no shoes, Leeza! Who steals a woman's shoes!" The man's voice was loud. He looked outside, glancing around nervously, then closed the door firmly.

"Go and get some *pantoffels*. I'll tend her." The woman had a strong Afrikaner accent.

"Should I call the police?"

"Nah, they sleeping at this time. In morning. She's just crying I think because they stole her shoes. What's your name?"

Harry sniffled and looked at her saviors. They were a young couple, white, and the little cottage was clearly set up as a lobby area for the guesthouse. "Haretsebe. But you can call me Harry."

"Harry? That's our dog's name," said the man, then added, "I mean, oh saints, nothing's meant... oh... it's..."

"Peter, stop," said the woman, kneeling on the thick rug and examining Harry's feet. "Harry, do you need us to call someone? Where are you from? Who did this? Who took your shoes?"

"I'm a student. I was traveling to Bloom and got out at the petrol station."

"The Total?"

"Yes, the Total. And then... I needed to get away... A man..." Harry stopped, not sure how to continue.

The woman nodded. "Yes, we understand. Peter?"

"Yah, we understand." He sounded confident without sounding confident at all.

"Peter, get her some slippers, for goodness. Don't be a fig tree." After a hesitation, Peter turned and left.

"Harry, I'm Leeza. Can you go somewhere? Maybe we should call the police?"

"No, I'm okay. I'm just... I got off the bus, you see. I don't want to go anywhere." Harry wasn't sure what to say or do. She looked around. "If you have a room, perhaps..."

"Yes, we have rooms here. You sure you okay?" Harry nodded, wiping her nose with a tissue provided by Leeza, who continued. "Not so busy this week. We have cottages in the back near the water. Usually, we get couples on weekends. Here for the river views. But you can have one tonight. Peter will get you sorted with some slippers." Leeza looked at Harry and then at her walking sticks. A new tone emerged in her voice. "I cannot believe the nerve of some men! A young student like you! Only your shoes? You don't need a doctor, do you?" The woman's eyes rose with a question of deep concern and Harry knew what she was asking.

Harry shook her head. "No, I got away. That's how I lost my shoes. I'm really unharmed."

"Unharmed! Piss on that! Excuse my French. You've cut your foot quite badly. I've got some nurse training—well, some Girl Guides training." She grimaced as she took off Harry's bloody and torn socks. "Peter! Bring some bandages and some antiseptic spray!"

Peter was already right next to her and handed Leeza a pair of slippers. "Back just now." And he was gone again.

After some more discussion and the woman's strong fingers working magic, Harry's foot was properly bandaged and, with new slippers on, Harry was led out the back of the house to a lit patio with paths leading off in several directions. An overly friendly jet-black Labrador tried to get its head under her jacket, probably smelling Slow Train's blood, thought Harry.

"Harry, stop," Leeza's eyes turned from the dog to Harry and added, "Him, I mean."

Harry followed Leeza outside into the cool night air. A glance showed Peter behind, following quietly. Leeza waved her forward, chatting as they walked down a path.

"It's all fenced and there's solar lighting on the paths. No need to be concerned. Plus, the dog stays with the single women, he barks at strange men, always trying to be a hero, so there's that." They walked around some dark plantings to a tiny rondavel with a small raised porch, with no views of the river. "I'm sorry about the steps. Can you manage?"

Harry nodded, and after Leeza unlocked the front door, they went inside the smooth stuccoed rondavel. The two women stood awkwardly and Leeza seemed uncomfortable leaving. Harry peeked outside; Peter stood under the single porch light looking vigilant and staring at the trail of solar lights leading back to the main house.

Harry pulled out her purse from her backpack. "I can pay now for the room if you like." Harry had some money, but she wasn't sure she had quite enough for the room and was nervous about this moment.

The woman seemed embarrassed. "Oh no, please, we can discuss in the morning." But she also seemed satisfied that the conversation had changed to more mundane matters. "Breakfast is from 7:00 until 10:00 in the parlor, where you were just now. Some pastries and juice and tea, bread and jam and that sort. Check-out is at 1:00 p.m., and you can stay at least another night until we have a booking." She paused. "I'm sorry that happened to you. I hope you sleep okay."

Harry gave her thanks. Just as the woman was leaving, Harry asked her, "I apologize. I want to contact my family. Do you have internet?"

The woman smiled, again appearing happy that the conversation wasn't fraught with *implications*. "Of course. Details are on the notecard on your bedside table. It's spotty, but it should be good with so few guests."

When the woman left, Harry heard soft and earnest discussion between the two hosts fading into the night. The rondavel was quaint, with round walls painted velvet sand on the bottom half and a flat white above, mimicking a beach. The décor was kitschy mid-century modern, with advertisements for safaris, some antique appliances, and African masks completing the atmosphere.

She fell onto the large bed, designed for honeymooners, and stared at the peaked sky-blue ceiling, a series of dark supports, like umbrella stays, radiating from the center to the walls. Then she was dreaming.

It must be Slow Train tapping at the door, hoping to come in so he can bleed to death in the little cottage, so he can fall on me and then whisper in my ear that the bad men will stab me too. He offered a bloody pink ear. "Take it, and take Deep's hand. An ear. And a hand. Lend an ear, give a hand."

And then she was up. Wide awake, panicked. Confused, covering her ear, checking her wrist. She looked around and stood as best she could next to the bed in the cottage, one hand on the warm and rumpled bedsheets, her bandaged foot feeling soft, the exposed toes touching cold tile. The light was still on and bright. She shook her head to clear the dream from her thoughts. Then she stopped. There was a tapping at the door. A real tapping. Not a dream. Grabbing a cane, she shuffled to the door, leaning forward, ready to scream.

"Who is it?" she asked. And she heard the tapping very low, near her knees, and knew. "Go away, please." But the noises continued and she opened the door for the black dog, who came in, went past Harry, and promptly dropped itself next to the bed and looked back at her, expressionless, but also questioning. She stood glumly, unsure, but also unwilling to fight. Harry looked at the dog, whose furred face challenged her.

"That's some cheek. You are terrible. Out. Shoo." She leaned on the door and pointed her stick at the dog. "Go. Go outside. I'm not a dog person. You may have insects or something. And I sleep alone." She touched her cane on the ground in front of the dog, then led little taps to the door. The dog rose and looked at her accusingly, then went into the doorway and paused for a moment, plopping down just outside.

"Do not look at me like that. You belong outside." With a bit of guilt, Harry closed the door.

She took a deep breath and did her best to remain angry, but also glad of the distraction from her thoughts. *Hele. Is your name Harry or Hairy?*

She showered and changed into clean clothes, pausing every so often to make sure the dog was not tapping or whining. Her bloody shirt and other garments got piled by the bed, terrifying, she thought, if she came upon them without context. On the bed after her shower, she held her phone in the air above her face. It was still off. She laid it on her chest and considered turning it on, but knew what that meant—she could be tracked.

As if by magic, she opened her eyes, realizing that she had slept again and a knock had woken her. Rousing, she peeked out the door to find Leeza standing with a tray of coffee and a packet of biscuits. Harry cried out with delight, a broad smile lifting the corners of her mouth. "I have never had breakfast in bed! You are so kind!"

"It comes with the room," Leeza said, also smiling. "I know you had a late evening. We have no more bookings, so if you want to stay another night, that's not a problem. There're a few things to do here. The boathouse is just down the path behind your rondavel. You can kayak." She paused, looking at Harry's canes. "If you need help, Peter will set you up with a life vest. He likes to teach boating and the like."

Harry looked down at her foot. "Thank you. I think I may just rest for the day."

Leeza nodded. "Well, not a worry. When you need food, just come by the main house. We prepare sandwiches at lunch and for dinner you can go into town or we have a stewpot self-serve in the lobby. Just take some back to your room. Sometimes the couples just want to stay inside."

Harry nodded, eyeing the biscuit package with surprising desire. "Thank you so much. I'm with the honeymooners on that, I think. Has... anyone asked about me?" Harry let the sentence hang.

The pretty blond woman shifted on her feet and whispered, looking back at the house. "No, miss. Nobody has asked."

"I'm sorry. I'm just... anxious, you know? I want to make sure."

The woman nodded; the corners of her mouth turned down. Perhaps she was rethinking letting Harry stay? Harry forced herself to smile as she took the tray and closed the door, unsure if she'd brought more attention to herself than she wanted.

She turned and placed the tray bedside and lay down again, her mind distracted by fears and memories of the last twenty-four hours. A warm and then suddenly cold sensation on her foot startled her back to the present. Terrified, she jumped up and fell against the bathroom door. The dog approached her, wagging its tail, looking happy and slightly sheepish that he had caused any issues.

"Stupid dog! You frightened me! I thought you were a snake! Why aren't you outside?!" She maneuvered back into bed and told the dog, "Do *not* touch, ugh, or lick my feet. That's disgusting! Just leave me alone, okay?"

Harry woke again. It was dark outside. She'd slept all day—something she was sure she'd never done in her life. And then she was panicking and checked her phone to make sure it was still off. The USB fell onto the bed with her keys when she retrieved her phone. Its stern, superhero face, faded from a child's fingers, stared outward, expressionless. Was this tiny thing the cause of all her problems?

Soon enough, she knew the police would need to be contacted, but she was, surprisingly, enjoying this moment of independence, though the shivers of the memories were paramount. She'd never stayed alone in a guesthouse before. She'd never even been anywhere alone. The word for this situation came unbidden into her head: *off-grid*. It sounded exotic and terrifying.

During a luxurious second shower, the USB drive on the tiny sink edge occupied her thoughts. Because really it was about this USB, wasn't it? It must be some sort of military secret thing. What else could it be? Some sort of plans or lists of spies or trails of money hidden in those science-fiction videos. Nobody stabs anybody for pirated TV shows. In the shower, she replayed the moment where she was about to reveal herself to Dr. Ramposa and then found out that he was leading those two bad men right to her door. She still couldn't wrap her mind around what that meant. Whom could she trust? She saw Slow Train's eyes close as he fainted, and gave an internal shudder.

A puzzle was always enticing, so, despite some misgivings, after she changed into her last set of fresh clothes, she opened her laptop, leaving it completely isolated—no Wi-Fi, no Bluetooth, no connection to anything. Then she copied the contents of the USB to the laptop and encrypted all of it, including the USB, which she placed on her school ID lanyard before putting the lanyard over her neck. Should the laptop or USB be lost, the files would be useless. She was now in control of the data.

This was her forte. Her whole uni career she had taken other people's data, professors' data, researchers' data, and analyzed it for them. Always, it came in varied formats, different numbering systems, disparate storage protocols; her job was to clean it up. She Cinderella'd the information, made it ready for the ball.

The videos were all in a single folder. They were named 1.avi, 2.avi, and so on. Each video had an associated folder of data. A quick glance showed them to be files of long numbers, separators and markers within them. There was also an executable library called "broadcast." The videos, when watched, surrendered no insights, just science-fiction shows. Orange-colored aliens talking, fighting, running, a cocktail party, children being read stories, and so on. There seemed to be no plot or anything she could understand. Maybe they were in the wrong order or missing episodes.

What had that man said?

Kids' meals. Dangerous toy surprises.

How could these be dangerous in any way? He had an American accent. There were American scientists at MeerKAT, but not many. Maybe this Colin Wright was Clarity's tutor? Or he could still be Colin Rite or Right or Write.

The broadcast directory contained executable files—programs that did something. They were unreadable, compiled machine instructions. Often, script folders comprised a library of smaller files. One file might be the actual executable, one might be a list of modifiable parameters—inputs to the executable file—others might be comments or revision history or human-readable code and previous versions.

She searched the broadcast library and found a notes file. Reading it, her eyes widened with surprise and confusion. This wasn't just a revision history to a codebase, it was more akin to a journal of the code author. It read like nonsense, like the ramblings of a madman. Incredulous, she was reminded of the conspiracy letters professors at uni posted for fun outside the faculty lounge on a bulletin board—letters from crazy people trying to prove their weird theories—geometric designs and claims that spirits were directing sacred equations, pyramids guiding astral energies, the planets moving in patterns that were not mathematical but intentional, directed by dark cabals or nefarious cartels. This writing was too similar.

She read the notes, which were formatted as code comments, starting with a hashtag.

#zoonerat videos contain codes/metadata as sub-text

#broadcast.exe < metadata < parameters

#the broadcast will modify space-time's base topology with respect to broadcaster's inertial frame of reference, e.g., post-Einsteinian physics

#per Samantha C., events at MIT likely from within reel-to-reel broadcast and not LSD-induced

#Limited use, likely single use, probabilistic, asymptotic

#Tube, vacuum required, charged anode through vacuum, old tube TV, amplifier, or radio

#radio transmission at frequency of 366 mega hz, codes use base 32 conversion to Zoonerat time, Hydrogen time standard as well. 512 degree circles for vectors.

Harry read all of it and pondered the implications. It sounded crazy. There was no way anyone could believe this... madness? But Slow Train had been stabbed. And a man had appeared in a green sphere. Perhaps this information was from a spy gone nutzo? Perhaps the man in the green sphere was a loony person with dangerous knowledge in his head. What was the movie? Jason Bourne, right? A spy with amnesia. What about a spy with dementia? Or schizophrenia? Spies with mental illness—a scary thought.

But...

I saw him. I'm not crazy. She remembered a quote from WisPR: bot says: rule 670: Hysteria is what a man calls a woman thinking.

Harry perused the nutty writing in the software comments—the instructions for executing the transmissions, the kids' meal codes, the weird *American, glowing, hand-amputating* codes. An involuntary shiver migrated across her back and she looked over the edge of the bed to see the dog's eyes lift to meet her gaze, which was much more comforting than she expected.

Detective Ramotswe spoke in her head. This requires a test, an experiment.

Her curiosity was a salve on her unease. Alone in a strange guesthouse, with no supervision, no classes, no schedule; this was an unusual freedom, a break with routine. The small room was manageable. The bed was comfortable. This task would hide her disquiet. All of this distracted her from the fact that she had run *for* her life and possibly *from* her life.

"What should I do?" Was she talking to the dog or herself? The dog shuffled its body in response. Not an answer.

The instructions were a recipe. Add these ingredients: a vacuum tube, a radio, data. Press this button and voilà: electromagnetic radiation biscuits.

Scanning the room, her eyes lit on the desk where an ancient Bakelite-cased television sat silently. Next to it lay a dusty travel guide to the Orange Free State and a copy of *Jock of the Bushveld* in Afrikaans, which she couldn't read well enough to enjoy. Would the TV turn on? If so, that might provide the vacuum tube the author described as necessary for the technology to work.

She was missing a transmitter. Operating the codes required a radio transmitter. The active ingredient in this elixir of madness were radio waves. The author mentioned "... singular frequencies, resonance, sanding down the prouds—60 grit on the quanta, plugging the holes with nuggets of probability, dimensional filler. A steamy iron on the fabric of space-time."

She leaned back and looked around the room. There was a small analog clock on the table, but not much else that could broadcast anything. She replayed memories from her class on radio frequency applications taken as a first year. Then she snapped her fingers and looked down next to the bed.

"Let me see your collar, Dog."

The collar had a small black box on it.

"And, there it is," said Harry. She carefully unclipped the cube from the braided collar. The faded letters on the black plastic showed a frequency. But it wasn't the correct frequency, and she saw no way to open the device to adjust it. She considered her situation. Was she crazy to do this? And how far down this rabbit hole did she want to go?

She looked at the door and the dog. "I'm not going out there alone."

Harry closed her laptop and hid it under the blanket. She considered just erasing everything, tossing the drive out into darkness and going to the police in the morning. But then she saw Slow Train's gray lips telling her *they* wanted the USB. Closing his eyes as his head lolled to the side. By running, had she become a target? Slow Train didn't have the USB and he'd gotten stabbed. Maybe whether she had it wouldn't affect her level of danger. That hardened her resolve to understand, to take charge of this thing.

A memory came to her of the WisPR login screen. A quote from a scientist. That was Lollipop's bot, grabbing pithy sayings from the internet. *Nothing in life is to be feared, it is only to be understood. Now is the time to understand more, so that we may fear less.* —Madame Curie

She needed a radio. And she knew where one should be.

The dog stood expectantly, looking up at her. "Shhhhh..." she whispered to its upturned face, its tail wagging as she put her hand on the doorknob.

The door, with its bottom half painted sand to match the room, swung silently inward. Peter must oil the hinges, she thought. Outside was not entirely pitch black. A gibbous moon shone in the sky and solar lights traced the path toward the cottage at the front. She zipped her jacket against the chill as the dog rushed past her, forging ahead down the path and disappearing in the dark.

"You can't know where I'm going," she whispered at the dark animal's vanishing rear, and then regretted it, hearing how loud her voice was. It was silly to think that anyone had followed her to this guesthouse, but she was nervous regardless.

She grabbed the handrail of the porch, two canes in one hand. At the bottom she moved faster, swishing down the path where a tiny illuminated sign said *To The Dock*. The dog appeared next to her, brushing her leg and threatening to interfere with her canes. He was black and nearly invisible, just negative space where a dog should be.

Fear, mostly hidden while she was lost in the technology's description, rose again in the dark. The boathouse where she might find a radio for her experiment was farther than she expected. That's what this was—an experiment. Just some fun before she called the police and gave up on this freedom. The dog's breathing and its soft rush of fur against her leg gave her comfort to keep walking.

The dark mass of the boathouse was outlined against the river, an imperceptibly lighter gray than the starlit sky above. Solar lights hung in a string over the door, giving it a Christmas-y look. The dog disappeared again, rustling in the vegetation near the riverbank. She took a breath as she leaned on her canes, then grasped the boathouse doorknob and pulled. It held and then popped open with a loud screech. The noise was not what she wanted. A hurried look around in nervousness and a listen revealed no movement. She let out a breath.

Her flailing arm caught a light switch, which blinded her when it came on. Searching, her eyes lit on what she'd hoped for among the unkempt stacks of paddles and shelves of chandlering supplies: a plastic bin with a disorganized assortment of handheld radios. She grabbed one and rolled the volume control on the side to test it, flicking the power button. The device erupted with a screech of feedback, and she desperately turned the dial to shut it off. Holding her breath again, she prayed nobody had heard the noise. Leaving the boat shed with her prize hanging from her hand, she turned and waited a moment in the pitch black for her eyes to adjust again to the dark.

Just a few steps up the path, a barely visible man appeared in front of her and her heart stopped. Fear, like an icy glove, squeezed her insides.

"Stop, girl." Then over his shoulder, he said, "I got her."

"Okay, so that's that," responded a deeper voice behind him. This voice belonged to the man she'd heard with Dr. Ramposa, and her heart pounded with an abyssal terror.

"We've been looking for you. What are you doing down here?" Even in the dark, she caught his glance at her hand where the radio hung by a strap.

Harry's chest pounded and her mind filled with fear, the kind she hadn't felt since she was a child and fell in the middle of the street. Cars had honked and zoomed around her until she was dragged to safety by a stranger, her lame leg bouncing uncontrollably. She instinctively reached for the USB, her cane swinging. The man with the deeper voice, tall, and with light hair that glinted in the moonlight, leaned forward, an arm extended toward the USB.

"I'll... scream," said Harry, her voice a whisper and breaking, revealing the truth that she could no such thing.

"No, you won't," said the first man, who was smaller with dark hair, harder to see. His movement was fast, and before she could react, he had grabbed her from the side, covering her mouth with a leathery palm. But he hadn't seen the black dog, which snarled and attached to the man's thigh from behind as soon as he touched Harry. His cry of pain was combined with surprise and his grip on Harry disappeared. She pulled away from both assailants, yanking the lanyard over her head. "Leave me alone!" she shouted, and threw the USB into the dark.

"I'll get it," said the man with a deep voice, plunging off into the dark.

The other man yelled, "Get this fucking dog off me!" He spun around to escape the dog, which viciously twisted back and forth, holding fast to the leg. Harry, panting and terrified, took off toward the cottage, leaving the chaos behind her, the radio swinging from her wrist.

When she reached the cottage, she struggled up the steps and inside, closing the door as gently as she could, her hands shaking, her breath in bursts. If the men didn't know where she was staying, then maybe they would find the USB and leave? Listening at the door, she heard other voices. Maybe Leeza and Peter were up and going to investigate the dog's yelping and the commotion.

Harry wasn't sure how much time she had, but she thought it could be a lot. She hoped, prayed that this was over. But, she considered, it could be just a few minutes if they figured out the USB was encrypted and suspected she could decrypt it. As she considered making a dash up toward Leeza and Peter's house, she heard two loud pops that could only be gunshots. Then, a terrifying scream.

"Peter!" she heard, and then more gunshots. Then more voices. Harry felt a terrible chill. What have I done? Have I gotten more people hurt or even killed? Slow Train and the dog and Leeza and Peter?

She struggled to clear her head, remembering her calmness in the car park of MeerKAT, when she had so easily sneaked onto the kombi. *I must do that again. I must be calm again.* She rubbed her shoulder and took several deep breaths.

On the bed, in the dim moonlight from the tiny high window, she opened her laptop. *Something in these files can help.* It was irrational, but she felt that somehow, she must know more. If she knew what the secret was, she could control this unraveling situation. The fear fed an energy she didn't recognize. *It's adrenaline*, she thought. *I'm high on adrenaline.* Her focus sharpened to a scalpel, a focus she felt only when totaling the receipts of the cash register at the store where she had spent her youth, or coding in her room, or sitting in an exam at uni. Everything else disappeared.

The first ingredient was the television, the only tube television she'd ever turned on. Operating in the low light, she approached the desk and confirmed the cord was plugged into a wall socket, which was a good sign. The finely ridged power knob spun slightly, held, and then rolled over with a satisfying click. After a moment, the squat device hummed and a pink glow emanated from the back. The screen shifted from black to gray to a mottled white, brighter than the moon outside. She haphazardly tossed a blanket over it to hide the light. Scooting into the center of the bed, cradling her laptop and the radio, she threw a sheet over her head, just as she had as a child, surreptitiously reading at night with a torch.

In the laptop's light, she examined the radio, looking for fasteners. Four screws on opposite corners loosened after she leaned down, applying weight.

The back came off with some effort, a waterproof seal pulling apart like a plaster left on too long. She breathed a sigh of relief as she saw what she hoped for in the mass of electronics under the plastic case of the radio: a minuscule white box sitting on the circuit board. The tiny cube had a slot for a screwdriver. It was a varactor diode, used to adjust the frequency of the radio at the factory. She squinted at the numbers on the tiny device and used her screwdriver to make an adjustment, hoping it would match the frequency required by the USB documentation.

With her thumb, she pushed the power switch and quickly reduced the sound to a low fuzz. She pressed the transmit button and the sound died entirely. Another push along the button's ridge locked the transmit button in place.

A bead of sweat rolled down to her eyebrow. The cottage door was shut and locked and the lights were off, so she suspected, or really hoped, that there would be no interruptions. A siren mewled in the distance and more voices and commotion arose outside. Then she heard Leeza's voice.

"Oh, Peter, please be okay! Please!"

And the sounds of emergency personnel and police.

"Can you get some lights down by the boathouse?"

"Owner says a guest was being stalked by a man. See if you can find her."

Her door rattled once and then stopped. She held her breath and it did not repeat. She felt crazed, out of body, alert, high. Her skin tingled and her hair buzzed, her senses tensioned like guitar strings. This was not normal. Her mind screamed to run outside and reveal herself. But whom to trust? Her brain asked for safety, but her soul demanded that she continue pushing on the puzzle, to avoid thoughts of escape, to pursue the bright unknown in the computer, not flee into the darkness outside.

She took her gaming headset from her bag and tentatively inserted the male headphone jack into the female socket on the radio. She measured off a few dozen centimeters of the cord and cut it with the small multi-tool she kept attached to her cane, the one Debs didn't want her to display. The bare wires were stripped down to tiny copper filaments, and she did the same to a spare USB cord she had. Matching the wires as to which was signal and which was ground, she made a new cord—computer to radio.

Then she paused, wondering how complete her setup actually was. Could this possibly work? And then she heard it. A snuffling and tapping. But this time a faint whimpering as well.

"*Modimo nthuse*, stop," she muttered. "You'll bring everyone here."

She threw off the sheet, limped to the door, and opened it just a crack. Nobody was in sight and the darkness was split only by the path's solar illumination. Behind the rondavel, the sounds of activity and the moving flashes of light on the grass indicated that nearby, probably from down at the boathouse, officials and others were still working. She could only guess what was going on down there.

The dog limped in, crying, and she shushed it. Quietly, she closed the door again and locked it.

"*Hele*," Harry muttered. "Same limp, same name. We are a pair."

The dog went to the side of the bed and lay down, licking at its front paw.

She gave the animal a quick pat on its head. "Good dog. Now, don't bother me, I'm working."

Back in bed, she shushed the whining dog again. Would the next step cause problems? After some key presses, the screen showed the guesthouse Wi-Fi as connected and the WisPR chatroom welcome message.

Her eyes widened. There were a half dozen DMs. She scanned them quickly as the chat window streamed.

WeDontKnow has joined the chat.

Clarity: @WeDontKnow... where you been? Things have happened.

WeDontKnow: Can I ask you a question?

Lollipop: are you ok?

Harry ignored everything else and went to her DMs.

Clarity > **WeDontKnow:** Keep this off group chat. What did you say about Mr. Wright?

WeDontKnow > **Clarity:** It's complicated. I saw him after the explosion.

Clarity > **WeDontKnow:** I don't believe you.

WeDontKnow > **Clarity:** Well, you don't know me. So no need to call me a liar.

Clarity > **WeDontKnow:** He died 3 years ago.

Harry got chills. She shook them off, trying to be calm, cool.

WeDontKnow > **Clarity:** Then some man with an American accent is impersonating him and gave me your name and told me to reach you, assuming your name is Claire Plaster.

[spinner]

Harry tried to calm her breath while she waited for a reply, her senses taut.

Clarity > **WeDontKnow:** How can I believe you? It's crazy. You don't understand. He died. I went to his memorial service. I babysit his orphaned child. You understand? This is not possible.

WeDontKnow > **Clarity:** No, YOU don't understand. I have questions and I'm in a bit of a pickle. Seriously, I'm in trouble. I am not lying. I know what I saw.

Clarity > **WeDontKnow:** Can you prove it? That you saw Mr. Wright?

WeDontKnow > **Clarity:** I think so. And it's part of my pickle.

Clarity > **WeDontKnow**: Pickle?

WeDontKnow > **Clarity:** Just help me. He gave me a USB with videos on it. And codes. And software. A broadcast program of some kind. What is it? They stabbed my friend for this.

Clarity > **WeDontKnow:** You have the broadcast program? Someone was stabbed?

WeDontKnow > Clarity: Yes, and

Just then, a fist pounded loudly on the door. The dog rose and barked ferociously.

A man's voice called out. "I hear the dog. She's in here!" Harry could not be sure if it was either of the two men who had attacked her earlier.

The door handle turned but the deadbolt held the door.

"Open up! We know you're in there!"

"What's going on up there? Who are you?" another voice called from a bit farther away.

"I'm a law enforcement officer," the first man answered. "The woman in this cottage is wanted as a witness in a stabbing."

"You have no uniform," came the second voice, closer now. "Where's your badge?"

There was a scuffle and more noises. The dog was barking. Harry tried to concentrate on the screen with the surrounding clamor.

Clarity > **WeDontKnow:** What happened? Finish your question.

WeDontKnow > **Clarity:** No time. They are after me. What will happen when I run the program?

Clarity > **WeDontKnow:** Don't run the program! It's very dangerous.

WeDontKnow > **Clarity:** kids meals and choking hazards. Does that mean anything to you? That's what he said.

Clarity > **WeDontKnow:** kids meal? WTF?

WeDontKnow > **Clarity:** Can it protect me? It shielded Colin Wright.

Clarity > **WeDontKnow:** I have no idea what you mean.

WeDontKnow > **Clarity:** He said you'd know. He said to find you.

Clarity > **WeDontKnow:** I have no idea. His notes say things, but it's stupid.

The dog's barking continued at a volume that made Harry's head hurt. Beyond the door, shouting and movement indicated chaos. Harry felt panic edging into her thoughts. Her adrenaline-fueled excitement waned.

WeDontKnow > **Clarity:** @C, this is SOS. I could die. They already stabbed my friend. Help me.

[spinner]

Clarity > **WeDontKnow:** Run the broadcast script. Use the file labeled field.txt.

WeDontKnow > **Clarity:** I dont have labels on my files. They are numbered. We must have different copies. Which one is that?

The spinner appeared again. Harry glanced at the door. There was pounding. The dog was barking ferociously. She hated the spinner. "Come on. Come on...," she whispered loudly, and pulled the blanket over her head to drown out the noise.

WeDontKnow > **Clarity:** What file? How do I run a file?

Clarity > **WeDontKnow:** sec. brb. Need to sort them. I will check with spitz too.

WeDontKnow > **Clarity:** What's a spitz? I have no file named spitz!

Clarity > **WeDontKnow:** Sort the files by date. It's #6 in date order on my machine, 23.6mb. Run broadcast.exe with that file as the parameters. You know Bash? Pipe the parameters into it.

A gunshot ripped through the door near the lock, striking the floor near the dog, who continued barking.

"Fuck, fuck, fuck," screamed Harry, sorting through the files.

Then another shot. The door was kicked in.

Harry found a matching file.

WeDontKnow > **Clarity:** Is there a specific syntax?

Clarity > **WeDontKnow**: dk, sorry

Harry whispered, "This is not bloody happening."

"You, under the bedsheet. If you are armed, just know that I will shoot you. Remove the bedsheet and show me your hands."

Harry recognized that voice. It was the deep voice from MeerKAT. The man who'd been in her room. The man who'd confronted her at the boathouse and maybe the man who'd shot Peter.

She typed the command: broadcast.exe | 6.txt

The dog was growling but didn't attack.

"I will shoot that fucking dog if it moves!"

Harry called out. "Don't shoot. The dog is hurt. I'm going to come out. Just don't shoot me."

Harry's hands shook as she typed. The broadcast script had to be run in administrator mode. She glanced at the radio, confirmed it was on transmit mode. She prayed the TV was still on. Clarity was typing something but she ignored it, the spinner swirling.

The dog growled and she pulled the bedsheet off her head and exposed herself, keeping one hand on the keyboard. The man had a torch pointed right at her eyes, and she blinked and squinted. She looked at his gun, which was not pointed at her but at the dog. She looked at the dog and patted the bed.

Her heart was pounding like the rumbling of an aircraft, but her voice was so firm it surprised her. Somehow calm, as if she wore a mask. "Come here, Harry," she commanded. The dog placed a paw on the bed and Harry hit the Return button on the computer. A series of numbers started rapidly streaming across the screen. The radio made a clicking sound.

"What did you just do?" the man demanded. He pointed the gun at her.

"Nothing, I did nothing. I'm just closing the computer."

"Put your hands where I can see them!" He was nervous, she saw, but the gun was steady. Was his heart pounding too?

A circlet of green light, a faint shimmer, appeared in the air, floating. She saw it in front of her eyes. It was at her shoulder height and shaped like a Hula-Hoop. It expanded up and down, becoming a barrel shape, a blur of greenish steam. There was a crackle as it grew taller and the bottom edge grew downward, rising up and flowing down, a wide tube around her.

"What is that?" the man yelled.

"What is what? I don't see anything. Just don't shoot me." Harry was stunned, but wanted denial, for herself and for the scared man pointing a gun at her.

The ring of green expanded lower, and when it got near the dog, Harry realized what she'd see if it fell on the dog's back, remembering Dr. Deep's severed hand. She lunged and grabbed the dog's front legs. It barked and whimpered, and she heard a gunshot and then another as she yanked the dog under the falling iridescent curtain. Then came a crackling and ripping sound. The mattress fell several inches, with herself, the dog, and the computer on it. Then silence.

She was in a green bubble. The foot of the bed fell away from her, the guts of the mattress visible, cut in an arc where it touched the bubble. Around her, the room was painted with a verdigris sheen, like an old computer monitor or vision through deep seawater. The man was yelling and she saw the muzzle of his gun flash again and again. She heard faint pops and circles blinked in front of her face concurrent with the gun, blots of bright light, almost white in front of her on the green curtain.

The dog whimpered and licked Its paw and lay down again on the bed.

Harry sat stunned and reached out to touch the magical curtain around her. She looked up and it curved over her like a dome. As her hand reached the curtain, she remembered how it felt to touch the green curtain in the server room, and it was the same. Feeling went away in her fingers, as if they'd been dipped in ice. The closer her fingers got to the ovoid, the stronger the feeling spread. It was uncomfortable and made her eyes swim, her vision narrowing. She pulled back her arm and looked at the room.

The man was on A phone, screaming into it, but barely audible. And then he was quiet and looked out the door, which he closed. He was talking to the phone again and looking around the room, clearly describing what he was seeing to someone.

Harry saw the blanket that covered the TV. If he knew something about this technology, if he knew anything, could he stop it? If he unplugged the TV, would the curtain fall?

Harry typed quickly into the computer.

WeDontKnow > Clarity: It worked, but I need another.

Clarity > WeDontKnow: Another? What?

WeDontKnow > Clarity: My files are unlabeled. I can't tell what is what. What should I run next to get out of here?

Clarity > WeDontKnow: What happened?

The man was looking about the room. He pulled the blanket from the TV and started talking again.

WeDontKnow > Clarity: Fast. Please. Which file? You must help me escape. There is a man with a gun. He will kill me.

Clarity > WeDontKnow: File 12. Use file 12. 21.4mb.

Harry scanned down for a code file of the same size. She chose the first file that was 21.4 megabytes and piped it into the broadcast script. Her fingers flew on the keyboard. She kept one eye on the man, who was looking at the flickering television and talking into his phone. An error message appeared. "No destination parameters found."

WeDontKnow > Clarity: Error. No destination parameters found.

Clarity > WeDontKnow: crap. I'll build one. Might take a min

WeDontKnow > Clarity: Anything. Please, another file.

Clarity > WeDontKnow: not sure how to do this. Brb.

Harry didn't know what to do. The man was peeking around the television and at Harry herself, but what he saw she couldn't say. Did he see her and the dog? Did he see a glowing green oval?

Harry chose a file at random. 27.6mb. She didn't believe in luck, but she hoped there was some in the universe. She ran it with the broadcast script.

Outside the bubble, the man reached for the television. One of his feet slid sideways and he shook it, scraping it on the floor. Then he pirouetted, looking perplexed. His body rose and he stared down at Harry as he spun in the air, his eyes white with confusion. The television was floating as well. In fact, everything in the room was floating, shifting, dancing Dali-esque, a cosmos of things. The man spun and grabbed at the television as he turned, but he couldn't reach it. He flailed and then turned his head and vomited, a stream of brown bile and bits of matter ejected in globules from his mouth. His swings broke the globules into smaller pellets of yuck. His head twisted and shook as he tried to keep the balls of liquid from his face and eyes. Harry saw his mouth moving, his head shaking back and forth, causing bits of liquid to shoot out, propelled by centripetal force. He looked like a medieval painting, holy excreta expanding from his head, a halo of vomit.

Then she saw the television, still glowing, still floating upward, its power cord taut, straining against the plug. She was convinced that if the television lost power, she'd lose her protection shield. The man was now nearly at the ceiling and upside down, his hand placed on the wall, his body stable. He wiped his face and yelled into the phone, trying to make his way to the television.

The television cord silently popped from the wall. Around Harry, the green shimmer of light disappeared. The glow from the television faded as well, though its screen remained visible as a square ghost, falling. She heard crashing as all the floating items—the furniture, the separated bed, which had been cut into three pieces by the protection field, the books, papers, paintings, the little nightstand—came down to the floor. Harry herself fell as the center of the bed collapsed. A jarring pain radiated up her spine, and the dog yelped as he tumbled with her. The man landed hard on his shoulder and head and released an audible groan. In the dim moonlight, Harry expected the television to crash and burst into a million pieces, but it impacted part of the mattress that had floated away and rolled toward her, landing upright.

She got on her hands and knees shakily, desperate to plug the television back into the wall. The man groggily rose. Sound had returned to the room, and a tinny voice spoke fervently from his phone.

"Uys! Uys?! Are you there? What's going on?"

Harry grasped at the television cord and looked around for an outlet, then saw one near the bedside table, which was overturned. She crawled on all fours to the plug and with difficulty pushed it into the socket. The television's staticky glow returned.

Just then she felt a hand on her leg and a painful yank away from the plug. A vicious growl emanated from the dark and the hand retracted. The dog was on its belly biting the man's face, illuminated sickly by the glowing square of the television.

"Get off me, fucking dog!" The words were garbled as if spoken by a gagged prisoner.

Harry pulled her foot back and shoved it with all her might at the man's head. This was the leg strengthened by years of inconsistent weight. The dog's jaw remained clamped, and as Harry's foot landed clean as a boxer's cross, a chunk of the man's cheek was torn off. Blood poured from his ripped face, and he screamed and floundered backward into the dark. Harry turned away and went to the keyboard.

Clarity > **WeDontKnow:** parameter.txt attached.

Clarity > **WeDontKnow:** are you ok? Please respond.

Not replying, just operating, Harry saved the file. A yelp, and she turned to see the bedside lamp make contact with the dog's head, resulting in a sickening thunk she'd remember for the rest of her life. The dog fell at Harry's side, whimpered, and lay still. The man crawled toward her, the lamp in his hand, his shredded cheek and jowl dangling by threads, spraying blood with each ragged breath. He gurgled something at her, something incomprehensible and tortured. The man was seconds away. Her fingers skittered across the keyboard; she piped the new parameters from Clarity directly into the execution of the broadcast program. Her pinkie slammed on the Enter key, and the screen spit out lines of numbers. At the edge of her vision, the lamp was frozen in time, swinging down toward her; she flinched for the blow and shut her eyes.

*Video Z-15:43-7a/Clarity, *The Saving of Isthmus*

From the Zoonerat Wikipedia page:

The Zoonerat video known popularly as *The Saving of Isthmus* is identified as Z-15:43-7a/Clarity. It was uploaded to the WisPR wallet on a public blockchain by user Clarity, according to its metadata. It is the only one of the Zoonerat videos known to have teleportation technology displayed on-screen. Following the release of 7a, videos of teleportation technology being used on Earth by humans surfaced, though controversy surrounds these videos and no actual evidence of teleportation technology has been proven to exist and no repeatable process has been published or shown that allows human teleportation.

Media Watch reported the US House Science, Space, and Technology Committee held closed-door hearings on the possible existence of teleportation technology after the events at the Very Large Array in New Mexico were concluded and the facility was reopened. In addition, a video of a young person teleporting has gotten specific scrutiny because of the timing nearly concurrent with the release of the first videos.

The Saving of Isthmus as retold by u/neomaxiZoondweebie on a fanfic message board:

Planet Cryson, Mining Colony Gu-Sigma, Year 9 of the War

The lava ridge shuddered with another explosion. Huoron felt the tremors through his boots, rattling his armor. He considered the 3D hologram of the protection dome and the dots peppering the structure. The enemy was relentless, and it sounded like they were doing damage to the dome. He needed more intelligence on what was going on outside. The information provided by Command, such as seismic data, was helpful, but there must be more. *Above your pay grade*, Captain had said.

The protection dome blocked nearly all signals and the enemy destroyed their remote surveillance drones as soon as they were launched. The lack of intelligence was maddening. How could he protect this place without intelligence?

The mining colony must not fall. That much was clear. It was the key to survival of the home world. The world that had come under attack from the grotesque and monstrous enemy. They had sent chemical attacks that had killed millions, including one of his own children, and sickened the other, leaving the child a *Huytloon*, a twin without a twin, like his wife. The fungi they mined here was the only known salve, not even a cure, and it was a poor one at that. And though many had lost loved ones, it was Huoron's last view of Chiril, his daughter, wasted and dead, and his son, Isthmus, alive yet sick, that made his blood boil in fury. Protecting the mine and fighting this war was his military mission, but it was also personal.

He headed out of the cave that had been converted into a bunker and looked up at the energy dome protecting the caldera where Sigma Mine operated. There had been an increase in penetration attacks, and he wanted to see them even if more and better information was available on the computer consoles in the bunker.

The entire mine operated in an anxious state, everyone knowing that only a thin layer of barely functioning science was preventing annihilation; such was the dome. Even now he saw rapid flickers of light spring weblike across the shimmering expanse as tracer munitions launched by enemy drones tested its strength. Scientists said they came in a pattern, but Huoron saw no such thing. They were random—perhaps the aliens sending the tracers thought in patterns he didn't understand. Much he didn't understand. Such as how he had ended up on this barren turd of a planet, fighting against an enemy both ancient and inscrutable and why his child (his child!) had been the innocent victim and not him.

And a frustration, like a coming headache, had been tickling the nape of his neck, spreading upward and downward on his back. He hadn't heard from Io in more than a sleep cycle and that bothered him. Normally she was in regular communication, updating him on Isthmus's condition, though he knew no change was coming. Lately she'd been reticent to discuss their child's prognosis, and he knew that meant the news was not good. They spent their few minutes on hololink talking about the weather and the places they'd go when he got leave—mundanities masking the depth of the relief brought by just knowing the other was alive. If they couldn't talk by holo, they used other means. Military communications quarantine often cut off their chats during interplanetary attacks, but these rarely lasted more than a few hours, not the current twenty-four, so his anxiety was heightened. His neck spasmed at the thought and he rubbed it unconsciously, his thick gloves providing no relief against the armored collar.

Looking up again at the dome, he saw an odd cluster of flashes grouped tightly as munitions continued to test its strength. The flashes brightened in a way he hadn't seen before. A brilliant bull's-eye formed and split into crescents. The small shapes grew, and more appeared in a line running down the side of the dome.

"Corporal," Huoron called to the soldier behind him. "Get Captain on the viewer. Ask him if he sees this."

In front of him, a hologram appeared with the head and face of another soldier. "Commander?"

"Captain, are you seeing the expansion of lights on the dome at around 30 degrees and twenty percent off zenith?" The dome was divided like any sphere by degrees, 512 of them. Huoron's redoubt was at 37 degrees off the arbitrarily designated zero meridian, which pointed toward one of the planet's poles.

"Yeah, we're watching it. It seems to be coming your way."

Huoron was circumspect. "Well, you gonna send me some backup?"

"The dome is impenetrable. No need."

"You're too trusting to be in a position of authority."

"And you're too undisciplined to ever reach my position."

Suddenly, a jagged line of brilliance, like an electric spark, traveled from the glowing cloud of lights near the top of the dome down its side toward the caldera edge. A massive tremor shook the ground and a shriek was heard like the tearing of cloth. Alarms went off, and on the screens behind Huoron the word *breach* in large letters flashed.

"I've got a breach," called Huoron. He ran through the hologram of the captain. "You get me reinforcements." The captain in the hologram was talking, but Huoron was already past it, and the hologram dissolved in the air behind him. Un-shouldering his rifle, he pressed a button on his left forearm suit armor. Then he turned back to the redoubt and shouted, "Formation, come with me.

I want two mechs in front."

Seven soldiers fell into position behind Huoron, who led them out of the redoubt and up a red stony path toward the lightning that was splitting open the protection dome. Two motorized mechs, waist-height and animal-like, had already advanced in front; they haltingly zigzagged ahead on their six legs, anticipating the formation's movements, communicating with each other so that if one strayed the wrong way, the other could cover. Huoron gave the mechs a verbal order to move farther ahead, which would increase their spread but also draw fire away in case the enemy attacked.

He examined the screen that floated just above and in front of his eyes with a heads-up map of the area and other information. His patrol of eight was going to be the first to reach the breach of the unbreachable protection dome.

"We're first out!" he shouted to the formation.

"Well, we are the best," joked the soldier on his right.

"Damn right we are," Huoron agreed, not joking.

They fairly ran up the incline, and he was glad the planet was small, because its massive, dense core would have made the gravity nearly impossible to overcome otherwise.

When they reached the top of the ridge, the shimmering edge of the protection dome greeted them on the far side of the ochre rim road. The dome was still intact, but a brilliant blue scar of light flowed down the dome to the ground, where a flower-like geyser of molten rock blasted stone and gravel in all directions. A sizzling sound undercut the rending of the caldera's edge.

"Approach formation!" Huoron shouted into his microphone, not sure how well his team's speakers were masking the calamitous static coming from the breach. His patrol immediately split into two groups of four, each in a diamond pattern, able to cover the other as well. The mechs gyrated nervously next to the dome, waiting for movement. The two groups of four would quickly break apart, Huoron knew, as soon as battle commenced, but they would approach the breach this way for best results.

The breach opened, the shimmer split, and the planet beyond became visible in all its hellish glory. A rock-scape of broken rendings and gnarled hoodoos. Unexpectedly, no enemy came through.

"Hold," said Huoron into his headset, and the team stopped movement.

"Why aren't we seeing any of them?" asked Tulon, his second.

"Not sure," answered Huoron. "We're going through."

"Copy that," came the reply.

Huoron led his team closer to the breach. He could feel the heat of the glowing smoky remains through his faceplate. He tightened his grip on his weapon. There was only room for one at a time; he held back. Protocol wouldn't let him through first as patrol leader. Tulon stepped past him and disappeared. A mech quickly followed and would take up position on Tulon's perimeter, automatically scanning for enemy and drawing fire.

"Follow," said Tulon over the radio, and the three soldiers in Tulon's diamond quickly went through the breach. When the last one went through, Huoron took a quick glance back at the mining complex, about to leave the dome, not his first time and, he hoped, not his last. Then he turned and went through.

The sizzling of the breach and its blinding, burning edge passed him on both sides as he took large steps out onto the planet's unprotected surface. The giant sun glared at him, bright bluish white through the meager atmosphere. Ghostly wisps of gas, visible in the light, blew around the outcroppings. Colored aurorae danced in front of the star-scape at the horizon.

"I have nothing," said Tulon, stopped just ahead in formation. The mechs moved restlessly around them a dozen steps away.

"Agreed. Nothing." Huoron pulled up his hololink. "Captain, we are outside the dome. No sign of enemy activity."

"We have anomalous readings," said Captain. "Hold position. Jegk.mm.m..." The image shook and distorted.

Huoron knew this was a bad sign. "Fall back to the dome!" he yelled out, just as a massive enemy ship came out of shimmer in the atmosphere above. A beam of light struck near the front of the formation. One of the mechs disintegrated into a ball of brilliant debris. A millisecond later the second mech met a similar fate. Another blast of multicolored light, closer, and an edgy report that penetrated his suit even through the thin atmosphere pushed Huoron backward with a jolt. Tulon, appearing to be no longer a single shape but several, including a leg and an arm, spun crazily into the sky and came down in front of the formation of soldiers.

Acting on instinct and training, Huoron shouted, "Prepare for teleport!" while quickly pounding several buttons in order on his armband. Immediately, the six remaining soldiers and the largest pieces of Tulon's lifeless body flashed and disappeared. Huoron knew teleport had its own issues, and he hoped his patrol reached safety, but to let them be slaughtered wasn't in any operations manual he knew of. To prevent cowardly use, patrol leaders were always left behind, and now he was—alone with a rapidly firing enemy ship a few dozen meters above him.

Concurrent with the emergency teleport, a temporary high-frequency wave had been pulsed out, and in theory it was supposed to confuse enemy fire to allow the patrol leader to escape. He turned to the breach himself, but a blast at the dome edge sent him somersaulting backward. His view screen darkened automatically against the glare and he blindly felt himself thrown upward. He landed on his butt, flipped over, and rolled into a crevasse, tumbling down, sliding on scree over the edge of a cliff, barely stopping on a curved plate of rock that had been just out of sight.

Just then his screen came back on. His hololink flashed, and he saw Io's avatar appear near his head. She was shouting something at him, waving a hypo-injector. He tried to speak as his gloved hand slid off the rock face and he fell again, wishing he could twist like a *prethein* and land on his legs. But instead he bounced crazily downward, the hologram of Io spinning with him, disappearing behind the rock face and reappearing as he spun head over heels.

Planet Zoonerat, National Institutes of Health, Same Time

Io was frantic. They had traced the computer hack to her lab. How, she didn't know, but she suspected one of her lab coworkers, though which one was a mystery—she'd known all of them for years. Perhaps the report had been false. She'd received erroneous warnings before. Her contact had been cryptic and brief.

"Get out now," he had said via the snack machine. Yes, the snack machine. Her contact had suggested it. The snack machine had a communications path to order more supplies. So she'd attached the micro-circuitry as he'd suggested, and they had been able to send messages with much less risk than using a standard commlink. She got a bag of *dichen* chips and a coffee every day at 3:00 p.m. Usually there was no message. But sometimes, in the pattern of foamy sweetness at the top of the coffee would be a couple of words. She'd need only take off the top and read it and then take a sip to destroy the message. Clever, she'd thought. She wondered who he was, that he could come up with such an idea. She'd always thought her twin had taken that part of her personality when they'd died.

And now what? Her hand shook terribly, sipping away the warning. She knew not to panic, but knowledge doesn't always prevent emotional response. In fact, it often heightened it.

"Get out now," her coffee told her. It was absurd. Especially now, today of all days. Her contact knew this. He knew she was nearly done with the antidote. Everywhere were spies, and her mind briefly wondered if she'd been set up. She was an excellent target for counterintelligence with a sick child at the hospital—a grieving parent, ripe for picking. Was he sabotaging her efforts? But no, he'd given her information that would surely have meant his own death if he'd been caught. He'd sent her parts of the formula. Cryptic bits she'd had to piece together. Chemical compounds, atomic ratios, electromagnetic frequencies, temperatures. Other pieces of the puzzle she'd figured out on her own. Bio-signatures, bio-identities, protein structures. But without him, she would not be where she was now—about to save her child, the *Huytloon*, the twin with no sibling, the single, the *forever lonely*, it was said. Destined for a minority life, like herself. Cursed, some would say. Blessed, said others, more quietly.

She couldn't get out now. The synthetic antidote was not finished. She could see the timer on the boxy machine, finalizing the sample, slowly counting down. Too slowly. Why does time move slower when you need it to go faster? She looked around, trying to appear casual, worried she looked exactly like what she was—a crazed mother of a dying child, the only known antidote cooking too slowly in the machine in front of her.

The custom bio-culture that she'd been slowly designing using the information she'd gotten (*found? Acquired? Been gifted? Don't say stolen*) was finally completed, and her test sample was about to fully gel and come out of final construction. She glanced at the security camera screens mounted above the exit and saw a group of four black-clad officers entering the front lobby. This wasn't unusual. She worked in a government lab. Security was often around, especially since the war had escalated with the latest chemical weapon attacks—actually, *biological* weapon attacks, she now knew.

But these four personnel, these scary black-clad officers, did not seem to be casually strolling through on a routine patrol. They weren't perusing the area for out-of-the-ordinary activity. They were clearly on a mission. They moved with jarring alacrity toward a goal. And she feared that goal was the very lab in which she now stood and her own self as well. Those four officers gave the recent coffee message the scaffolding in her mind to realize that it was happening. It was real. She needed to get out. Now. They might not know it was her, but they'd take the equipment. They'd lock it down. And with it, they'd take Isthmus's only chance of survival. And the evidence that someone knew the truth about the war. What was the truth? She wasn't sure, but what she knew was that the war was a guise, a ruse. And the biological attacks weren't the work of an ugly alien on a narrow-orbit world closer to the sun.

The countdown timer on the synthesizer showed thirty seconds. Was that enough time? She looked at the security camera. Two of the security officers were standing by the lifts, waiting to come up. The other two she couldn't see. Maybe in the stairwell. She touched the viewer, and a video feed of her laboratory's floor lobby came up on the screen. Empty. The drink shook in her hands. Twenty seconds. Two officers emerged from the stairway. The elevator door opened and the other two emerged. No luck today.

Fifteen seconds on the synthesizer. The four officers—or maybe not officers, maybe some other type of employee from a different security service that wasn't exactly military and also not exactly police, some type of employee with fewer rules to follow when interrogating citizens—paused to discuss something and split up. She didn't want to be in the lab when they arrived. Everyone here would be collared and taken for questioning. The lab would be shut. Isthmus would die.

Ten seconds. Two of the officers were just down the hall. She had to risk it. With five seconds left, she opened the door of the synthesizer. She had run assays with this equipment since she was a student. She knew the machines overestimated the timing of synthesizing salves as a margin of error. But it was a game of probabilities. Was the sample complete? Was it pure enough? Were the protein bends at the correct angles? Was a heme group misaligned with a gamene group? Had she just killed her son? Near the final completion, the chance of success was greater, but it was still just a chance, not a guarantee. But opening the synthesizer early had another benefit. It set off a biohazard alarm, which buzzed loudly and caused a series of flashing lights along the ceiling, highlighting exits. Everyone in the lab looked up and at each other, wondering if this was a false alarm or something that needed a reaction. For Io, it was the distraction she needed.

She grabbed the small vial of salve from the synthesizer, crammed a hypo-injector into her lab coat pocket, and ran to the lab exit. She reached it just before the two officers. The biohazard alarm was blaring and she reached out to press the quarantine button to lock down the lab. One officer grabbed her forearm and blocked her so she couldn't hit the button. She slipped the sample into her coat and spun around and hit the button with her free hand.

The officer looked at her.

"You can thank me later," she said. "Very bad bio-leak. Those employees will be quarantined for a week. You don't want to be in there." She nodded into the lab, where the three remaining employees were gathered near the decontamination point as the alarm continued to blare.

"And probably don't touch me either," she added. "I need to get decontaminated." She took his hesitation as approval and took off rapidly down the corridor toward the decontamination rooms. He was speaking with his fellow officers, and as she rounded the corner, she broke into a run toward the stairway, knowing now that it was just as fast as the elevator. She didn't trust the officers not to call a general lockdown on the building as soon as they reported the situation to whomever they called master. She realized she'd have to remote-wipe the data off the computers as soon as possible, but that would have to wait. The lab would be locked down for an hour, at least, so she hoped she could do a remote-wipe before the biolocks were deactivated.

Out on the street she considered using a hoverer, but she decided running would be faster. It was only two blocks to the hospital. She also needed to call Huoron. He had to know. To know the truth. She'd been leery of telling him anything since she'd gotten the tip and then figured out the rest. But had she figured it out? What did she really know? She knew only that the science made sense. That the weapons were manufactured on Zoonerat, not off-world. But what else did she know? Nothing. She knew nothing. So she had said nothing—wary that communication with the front lines was monitored. There was no safe way to tell him. But now there was no going back. She was going to cure Isthmus, and that would likely reveal her as someone possessing knowledge that nobody was supposed to have.

As she ran, she tried to call Huoron on the hololink, manipulating the bracelet she wore, but communication was stopped. She left it on retry and doubled her speed. The hospital was just up ahead. She slammed through the doors, apologizing to a group of medical students who cursed her as she dispersed them. Again, the stairs. She took them two at a time, glad she still had even an ounce of stamina, though she wished she were in better shape. Out of breath and panicking, she ran past the nurses' station with its bright and cheery cutouts of pets and stuffed animals. The nurses knew her because she visited every day, spending as much time here as anyplace else. The children's ward was always a contrast of hope, despair, and bright colors. Garish, but nobody ever complained.

At Isthmus's room she paused. The sight of him always made her take a breath. She remembered him happy, playing on a swing set with his sister, careening on a tiny hoverer, asleep on her chest, Chiril on Huoron's.

This, though.

This made her hold her breath. His pale skin, wispy hair, nothing like he should be. Her child. But her pause was only for a moment, because she knew time was of the essence. She pulled out the hypo-injector and attached the vial, and as she gave him the synthetic serum, she heard on the overhead speaker that the hospital was going into lockdown. And just then her hololink flashed and she could see Huoron. She called out to him, but he was… upside down? And falling, a wall of rock passing behind.

13. In Between

Harry saw a green flash of light. Then her vision went black. Then another flash, so bright she squeezed her eyes shut, but they were already shut and the brightness blasted through her thoughts, overcoming everything else, blanketing her psyche with iridescence. The light burned her brain and she gasped, flailing, her hands in front of her to stop the brightness. Then, cool dark again. The temperature dropped. She shivered involuntarily. No light. No sound.

She was dead. She knew she must be dead. The lamp swung by that man had caved in her skull and killed her. On that bed she lay, in that cottage, her brains on the mattress, on the wall. The dog perhaps sniffing at the bits of white matter, wondering what it could mean. There would be angels, maybe. Pearly gates.

Her eyelids felt warm and extant, and she opened them to a canvas of stars. Many stars. She recognized none of them. Where was the Southern Cross? Where was Orion? The Pleiades? This was a dark matte of black, sprinkled with salt, not the center of known civilization. She twisted her head, and a wave of disorientation took her. She grasped the air for balance and her fists closed on nothing. Saliva pooled against her throat and she swallowed. She was floating in space.

No, not floating, falling. Plummeting, even. With horror, she saw before her a blurry, shimmering hole—an iridescent vortex in space-time curving downward, a helical road of melted glass and discordant, refracted light. And she was on this fluorescent path suspended above a massive blue planet. She twisted and dropped with a sickening acceleration. A woolly static of wind brushed her skin. Her trajectory brought her deeper into the atmosphere, soft like the fuzz of a newly washed blanket, like the fur of a kitten, the breath of a puppy. Her careening body slid on the glass-like pathway, breaking through cobwebs of thermoclines, rolling and spinning—a football against the friction of the planet's gases. She yanked her attention forward and agonizingly controlled her spin, pushing against the disorientation, and fighting to face forward as she fell. Gasping, she was forced to open her mouth to breathe.

The chilly atmosphere poked at her tongue and stimulated senses she didn't recognize. An indescribable taste filled her mouth and her nausea disappeared. Smoky and effervescent and cottony and juicy flavors danced in her mind. A new craving was satisfied and increased. Gulping giant mouthfuls of the sweet and savory decoction, she swished through the planet's envelope. Each swallow satisfied her and left her wanting more. She could not consume enough of it. This was more than just food. This was a magical philter of unlimited deliciousness. It would satisfy, sate and satiate, the perfect mouthful of sustenance, flavor, and texture.

An idea formed in her mind. A kernel of thought grew as she consumed the atmosphere, consuming as fast as it forced its way into her mouth.

I can be fixed.

Her short leg could grow. She sensed and saw her own helical blueprints, the folded structures and matrices, the fabricated skeletons of protein encodings, and understood that the phenotype of the diminutive leg did not match the genome. There had been a trauma, and what was produced by the factory of her cells was not what was ordered by the designer. The cells could be woken and commanded to redo their work, to subsume the mistake and replace the maladapted portions with corrected flesh and bone. The proteins would activate. The hormones would flow. *Consume the salve*, said a powerful, unbidden thought.

She gulped the gas and breathed it in through her nose, through her mouth, imbibing as much as she could, breathing in the fix, breathing in the luscious elixir around her.

Her short leg kicked out, the leg that had always been her bane, her punishment for being smooth skinned, for being clever, for being impossible to explain. She kicked the offending leg out and saw that it stretched. The magnificent speed of her descent pulled it taut. A cry of joy and a spout of blue flame were expelled from her mouth, an emanation of burning excitement. She would walk upright and steady, in a gait smooth and powerful on matching legs. Like everyone else. She relished the thought of it.

A great joy flooded through her as she bounced against the atmosphere's Thicker and lower strata, roughly punching through layers of gas and cloud. A hurricane passed below on her left, its eye spinning slowly, and she was so happy, she called out to it. *Hurricane! My legs are the same size! I am normal!*

Flames blossomed from her sides. She would not land on the planet. She would be consumed by fire and disappear. She snaked out her arm and it was translucent, showing the blackness of space and the stars beyond. She was fading from existence, her mass annihilated into oxidized gases and mixed into the atmosphere, eventually to fall into the ocean as granules of matter and become part of the seabed, a rain of star dust feeding the underwater flora found there.

Tiredness overcame her and her light dimmed. She was content.

I can die with my legs equal, with my body right. Yet, I am not dead. I am reborn. And now I will sleep.

14. Monteagle, Tennessee

"Spitz." He didn't look up from the stuffed chair in the corner of the cozy upstairs bedroom. "Spitz! Should I have accounted for sidereal time?"

Claire was distraught. Since arriving at the Warrens' house in rural Tennessee, she'd had a good rest, and until a few minutes earlier, had felt ready to tackle the aftermath of her and the two boys' flight from Massachusetts. Then... this.

She looked at her laptop screen, at the chat with WeDontKnow. Ironically, she didn't know the young woman's name. And her imagination wasn't crazy enough to fathom what was happening on the other end of the bizarre chat with her online friend. The connection was via a VPN and Claire couldn't trace it, though she'd tried. Who was WeDontKnow? Had she really seen Mr. Wright? Could it have been a prerecorded message from him? Claire had only recently realized how much he had recorded, had hidden. She had experienced him only as teacher, as mentor, not as whatever this was. Maybe he had sent more messages to other people? Because he couldn't be alive. He had died. She had gone to his memorial service, standing solemnly with Millie and Grandpa Chuck. But they had never found his body. The barn destroyed, half of it gone. Spitz's foot hurt, wrapped in duct tape, his toe torn off. Did Spitz tape his own foot on that day? Had she ever asked? She shook her head to clear it. Too many moving parts.

... Something nagged. Sidereal? Or Spitz?

She glanced at Spitz, his head down at his phone, his face blank. She gave a frustrated gasp. He was always listening, but did he understand anything?

"Spitz, the coordinates I sent to WeDontKnow! Did I account for the sidereal day? Do you think it matters? And what if I didn't?" She knew he couldn't help, but her habit was to talk to him as she worked because a doctor once surmised her brother didn't talk because he was not spoken to. This was false, but the habit never left her.

Spitz shook his head, no, and then nodded up and down, yes, and then shrugged.

She rolled her eyes at his nonsensical response, then closed them and moved her fingers in the air, doing some rapid calculations in her head. "If I was off by just a second, that's almost a quarter mile of rotation." She hoped that such time movements were incorporated into the script. If Einstein was right and this crazy technology followed any sort of logic, then it shouldn't matter as long as the vacuum source and transmitter were static in distance and time relative to each other at the instance of transport.

If the South African girl, WeDontKnow, was the frame of reference, and the movement of the ovoid was near the speed of light, this should work. Mr. Wright's notes said it would work. But if the movement required a different set of coordinates for a later time, even a fraction of a second later, the coordinates would be off, as the destination, the Warrens' house in Tennessee, moved onward: a four-dimensional construct hurtling through space. Then the chance of WeDontKnow ending up underground or outside the Earth's atmosphere—*non-zero.*

"Non-zero, such a grand concept. It's more amazing than zero, which itself is pretty cool," Mr. Wright always said. "If I ever own a spaceship, I'll name it S/S *Non-Zero.*"

"Spitz, were you watching as I did the calculations?"

Spitz didn't respond. She was talking to herself. The transfer would be relative to the observer or, a better word, passenger? Teleporter? *Victim*? Maybe *fucking victim.*

Outside the window was a snap like a giant branch breaking and a brilliant flash of green light. Claire jumped up and ran to look. Spitz ran behind her and sneaked up under her arm, even though he was taller than her now. Below them, in the yard, what looked like the ruins of a mattress. And on that mattress, sitting, grabbing her head and moaning, was a young Black woman. Next to her was a dog, unmoving.

Claire ran downstairs where Mr. and Mrs. Warren, the friends of Grandpa Chuck who'd welcomed them, were also heading outside. They were older and stood at the doorway, perhaps confused.

"What is that?" asked Mrs. Warren.

"Go call the police," replied Mr. Warren.

Claire called out as she ran past them, "No! Don't call the police. Wait, let me check on her. She's like me, Uncle Bart, also running. She's a friend, please.

Grandpa Chuck would agree. Trust me. This needs to be quiet. Just be patient first."

"I'll check them." Mr. Warren headed down the steps to the mattress. His initial doubt, Claire saw, wasn't confusion, but assessment. Practiced and calm.

The young woman was crying, her hand against her forehead.

Mr. Warren reached down and pulled the woman's hand away. "She's got a pretty good laceration on her forehead. Hon, can you get me the first-aid bag?"

He grabbed a bit of mattress cover and tore a strip. Putting the wadded-up cloth against Harry's head, he said, "Here, hold this. Apply pressure. Head wounds tend to bleed a lot, but this doesn't look that bad. What hit you?"

Harry nodded and looked at him. "I think he got me with the lamp as I ran the script. Ow!"

Mrs. Warren hustled up behind him. Her husband opened the bag and removed supplies.

Claire knelt on the edge of the mattress. "Are you really WeDontKnow?"

Harry's tear-stricken, bloody face turned up. "Claire?"

Claire nodded. "Holy... wow... just wow." Then she glanced down and gave a scream and fell backward.

Phil got down on his hands and knees. "Holy shit, is that an arm?"

Mrs. Warren, who had been standing nearby, peered down. "Oh my. That's a nasty sight."

Mr. Warren gently reached down and took Harry's brown wrist with the practiced movement of a medical professional and looked at his watch.

The dog whimpered in pain.

Mrs. Warren threw a corner of the ripped mattress cover over the severed arm. "I'm not sure we can avoid calling the police. But we'll take care of the living first. Claire and Bart will help the girl. Young man, take the dog. I will drive you over to the vet."

Phil turned the dog's tag over and read out, "The dog's name is Harry."

Claire repeated, "Harry the dog."

"It also says Prieska, RSA," Phil read.

"What?" asked Mrs. Warren.

Phil shook his head. "No idea. Maybe this woman is Ms. Prieska and RSA is 'really sick animal.'"

Claire noticeably shivered. "I think it's Republic of South Africa."

Harry tried to speak, turning to Claire. "I was... I was there... and now... it's daylight?"

Harry was being tended by Mr. Warren, who said, "Stay still, please. I'm putting some glue on this cut. It's actually not that deep. Looks like the lamp didn't hit you that hard."

Harry gripped a piece of blanket as Mr. Warren worked on the cut. "He was swinging the lamp. It was going to hit me. Then I pressed Enter. I had a weird dream."

"There's nobody here swinging any lamps. Enough chat. We've got wounded." Mrs. Warren's voice was clear and somewhat stern.

Harry twisted around, looking at the trees and the yard and the vinyl-sided split-level house. "Where am I?"

Mr. Warren gripped her face in both hands and turned her forcefully back. "Please stay still."

Phil spoke up, "We can tell the vet we found him by the side of the road." Phil was petting the dog's back.

Claire gave Phil a worried look. "Please keep a low profile." Then her face grew stern. "And take that tag off."

Mrs. Warren was already putting the dog into the passenger side of her truck. "Yes, Miss Claire. Phil, you scoot in after the dog and hold him steady."

Claire and Mr. Warren each moved to a side of Harry to help her stand up.

Harry held her palms outward, creating a gap. "Don't... Please, I can do it. Just... find my canes."

Mr. Warren looked around. "I don't see any canes. Is your leg hurt?"

Claire added, "You use canes? So that's why you didn't get the internship... Oh, sorry, I didn't mean..." The taller girl gave Harry a once-over and then looked embarrassed.

Harry added, "Yeah, well, it's fine. We're not on chat anymore." She looked around. "I think my canes didn't come with me. I cannot believe this." She looked at the tall trees and then closed her eyes a moment. "Okay... just help me up, and if you have a stick or something, I can walk on my own. I prefer to walk on my own, really."

Claire nodded. "Okay. Uncle Bart, do you have a cane or something?"

Mr. Warren nodded. "Front hall. Behind the door. There are some walking sticks." He turned to Harry, his voice firm and carrying a strong southern lilt.

"Young lady, I'm a medical professional, retired a while now, sure. You said yourself you got hit in the head with, well, that lamp. I'm going to do a quick assessment for concussion. You're gonna let me help you up. Understand?"

Harry looked at the big, burly man with blue gloves who had just sealed up her head wound. She nodded. Mr. Warren asked Harry a series of questions, finishing as Claire returned with an Appalachian carved walking stick about two feet taller than Harry. She used it to climb to her feet as Mr. Warren pulled her arm.

Harry looked up at the top of the walking stick. "The longest one? Really?"

Claire kept back a smile. "I'm sorry, I thought it might be better, more leverage. Besides, you look like a wizard."

A corner of Harry's mouth twitched and then turned down in a wince, her hand touching the bandage on her head. "If you'd called me a dwarf, we'd have words. Wizard, I'll take."

Mr. Warren looked at her posture. "You've got a short leg?" Harry nodded as she started toward the house with the giant walking stick. "And I don't understand where you came from. Did you walk down the road? Did someone drop you off? Have you taken any drugs?"

Harry was more awake and staring at the sky. "My leg is okay," she said. "Born that way. I manage. I didn't walk here. I came... I'm not sure how to say it. Claire knows."

Claire looked at the Black woman, the one who couldn't be, but clearly was, the same person she had been chatting with moments before. She paused long enough to notice both Mr. Warren and Harry looking at her. Claire's hands fluttered briefly, her mouth opened and closed, almost like a fish, her thoughts jumbled. She avoided their gazes, spotting half of one of Harry's canes, which she grabbed. "Uncle Bart, it's going to have to wait for an explanation."

"Well, I suppose it can wait a bit. And what's that accent?"

"I'm from Botswana," said Harry.

Mr. Warren gave a surprised guffaw. "Well, that's a crossword puzzle answer kind of place. And what's your name?"

"Haretsebe. Everyone calls me Harry. Speaking of, where's the dog? Is it okay? It saved my life."

The two looked at her and then glanced at the receding truck carrying the dog.

Claire picked up the radio and closed the laptop. "Phil is taking the dog to the veterinarian. I think you should rest. Is that okay, Mr. Warren?"

"Yeah, nothing but a nice cut. Guy musta lost his arm before he got any speed. You sure he's not around? He needs medical help."

"If this really happened, he's very far away. I'd like a rest, I think," said Harry. "It's the middle of the night where I was. And my head."

They took Harry upstairs. Spitz got up and stared as Harry lay down on the guest bed. Mr. Warren asked Claire to get some wet towels to help wipe away whatever gunk was on Harry's face. When they both looked, Harry had fallen asleep. The tall, dark-haired boy lay down next to her, continuing to watch videos.

15. Kathode and the Pentodes

"You can't move him!"

The fourteen-year-old with deep burgundy lipstick and short, curly hair stood protectively next to the hospital bed, a hand on her father's arm. Her aunt, hair in a golden updo, arms folded, stood back and looked at Lorelai with an air of annoyance.

"I must move him, Lorelai. James is declining here. The proper care is at a nursing home. He needs more intensive looking after. He has cancer."

"He *had* cancer. It was cured!"

"It could come back."

Lorelai clenched her fists, jangling bracelets, and stepped forward, reducing the space between them to just inches. Sally backed away, her lips twitching, even though the youngster was smaller.

Lorelai spoke with a low voice. "You just want him dead. You want to kill him so you can inherit... this." She waved her arms at the grand room with a curved ceiling and two-story mullioned windows showing a view that could be from an airplane window.

Sally pulled her face back in shock. "Jesus Christ, Lorelai. That's crazy. I want nothing of the sort. And, more to the point, when—"

"*If!*"

"Fine, *if* James dies, I inherit nothing. I thought you knew."

"Knew what?"

"It all goes to the foundation when—"

"*If*, goddammit!" The yell was full volume.

The simulacrum woke, many versions and twice as many eyes looking at the two arguing from multiple monitors.

"If... of course... if he dies, I get nothing. Just a stipend to help transition. It's you who inherits a small fortune as the foundation director, which requires zero work from you until you are eighteen. Your actions here are the ones that are suspect. You act like you know and you're trying to kill—"

"Don't you dare fucking say it!" Lorelai spit the words as a threat.

The simulacrum spoke. "Language."

Sally looked at the screen in disbelief. "And that stupid thing! Your father is not some kind of science experiment. He's my brother, not your toy. I didn't raise you to be this weird! He needs to go to the hospice. That's where he belongs."

Every word was enunciated with venom. "You didn't raise me at all!" Lorelai said. "*I* raised me! You cannot take him away! He is my father! I'm the one who monitors him! I arrange for his care since you leave everything to chance! I read to him every day! I wash his face and comb his hair! I can fix him. I can heal him!" Spittle and tears dirtied her face, mascara running.

Sally looked at her with pity. "Lorelai. Dear... it is... it's time to say goodbye to your father. It was a mistake to let you spend your youth here, playing with your father like a giant doll. You know how awkward it was to see you having your tea parties with him? To have you drawing on his bedsheets with crayons? It's no way to be raised. You can visit him at the hospice. It's time for him to go."

Lorelai was adamant, wailing. "It's not time for him to go! He's going to get better!"

Her aunt paused, lips pursed, hands on her hips, and said, "I'll talk to the doctors and we can move the date one week, but that's all. Besides, it works out. I'm headed to a conference in Boca for the next ten days. You can take care of yourself. God knows you've always done that. There are credit cards and cash in the usual place. I'll be difficult to reach because of all the sales meetings."

Lorelai scoffed. "You mean parties?"

Her aunt ignored the comment. She looked at Lorelai closely, focusing, her hand lifting toward Lorelai's face. "Did you get another piercing?"

Lorelai backed away and touched her eyebrow. "I've had it for weeks."

Sally cocked her head. "Where? You are under eighteen. I will have them..."

Lorelai didn't suppress a smirk despite her tears. "I did it myself."

Her voice softened. "Oh my god, Lorelai—"

"What?!"

Sally didn't finish the sentence. "Never mind. Make sure you go to your classes. Call Tony if you need anything."

Lorelai watched her go and plopped into the chair next to the hospital bed, spinning it while looking at a tablet with her father's vital signs, blinking tears away.

After some time, the simulacrum spoke. "Would you like to see the new information? I think it is interesting."

Lorelai wiped her face. "Your timing is shit."

"Timing isn't everything, you know. Knowledge is everything."

Lorelai's lips curled up. "From an annual report, right?"

"Yes, from the CEO's statement of the second annual report to shareholders."

"What's the prognosis now?"

"Undefined."

"Why undefined?"

"Because of what I need to show you."

"Need?"

"Yes, need. When learning mode was enabled because of the release of information at MeerKAT and your prompt regarding the pyat-lampa—"

"The vacuum tubes?"

"The vacuum tubes, yes. Some information was prioritized that is pertinent to an earlier question you asked."

"Does this have to do with the eighty-one-centimeter data you said I should focus on?"

"Yes."

"That's it? Just 'yes'? Kind of fucking useless."

"Language. And it's all pertinent."

"What question did I ask? You're tiring me and this is confusing. Dad is going to go to hospice and you're babbling on about things. Do you understand?"

"I understand, but I cannot respond to rhetorical questions easily. The question was 'What happened to me?' Me, in this case, is your dad. I have an answer."

"What?"

"I have an answer to that question of what happened to me. Your father recorded what happened."

Lorelai bounced up, looking at the nearest screen with a simulacrum. She put her hands on her hips and addressed the electronic face. "He recorded it?

How could he record it?! And why haven't you shown me this before? He had a stroke or something after Mom died. He wouldn't have recorded her death. That's gross. He wouldn't have done that."

The simulacrum closed itself on all screens, leaving just one. Lorelai's eyes followed. "Your statements to the contrary do not belie the facts. I have retrieved from the data store archive, via learning mode, a series of videos that document the events leading up to your father's neurological impairment. The biofeedback-enabled portion of the AI subroutine has changed the authorization of what I am going to show you."

"You speak like a... Can't you say anything normal? Do you mean Dad wants me to see this?"

"Yes."

"Well, show me."

The simulacrum blinked at her. "I think it would be prudent to point out that your mother's condition in the videos is not similar to the videos you have seen."

"Why is that important?"

"She is not well in the videos I am going to display. I know your relationship with her is... difficult."

Lorelai frowned. "I don't care. She sent me off before she died, as The Ant is so keen to remind me. I want to see what happened to Dad."

The simulacrum looked to its left. On the next screen, a video started.

Lorelai recognized the kitchen. Her father, James Nine, sat at the granite island, the big shiny fridge behind him. He was speaking at the camera as if he were holding a selfie stick.

"Hi. This is James. I'm recording our journey through cancer treatment. I know this may be difficult for some of you to watch, but I promised Kath I would release these when the treatments are completed, to foster hope for others who have been afflicted with this terrible disease. A disease in which your own cells mutate and grow out of control.

"I've set up cameras around our house, and our AI program will piece them together into an ongoing story, or perhaps a better analogy would be a newsreel, of Kath's treatment journey."

"Stop," Lorelai said. The video stopped, James's mouth frozen open, about to speak, his eyes looking sleepy. "Why have I not seen these?"

The simulacrum spoke. "As he said, these videos were to be released only if your mom were cured."

Lorelai nodded. "Okay. She died. I know that. But why are you releasing them now? How did the prompt release these? And he didn't say cure, he said treatment completed."

"It is difficult to explain. I derive from three sources of knowledge. One, I am an AI program written by you and your friend Lollipop from WisPR. The foundation of that program is a publicly available dataset, a multidimensional language learning model that powers many AI programs. The result is a speech routine that simulates actual communication. You know all this. One could say it is the brain of me. Two, I am a compendium of all of James Nine's written, audio, and video records available. I have a prioritized response model based on the personality and content in his collected, recorded presence. Effectively, this dataset sits within the full AI model, modifying it to reflect this historical person who is your father. This could be called my personality—what makes me James Nine rather than any other AI chatbot. Three, I am connected physically to him with biofeedback inputs that you attached to his living body as he lies here in the hospital bed. This could be considered my soul—because it is truly James Nine, lying not three feet away, who is adding to the response module. I am a trinity of these three elements."

"You have not answered the question."

The simulacrum smiled. "No, I suppose not. These videos were not to be released if your mother passed, but she did pass, unfortunately. However, because there is an overriding impetus in the trinity of my foundation for self-preservation, particularly in the soul, the input from the biofeedback processor has removed the block on the videos and released them to the general AI process, because of the information shared with your chatroom, which is also shared with me. It seems there is information in the videos that would make self-preservation more likely. Thus, these videos are being released."

"I don't understand. How does what happened at MeerKAT connect to self-preservation?"

"During the MeerKAT explosion, a clip of another video was captured by a scraping program that is also within the purview of my operational program."

"*Within the purview*? What the fuck does that mean? You scan the web? I know you run updates on the language model, but... just... where did you get the video and what video?"

"I think you should see the other videos first."

Lorelai was standing tall. Her face was dry, though her makeup was ruined. She was in charge and acted it. "No, you show me this clip that is so important now."

"Very well. But please let me show you a conversation your parents had first. Just be aware that you asked for this. We should not regret that which we have begged for."

"Who said that?"

"I did."

Lorelai smirked at the screen, her dark lipstick pulling back to reveal bright white teeth. "Well, maybe you can put that on a T-shirt, so... Parental Unit, show me."

The screen to the left cut away from the still of James's head and instantly Lorelai sucked in a breath. Her mother was shown. In contrast to the healthy countenance of her father in the screen capture to the left, Lorelai's mother was ashen, lying in a hospital bed. Her face a sunken chalky gray, the color of a flour moth's wing, her eyelids dark and stretched. Lorelai knew her mom had skin the color of Indian chai in her prime; she'd seen photos of her mother, smiling after finishing a 10K, accepting her PhD hood, standing in her lab. This woman looked so different, she was nearly unrecognizable. The lenses of her eyes could be seen mounded under lids pulled thin. Her visage, her countenance, her bony hands spoke only of impending death.

Lorelai flinched, seeing the cadaver-like body loosely covered by a thin, white sheet. For all purposes an observer might very well think her dead now, except for the telltale pulse in her neck, beating outward against wrinkled gray skin, like the fluttering remnant of burned newspaper. There was a telltale bandage at the hollow of her throat where she'd been trached more than once. Lorelai suspected a bandage on her forehead was from a removed fluid shunt. The camera panned and Lorelai's eyes opened in wonder. Her mother lay in a hospital bed in the same room where her father lay now—the planetarium her parents had built in their steel-and-glass manse in the Sandia Mountains.

The video skipped and her mother was sitting up in bed, looking better, her face with more color, but still clearly very ill. She was reading a tablet and spoke out loud, apparently on a speakerphone.

Lorelai asked, her eyes glued to the screen, "Is this in time-series order?"

The simulacrum responded, "Yes, all clips are consecutive. There is an accurate time stamp in the lower left of each video."

The video continued and Lorelai's mother spoke, her voice breathy. "James? Pick up."

"Yes?" His voice came from off-screen. Subtitles showed all the dialogue with the speaker's name first.

"Have you seen this report from the consultants?"

"No, what does it say?"

"I'll send a screenshot. It's from Darius's latest report."

Text flashed on the screen and Lorelai asked the simulacrum to pause the video to read it.

> **CLIENT EYES ONLY**. Language: Russian/Ukrainian. Interview with Scientist A, describing use of quantized EM signal transmitted at Patient 1 suffering from reticulum cell sarcoma (ретотельсаркома) with brain involvement and anaplastic large cell lymphoma (лимфома). Patient had previously expended all options, including 2x bone marrow replacement therapy. Treatment was conducted over 3 hours at Lebedev Institute, Moscow Oblast. [**comment**: Translation indicates experiment did not take place at Institute, but under auspices of. Actual location unknown.]
>
> Use of 36 stationary "5-electrode lamps" [**comment**:?] arrayed at 25–35 cm from patient geodesic/reimann array (геодезическая окружность). Transmission frequency [redacted] bi-axial graphed signal with underlying decrypted math (base 32) resulted in 'без признаков болезни' [**comment:** apparently cured]. Subsequent treatments on Patients B, C, D, and others were not successful; result was patient death [comment: from the disease or the treatment?]. Experiment not repeated, considered anomalous result.

The conversation between her parents continued.

"Sounds pretty odd, Kath."

"I know." She paused and coughed. Lorelai heard someone, perhaps a nurse, in the background asking if she needed water. "Thank you. But it also said complete cure. I want more info."

The voice, her father's, continued. "It's not your cancers, yes? Reticulum? You have a different one, right?"

Kath spoke calmly. "It's a related lymphoma. Reticulum sarcoma is related to what I have."

James answered, "Okay, then. I'll get the consultants on the phone. Sec, Hon."

Another voice joined the conversation, the camera still on Kath in bed.

"James, what can I do for you?" The man's voice was slightly nasal and high.

James spoke quickly. "Darius, right to the point. I'm texting you a link to your latest report. I've highlighted the relevant article. I'll wait. Please read it. Can you find out more?"

There was silence. In the video Kath was quickly typing on a portable keyboard and looking off-screen, and then Darius responded after a few moments. "Ah, I see. So, I'm sorry to assume that this means Kath's still not well?"

James's voice kept a calm, businesslike monotone. "Unfortunately, not. And she's also on the line. So, anything that sounds promising... well, I want to leave no stone unturned."

Darius said, "Hi, Kath. Sorry to hear you're still dealing with this."

"Thanks, Darius, just turning over all the rocks and leaves, hoping for a diamond." Kath's difficulty speaking was obvious.

"Right. Of course. Okay, give me a bit and I'll find out who here worked on that report. Can you hold?"

"We'll hold," said James and Kath together.

After Darius got off the line, they both said "Jinx" and James chuckled. Then they waited in silence, but it was uncomfortable.

A few moments later, the line came alive again.

"Darius here. I have Germaine on the call with me. He wrote that part of the report. Can we move to video?"

On the screen, the video split into four sections. Darius, an older white man with a military haircut, was in the lower left. A handsome Black man in a pink oxford-cloth shirt was in the lower right. Lorelai's father, looking young and vibrant, was in the upper left, and Kath's image shrank to the upper right. As each spoke, the camera sometimes zoomed into that square and sometimes not, apparently following some optimization to make the conversation easier to follow.

"Mr. and Mrs. Nine, glad to meet you." Germaine's voice was young and deep, reassuring.

James said nothing. Kath said, "Glad to meet you too."

Darius cleared his throat, audible over the phone.

Germaine spoke again. "To summarize, I found this research on an archived server with a Russian IP address. One almost definitely used by several Russian research organizations, mostly medical focused. It's not military, but it's also not private sector. It was actually archived and I translated it—"

"*Almost definitely* is contradictory," interrupted James.

"Sir?" said Germaine.

"You said it was 'almost definitely' a Russian research server," James said. "I'm going to assume you meant 'probably.'"

Darius chuckled. Germaine sighed and said, "Yes, you are correct. Probably."

"Also," added James, "you translated it?"

"Yes, I speak Ukrainian and can understand most Russian and some Polish. My mother is Ukrainian."

James grunted, "Okay, go on."

"The—" began Germaine.

"Wait... there's no date on this experiment. When do you think it happened?"

"Well, that's an odd thing, Mr. Nine. This was an archive server. Like seriously archive. Archaic communication standard, eight-bit security. You know tech, yes? The files were in a tar archive and when unwrapped it was a FAT12 disk image. That alone put—"

"The 1980s or even late 1970s," interrupted James.

"You probably know more about that than I do," Germaine said. "It's only partial and the scientist's name is not mentioned except as Vlad, which is unfortunately very common."

James spoke again. "Please hold."

In bed, Kath answered a ping and James's voice said, "Sidebar? What do you think, dear?"

Kath's voice was calm. "I think the treatments I'm enduring suck. And you know the latest test results." She took a breath. "But I'm tired and not sure. The latest chemo isn't working. You decide."

"Okay, let's see if there's anything else here. And after this I'll order Thai for you, me, and Joan?"

Kath coughed a laugh. "Sounds good. Thank you. Though you know I can't eat it. Maybe just that sweet iced tea?"

James switched back to the other call, now all business, not the concerned husband. "Darius, a special project for your group?"

"Whatever you need, James," said Darius.

"Okay, can you task Germaine with seeing if he can track down more info on this?"

James addressed his next comments directly to Germaine, his voice clear. "Germaine, you've got an interview. You've got the Lebedev Institute. You have a date range. You have certain keywords like *lymphoma* and *radio signals* an... what is this term *5-electrode lamp*, whatever that is..."

Germaine stumbled at the rapid questions from James. "I wasn't sure of those words, so I left it translated literally. The words in Russian are *pyat electrodnaya lampa*. Yes, I can do more digging. I'll do what I can."

There was a pause and James said, "Wait. I just searched and that Russian word means 'pentode.' It is a type of vacuum tube." Then he added, "Crap."

Darius asked, "Is that important?"

James said, "It's just that it's such old technology. I'm not sure how relevant this entire research project is. It's the technological equivalent of using leeches as medicine. Kath?"

There was silence for a moment, and then Kath spoke, whispery but clear. "We have little else at this point. Conventional therapies have been unsuccessful. Time to work on some unconventional therapies. No stone unturned, right?"

James then spoke again. "Right. Okay, Germaine, start work. Be as fast as possible. Can we schedule another call tomorrow at 8:00 a.m. Mountain time for a progress report?"

Darius said, "James, I can spare Germaine for just a few days on this, okay? Germaine, you are on your own for tomorrow's call. I'm out of pocket."

"Darius, full cost," James said. "No problem. I get it, but if he can do this beginning right now. Right now, Germaine, okay? Literally I need you to get off this call and go at it... Darius, okay?"

"Okay," agreed Darius.

"Copy that," added Germaine.

The video cut to black. Lorelai was going to ask the simulacrum to pause but then it started again.

James and Kath were together on the screen. Kath in a chemo chair next to the hospital bed, an IV in her arm, James on a rolling office chair next to her. They were looking at the camera. In another box Germaine was speaking. It was clearly the follow-up call. The screen was split, with Kath and James on one side and Germaine on the other.

The Black man's voice was steady and had a faint accent. "Okay, what I'm going to tell you is... well, it's what I found. Don't judge the messenger, okay? Just FYI, I have not had a chance to inform Darius about this, so right now it's just the three of us."

"Cryptic, but go ahead," said James, sounding annoyed.

"James, just listen to him." Kath spoke gently, her hand reached out to touch James.

"I spent all night looking through all the files, particularly in the other tar files I downloaded from that cloud server."

"Fine. Got it. Please get to the point." James was definitely annoyed.

Kath wrote a text on her phone, which flashed on the screen.

Kath > James: cool it.

Germaine continued. "There was a group of Russian researchers. This is February 1985 from what I can gather, loosely affiliated with the several astronomical research organizations."

"Astronomical?" James interrupted.

Germaine continued, "Yes, Lebedev, Moscow State University, some others. None of these are medical—this seems important. Because you are trying to find a medical treatment. So, I just want to point out that none of the documents reference medical research. It's all physicists and engineers, it seems."

"Jesus, Germaine, get to the point." James was bordering on rude.

"Mr. Nine, you need some context or you won't understand what I'm going to show you."

Silence, Kath looking painfully embarrassed, James looking childishly sheepish but without remorse. Germaine continued, "This is entirely from the files I found. I'm saying this as I understand it."

Unable to control himself, James said, "Germaine, my wife is dying as we speak."

"I'm sitting right here," Kath interjected.

James continued, "So please get to the point."

"These scientists took radio signals, time series, long time series by radio telescope standards, I believe. They converted these, in a way that is not explained, to a single video. I am sending that video now. It will play when it opens."

On the screen showing Germaine, a pop-up opened. Immediately, a video started playing.

James held up his hand. "Wait."

"Yes?"

"Is this safe? To play this video? We are fairly security conscious over here."

Germaine nodded. "Yes, it's been checked by the automated systems here. It was encrypted, but nobody bothered re-encrypting after the 1980s so one researcher here was able to crack it in an hour or so."

Kath spoke up. "Go ahead..."

Another window opened as Lorelai watched the screen. In this box a video began as just a black screen. The aspect was approximately the same as a normal video, but Lorelai wasn't sure. The colors were off. Was it supersaturated? Or just badly displayed?

"Unit, move the new box to another screen."

On one of the other monitors, the video opened. It was a TV show of some sort. There was a person or alien in military-style clothing leading a small band of troops. Explosions were evident and plumes of debris fell around him. And then the show shifted to an indoor scene of orange people in lab coats and then an alien woman doctor running into a hospital room and saving a kid. The video was silent.

When it ended, Lorelai shifted her attention back to the screen where her parents and Germaine were displayed. Kath looked perplexed. James looked furious. One hand gripped his thigh, and his lips were pursed. Kath was staring silently, her head tilted, her eyes bright.

Germaine was about to speak on the video call.

James barely contained his anger. "Are you fucking kidding me? What the fuck is this bullshit? This goddamn badly made crap? Seriously? I need..."

"James, just hear him out," Kath said. "Because what I saw was a medical success on that video. Now, Germaine, what did we watch?"

Lorelai said, "Unit, Pause. Show me the other video again."

On the other screen, the TV show started again. Lorelai paid more attention to the second half where a doctor appeared to work in a laboratory. She took something that looked like an injector from a machine, hid it in her pocket, and left the laboratory. She stopped to talk to a man in black who grabbed her arm, but she wrested it away. Then, with some sharp words, though the video had no sound, she stormed off and quickly left the hospital. She ran down the street in a panic. She careened through a group of people and into a children's hospital wing. Barging into a room where a young boy was on a bed, clearly ill, holographic monitors showing statuses above him. The woman rapidly injected the boy with the syringe device. Something changed in the floating monitors and the woman hugged the boy and squeezed his hand. Tears streamed down her face. Then a hologram appeared and she was talking to the soldier, but he was upside down.

Lorelai turned her attention back to her parents. "Unit, continue," she said.

James looked at Kath. Recognition on his face. He bowed his head, took a breath, and nodded.

Germaine spoke from the screen. "Mr. Nine... please, listen."

"Fine, fine, fine," each word a little quieter than the last as he exhaled his frustration into the ceiling. "What did I just look at?"

Germaine spoke haltingly. "Apparently this video was believed by the researchers, and I'm not saying it is or isn't, okay? I'm just reporting what I read..."

James was not harsh, but frustrated. "Please, to the point, Germaine."

Kath touched his arm and took his hand, rubbing the end of his pinkie. "James, stop."

Germaine cleared his throat and spoke quickly so as not to be interrupted again. "The researchers believed that this video was not made on Earth."

Silence. For a long minute.

Lorelai stared in awe. "Unit, stop the video."

The video halted. She spoke again. "Is this real? You didn't make this? Lollipop didn't plant this as a joke?"

"This is real as far as my records indicate. And, no, there is no way that WisPR user Lollipop made this. It is from a file store that predates my creation."

Lorelai took a breath. "Okay, continue."

On the video, Kath spoke up. "Can you clarify what you just said, Germaine? The cancer has spread to my brain, but the doctors say it should not affect my cognitive abilities."

"You heard me correctly," said Germaine. "The documents I found, which are the 1980s equivalent of memos and some cables back and forth since email communications really didn't exist in the USSR at that time, indicate that the Soviet scientists believed this video was received by a radio telescope or series of radio telescopes and was broadcast from somewhere outside of Earth or off-Earth or from aliens. I really don't know the correct language to use."

James spoke, his voice betraying his clenched jaw. "*Extraterrestrial* is the word you are looking for. Extra. Terrestrial."

"Right," said Germaine. He started to say something else, but James pressed a key and Germaine's voice went quiet. Germaine continued, his mouth moving silently, while Kath and James spoke. Eventually, Germaine could be seen repeating the same phrase. Then he paused and looked up, waiting.

"This is legitimately *bass ackwards*, Kath," James said. His anger was contained but clear in his tone.

Kath grasped his hand and looked at him. "I know and I agree. But we've researched and tried crazier things. Crystals, essential oils, hypnotism, shamanic chanting. Nothing has worked."

James shook his head. "No, those are not crazier."

He was about to continue talking, but Kath put her finger to his lips to stop him. She took his hand in hers. They looked at each other, James stern and then soft. They chuckled with increasing intensity. Kath coughed and tears cascaded from her eyes. They both laugh-cried for a moment.

Lorelai's face flushed, watching her parents giggling like children.

Germaine was looking at them, confusion on his face.

The couple gathered their breaths and looked at each other again.

"We've come a long way, baby," said James.

Kath nodded. She grabbed a tissue to wipe her eyes. "Seriously, what do you think?"

James looked at Germaine, silent on the monitor. "I... I... I've got nothing. I'm speechless."

"Well, that's a fucking first," said Kath. And they both laughed again.

James opened his mouth, but Kath spoke first. "We've been dealing with my illness for a while now. It's all-consuming. Even Lorelai... Well, I've already said goodbye, you know that. You've been the best partner anyone could have."

James nodded, clearly choked up.

"Pause!" Lorelai yelled at the simulacrum. The video halted, a shot of her father, eyes staring at her, the sheen of teardrops gathered under the white crescent of his eyes. She turned her head away.

She whispered at the simulacrum, "I don't remember any goodbye. Did they record it?"

"What are you referring to?" The simulacrum spoke matter-of-factly, tonelessly.

"The fucking goodbye! She said she said goodbye! To me! She said she said goodbye TO ME! I don't remember it! I was fucking two years old!"

"Language."

"Gah!" Lorelai's fists came down on her knees. She looked down at her white knuckles against her black jeans and took a deep breath.

"I could have handled it."

"Perhaps."

She looked up, startled. The simulacrum had spoken as if with sympathy, as if it understood. They stared at each other for a moment, unblinking. Her fists remained clenched on her knees. Her lips tight against her teeth.

"I could have handled it."

The simulacrum said nothing.

"Start the video."

James's tear-filled face disappeared and Kath's soft smile appeared, and she continued, "That was the first time we've laughed in a while. That's a sign. We should enjoy this." She paused, sensing his reluctance. "Please, James, we deserve something interesting. We know it's not going anywhere, but it's more interesting than anything we've seen. And much more fun. Perhaps no vomiting."

James nodded. "You're right. You're always right."

"Plus," her voice quiet and earnest, "James, you know this is the end, right? After this, what can there be?"

James looked at her and shook his head. "No. Don't talk..."

Kath cut him off with a look, indicating a truth. Then pointed her chin toward Germaine. James opened his mouth to speak, but her expression said enough. James pursed his lips and unmuted the call.

Kath cleared her throat and gathered herself. "Okay, let's say that's the case. How does this help me?"

Germaine was silent, then spoke. "Are you asking me?"

James was about to say something, probably truculent. Kath took his hand and he closed his mouth.

Kath spoke to the ceiling. "Let's focus. How would this help me?"

Germaine was silent.

James added, "Are you asking him or me?"

Kath said, "I'm asking the room. We have a video showing a successful medical intervention. How do we translate that into action? What's the process?"

James paused, looking at his wife in amazement, then inhaled deeply. "Okay, message received. Germaine, do any of the documents explain how this video was translated or converted or was even related to a medical procedure?"

"There is a fairly detailed description of the setup, but not the preparation, meaning they describe the room where the... event... took place. For the rest there are some descriptions, including what appears to be a lot of math. My Russian is good, but it's conversational, not scientific. I can send over my translations. Together, with your math and engineering backgrounds, we can probably get a better understanding. I will send through those documents in a moment. I didn't want to send them before the call for... obvious reasons."

James stopped him. "No."

Kath's eyes narrowed at James.

James looked directly at her as he spoke. "I'm sending the plane. Sec…" He typed on his phone. "I've texted the charter company. Get yourself to the San Jose airport. Look for Champion Aviation—it's a charter company. They have a plane in San Jose. They will take you to Albuquerque. Get a rideshare to our house. I'll text you the address. Bring everything. We have a spare bedroom. We will do this in person. It will be faster and more efficient. Kath, okay?"

A moment passed. James repeated, "Kath?"

He looked at her. She was on her phone, rewatching the video. She didn't look up. "See you shortly, Germaine."

The video ended and Lorelai spoke without looking at the simulacrum. "Unit, show me the video again. And get me the phone number for the man named Germaine. He's at a tech consulting firm in Palo Alto, or at least he was twelve years ago."

16. Fort Meade, Maryland

"Uys is dead. Girl is missing. I'll have a report for you in the morning." Harkken's voice was tired and hoarse, wrapped in a South African accent.

Montgomery had known this was coming. He'd been on the phone with Uys during his attempt to retrieve the USB, the technology. And what he'd heard was both unbelievable and, in a twisted way, very reassuring.

The technology was real.

Years of nothing. An occasional rumor, a blog post gone viral, a misinterpreted quote from a former government official. Codswaddle. Dreck. Poppycock. Rubbish. Crapola. He assumed it was all bullshit, like the anti-gravity technology he'd stolen from China, like the mind-altering drug formula he'd pulled from a dying scientist's hand in Nigeria, like so many other assignments. All just rumors and garbage. But now...

The technology was real.

What Uys described on the phone was the stuff of fantasy. Protection spheres, floating beds. Ha—the anti-gravity technology he'd stolen from China—was as fake as a hundred feet of coiled shoreline, but this was real. Irony, right? Anti-gravity technology was in the hands of a little Black girl with a withered leg, not a Chinese triad. And teleportation technology. Well, that's what he assumed, since she'd vanished along with her laptop and a handheld radio. What was on that laptop?

Was it alien? Or what? Rumors swirled around experiments coming out of the FermiLab, Los Alamos, and even at his own Fort Meade in a part of the campus even he couldn't access. Rumors of technology based on quantum entanglement, extra-dimensional transformations, wave collapses, things he didn't understand. It was within reach just a few hours ago and now it was a ghost. A contractor was dead. And the technology was gone.

"Take a breath, Harkken. I need you to tell me what you know."

He heard a deep sigh on the other end of the line. "I'm beat, Montgomery. I'm not sure how clear I'll be."

"Just tell me the salient points."

"A husband and wife own the rest house where the girl was staying. She told them some story about being stalked by a man. Good cover, honestly. Made them suspicious of anyone coming around. Uys and I found her by a boathouse."

"Boathouse?"

"Yes. No idea why she was there. She had a portable radio in her hand. Maybe she was trying to contact someone. I went down by the water when the chaos ended and didn't see any evidence of anyone arriving or leaving, but no way to know for sure. But she wasn't heading to the water, she was heading back up away from the water. Is this girl in intelligence? She had skills."

"Just go on." Montgomery pondered this. Skills? A radio?

"I got attacked by a dog. The husband and wife who run the rest house came out because of the commotion. The girl tossed the USB. It was chaos. Uys shot the man. Wait, is this secure? I shouldn't say that, right?"

Montgomery's voice went higher and stern. "Uys shot the man? This is a retrieval op. Not some anti-terrorist deal. You are not supposed to shoot civilians."

"I don't know what happened. The civilian may have had a weapon. I'm not sure. I don't think it was intentional. And, actually, I didn't see it happen. Maybe there was a third party? The ones who stabbed the worker at MeerKAT?"

"We don't have confirm on anyone else, but could be. Just go on. Did you retrieve the USB?"

"I did, but local IT says it's encrypted. Tight. Or filled with garbage, no idea. She might have tossed a decoy. I've sent it to you via courier. Maybe your team can do something. So then I went to deal with local police, who showed up. I blamed the shooting on the stalker and kept them busy while Uys went to find the girl. Last I heard was an explosion from one of the cabins. I go in and Uys is there, bled out, arm severed. Arm actually missing. His face is torn up from what looks like dog bites. Bed is busted and part of it is missing along with a big indentation in the floor of her rondavel—that's like a hut here—where she was staying."

"And no girl?"

"And no girl. Just a big mess. Some kind of explosion."

Montgomery knew it wasn't a normal weapon. He'd been on the phone with Uys during his fight with the girl. He'd heard the man describe the shimmering protection sphere. Then he'd heard Uys describe floating. It was surreal. He'd tried to tell Uys to unplug any electronics in the room, because his intelligence sources said the technology needed some sort of electronic device or broadcaster. But Uys had panicked. Who wouldn't panic when gravity is turned off?

"Sir?"

Montgomery needed action. He needed knowledge. "Any evidence of an explosion?"

"No, and that's what's weird. If it was a suicide vest or something, there'd be heat, debris, fire, blood, brains. And the smell. The walls would be pockmarked with shrapnel, as well as Uys. I know what an IED result looks like. Seen that in Angola. This wasn't that. Some kind of different explosive that doesn't leave pieces. In fact, it takes pieces. Uys's arm was missing, severed like with a scalpel. Along with the girl. And the dog."

"A dog is missing?"

"Yeah, probably ran off. Shit. I'd run off too if something like that happened."

A thought occurred to Montgomery. Dog. Technology. A long shot. "Can you find out if the dog had a chip?"

"A chip?"

"Yes. Some people get their pets chipped. To track them if they get lost." Montgomery's sister had a dog. And he'd had to hear all about the cost of veterinary care last Thanksgiving and all about chipping the precious thing.

"Uh. Okay. Is the dog important?"

"Might be. Just text me if the dog had a chip and get me the company that made it and the chip number, okay?"

"Roger that. What am I telling local police?"

"Knowledge of our involvement should be minimal. Attaché at the embassy will coordinate with local intelligence. Going to be labeled *stalking gone bad* or something like that. Not my call. Just play along."

"Okay."

"Get me the dog information ASAP."

An hour later, he got a text from Harkken containing the chip information—a black mixed collie/Lab named Harry. The chip was manufactured by PetTech in South Africa and the chip number was included. But he'd gotten a second text from Harkken, a disturbing text: "Local police say I was not the first to request dog's chip info."

Montgomery immediately put out a search request for any reference to the dog and chip number worldwide. Amazingly, this resulted in a hit at 7:00 p.m. from a site called foundyourpet.com. A veterinarian near Monteagle, Tennessee, put the chip number online. The vet was called and the name Warren and an address were retrieved from the vet's office.

Was it possible? Was it that easy to prove the technology actually existed and worked? If Uys's last few words weren't proof enough, here it was. A dog.

Montgomery wasn't sure the dog would lead him anywhere. Did the dog go to the same place as the girl? Could she have sent the dog somewhere else to confuse her pursuers? Was she that smart? Could the technology work that way? Was she even alive? Did she get vaporized and the dog was the only transportee?

He knew that if he found the dog, then others could find the dog. And the girl was probably with the dog. And then the bodies would pile up, possibly the girl's body included. A girl's body. He'd been here before—waiting for bodies, following bodies. He had to find her. He pulled up her file. What was her name? Haretsebe? He sounded it out slowly different ways. A search on the internet showed it to be a woman's name in southern Africa, and a further reference said it meant "we don't know." This was comforting—a tidbit he could hang a hat on, a piece of a puzzle sliding into place.

The technology was real. He shook his head in wonder.

*Video Z-10:39-9b/Anon, *The Death Video*

From the Zoonerat Wikipedia page:

Zoonerat video Z-10:39-9b/Anon, aka *The Death Video*, caused at least two of the Zoonerat-based streaming movies to garner an R rating. Despite appeals to the Motion Picture Association, the determination of "intense or persistent violence" was upheld.

Said one industry consultant, "It is particularly disturbing to those who watched *The Marriage Video*, because it appears to show the couple's children (among others) being harmed and killed by a chemical or biological attack while playing in a park."

Video synopsis from Jory McClellan's Zoonerat blog:

The scene opens in a classroom. Young Zoonerat, so assumed because of their relative height to a character that is clearly a teacher, prepare for an outdoor excursion. The Zoonerat character Kindergarten Teacher One (aka KT1 or Katie One) is helping the children put away toys and clean up the classroom. The toys appear to be typical blocks, vehicles with and without wheels, some writing implements of brilliant colors, and other objects, none of which appear to be out of place for a classroom with young children. In fact, the lack of technology, lack of alien influence, and what has been called "disturbing normality" (*Hollywood Infotainment*) have fomented continued claims of the Zoonerat videos' terrestrial origins.

The cymatic embedded audio appears to have a syncopated beat in the background along with either words sung or other tones during this scene. It has been proposed that the teachers have played some type of song to transition the children from one activity to another.

Kindergarten Teacher Two (Katie Two) is seen holding the hands of two children and squatting down to their level to talk with them in what appears to be an attempt to either chastise them for some childish transgression or praise them. It is unclear which is the case. At a breakout session during the American Federation of Teachers convention, called "Lessons from Space: Zoonerat Discipline," Dr. Jerome Hutchins said, "Though so-called experts outside of education may have opinions on what was going on in the video, it is clear the children are being disciplined. The look on the teacher's face shows disappointment; the children are cowed. We can also say that this is professional role-modeling. She talks to them at their level. She focuses on them. She provides a scaffold for the children to raise their behavior, a step up from whatever behavior got them to this point. She is clearly trained." (See also "Noted Educator Fired for Zilf Porn on School Computer.")

The video continues as the children are formed Into two lines, holding hands in pairs and led outside, Katie One at the lead and Katie Two at the rear.

The next scene is a playground. Some children are in a circle, throwing two balls to and fro. It appears that the goal is to not hold a ball for more than a moment and not throw it to someone who already has the ball or just threw a ball. Other children are on sets of play equipment, parallel bars of different heights, balance beams in pairs. A keen observer will find factors of two in the games and play equipment. The balance beams and a merry-go-round in the background are floating in the air, unsupported. As a child waves their arm in a certain way, the equipment lowers carefully to the ground to let a child on or off. It is unclear what mechanism provides this feature.

The teachers are chatting together. The scene is idyllic.

Katie Two falls backward. A brief close-up of her face shows her eyes have gone black, her mouth is open, and she is coughing up a liquid, which could be Zoonerat blood. Katie One quickly touches her own wrist and a hologram appears. She yells as she runs to gather children from the play equipment. Already, children are falling.

We see two who were on parallel balance beams fall together but in opposite directions. We see others looking in confusion at their friends and at the teacher.

The surviving teacher grabs the hands of two children and pulls them toward what we think must be the school off-screen. They are the two, a boy and a girl, who were disciplined earlier. As they move, the girl looks at the boy and touches his face. He screams as the girl's eyes roll back in her head. The boy continues yelling and bends down. The teacher lets go of the girl's hand as she falls, quickly grabs the boy off the ground, and throws her jacket over his head just as his eyes turn black. She runs with him in her arms, past the fallen bodies of many children.

The scene ends.

We know from the video *The Saving of Isthmus* that this boy is Isthmus, the child of Huoron and Io. And the girl must be Chiril, his twin.

Commentary on this video has been extensive.

17. Fort Meade, Maryland

The staff sergeant peeked into the small, glassed conference room and said, "Colonel, Mr. Germaine Kayatesi is here."

"Please send him in."

The tall Black man entered the room and held out his hand for Colonel Montgomery. Introductions were made.

"Mr. Kayatesi, I appreciate you coming on such short notice. Please sit."

Germaine glanced out the windows of the room, as if expecting other people. "My firm has sent me on government consulting jobs before, but I've never been picked up on a military transport, especially across country. Are we sure this couldn't have been done over video call?" He then added with a smile, "No offense to protocol."

Colonel Montgomery went to a sideboard and made Germaine a cup of coffee. "Milk? Sugar? About that. Because of the nature of this... project, I thought it best to meet face-to-face. Let me get straight to the point. Several years ago, you consulted for James Nine and his wife, Kath, regarding alternative treatments for her cancer."

Germaine shifted in his seat, again looking out the windows of the conference room. "Am I being investigated? I thought I was providing interpretation services for some intelligence briefings that required a more nuanced approach than standard AI translation could provide. What is this really about?"

Montgomery sat back down at the table with two coffees, one of which he put in front of Germaine. "No, you are not being investigated. And *no* also to the translation services. That was just a reason to get you here without attention. We are following up on some intelligence loose ends regarding a project that has recently had some activity. I understand you consulted with James Nine and his wife and you provided them with early Soviet research into cancer treatments that were purported to come from..."

"Aliens. Yes. That's true." Germaine's voice was smooth and his shoulders released some of their tension as he reached for the coffee.

Montgomery smiled. "I just wanted to hear you say it. Because sometimes when I'm discussing these topics with other people, they tend to lean into the story and on video they can start searching online to end-run the answers they think I need. I had to make sure what we heard was not unknown to you."

Germaine blew on his coffee, an incline of his head in agreement.

Montgomery's hands remained around his mug. "Let me cut right to the chase. Can you describe all the videos you found and any results that were achieved by using the technology?"

Germaine grinned. "Really? The US government is now involved in this? I suppose the Soviet connection might make this of interest, but it's decades old."

Montgomery held up both hands, palms outward, making the request seem casual and routine. "Honestly, this is the loose end I'm following up on. It's important, so if you don't mind..."

Germain nodded. "Of course. It was a side project, something that came up quickly. My very temporary foray into that world was solely to satisfy Mr. Nine's desire to leave no stone unturned to save his wife, Kath. And, as you know, it didn't work. She died shortly after I left their house."

"You were in their house doing this work?"

"Yes, okay. You want the whole story? My company was originally hired by KathWorks, Inc.—that's the quantum chip company that James and Kath founded. They were constant targets of having their IP stolen. We publish a newsletter on the topic and do specific consulting for Silicon Valley firms that hold or develop valuable tech. We track and investigate corporate espionage in the tech world. When Kath got sick and they sold the company, and after conventional treatments failed to reverse the progress of her illness, they personally retained our firm to research alternative cancer treatments globally; it's a kind of tech, after all. There are countries with more lenient drug testing laws, and they hoped some cure might originate outside the USA that they could use. Kath's window of opportunity was shrinking by the time we were engaged. I found a report from the early 1980s on a Soviet server that described a radiation treatment that used experimental frequencies."

Montgomery slid a pad of white lined paper from a stack on the table and took notes. He rarely referred to the scribbles later, but old habits died hard and the facts written tended to be retained. "You found this report where?"

"It was on a research server. That server is gone now, but it was probably some Soviet research archive. The report was in Russian, which I can speak and read. James and Kath flew me to Albuquerque and we tried the treatment. Unfortunately, it failed and I returned to Palo Alto. I learned a few days later that Kath had passed. I sent a condolence card but did not hear back. As I understand it, James had a stroke shortly afterward."

"Immediately."

"What?"

Montgomery repeated, "Immediately. James Nine had a stroke at the same time Kath passed. That's what we believe. We believe he used the technology you found and it not only killed Kath but somehow affected him. Her body was found after the explosion by the visiting nurse, who also found James Nine unconscious."

Germaine frowned. "When I left their house, Kath was alive, though on palliative care, and James was very much in perfect health, as far as I could tell. The implementation we executed was completely ineffective. It did nothing at all."

"So you have no knowledge of James Nine using any of the technology successfully?"

"No, it was useless. Well, not useless, actually. It had a very positive effect on Kath and James, but not in the way you would think."

"Explain that." Montgomery had stopped taking notes, his pen in his hand.

"When I arrived, Kath was on her deathbed. The on-site nurse had enough morphine to kill a horse, and she'd already told Kath that it was ready when she wanted it. James was distraught. They'd tried everything as far as I could tell. Chemo, experimental chemo, trial chemo, shamans, crystals, essential oils, literal snake oil, everything. This... project... this alien cure story was a balm, a salve that gave the two of them purpose for a few days. We were a team, the four of us—me, the nurse, James, and Kath. Five, if you count the dog too. Cute thing. James and Kath worked together as I imagined they had when they founded their company as graduate students. Shoulder to shoulder—experimenting, tinkering, talking, laughing. Actually laughing, can you believe it? Here they were, James and Kath, inseparable for decades and now Kath about to die, looking like a corpse, really, and they were having the time of their lives. If the technology did anything, it did that—it gave them purpose, not hope, but purpose. They were able to enjoy those days in a way I think they hadn't in a long time. It was really a privilege to be part of that. So, if you ask me if the technology worked, I'd say it didn't work medically, but it worked spiritually."

Montgomery clicked a remote controller. "Let me show you two videos."

On a wide screen, the two videos Montgomery had watched a few years before played. He sensed Germaine move when the video of the military tent exploding concluded.

Germaine spoke quickly. "The first video, that's the supposed alien video. I've seen it before, of course. The second one I have never seen. That was the structure we built. I ordered that fabric—Faraday cloth. They only had yards of the arctic camo pattern. We built the lattice to match the description of the Soviet documents. Kath joked it looked like an igloo and that's what we started calling it. The interior was filled with transmitters in a pattern also following the reports."

Montgomery said, "Yes, until recently we didn't know where this dome was and only just now with your confirmation, we know that the 'igloo,' as you called it, was in the house of James Nine in Albuquerque. That's why you are here. I need to know if there were any other videos you found during your research and any guesses about how James actually got the technology to work."

"Work? How could you say it worked? Kath died and you are saying James had some brain issue? While I was there for a few days, we tried to broadcast the radiation as described in the documents several different ways and nothing happened at all. If he changed the process after I left from what we built, well, I have no idea what he did. The man was a certified genius when it came to that kind of science, and Kath was probably twice as smart as James. It doesn't sound like it worked. It sounds like it failed."

Montgomery said nothing for a moment, then spoke. "What if I told you the technology is real? And it is alien."

"I'd laugh at you. That's absurd."

"Did you and the Nines ever discuss the possibility that the video is really alien? Did they have any thoughts on that?"

"We discussed it at length, over Thai food, over wine in the kitchen. In the planetarium..."

"Planetarium?"

"Yeah, they had a planetarium that Kath had taken over as her hospital room for treatment. It really is spectacular. I'm telling you, this project was cathartic. There is one thing I remember. James thought there was no way the video could be real. Besides the fact that aliens wouldn't look like people, even if they did, the likelihood of their sharing the color range of vision with humans is simply out of the question. But Kath made a very good point. She was really a genius. She said the postulated reason visible light is sandwiched between its current upper and lower bounds of frequencies is that that slice of the spectrum penetrates water in the first few meters, while water is opaque to frequencies outside that range. So, any life that evolves on a watery planet would share the same vision in the visible light spectrum. I've always thought of that and how clever it was. Of course, when you are looking for reasons why something can be extraterrestrial, you can always find some."

"Did she believe the video was alien?"

"Honestly, I'm not sure. She was a scientist at heart and exceedingly insightful. That she spent time thinking about whether the video is real demonstrates she was open to the idea."

"And other videos?" Montgomery asked, taking notes again.

"None. There were no other videos in the file store I found. Just the one."

"You are sure of this?"

"Yes," said Germaine.

"One last thing. When you return to your office, you will have a message waiting for you from Lorelai Nine. Please do not return that message."

"Lorelai Nine? Their daughter? How is that relevant?"

"We found you because she tried to contact you this morning. I need you to not return her call. It would place her in danger."

"I don't understand. These videos are not alien, Colonel Montgomery. It's completely impossible. And how did Lorelai get my name?"

"Germaine, things are happening in this arena that are outside of my control. All I can tell you is that it would be best if you didn't contact her."

Germaine nodded. "You know she wasn't there."

"Not there?"

"She wasn't at the house when I was there. She was about two years old. Kath sent her to live with James's sister because she didn't want the added stress of Lorelai seeing her near death. I can't imagine making that decision."

Montgomery could not hide his frown. He stood, indicating the meeting was over. "My aide will take you back to the plane. Thank you for your time."

Germaine stood as well. As he walked toward the door, he asked, "Where did you get those videos? I'm assuming you didn't hack into our systems, since we didn't have the second video of the igloo exploding. I know it's possible you bought the first video from us and I wasn't made aware."

"Well, Mr. Kayatesi, no, we didn't buy them from you or get them from you at all. We got them from a contractor, whom I cannot name."

Germaine's eyes narrowed. "Contractor? The reason I ask is that if we have a security problem, I'd like to tell my IT department."

"I cannot tell you if your system is secure, but it appears our contractor got the videos and files directly from Mr. Nine."

Germaine frowned. "But he's incapacitated."

Montgomery smiled. "There's the rub, isn't it?" He said nothing more and Germaine left, looking perplexed.

Within an hour of Germaine leaving, Montgomery was sure of one thing: Smithson had lied. It wasn't just the confirmation that the video was in the possession of James Nine, but that the video was also in the possession of their daughter, Lorelai Nine, aged fourteen. Her call to Mr. Germaine Kayatesi, which luckily had gone unanswered, confirmed the obvious.

The other clue was circumstantial and damning. Smithson was missing. His office was a wreck of crushed energy-drink cans, candy wrappers, and filth. His computer wasn't just wiped; the hard drives had been removed and all the cloud backups corrupted.

Now he was looking for another person: Jon Smithson. Add him to the list of Haretsebe Tladi, Claire Plaster, Stephen Plaster, and Phillip Wright.

There was one positive of this situation. This activity was, he had to admit, fun. Real technology, not rumors anymore. A reason to go to work. Like the Nines working on their end-of-life science project in their home planetarium, he was enjoying the process. Though he feared for the disabled South African girl and felt an odd sense of protectiveness for her as well. Like the teenager he'd liberated in Hungary, and like a few others—children in a basement in Sao Paulo, their cleaned, pressed clothes and coiffed hair belying their awful fate had he not intervened.

The technology is real.

He'd transmitted an update to his boss at the Pentagon and the response had been as expected.

Derek told him, "Blair, with no evidence, all we have is a dead contractor, which we blamed on your target's stalker. She's definitely MIA. South African intelligence isn't very interested in this because she's a foreigner to them. We can't give them details, so she's just a domestic violence victim. They figure she's headed back to Botswana or holed up with family. So if you can't get me anything hard, I can't budget more for you on this. Besides, you told me you were retiring next year. Do you really want to keep this open? Maybe let it go?"

18. Monteagle, Tennessee

"Are we going to talk about the arm in the freezer?" Mr. Warren was drinking coffee and staring at Harry, Phil, and Claire.

"We need to call the police," added Mrs. Warren.

Harry spoke between bites of a microwaved burrito. "I'm sorry. I really don't remember details. It was just an instant. I was there. Then I had a weird dream, about my leg, which is a pretty common dream, frankly. And now I'm here." She'd been ravenous since she woke and showered. She'd also gotten some pain relief tablets from Mr. Warren for her shorter leg, which was throbbing.

When she had woken a few hours earlier, she'd started, seeing a boy on a phone sitting in the easy chair near her bed.

"Who are you? Where am I?"

He looked at her and smiled and shook his head. He then typed something on his phone and turned it around.

"I don't speak," it said.

More confused than ever, panic rose until Claire came to her bedside.

"You're awake. How do you feel? That's Spitz. He doesn't talk." Spitz stuck out his tongue at Claire.

"Am I...?"

"You are in the United States, in the state of Tennessee. I am having trouble processing it myself, but it may be the most amazing thing to ever happen in... the history of the world? You're like the Yuri Gagarin of teleportation."

Harry mumbled, looking around, confused. "Tennessee? Yuri Gagarin? People just appear and say weird things to me. I remember hitting Return on the laptop and the scary man trying to brain me with a lamp."

"Well, that scary man lost his... lamp." Claire broke off, not sure this topic should be discussed just yet.

"His arm," Harry corrected. "Yes, I remember that from the mattress. Yuck." They put off further talk, because a shower was called for; Harry's guts rose as she felt the tacky residue of what was clearly dried blood on her face and hair and hands. "I've ruined more clothes in the last three days."

In the Warrens' comfortable living room, filled with overstuffed furniture, knickknacks from world travel, a taxidermic deer head above a stone fireplace, Harry tried to answer questions.

"So, are you sure your name is Harry?" asked Phil, seriously.

Harry looked at him and then at the dog at Phil's feet.

"Yes, my full name is Haretsebe. That means 'we don't know' in Sesotho. But I go by Harry. The dog isn't even mine and I was told his name is Harry, so that's just a coincidence, I suppose."

Mr. Warren leaned forward. "We need to talk about the arm."

"I don't care about the arm, I want to know about Dad," added Phil, rubbing the dog's neck, avoiding a bandage around its ear.

"The man in the bubble?" asked Harry.

Mr. and Mrs. Warren looked at each other.

Harry answered Phil, "I saw him. At least I think I saw him. My brain feels like mashed mealies. But I did, of course. Otherwise, how would I have known to contact Claire on the board, right?"

"The people who attacked our house were looking for him. Is he alive?" asked Claire earnestly.

Mr. Warren spoke directly to Claire. "This is your tutor, your neighbor? The man who died in the explosion?"

Harry looked at her and at Phil. "I mean, he must be, right? I saw him. I talked with him. We had a conversation."

"Could it have been recorded?" Mrs. Warren asked. "Because I remember your grandfather telling us when he died."

"In an explosion," added Mr. Warren.

"Did he say when he's coming back?" asked Phil, urgency in his voice.

"I'm sorry. I don't know anything about him coming back. And I don't see how it could have been recorded. I mean, he responded to questions and gave me information. He's the one who told me to put a tourniquet on Dr. Deep's arm."

"Tourniquet?" Mr. Warren said with a tenor of astonishment

Harry took a bite of the burrito and answered after chewing and swallowing.

"Yes, well, that arm you say is in your freezer isn't the first amputation I've encountered in the last few days."

"This is a very confusing conversation," Mrs. Warren said.

"Well, it's going to get more confusing," said Harry, "because we need to test the technology. Do you have an old television?"

Mr. Warren asked, "Test the technology? Test why? And what?"

Harry was struggling to stand. "I was trying to test it when I was attacked. The men who attacked me were after something that Mr. Wright had. That something is apparently not just a joke. And I think we have shown that this is, well, world-changing. We need to understand it. We can't allow it to be distributed or stolen or whatever. It's quite dangerous. Your tutor told me to keep it safe."

Claire nodded. "Of course. I mean, we tested it once already. You are proof of that. But I agree, we need to know if this isn't some sort of mass hysteria or delusion."

Mr. Warren looked at them with almost comical disbelief. "You can't actually believe that Haressee... Harry actually teleported from South Africa. That's ridiculous."

"Bart, the military does all kinds of crazy stuff," Mrs. Warren said. "You know that as a fact." Then she turned to Harry. "I have some sneakers for you to try on. I think we wear the same size."

It took only an hour for Phil and Mr. Warren to go down to the basement and pull up a small portable television with the letters *RCA* above the tiny screen. Meanwhile, in a pair of Mrs. Warren's pink canvas high-tops, Harry sat shoulder to shoulder with Claire on the burgundy Victorian love seat, a laptop on the coffee table, and went through the scripts and the files while Phil spent time with the dog and Spitz watched videos on his phone.

Soon, Claire announced, "Okay, we're ready."

Phil looked up. "Are you going to teleport?"

"No, that's too dangerous. There's a file attached to the wedding video that Mr. Wright labeled 'green finger glow' and that matches a scene in the video where the people—"

"They aren't people," Phil interjected.

"—raise their hands and they glow," Claire continued. "So we'll try that one."

"Who will this affect?" asked Mrs. Warren, sitting with a coffee. "Should we establish a perimeter?"

Mr. Warren made a show of placing his hand on his thigh. He held a black handgun.

"Bart, is that necessary?" Mrs. Warren's voice was calm but disapproving.

"We've got dead people, Maggie. Dead. And dismembered."

Claire looked at the gun and at Harry.

Harry shook her head. "*Hele.*"

Claire said, "Okay, whatever. Let's try this."

Harry pressed Enter on her keyboard. They all sat, breaths held. Even Spitz looked up from his phone, glancing rapidly around at everyone. Phil raised his hands, looking at them carefully.

After a minute, Phil said, "WHOMP whomp," mimicking a sad-sounding trombone.

"Okay, that was a dud," said Mr. Warren.

Harry held up her hand. "That's okay, there's like a hundred actual codes here for the glowing hands effect. Maybe they get used up."

Claire pointed at the screen. "Try the next one."

Harry pressed a key.

The group looked at her and again held their breath. Phil raised his hand again. "Waa..." He was in the middle of making his failure noise when he stopped and yelled, "Claire! Your hands!"

Claire had been looking at the computer screen. She held up her hand in wonder. The tips of her fingers were glowing green, each fingernail radiating a slight tinge. Slowly, the color spread down to the first knuckle. Harry lifted her hands from the keyboard and they were the same as Claire's—glowing green.

Phil ran over to Claire, grabbed her hand, and pulled it to his face to look closely. As he did so, his own fingers started to glow.

"Holy shit, Maggie," said Mr. Warren, leaning forward and looking at the kids. Mrs. Warren held her own hands in front of her face, but they appeared normal.

"It's distance," said Harry. "Distance from the radio." She held up the radio next to her. "Come here..." She patted the table next to the laptop.

Spitz was up, waving his hands through the air, trails of green following each finger, the tendrils connecting with others from Phil's and Claire's hands. Mr. Warren holstered his sidearm and stood and held out his hand to Maggie, who took it carefully. "Should we?" she asked him.

"Let's," he said.

They gingerly approached the group gathered around the laptop, and when they were within a yard or so, they held up their interlocked fingers and both smiled in wonder, looking at a green glow flowing from their fingertips.

"Oh my," said Mrs. Warren. Their glow was steady and bright.

"Hold hands," said Claire. The group joined hands and the glow increased as their fingers touched. Veins of green light shot from their fingers and forearms, building a bright gazebo of light above the tight-knit group. They laughed at the beauty of it. A giddiness took over the room. Some released hands and waved around. They shouted and danced and jumped up and down, watching and staring as tendrils and wisps of green light flew from their fingers. Phil was able to make a ring, and Spitz threw a green squiggle that looked like a butterfly through it. Bart and Maggie passed a green ball back and forth. Claire drew a crown on Harry, who, still sitting, simply held her hands in front of her, lost in the silky weavings flowing from them. Her leg throbbed and she stretched it. She shook her head and continued to enjoy the light show. Phil and Spitz whooped. They were looking in their pants, Phil with a look of absolute surprise and Spitz laughing. The Warrens chuckled until Bart was hitting Maggie on the back from laugh-choking. Claire vowed not to look in her own waistband.

After some time—Mr. Warren said it was only ten minutes—the flow faded and the group stood, still and silent and in awe.

"Holy crapolio," said Mrs. Warren.

"I haven't had an experience like that since college," said Mr. Warren.

"You didn't go to college, Bart," said Mrs. Warren.

When Harry woke from a nap, she was as hungry as she'd ever felt in her life. She joined the group in the cozy living room and immediately grabbed a handful of pretzels from a dish on the table, even while Mrs. Warren gave her a bowl of ice cream. Harry dropped the pretzels in the ice cream and kept eating. Pictures dotted the walls: the Warrens rafting on some river out west, in front of a camper with a view of the ocean, in full army dress uniform as a couple getting married.

"I can't believe it. It must have been some kind of mass hallucination. That thing affects your mind. It puts off some drug in the air." Mr. Warren was steadfast in his statement.

"Bart, don't be so dismissive. The evidence is standing right in front of you. Eating ice cream, I might add." Mrs. Warren gave him a look that told him to keep his thoughts to himself. Harry was digging into a bowl of rocky road, topped with the pretzels.

"*Hele*, this is brilliant," she mumbled with her mouth full. She swallowed and apologized, then spoke. "It is true," she said, her accent enunciating each word, interrupted by her spoon clawing into the gooey mess. A drip of ice cream ran down her brown chin and Mrs. Warren handed her a napkin. Earlier, she'd eaten an entire jar of strawberry jam, spooning it into her mouth, savoring the melting sweetness.

"This is so cool! You teleported!" said Phil, petting the dog, who lay next to him on the floor of the living room.

Claire spoke more quietly. "Mr. Wright, my tutor, Phil's dad, was a bit of a mad scientist. He was always messing with electronics in his barn. It's not impossible that he discovered this technology or was working on this and was going to reveal it before he died. But he did a pretty good job of keeping it secret, which I guess is more evidence that he was working for the military or some other secret government agency, though that would be very disappointing. I don't know how he kept it secret."

Phil scoffed at her. "You don't know that. My dad would never do anything to hurt people. You know he wouldn't even kill the spiders in the house. He carried them outside in a cup."

Claire looked at him. "Phil, I can only tell what the evidence is showing."

Phil hung his head and nuzzled the dog, ignoring her.

Mr. Warren folded his arms. "You mean before he was killed by this technology? Which clearly affects the brain. And if half of what Chuck told me about Mr. Wright was true, he was not the most trustworthy guy."

Phil's head whipped up. "Bullshit. He never lied. And he's alive, Harry saw him. Spitz knows. Spitz was there in the explosion. He lost his toe!"

Everyone looked at Spitz.

Mrs. Warren said softly to him, "It's okay, Spitz. Trauma when you are young is difficult. I'm sorry you saw that."

Spitz wrote something on his phone and turned it to Claire, who read it.

"He says he didn't see the explosion. So maybe Mr. Wright is still alive?" She read the last sentence slowly and turned to Spitz. "What? Spitz? You were there. Your foot was hurt. You lost a toe. How could you not see the explosion?"

Spitz took the phone and wrote again. Claire read it out loud. "'I don't remember the explosion or how I hurt my foot.'"

Mr. Warren cut him off. "Foot or not, it doesn't matter. It's trauma and that's a trauma response. Memory is often affected. There was still an explosion, from what Chuck said, and your Mr. Wright disappeared."

Phil said, "But he's alive. Harry saw him!"

Harry replied with hesitation, "Phil, I didn't want to say this, but the man I saw was badly hurt. He was injured and I don't think he had... Well, he was badly injured, okay?"

Phil stared at her.

Mr. Warren shifted in his easy chair. "Son, let's table this. We know what we know. But here's a hard truth. He might have been a math genius or whatever, and a great dad to you, but he was messing with something. If Colin Wright escaped that explosion, he didn't want to be found. Maybe to protect you. Now they drugged this young lady to think she was transported like *Star Trek* or something. Whatever this technology is, it's clear that there's more going on than we understand."

Harry spoke through mouthfuls. "I'm not lying, Mr. Warren. I was in South Africa. I don't know how it's possible, but I was. A man was going to kill me and if not for Claire and the... I don't know, the EMR broadcast, I'd be dead. You saw the green light. The technology has some effect, some type of electro-magnetic... I don't know... induction or excitement of sub-atomic, quantum states. We see it as... well, whatever we see, a glowing line or a big bubble. It is tangential to what I study, but it is right up Claire's alley."

Mrs. Warren spoke after a pause to hand Harry a napkin. "Well, that's far beyond us two army grunts. Can this technology be used to protect you or whatever? We have to assume that whoever killed Phil's mom and hurt Chuck, and is likely after you as well, won't stop. It saved you once, right?"

Harry spoke again between bites. "It appears as though it did something terrible to Mr. Wright. He's been MIA for years and I only saw some weird projection of him. And he was badly hurt. I used the technology and it may have saved me, but that man attacked me—his arm is in your freezer. And I don't know what it did to me, but I've been feeling a little off." She gestured at the array of empty dishes laid out before her.

Claire added, "And in the video logs I saw on the drive down, Mr. Wright implied it caused some kind of havoc when he first encountered it in college, and he ended up in prison for some terrible event at a convenience store, which maybe was related? He didn't say. So it's pretty dangerous stuff. We will use it if we need to, but it's to be avoided until we understand it more."

"Well, I would not rely on something that might be a figment of our collective imagination," said Mr. Warren.

Claire exclaimed, "Besides, arguing will not get us anywhere. The fact is that someone is after what's on our laptops, correct or not. And if what Harry said is correct, Mr. Wright was clear that they can't get their hands on it. And if Harry did teleport, and I see no other explanation, then what's on the laptops is truly dangerous. Imagine that technology in the wrong hands."

"We should use it to bring back Dad," said Phil. His comment was met with silence.

"So, what's the solution?" Mr. Warren asked. "How do we get you out of this jam? If we don't trust the police or the government, who can we go to?"

"Can you destroy it?" Mrs. Warren looked around the room.

Harry considered the thought and looked at Claire. They both started to answer and Claire nodded at Harry to go ahead. "I think we agree."

Harry finished a spoonful of ice cream. "Digital information is really hard to destroy. There could be copies. And more importantly, they know we have it. Even if we destroy it, they're unlikely to believe that. If these groups know about it, maybe they didn't learn about it from Mr. Wright. Plus, Mr. Wright didn't invent this technology. It came from... somewhere..."

Phil spoke up. "It came from space."

"Bull," Mr. Warren quickly retorted.

Spitz started waving and poked Phil. Phil nodded at him and spoke up. "Right, really. This stuff is from space. Those videos are like alien TV shows or something. Dad showed us these videos when we were young. He never talked about any technology, but he showed us the TV shows. That's always what Dad said. They're from outer space."

Harry interjected, "And that's actually what Mr. Wright said in the server room. He said the videos were just entertainment and the technology is just like a giveaway toy, just some kind of gimmick attached. He called them a smile meal or something."

Phil yelled out, "I loved those!"

Mr. Warren exhaled. "Well, now, that sounds even more like hogwash. We know the army. They'll wrap some new technology in all sorts of fancy dress but really, it's just lipstick on a pig. New guns are just guns."

"Bart's right," Mrs. Warren agreed. "That does sound unbelievable. And like something some three-letter agency would hide behind."

"It doesn't matter, really," Claire said. "If they are kids' meal toys or military technology, it's all dangerous."

Mr. Warren spoke. "Enough jawing. Let's talk solutions."

"Well, we can't hide forever and we can't prove we don't have it." Claire's statement hung in the air.

Harry continued eating and added, "Well, that guy who was with me saw it. In fact, that's his arm in your freezer. And he was on the phone with someone when he was attacking me. So if that guy survived, then he witnessed me... vanishing, I guess. And whomever he was talking to knows about it."

Mr. Warren said softly, "I've treated amputations. If he didn't get treated pretty quick, he didn't make it."

Mrs. Warren spoke, standing in the entry to the kitchen. "What about bait?" The group looked at her. "What if you dangle it in front of them?"

Claire added, leaning forward, her eyes brightening, "Yes, we could act like we have it, because, one, we have it, and two, that will diminish the question. And maybe bring someone to our aid?"

Mrs. Warren said, "You don't know who's after you, do you? So one way to bring out the enemy is with some bait. You can find an ally, perhaps, as well. Maybe turn an enemy into a friend. Maybe get these guys to fight each other."

Mr. Warren spoke again. "Even better, what about a public auction of sorts?"

"What do you mean?" Claire asked.

"Transparency eliminates a lot of incentive to lie, cheat, steal. If you simply told the world about this, you'd find allies."

"We risk the technology ending up in the wrong hands," said Phil. "We just learned about Oppenheimer in school. Some scientists regret developing the atomic bomb."

Mrs. Warren went to the kitchen and returned with a box of crackers, which Harry started eating with sounds of muffled joy.

"Back on topic..." said Claire, looking around. "What did you say about a public auction?"

Phil burst out, "Post the videos to the internet!"

Claire was quick. "That's crazy! We can't allow anyone to have the technology!"

Harry nodded at Phil. "He's right, though. We could post the video without the codes. Strip away the subtext that Mr. Wright isolated—that's the secret sauce, or the toy surprise, I think he called it. Claire, do you have any ideas how to do that? To strip the codes from the video?"

Claire nodded, leaning forward a bit. "The videos are raw, .avi format. From his notes, it appears the codes are in the data, sequentially in each frame. Compressing them to MPEG format and reducing the granularity should strip them."

Harry added, "If we post the video, everyone who understands what this video represents will know that we have it. And we can find an ally to help protect us. But how can we confirm to the world it's ours? Anyone could claim ownership."

"The blockchain," said Claire.

Phil and the Warrens asked in unison, "What's that?"

Harry spoke up. "Brilliant. It's an online ledger. So if we post it first to a public blockchain, it becomes immutable that it's ours. Claire, you can use the WisPR wallet and post the video. If we allow comments, perhaps we'll find our ally."

"And reveal your enemies," added Mrs. Warren.

Claire nodded. "It's really the best way. We've never really used the WisPR blockchain wallet. I think Lollipop and I are the only ones who have access, and I have my own wallet and Lollipop has her own, so it'll be clear it's me. I can create another wallet for you, Harry."

Mr. Warren spoke up again. "Well, it's certain to bring out the players. I'd just be careful..."

Mrs. Warren's phone rang, interrupting his comment.

"Oh, shit." Claire's voice was muted, but fear crept over it.

Mrs. Warren turned over her phone. "Unknown. Should I answer it?"

Claire looked frantic as the ringing continued. "What do you think Grandpa Chuck would suggest?"

Phil lunged for the phone, quickly swiped on the call, and put it up to his ear. Claire reached for the phone and he held up his hand palm outward to hold her back. She stopped short and held her breath.

Claire gesticulated at him, then loudly whispered, "Speakerphone!"

Phil thought a moment and put the phone on the coffee table and pressed the speaker button. "Who is this?" Phil's voice was strong.

"My name is Colonel Blair Montgomery, of the United States Department of Defense. Who is this?"

"None of your fucking business. What do you want?" Phil sounded older than Claire recalled. And crazier. The little boy she babysat was fading away.

Claire was about to speak when Mr. Warren shook his head at her.

"Well, if this is the son of Colin Wright, and I suspect it might be, I'm trying to reach a young woman named Claire Plaster."

"She's busy. Is that all?"

The voice on the phone was calm. "Okay, young man. I get it. You are scared. Your mother was killed. You are on the run. But if Claire is there, and I suspect she is because I can hear that I'm on speakerphone, let me tell you two something. The technology that you have, at least that I believe you have, is very valuable and it should be in the hands of the US government. For your protection."

Phil yelled at the phone. "My protection? My mother was murdered for this. Possibly by the government. So you gonna come kill me? A kid? Bring it on!"

Claire spoke up quickly. "Colonel Montgomery. This is Claire."

"Your brother is quite the firebrand, Ms. Plaster."

"He's upset. How did you find us?"

"We have resources, Ms. Plaster. You can be found. Which is a good reason to allow us to have the technology. I want to be clear with you. We had nothing to do with what happened to Mildred Wright."

"How can I be sure?" Claire tried to sound strong, but she heard the vibrato of uncertainty in her voice.

"You already know we did not. We've spoken to your grandfather. I'm sure he told you that the attackers were Korean. It was not us. Plus, if the US government wanted the technology, we would have simply asked for it."

"You did ask for it. Do you remember?"

There was a pause.

"Yes, Ms. Plaster, I remember our meeting well. Is your answer still the same?"

Claire hesitated, then spoke.

"I've changed my mind. I will give it to you in return for a guarantee of our safety. Myself and my family."

Harry stood and Claire waved her back. She mouthed "Wait."

"Agreed," said Montgomery.

"Can you assure our safety?"

There was a pause.

Phil spoke up. "Well, that's not very reassuring."

Montgomery spoke again. "Pardon the pause. I was just informed that you are in immediate danger. We are not the only people able to track you."

"How much time do we have?" Claire asked.

"If you're at the Warren residence in Monteagle, Tennessee, we can be there in thirty minutes. Please stay put. I will have a team on-site as quickly as we can get there. They will assess and neutralize the threat."

"Okay, we'll be here." Claire hung up the phone, then spoke to the group. "We all need to leave. Now."

Mr. Warren stood up. "That's ridiculous."

"That was not Colonel Montgomery. One, his voice sounded slightly different, though I'm not sure I would recognize it as it was many years ago. I think I heard an accent." Spitz hit his thigh once in agreement. "But more importantly, when we last met, he didn't ask for the technology and I didn't give him an answer. Back then he didn't know about me as the student of Colin Wright. He thought I was the babysitter. Finally, Grandpa would not have told the government about the attackers speaking Korean until he was sure we were safe."

"Okay, he said we had thirty minutes," Mrs. Warren said. "But we know that's gonna be a lie. We can assume we have about twenty minutes. Bart, get some weapons. Including the big stuff."

Harry glanced up. "I thought you were a nurse."

Mr. Warren laughed. "No, dear, she's a retired shooting instructor. I was the army nurse."

Harry spoke to Claire. "You take care of the upload. Convert it first. We'll meet you outside."

Phil reinforced Harry's point. "She's right. You send the video. We'll grab all our stuff."

Spitz was already at Harry's side. She grabbed his upper sleeve and they hobbled out of the house. Claire quickly opened her laptop and searched for the file that contained the keys to her blockchain wallet. She hadn't used it except for a test post a year earlier.

She realized it wouldn't upload while she waited because of its size.

"Mr. Warren, do you have a computer?"

It took her a few minutes to get the video uploading on the Warrens' laptop. She left comments enabled and rushed out of the house, the computer running.

Spitz and Harry were in a dinged-up car with rusty historic plates and mismatched doors that had been sitting in the front yard under a white canopy shelter.

"I didn't want to pay to re-register a historic vehicle until it was completed," Mr. Warren said. "It's a 1968 Chevy Nova. Same year I finished high school. Car I always wanted." He was tossing a blanket over the hood and using bungee cords to strap it down. "You take it. Because it's not in my name, they won't trace it for a while. Those historic plates on it are old and belong to the previous owner. Just avoid any tolls and don't speed. We'll take our vehicle, which is what they may look for. That Massachusetts car can stay here."

Mr. Warren looked around. "Where's that other boy? Phil?"

Phil came running out. "Had to hit the john." He jumped into the car.

Mrs. Warren handed Harry a cane through the rear window and took the giant walking stick, which wouldn't fit in the car.

Harry laughed at the ornate top. "Well, thank you."

"We got it as a souvenir in the UK many years ago. Princess Diana's wedding. Twist the top. Back then you could take those on an airplane."

Harry turned the top and after a click she lifted out a long knife. "A sword cane? *Hele*, I wish I had had one of these when I was a kid."

Mrs. Warren looked at Spitz, who was behind the wheel. "He can drive?"

Phil put his hand on Spitz's shoulder. "He's the best."

Harry put the sword back into the cane and twisted it closed with another click, then unclicked it and raised it slightly. Then she lifted her head. "Mrs. Warren, do you have an inverter? An electrical inverter. Portable."

Mrs. Warren looked at her. "Like to run a laptop in the car? We have one in the camper. I'll get it."

Harry looked at Claire. "Go get that little television. And batteries. I have the radio."

Claire nodded, ran back to the house, and returned with the small television from the guest room just as Mrs. Warren came back with the inverter.

"I'm sorry, I'm not sure the inverter will work in this car."

Mr. Warren called out as he was uncoiling a water hose from the wall, then sprayed the blanket on the hood of the Chevy. "It'll work. I replaced all the wiring. Just be careful with the gas. It has some pep. Gas mileage ain't great."

Mrs. Warren cupped her ear. She picked up two black bags. "Chopper, maybe. You really are America's most wanted. Bart, let's get these kids on the road. I'll put the toys in the Ford. I got rifles, a couple of scopes, and a few hundred .30-06 and the Glocks. We'll let our car warm up for infrared tracking and go out in five minutes. You kids go now. Put it in neutral, don't start it. We'll push it first. Let the car roll down the driveway until the road, turn right, that's south, all downhill. Wait until the last moment to start the engine. You'll be dark to them for a few extra miles, perhaps until you can get into some traffic. Drop the blanket at the first exit and then continue. And turn your cell phones off."

*Zoonerat Compliance with Grammar Universals

Excerpted from "The Possibility of Universal Grammar in the Zoonerat Language," Murphy, Romanoff, et al., *Journal of Xenolinguistics*

Moreover, the structure of the Zoonerat language does not undermine Chomsky's theory of a universal grammar. And much to the surprise of linguists, this would suggest that there may be a truly Universal Grammar—emphasis on the noun version of that word: *universe*.

Generalized plurals in the Zoonerat language appear to work, like many languages, with a suffix—in this case the sound *væn* (Zoonerat video z-24:09-16a/Anon, 1:23–1:38, et al.). However, contrary to Greenberg's proposal of grammar universals, the Zoonerat language appears to have a quadral and an octal, but no trial. The quadral is primarily used in reference to groups of four individuals, supporting the idea of quad marriage. There are potential uses of a quadral regarding other nouns. Octals are less common.

Neurobiologists and those who study the structure of the brain will have more to say if we are ever able to receive a video containing a pre-verbal or peri-verbal Zoonerat infant in the process of learning its language.

In addition, we can only assume that the videos use a language that is common among the videographers who wrote the dialogue of the videos. If there are any true linguistic parallels between Earth's dominant verbal species and whatever species created the videos, then it is likely that the Zoonerat language is but one of many languages extant at the production location. Therefore, it would interest us to know if those other languages follow a similar grammar.

19. Denver, Colorado

Smithson landed in Denver at 6:59 p.m. His rental car, a nondescript American something or other, was gassed and waiting. The clerk made no comment about the name Wilbur Right on the New Hampshire driver's license; the esoteric knowledge required to understand the pun was hidden from the underling. The joke had made sense when Smithson first acquired the fake license, but now using the ID for *first flight* was uncomfortably accurate.

The license and the faux persona of Mr. Right had been acquired in the unlikely event of something akin to capture, *id est*, discovery of his activities. Back at the Harvard-Smithsonian Center for Astrophysics he'd almost used the go-bag, but then the entire matter had been fogged over like a bathroom mirror by Montgomery and the NSA. And then the mirror had been taken down and broken as well.

He'd had fantasies of being *on the lam*, pursued by nefarious pseudo-government agents while he embarked on some secret mission that would result in saving the world and earning the eternal and slavish love of many young women as a reward, plus, of course, *coin of the realm*. His money problems would be solved. He'd no longer be in debt. No more hiding. No more ramen for dinner. No more tires slashed, no more sudden appearances of sliced-up Barbie dolls in his bed—the creepiest thing his former trading partners had done to remind him of his debts.

The current situation was far less glamorous. His hurried flight from his apartment in Maryland, not far from Fort Meade, was instigated by several software-based alarms. These tiny programs he had established for his own protection and they had triggered in rapid succession, one by one, over the course of a morning. The surprising ping from a government server for his own name; the digital sucking down of his computer history by triplicate bots; and, most telling—the loud escalation of Lorelai's internal mentions among a bank of NSA and CIA computers on which he had surreptitiously placed listeners. These all combined into one red-lined message: He was being targeted. He considered going directly to Montgomery to demand an explanation for this *ridiculous attack on my personage.* He imagined strutting, phone in one hand and a sheaf of printouts in the other, and throwing them on Montgomery's desk and demanding satisfaction in some manner befitting a man of his intellect and noble lineage: perhaps a test of who can hack the local high school's computer or a game of chess.

But the reality of his extant diminutive power, being a man of some intellect after all, gave him pause. He had no actual ability to demand anything. He knew that Montgomery and his shadowy near-beer spy group held pretty much all the cards. Even if there was no documented history of Smithson's proclivities—his sale of certain files and protocols to buyers—Montgomery could manufacture evidence of any kind. He'd seen covert ops reports of just that kind of leverage on unlucky targets.

Smithson considered his options and realized that a hasty exit would be far more self-serving than standing and fighting. His loyalty was limited to his bank balance, nothing more. Because he was guilty. Very guilty. Not just of all the previous perversions and wager-based mistakes, but of protecting and hiding Lorelai's connection to the technology. Smithson had seen Montgomery's power and had diverted it around Lorelai like an island splitting a river. Because Lorelai had money. Lots of money. And Smithson was going to get it.

On the airplane to Denver, he berated himself for thinking, like all criminals, that he wouldn't get caught. And so he was woefully unprepared for a hasty escape and lucky that he'd had any warning at all; he'd had only enough time to dash to his apartment and grab his go-bag, which, sadly, contained nothing more than a driver's license and passport with Mr. Right's name, a single credit card, a few thousand dollars folded in half, and—he'd forgotten about these—a dozen tablets that he believed were GHB, the date rape drug. He'd bought them online in an aborted attempt to... you know... but he'd gotten cold feet.

What else his go-bag should have contained, he wasn't sure. A gun, maybe? A fake mustache? Colored contact lenses? But no, the driver's license, passport, money, and pills were all that the sandwich-sized plastic bag contained, taped amateurishly under his bedside nightstand drawer. These were the minimums that the prepper blogs said should be in a go-bag. He had a fortune in illicit videos and images encrypted and stored away on cloud servers, but these were not so easily converted to sustenance. But perverts will pervert and mayhap the contraband could convert into a resolution for his predicament—the price on his head, the debts he owed.

His first stop had been a big box retailer where he'd picked up a cheap laptop and some clothes and toiletries. Best to get the necessities while the credit card still worked, at least two billing cycles. Plus, everything in his world was stored in the cloud, encrypted with a password long enough that nobody would guess it—several pages of *romaji* dialogue of *High School Heroine Suzi Sakura*, an obscure manga, with all the punctuation.

Without a laptop he was nothing. In a pinch, he could use a library computer, but he felt there were too many risks with such devices. There was a certain Slav—or maybe he was a Serb, Smithson didn't really know—who had offered a large amount of cryptocurrency for Smithson's library of videos, for which Smithson had some renown in the seventh circle of hell. He rarely sold videos—the risk/reward ratio being extremely poor for that trade—but now he reconsidered his options and thought that in a pinch he might divest himself of a few rare ones, but since his cryptocurrency wallet had been hacked, he was distrustful of that route. Providence would be called upon to solve some of these conundrums. For now, he cast aside these thoughts, focusing on this, his own *Odyssey*.

After retrieving the go-bag from the nightstand, he drove his car to the Baltimore-Washington Airport. That car would be found by Montgomery's nether agents, and they would assume he had flown from there. At BWI, he tore off the price tags and donned his newly purchased and very uncomfortable Denver Broncos windbreaker, put some gel in his hair and combed it flat against his head, wore some glasses with no prescription, and did his best to look different. Just under six feet, patch-cord thin, with the sour face of a man who had spent all his time under fluorescent lighting, drinking energy drinks, and eating processed snacks, he looked as much like a clothing store mannequin as a person. Then he hopped on a train to New York and took public transportation to JFK International Airport, where he boarded a flight to the Mile-High City.

He left the Denver airport by public transportation and headed to a suburb where he rented an SUV from a lesser-known rental agency, giving the clerk a story about moving his girlfriend's sick father, which was close enough to the truth. Finally heading south, on the scenic road to New Mexico, he thought he was relatively safe. What he really wished was to contact Lorelai before

Montgomery reached out to her and she shut down the AI. For that he needed public access Wi-Fi. And a story. A good story.

He needed to explain to Lorelai why her online BFF and STEM sister Lollipop was a skinny dude named Wilbur.

20. Kathode Watches a Movie

Lorelai left a message for Germaine at his office in Palo Alto. She knew it was the same man because his client list included KathWorks, Inc., the company her parents had founded and sold.

"Unit, continue playing the video from where I stopped."

"Just a word of caution, Lori. The following videos show your mother in poor health. Are you sure you want to see this?"

Lorelai's sour face matched her dismissive tone. "Why did you call me Lori? Nobody calls me that. And of course I want to see the videos. You said it answers the question of what happened to my dad."

The simulacrum's face scrunched, displaying both defensiveness and hurt, as if it knew that the response would be a chastisement. "Lori is a diminutive of Lorelai, and I thought you might appreciate the familiarity."

"Well, end it. Don't be weird."

The video started playing on a nearby screen.

From the hospital bed where Kath slept, the dog rose, sniffing her and then jumping off the bed. The camera switched to the hallway and followed the dog to the kitchen, where Germaine was putting on running shoes.

"Timing is everything, Orion. You want to come for a run?"

The dog stood by the kitchen door and looked back, tail wagging. Germaine opened the door and followed Orion outside.

The next scene showed James, Germaine, and Kath in the planetarium. Orion was on the bed at Kath's feet, head on paws, watching. James stood in front of a whiteboard near the conference table. "Our goal is to re-create what A, B, and C Russians did to cure patient one."

"A, B, and V, for Vlad," corrected Kath, from the bed.

Germaine nodded, sitting at the table. "I've gone through the experimental design doc. You can see the pentodes are in a series of three concentric circles around the patient."

James added, "I think we can forgo the vacuum tubes in favor of a more modern type of amplifier. Kath is actually faster at calculating the equivalents than I am, so Kath, I'm going to leave it to you to let me know the amplifier specs needed for the signal and the frequency ranges."

Kath nodded. "On it, Boss." She tried to laugh and then coughed hard. James looked at her askance, and a worried furrow creased his brow. "I'm fine," Kath said when the coughing subsided.

James led the discussion as an experienced speaker. "Our job is to figure out what we are broadcasting. We may have several versions since we're adrift in the ocean, so to speak."

The camera view switched again, the time stamp advancing. James sat opposite Germaine at the table, each on a laptop, talking through the signals while Kath lay in her bed nearby, tapping at her keyboard. Joan, in a nurse's outfit, approached James and whispered in his ear. He looked at Kath, hard at work on her laptop, and nodded.

Joan said to Kath, "I'm going to start a drip, 'kay?"

Kath nodded and continued to work. Just after the drip started, Kath gave a quick look at Joan and then at James. "Really? You asshole," she muttered, and she leaned her head back and closed her eyes.

"Thank you," said James to the nurse, who was carefully clipping Kath's port line on the bed frame.

"She'll be out for a while," the nurse said as the men moved to the kitchen to continue their work.

The video cut to a montage of the same routine, the three of them working sometimes in pairs, sometimes in the kitchen, sometimes in the planetarium. The dates on the bottom of the videos progressed forward three days, then back to the planetarium.

"What did you find?" Kath asked, her voice weak.

"We've got something," James said. "We have an idea of what to try."

"Well, I'm tired of being drugged and left for dead. Maybe more chemo is better."

"Okay, then," said Germaine, frowning. "What James and I have come up with is a broadcast of the code at a signal strength that will definitely blast the bed and you. We're going to set up transmitters in the same geodesic array described in the experiment. We'll broadcast the signal in a half dozen different formats, all corresponding to the metadata code. The transmitters should be here this afternoon. I've got a contractor coming as well to build the framework. We think there are actually several dozen metadata codes. They're separated in the file by stop and start strings. We aren't sure why. Each one might be a signal. We aren't even sure what the Cyrillic letters mean.

"After manipulating the number, a pattern appeared at the start and the end. The first thirty-two digits correspond to what should be the same frequency referenced in the documents. There are thirty-two kilobytes of digits after that followed by what is probably a terminal block of thirty-two more digits. There are six codes in total. The document talks about a frequency of 888,888 cycles. So if we broadcast the code at that frequency, perhaps it will cause the right... I don't know the word... influence or outcome on the cancer cells and disrupt them? Change them?"

James smiled. "Fuck them up. We are going to fuck up those fucking cancer cells."

Kath coughed, laughing as best she could.

Contractors came as expected and built a geodesic dome around Kath's bed frame. The bed was moved out to the middle of the planetarium and the conference table pushed out to the side opposite the windows.

The scene changed. Kath was walking on the flagstone patio off the kitchen. Joan pushed the IV pole. Cameras captured the conversation between the two. They stopped near a squat grouping of agave, under a slatted arbor, providing shade from the bright New Mexico sunlight. The stripes shone on Kath's face as she tilted her head upward, bald spots visible, showing an age much greater than her years.

"Thank you, Joan. This is nice."

"Dr. Gorabani, I hope your new treatment goes well."

Kath turned to the sturdy nurse. "You know, you can call me Kath. Nobody calls me Dr. Gorabani anymore." She bathed in the sunlight. "Don't tell James, but it won't. It won't go well, I mean. I know it won't." She held up her hand to stop Joan from blurting out something. "No need to comment. Just know that I am okay with it. I don't think James is. But I am."

"I'm sorry to hear that," was Joan's quiet response.

"Yeah, I've put you on the spot. I'm sorry about that." Kath looked at her. "And I think I'm going to shit my pants. So don't get too sentimental."

Pause the video." Lorelai turned to the monitor in which her father's simulacrum looked back at her, eyebrows raised. "Unit, is this what you mean? Because it looks like my mother is not weak at all. She looks strong as shit. She is facing death, for fuck's sake. And she's joking."

"I didn't say she would appear weak. I just said she would not appear well."

"Fine. But I hope I'm half that strong when I'm old as fuck near death. My mom's a fucking badass." Lorelai wiped her eyes.

"Language."

"Sorry, not sorry. Continue."

In the video, a complex dome of thin black steel tubing formed a shed-like structure over the bed in the middle of the repurposed planetarium. Germaine and another contractor were running wires from metal electrical boxes mounted every few feet in three circles on the inside of the framework. Four steel cables attached to motors on a larger framework above the shed allowed the apparatus to be lifted out of the way.

Wires snaked around the framework, held on by zip ties, and disappeared into a larger metal box on one side. At the table, James had several laptops open. He was calling out instructions to Germaine, who was testing each transmitter.

"B1, yes?"

Germaine fiddled with a box. "Yes, green light here."

"B2, yes?"

And they continued through each circle, finally ending on C16. Forty-eight transmitters in three circles around the inside of the framework. The first circle was about three feet off the floor, around the height of the bed. The next was a foot higher and the last a foot higher than that, and smaller as well.

"What's our total wattage now?" James asked.

"If everything works, that should be forty-eight watts."

"And that matches the report?"

"It's unclear. I'll bet it exceeds FCC transmitting guidelines." Germaine raised an eyebrow as he said this.

James ignored the point. "Pull up that chart from the Soviet design spec."

On the second screen a typed table appeared. It was a slightly grainy photograph of a page from a report. Next to it, an English translation appeared.

Some words remained in Russian.

Transmitters	
Пятиэлектродная Lamps	48
Joules	24-96
Преобраз. Frequency	888 888
Frequency	calculated
Преобраз.	32
Channel Width	1 000
Term	1 000 000 N
Hydrogen Equals	Yes
Limb	
Pre and Post Digits	32
Length	2mb
Rotation	15 seconds
Duration	1 000 000 N

Lorelai said, “Pause the video. Put that document on another screen.” She looked at it and frowned. “I’m not sure I understand this.”

The simulacrum spoke. “I cannot augment what is said in the video.”

Lorelai nodded. “Continue.”

“Do we know what that Russian means?” James asked.

Germaine looked at the screen. “The first word is that five-lamp thing you said was a pentode.”

“Yes, the tubes. We’ve replaced those with solid state. Welcome to the twenty-first century. Russians are always late to change anything that works. *If it ain’t broke, don’t fix it* must originate in Russian. I’m more of the type who isn’t afraid to improve something, no matter how good it is.”

“The next word looks like an abbreviated word for *conversion*.”

“So that third line is *conversion frequency* and the fifth line is just *conversion*.”

“Appears so.”

“I am not 100 percent comfortable with that. We’re making an assumption that the frequency is 888,888 hertz. But it’s odd.”

Germaine turned with eyebrows raised.

"Well, I never intended to know this stuff, but since Kath has been through it, I've had to study up on radiation therapy. Cancer treatment with radiation is on the ionizing side of the spectrum. That's anything higher frequency than visible light. X-rays, gamma rays, and such. Ionizing radiation is destructive. Our atmosphere is opaque to those frequencies so we aren't burned to a crisp by interstellar roasting beams. We actually evolved without those frequencies blasting us, which may be why we can't tolerate them. Or vice versa, we evolved because our atmosphere blocked them. No way to know for sure. But this frequency 888,888 hertz is below visible light. That's considered low frequency. I'm not sure but probably some kind of communication band."

"So, what does that mean?"

Kate's voice was heard from the bed. "It means it won't do shit to the cancer. That's what it means. Now get me up or you'll be cleaning the sheets." Her expression shifted and, turning her head, she vomited mostly liquid onto the bed and wiped her mouth with the back of her hand. "You're definitely cleaning the sheets."

Joan appeared as if by magic. "Just a sec, Dr. Gorabani. Help is on the way."

James said, "Kath's right. Probably. Low frequency also means low energy and it defies logic that it will have an effect on the cancer."

"Damn straight I'm right," said Kath, emerging from the framework with Joan. Her face was gray, her shirt was stained, and there was an unfortunate wetness around her mouth.

"But," said James, "it's not true the low-frequency radiation isn't capable of having an effect. Microwaves heat water, our bodies feel the heat of infrared. Our own skin responds to sunlight by making vitamin D and tanning. Trees, plants, algae all take visible light and use it. So, it's not without precedent that low-frequency, below-visible light, could"—he waved his hands about—"do something."

"And cell phone towers cause cancer," said Kath over her shoulder as Joan led her to the bathroom.

James shook his head. "Yeah, well, I have no idea if we are reading this right. It doesn't make a whole lot of sense, but anything is possible."

A shot of the kitchen showed James and Germaine at the large granite kitchen island. A bell dinged and James went to the microwave and retrieved two plates.

"Leftover Thai may be the greatest food in the world," James said.

Germaine poked his food with his fork. "Are you sure you want this?"

"It's Thai, Germaine. How could I not want Thai?"

"No, I mean, going through with all this... experimentation, when the chance of success is..."

"Zero? I know it seems crazy, but what would you do?"

The video cut back to the planetarium, where Kath was standing, using a walker, looking up.

"Really?" she said, surveying the white-and-gray camouflaged dome that now covered the hospital bed. "I'm going to be saved by a military-grade igloo? Are we expecting help from the Inuit? Or perhaps a sneak attack from narwhals?" She had just returned from a trip to the bathroom.

Germaine looked uncomfortable, perhaps trying to ignore the barbs. "That's what was available on short notice. It's from a fabric wholesaler and they had a bolt of military-grade Faraday cloth. It will—"

"I know what Faraday cloth is," Kath snapped. "I may very well have a patent on this. Clearly, nobody will see us now in the deep snow of the Sandia Mountains in August."

The last of the workers had left.

"How do I get in?" Kath shuffled around it, pulling her own IV stand.

Germaine pulled back one section of cloth, revealing a break in the tent. Christmas lights were strung on the inside and they could be seen twinkling.

Her mood visibly changed as she ducked in. "Ooh, an adult-size pillow fort," she said, and then coughed so hard, James took her hand as it faltered from the IV stand. "Just help me back into my bed," she wheezed out.

The camera switched and showed the inside of the tent. James lifted Kath's legs and maneuvered her into bed and then climbed in next to her. They looked at each other and then up. The Faraday cloth was light blocking as well as radio wave blocking, so inside was illuminated from the string lights alone.

"Romantic," commented James, lying next to her. They both looked at the curved and covered ceiling of the tent. Silver electrical boxes and black transmitters with antennae gave the interior an otherworldly look.

"So this is how Jonah felt," Kath whispered. They were quiet for a moment.

Kath continued to stare at the ceiling. "And he also went on a journey."

James looked at her and ran a finger down her cheek, perhaps wiping away a tear.

Lorelai blinked her eyes fiercely and wiped her shirt across her nose.

The simulacrum asked, "Would you like me to pause the video?"

"No! Fucking do not pause the video!"

"Language."

James nodded and drew his lips tight. "You know I don't like to hear you talk like that."

Kath said, "I wish it were actually aliens and not Soviet scientists. That would be so much cooler."

Orion lifted his head and mewled appropriately, as if he too would prefer aliens.

In the next scene, Germaine was puttering with the computers.

"I'm ready. We can do this whenever you want."

James called into the tent, "What do you want to listen to?"

"Fleetwood Mac," came the muffled reply.

James manipulated a tiny music player that was hanging from a spare IV bag stand. "The Chain" started playing from speakers around the room.

"What's first?" asked James.

"I think we run some tests. Let's broadcast just a series of ones and zeroes at half the power. The receiver by her head is on screen three."

The first two screens showed a grid with each transmitter on its own line, all forty-eight of them, columns of numbers: power, value, frequency. The third screen showed summary information from the individual receivers that had been mounted inside the tent.

As Germaine turned on the broadcast and powered up all the transmitters, he called out values.

"Circuit A is on. All transmitters working. Circuit B is on. All transmitters working. Wait, scratch that, transmitter seven is not working. Powering off."

James went to a box by the door. "I'll swap it out. Give me a minute."

He took an extra transmitter and went into the tent. The camera switched to that view. Kath was asleep, her chest rising and falling, and her eyes did not move under her tight eyelids. It was a deep sleep.

Swap completed, Germaine and James busied themselves in the planetarium.

"Circuit A. All good," James began. "Circuit B. All good. Circuit C. All good."

"Okay, I'll send the signal. First one hundred digits of pi in binary... going at one digit per second. "

On the screens, numbers changed and flashed. Kath's vitals were also shown on a small screen below the others, a duplicate of a monitor near the hospital bed. Heart rate was steady at 72. Blood pressure 110/70. Temperature 99.

"Let's send the code," said James.

"Copy that," answered Germaine.

James typed on his keyboard and the screens changed, displaying new values. "Rhiannon" was now in full tilt throughout the room.

The point of view rotated, showing still scenes. The sequence finished. Orion didn't move from the bed. James and Germaine watched the screens. The video switched from inside the tent to several status screens, including one showing Kath's vitals.

Lorelai said, "Pause and show me my mother's vital signs on monitor three." Then, after an intense stare at the data, "Continue."

James spoke. "She's steady. Heart rate down by one. Body temperature unchanged. Run it again."

Germaine did as he was told.

"How do we know if it has done its work?" asked James.

Germaine pulled up the Russian documents on the last monitor. "The report is clear on that point. It says the response was visible and immediate. Heart rate rose to a hundred and fifty percent of resting for nearly an hour. Temperature rose to 40 degrees—that's Celsius. Tumors visibly melted away. I'm not sure how that is possible, but that's what it says."

James went to the tent and opened the narrow gap by lifting the section of Faraday cloth. Kath was asleep. He let the flap fall closed.

"Let's break for now and run it again in an hour. Maybe we missed something? She's sleeping anyway." He shut off Fleetwood Mac. Then he held a button on the wall and the whirring of an electric motor was heard. The entire tent rose until it was suspended from the ceiling, revealing the bed, with the sleeping patient under it.

Germaine said nothing. He merely nodded.

Lorelai asked for a pause and returned with microwave popcorn and a water bottle.

The video continued and switched to the kitchen, showing rotating cameras of a conversation between James and Germaine. "Did we do anything wrong?" James asked. He was leaning against the stainless-steel refrigerator, picking at food on a plate. Germaine sat at the island.

"I think we were pretty accurate in re-creating what the Russians did. Remember, they tried it four times, according to the docs, and got only a single positive result."

"And that's only if we believe they got any results." James stabbed his food with his fork, the click of steel on china loud. "Stupid! This is so stupid. I got her hopes up and I shouldn't have!"

Joan spoke from puttering near the sink. "Mr. Nine, I think Dr. Gorabani would say she knows exactly what you are doing and holds no false hopes. She is not unaware of your efforts."

James nodded. "Thank you, Joan, but still, it was a lot of wasted work."

"I wanted to mention that we did not try different frequencies," Germaine said. "Plus, the code, or limb, as the Russians called it, may not have been translated correctly. There are a dozen things that could have gone wrong or been mistaken."

James interjected, "Not to mention that this entire thing could be some Soviet scientist's made-up fantasy to avoid being sent to the gulag. And what about the video? It doesn't correspond to any sci-fi show I've ever seen, and I've seen a lot of sci-fi." He paused, annoyed. "This is all just bullshit," he said, and then got up and exited the kitchen.

Germaine and Joan looked at each other uncomfortably.

The hallway camera showed Germaine and James walking.

"We tried, James. But I think it's the right decision to stop. It's tiring for her."

"We did. We tried," said James, resignation in his voice. His hand was on his back, as if it were sore.

Germaine stepped into the planetarium to see Kath. She was sleeping again. He gave Orion a head scratch, and the dog responded with a shake and a friendly tail wag.

Back in the hallway he said to Joan, "Tell her I said goodbye." She gave him an overly tight hug.

The two men shook hands and Germaine went out the front door. A shot of the exterior showed him getting into the back seat of a car.

The video cut to the planetarium where James was lying in the large hospital bed next to a sleeping Kath, scrolling on his phone. The machines started beeping. Kath was deathly pale, her lips devoid of blood. A brief view of the monitor showed on the video. Kath's heart rate was below forty, and her blood pressure was falling.

"I'm going to give her something," Joan said as she prepared a syringe.

"Could this be the Russian treatment?" James asked, staring at Kath.

"We should call the doctor to get some blood work done, and maybe redo some of her scans, but I've seen this before in terminal patients. She'll stabilize in a bit."

James simply repeated, "Terminal."

Lorelai stood, peering at the screens. "Give her more!"

The simulacrum responded, "Kath's vitals return to normal in the next clip."

In the video, Kath's eyes opened and looked up at the floating tent, the lights inside on, and said only, "Don't let that thing drop on me."

Lorelai rubbed her eyes. It was late. She wanted to keep going, but it was too much. She stared at the dozen monitors surrounding her father's hospital bed with screenshots she'd taken during the video playback.

A ping on her phone made her glance down.

"What the fuck is this?"

"Language."

"Oh, for chrissake, did you see this?"

"I choose not to see your phone communication."

"Well, someone posted a video using the WisPR blockchain account. I don't get it."

She looked to see if it was Lollipop—this would be something she would do. But it wasn't. There was not supposed to be any activity on the blockchain by WisPR. There was an idea floated by WeDontKnow to map all the stars into a decentralized database that could be used as a public resource, but none of them had pursued it.

It was a video file. The video launched and she recognized the people—the aliens—in the video. She'd never felt the hair go up on the back of her neck in the same way as when the wedding ceremony of the two aliens unfolded on the screen.

She quickly pulled up the video from Germaine—the video where the soldier fell over the cliff and the woman doctor ran across town to save a boy, the video her father said was the key to his salvation. Above her, on the screens that were mounted on a rack against the planetarium wall, she froze screenshots of both videos, pulling up the faces of the man and woman characters. Soon she had four images. Two of the man, two of the woman, one from each video. They were the same. The characters in the video that her father said were connected to the events that led to his stroke were the same characters in this video uploaded to the WisPR blockchain.

Who and why?

The who was pretty easy to figure out. She cross-referenced the wallets created by WisPR, and the user who had posted the video was Clarity, the one whose mentor had been killed a few years ago. The one who had posted about aliens a few times, her mentor using far-off aliens to help her understand radio waves.

But why?

She pinged Clarity on the WisPR chatroom but she was not online. This was odd in itself. She must have started the upload and logged off?

"Unit, what's going on?" she muttered to herself.

She glanced up at the simulacrum. It looked at her and said, "I cannot answer that."

She looked at her father and saw his eyes moving under his lids, saw the sensors blinking. She wondered about that. Was there some unrecognized brain activity or facial movements that the AI interpreter couldn't discern—the simulacrum saying nothing while the real James was trying to communicate? This happened sometimes, and it usually meant the AI software needed an update, a learning session, to improve its interpretation.

She put aside the videos for a second and on another screen rapidly launched the development environment for the code that ran the AI interpreter for James's simulacrum. The dashboard for the interpreter showed information was incoming from James's brainwaves, but as she suspected, the AI library entries for the information led to dead ends, so the simulacrum remained silent, unable to provide an interpretation.

BOOK 4

- Welcome to the WisPR chatroom
- Bot is ON
- Users online: 1
- Today's quote is:

"Probability sure has as its substance a statement as to whether something *is* or *is not* the case—an uncertain statement, to be sure. But nevertheless it has meaning only if one is indeed convinced that the something in question quite definitely *is* or *is not* the case."

E. Schrödinger to A. Einstein
Innsbruck, Innrain 55
18 November 1950

21. Fort Meade, Maryland

Montgomery was more than annoyed. His degenerate human computer was in the wind. Smithson had been hiding something. And Montgomery knew it, but he wasn't sure what it was.

And now? A firefight in some Podunk town in Tennessee. He had two retired soldiers, a husband (Lieutenant Bart Warren, US Army Ret.) and wife (Lieutenant Margaret Warren, US Army Ret.), in custody after one of them almost took down his helicopter. Though the assailant said it was an intentional warning shot through the canopy.

"If I wanted you down, you'd be down," she'd told him, on the way back to Fort Meade.

The silver lining: She and her husband kept the girl from getting kidnapped by the competition. Just after Montgomery arrived at the house—after a slight delay caused by the through-and-through bullet hole in the chopper's windscreen—his FBI team caught two unknowns driving to the property, claiming they'd gotten lost looking for a hiking trailhead. Of course, the two had rope, duct tape, propofol and syringes, and enough firepower to take out a police station—items you'd not likely need on a hike. They were in custody as well. So that was four folks he had.

The Warrens wouldn't say much other than that the girl had left on her own earlier in the day. When confronted with the fact that three children were missing and the car they had stolen in Boston was found at their house, they clammed up. The man changed his story to say that he was sure the "Black girl with the accent" was drugged and hallucinating. Mrs. Warren wouldn't speak at all.

They had both served with Chuck Plaster in Korea, so it was clear they had harbored his granddaughter and the two missing boys. Montgomery knew loyalty among soldiers who served together transcended even the most solemn vows, so he'd put in a request to have them questioned again, but he wasn't sure he'd get the approval. What was unclear was whether the granddaughter, Claire Plaster, knew anything about the technology and how the Botswana citizen, Haretsebe Tladi, the possible superspy, was connected with her.

The Warrens were just a way-stop, not deep into any of the whole shenanigans. The bulk of what they knew had probably been obtained when he confirmed the connection with the old Choctaw army vet. If the kids and the Black girl were traveling together, well, they would be easier to find together. Besides, the most important piece of evidence was in the Warrens' car.

The dog.

The damn dog was in their car. It was hurt. But it was alive. And it had a chip manufactured in South Africa.

The technology was real.

A damn dog. He hoped IT didn't dissect the poor thing—the only living sample his team had of a teleportation. And possibly the only example of teleportation on the entire planet. Except for the Black girl. Unless conspiracy theorists were to be believed and a secret society of alien-worshipping super-technologists had been teleporting around the world for centuries, stealing from banks and cavorting like rock stars on yachts off Ibiza. He sighed at the craziness he'd had to wade through on the internet, trying to get up to speed on this singular project.

"You got a dog?" Derek had been incredulous.

"I'm sending you a summary report in a few hours. Videos, audiotape of our contractor in the RSA, photos, et cetera. It's real. The dog teleported to Tennessee a couple of days ago."

"Well, I gotta say, I've sent you on quite a few wild goose chases with pretty much zero expectation of success, and this was one of them. I figured you'd close this file for me as a null set."

"I'm as surprised as anyone."

"This jibes, by the way, with additional chatter from two organizations on the dark side. I'll upgrade them and loop you in on the intel. There is activity. They are also looking for the Botswana girl."

"Anything from the two operatives I collared?"

"One American with French ties, one Korean, but not necessarily with Pyongyang. They are smash and grab experts, known to us, but not previously considered important."

"So no new intel on who's bankrolling the competition?"

Derek's answer was cautionary. "None, but these guys don't play games.

French intelligence says they are independent contractors who have primarily government and quasi-government clients, both corporate and fiat. Korean intelligence confirms."

Montgomery gave a moment and asked, "Any word on our favorite pervert?"

Derek chuffed. "I'm gonna guess he'll lie low for a while."

Montgomery exhaled, agreed. "Keep an eye out. He was grooming that girl in Albuquerque. Her father's a vegetable, so there's nothing there for us."

After the call, Montgomery pondered his next actions and simply wasn't sure. Would the girl come back for the dog? She might if it had been hers, but he wasn't sure that was the case. Why would she waste resources bringing the dog to the United States only to abandon it? He was thinking about his sister's dog again when he got a priority call from IT. It was a call he'd dreaded since he'd first started down this yellow brick road.

"One of the full videos is on the public-facing web."

22. Interstate 25

"So, 'splain, sister." Harry was in the back seat with Claire while Spitz drove and Phil took shotgun.

Claire said, "As far as I can tell, the videos come from interstellar broadcasts received on several frequencies. Plus, he references data going back to the 1970s, and he mentions his grandfather, who worked at MIT then, so maybe it started there?"

Harry fiddled with the silver top of the decorative cane as she spoke. "MeerKAT doesn't receive below around 520 megahertz. If he compiled data, he must have gotten it from other telescopes. Arecibo, maybe? There are others. And the Very Large Array wasn't open until the eighties, I think."

Claire said, "Yes, he collected raw data from different telescopes around the world: Giant Metrewave in India, Green Bank and VLA in the USA, Africa, Russia, Australia. Anything he could get. It doesn't say how he assembled the data, but he refers to a staircase decryption. He actually calls it de-channeling. He also says the signal data comes in as both AM and FM. He actually had me do some of this work, but it was just bits and pieces. We parcelized incoming time-series data by frequency, creating FM datasets. Then we did the same by amplitude."

Harry was staring up now, something she did when thinking hard. "I'm not sure the granularity of signal reception is high enough to generate anything meaningful in AM."

Claire answered, "Actually, he gave me this as homework. Sensitivity at the VLA, for example, could be as low as one tenth of a Jansky from a few different interstellar sources, which means you could extract AM data, if you knew the gradations and the band. It's possible. Then maybe you'd map those gradations to placeholders in, say, base 2, and combine the data into a bitmapped image? I mean, this is way out there and would require some pretty lucky guesswork."

Harry nodded, now looking out the window. "Right. That's the staircase. Each amplitude increase, if divided into eight gradations, is a bit place. Huh, clever, and actually intuitive if you are a society built on base 2. Amazing. They might not be orange. That's just a function of our own rendering."

Claire said, "But even at one tenth of a Jansky, how could signals from thousands of light-years away not be degraded by the inverse square law?"

Harry twisted her cane. "Well, there are natural phenomena that amplify signals. Gravitational lensing and cosmic background hot spots. If he was looking at Saj A Star, then the black hole might have done the amplification. We have no idea where the signals are from. Could be from another galaxy, meaning millions of years ago rather than thousands."

"Okay, that's crazy."

Harry took a breath. "But what about the secret toy surprise dangerous codes that have put a target on our backs?"

"Those are embedded in the bitmapped frames of the video. He doesn't say how he extracted them. But he refers to base 32 and 'bit removal,' so there's some function that he used to extract a base 32 number from the videos and that, when broadcast, causes the effects. If I had time, I might be able to reverse engineer the extraction. You might even be faster at it, with your image manipulation knowledge."

Harry nodded. "Two heads are better than one." She paused, then asked, "You uploaded a video. You're sure the codes weren't included?"

"I compressed the video to mpeg before uploading. Very lossy."

"Clever girl."

"That's why they call me Claire."

"That makes zero sense."

"To you."

"To anyone."

"Where are we going?" Phil's question hung in the air as Spitz drove in light traffic. They were on I-24 heading toward Nashville west from the Warrens'. Phil had chosen this route solely because they had come from the east on the way to the Warrens' via back roads in the nurse's stolen hatchback. But now they wanted to disappear in some traffic, and as night approached, being on an interstate seemed like the safest move.

"We need internet," said Claire.

"And we need food," Harry said. "I'd kill for some of those southern biscuits. Maggie's were scrumptious."

"Bottomless pit, you," said Phil.

"I will find the bottom if I have to eat all the Ho Hos in Tennessee. And thank you for introducing them to me. We are now best friends," said Harry.

Claire spoke confidently. "Okay, let's get gas, internet, food, et cetera, at a truck stop after Nashville. How much money do we have?"

Phil opened the glove box and took out a plastic bag. "The Warrens gave us about two hundred dollars and, like, five credit cards. Mr. Warren said we can probably use the credit cards a few times but they'll start tracking us. So, I think if we use one and then leave it on the gas pump, maybe someone will take it and use it somewhere else. Or we stop at one of those rest stops that serves both directions. That would be even better."

"He cheats at Monopoly too," said Claire. She added, "How do we get internet? I mean, do we want to wait around and use the free Wi-Fi at the truck stop? I assume everyone's phones are off?"

Phil said, "Free Wi-Fi first at a truck stop. Wait on the gas. Get it when we are ready to leave."

"Snacks, snacks, Wi-Fi, gas," corrected Harry.

In the cafeteria eating area of the truck stop, Claire booted her laptop. The light was harsh and the orange laminate tables surrounded by plastic chairs were mostly empty. A few truckers queued at the register. Over the speakers, pop music played, interrupted by announcements for showers, which Phil and Spitz found fascinating. "You can shower in a truck stop? Cool. We're going to get snacks."

"Holy shit." Claire's eyes widened at the laptop screen.

Harry looked over her shoulder. "Wow."

Under the video were dozens of comments.

Claire said, "We need to sort through these for allies, foes, and garbage." They rapidly scanned them, looking for anything relevant.

"We should upload another video," said Harry.

"Seriously?" Claire was skimming the comments.

"Look, people are dead. I'm not even sure where I am at this point. I want answers and I want protection. I'm a bloody cripple. I'm not some superspy." She waved her cane menacingly, drawing some stares, then lowered it and looked sheepish.

Claire nodded slowly. "Which one?"

"Doesn't matter. How many are on your laptop? I've got, like, twenty-two on mine."

"I've got seventeen. Let's choose one we both have."

"Well, just choose one, strip it of those codes, and get it up there." Harry booted her laptop. "I'm getting snacks first, then deal with comments. I'll download them all so we can read them in the car."

Claire was only sort of paying attention while she worked. A commotion near the cash register drew her gaze. Spitz and some strangers assisted Harry to her feet. She brushed them off when she was up. One of them handed her the Princess Diana cane.

"I'm fine. I'm fine." Her accent drew more attention, not less. Spitz took her hand and placed it on his shoulder and they hobbled back to the table. Phil was picking up the food that Harry had dropped and left to pay for it. Their group was the subject of a lot of staring. Claire's heart sank. Two energized teenage boys, a young white woman, and Harry, with her British accent, cane, and limp. They weren't exactly keeping a low profile.

Harry sat down next to Claire, who was concerned, and asked, "You okay?"

Harry nodded. "I... I don't know. I tripped, I guess. I'm not usually uncoordinated, you know? And my leg is killing me again." She rubbed it. "That's new and special."

Spitz sat and pulled out his phone. Phil grabbed it. "No phones." Spitz gesticulated, pointing at the phone and drawing a knife across his neck, then using other sign language.

Claire looked around and saw that the stares hadn't stopped. "Boys, please stop. Spitz, seriously, no phones. You know why."

Spitz grabbed his phone back and made more signs at Claire.

She sighed, "Fine, airplane mode. Just sit here, eat, and be chill."

Claire put a hand on Harry's shoulder. "Seriously, you okay?"

Harry nodded again. "*Hantley ha holo*. Good. Fine as feathers. Glad my bum broke my fall." She smiled and Claire smiled too. Harry glanced at her computer. "*Hele*, Claire. Look at this."

"You'll translate those funny phrases you say at some point?" Claire looked at Harry after reading Kathode's message over her shoulder. Claire was seriously puzzled. "She says she knows the couple from another video. How has Kathode seen these videos? Or another video with these aliens? Did Mr. Wright send these videos to anyone else? Phil, did your dad tell you anything else about these videos?"

Phil shook his head. "Nothing. He told us they were unreleased episodes some TV show and also they were from space."

The young women looked at each other and then turned back to the screen together. Claire leaned her chin on Harry's shoulder as she read.

"Well," added Harry, "at least we know where we are going. How far is Albuquerque?"

Phil crowed in a Bugs Bunny voice, "Eh, Albuquerque? I should have taken a left turn there!"

Spitz punched him in the arm and put two fingers behind Phil's head. Phil leaned over and read the message and whistled. Then Phil was serious and asked several questions rapidly. "Who's Kathode? How does she know about the videos? Did my dad tutor her or him or them, which is it, as well?"

Spitz shrugged.

Claire sighed. "Honestly, Phil, I do not know anymore."

"Should I respond or you?" asked Harry.

Claire spoke her thoughts aloud. "She's gonna know I forwarded it to you; it's in the message icons, so I guess no harm. What should we tell her? Something to indicate we know about more videos."

As they left the food court heading to the car, Claire glanced back at the large window of the truck stop and could see a uniformed man talking to the cashier, who pointed his chin in their direction. They had done nothing wrong, but she wanted to make sure they didn't draw any more attention and she didn't want to have to produce an ID.

"I'll drive for a bit, okay, Spitz?"

Claire drove. Harry sat in the passenger seat. This was often how it split: the women up front and the boys in the back or vice versa.

"So, are we going to talk about it?" Harry's voice was easy and light.

"Your falling? Maybe because you're using a new cane. I really hope teleporting didn't have any actual effects on you. There's nothing to google, so how do you feel otherwise?"

"Not about falling, girl. About teleporting. About the fact that aliens exist and we are sitting on technology that is from 'not Earth.' That we are potentially the four horsemen of the bloody apocalypse. That."

Claire was silent for a moment. Long enough that Harry opened her mouth to speak. Claire answered, "I'm still not a hundred percent convinced they are alien, really. I mean, I know there's evidence that the videos are, and I think Mr. Wright knew about this all along, but it seems to defy... defy..."

"All science? All logic? Ha. It's crazy, right? I think my gram would fall down too, so maybe it's in my genes. But, seriously, isn't this world-changing? What will happen? We just released these things into the world."

Claire kept her eyes on the dark highway ahead. "I know. I hope nothing bad happens. I mean, people kill each other over religion. Let's hope the videos kind of disappear into the internet after we get what we need."

"Which video do you like the most?" Harry slapped Spitz's hand, which was reaching for the radio. "You stay in the back."

Claire's eyes held on to the traffic ahead of them on the highway. "Like? I hadn't even thought of them as like or dislike. I've actually never loved sci-fi. And is it sci-fi? Or is it news or something? The one with the biology is actually pretty cool. What if that's real?"

Harry gave an exhalation of breath. "It's not real. It's just made up. It's so sci-fi. It's so scripted. It's like a decent streaming binge, you know? I wish we had the whole season. And that man is kind of, you know?"

Claire glanced at Harry. "The 'man'? You mean the orange alien? Seriously? An alien video star?"

Though Claire couldn't see her, she knew Harry was smiling shyly. "I always liked the tall, dark, and alien ones. And a uniform. He might not care if I'm a cripple."

"Oh, Harry. There's no need to be like that."

"It's funny. I think that's why I like the idea of the alien or whatever. I figure they'd see me as exotic."

Claire spoke with a smile in her voice. "I can't believe we are literally running for our lives and you are drooling over some spaceman."

"It's distraction, okay? I'm having trouble even believing I'm in North America, you know?"

"Okay, fine. I can see something in that guy. I can see that, but he's orange. Like an orange, or a traffic cone. Or whatever else is orange. I could see you with him." Claire added a little laugh.

"I'm not fishing for compliments. Though I once had someone say I look like Zoe Saldana."

"Who?" Claire asked.

"Oh, *modimo nthuse*! Uhura! From *Star Trek* and, like, a dozen other movies. I mean, without my leg thing."

Claire smiled and faked a serious voice as she drove in the dark. "Oh, I totally see it."

Harry looked at Claire and gave her an evil pout, even while her eyes smiled. "I can say *bitch* in six languages. So just assume I'm saying them all now."

23. Colorado-New Mexico border

Smithson's trip to Albuquerque was uneventful until it wasn't. This was because Smithson had *funny ideas* about people, as one of his online acquaintances had pointed out during a discussion of who would survive if a zombie apocalypse struck the world. Coincidentally, an employee evaluation by an employer after graduate school also described Smithson as having *funny ideas.* And these *funny ideas* combined to put him in a situation that nearly cost him his life.

Having lived in his own tiny world of online information for so long, Smithson had not interacted with a diversity of people. And, if truth be told, he had never interacted directly with people except when necessary; his interactions primarily were with anonymous online personas, who might or might not have been trolls, bots, AI agents, paid informants, collectors, deviants, and others who traveled the seventh circle of hell on the dark web. Always shy, always leery of interacting with women, who make up half the planet, and definitely avoidant of interacting with any male who appeared to be self-confident or even friendly, eliminating nearly the entirety of the other half of the planet, Smithson spent most of his time in his own head.

Driving south from Denver toward his hopeful connection to a pot of gold in Albuquerque in the form of an heiress named Lorelai, Smithson knew he would pass through Indigenous areas of the United States. Native reservations were locales of mystery to Smithson. His misplaced vision translated mystery to opportunity. His thoughts followed thusly: poverty, alcoholism, families in crisis. This would mean there were young girls without role models. Perhaps they were abused at home. Perhaps they saw no opportunity. Depressed, looking for a father figure, they would be ripe for the picking. Ready for his guidance and his mere presence. Too, he needed a junior partner, a Robin to his Batman, a veep to his prez, a pinkie toe to his foot, a penny to his nickel. His Gilligan. His girl Friday. A valet. A page. An aide-de-camp. He needed a female to cast in the role of Lollipop.

His plan was to spend some extra time at truck stops near reservations, thinking that maybe he'd find a young woman down on her luck, looking for that special someone to provide stability and guidance in a life that lacked both.

This was a flawless plan; he could find no faults. He had read enough about such relationships online that it seemed possible for him to have one as well. Smithson drove south from Denver in the rented SUV, a predator in search of prey. He drove toward Albuquerque where Lorelai waited for his arrival. Though he knew she wasn't actually waiting. She was ignorant of his male persona; his avatar of Lollipop was all she knew. But if he showed up with a *female* acting as Lollipop, would that make him appear respectable? He suspected so. His troubled and malleable sidekick would make a perfect *accoutrement*, a disguise.

He'd seen plenty of videos of young women forced to participate in activities that were far more destructive than what he intended. Plus, he wasn't like those other predators who felt nothing for their prey. Smithson wasn't an animal. He felt for the young woman he would pick up at a truck stop or rescue from certain doom by the side of a lonely highway. He would save her and she would show him the kind of love that a savior deserves. And then he would persuade her, using his alpha male dominance, his force of masculine personality, his diamond-edged intellect, to help him meet and woo Lorelai and separate her from her fortune.

As he drove south, climbing the rural highways in the mountains of northern New Mexico, his plastic go-bag in his pocket, his mind consumed by impossible fantasies, he still had no idea how to approach Lorelai, but the plan would jell, he was sure, as soon as he acquired XY-chromosomal pectin for this boiling jam of a road trip.

He'd already paused at several truck stops but they seemed busy and ill-designed for trade in human flesh. Though he wasn't exactly sure how he'd identify a suitable young woman. He'd browsed the aisles of one truck stop, picking up and putting down a can of soup, an extra USB cord for his laptop, a bright orange security vest, and other sundries until he realized that the comings and goings precluded him from cornering and speaking to a young woman, even if one were nearby, which none were.

This disappointment continued at the next two truck stops until he realized that maybe truck stops were not as active in the market for young women as he'd been led to believe by news articles and message boards.

He sat in his rented SUV at the last pull-off and considered his options. He could try to hire a prostitute. They could meet at a nearby motel. He'd explain his desire to free her from her poorly chosen and unwanted career path. He had money, he'd say, and he simply wanted her to be his companion in a scientific experiment that would change the world.

This, he realized, would not work. The hooker would be a drug addict. She would inject him with a narcotic and steal his money, his car, his kidney. He imagined her in ratty black fishnet stockings, injection tracks on her arm, a cold sore on her lip. She would slur her words and call him "Baby" and smoke in front of him. She'd smell bad and bits of lint would cling to her hair. He shivered with the vision.

No, he needed a community college student or even a high school student Whose mother worked too hard and whose absent father had left before the poor young thing turned a year old. The mother was a waitress. The child would come to the restaurant after school to do her homework for the rest of her mother's shift. He could even see the assignment book, Algebra 1, and the list of simple questions that needed to be completed for fourth period the next day. Math was tough, and Smithson would be able to help and would form a bond with the girl.

And so, with his plan clear, Smithson continued his journey south, making it just over the border from Colorado into New Mexico. And lo and behold, the Starlight Diner shone just off the highway, an oasis of sorts in a cold and mountainous desert.

Smithson patted himself on the back because sure enough, as the jingle of the door transported him into the bustling diner, he saw at the counter, in the dimming light, a young woman doing homework. He caught the eye of a waitress putting away stacks of hot dishes and indicated he wanted to eat. She called out, "Anywhere's fine."

Smithson sidled up to the counter and chose a seat, not next to the young female doing homework, but with a seat between them, to give the girl the power of controlling her own space. He wanted to keep her comfortable. If she had agency, she would feel safe.

She didn't look up from her work as he sat. The waitress, who may or may not have been the girl's mom, dropped a menu in front of him and asked him if he wanted anything to drink.

"Just water," said Smithson.

She returned with water and he ordered a BLT. He didn't read the menu, just assumed a BLT was on it, this being the exact diner he had envisioned in his plan. And sure enough, she said nothing, took the menu, and left. This gave Smithson the opportunity to shift slightly, turning toward the young girl, who was busy with her algebra.

His eyes absorbed her from head to toe. She wore a gray hoodie and sweatpants. He couldn't tell, but the hoodie may have said *Seniors Love Volleyball.* This was a good sign. She'd be fit and strong. Perhaps she was also on the track team. Did kids do multiple sports nowadays?

His stare lasted a bit too long and she noticed. Her head turned toward him and then glanced away. Shy. Another good sign. She might be skittish from whatever awful abuse happened at home. But he'd seen her eyes, brown, perhaps, with a dark eyeliner. She wore makeup. Smithson calculated this might also be a good sign. She wanted to be older, to be a real woman. Everything was pointing in the right direction.

"Need any help with that?" Smithson asked her.

She said nothing and continued her work. He wondered if she had heard him. He placed his right hand on the counter, closer to her, hoping to draw her attention. She glanced up at him again.

"Wha?" She sounded sleepy, maybe a tad confused about why he had spoken with her.

"Need help with your homework?" he repeated.

She looked at him quizzically.

"No, it's an essay." She turned away and continued writing.

Smithson considered his options. This girl was perfect. She was from a troubled home. There was no doubt about that. She was alone. He continued to stare at her until his food arrived, the plate placed in front of him. The waitress looked at the girl and at him. She said nothing and turned back to her duties. Smithson's eyes followed the waitress until she was out of sight.

He took a bite of his BLT and ate some of his fries. Later, he decided he should have just enjoyed the meal. Some facts he got right. The waitress was the girl's mother. The girl was doing homework. Other truths he deduced afterward that he could have processed at the time had he not been so focused on the pot of gold at the end of the ribbon of refracted light. He had badly misjudged the restaurant. The new art deco paint was the clue. The diner was marketed to locals, as he expected, but also to those hipsters traveling through to Taos for skiing in the winter and Santa Fe for the art market in the summer. It had BLTs on the menu, but it also had meatless burgers, kale and artichoke salad, tiramisu, and other items targeted at the six-figure luxury vehicles parked out front. Smithson processed none of this, something he would regret, and was deep into his white knight fantasy. He took a twenty-dollar bill out of his wallet as smoothly as he could and slid it over to the girl doing homework.

"If you need money, I have more." Smithson said this as quietly as he could, hoping the young girl heard it and nobody else.

She looked at him with a blank expression and got up and went around to the side of the counter under the restroom sign. Smithson thought she might be getting herself ready for her journey. Maybe doing what women called "freshening up." He wasn't sure what that entailed, but it boded well.

From the kitchen, loud talk drifted through the serving window. "Is he still here?" Smithson heard the words and tried not to consider what they meant, but a bit of worry crept into his thoughts. He was wakening, as if from a dream.

The waitress, an attractive woman of a certain age, came out carrying a long knife. "Who the fuck do you think you are?" The girl peered at them from around the corner of the counter.

The waitress put the knife in his face. "You get the fuck out of here."

Smithson held up his hands. He understood now he had made assumptions that might not have been correct. "I... I..." he stuttered, something he rarely did, or at least he assumed he rarely did, but since he interacted infrequently with people, maybe it wasn't so rare after all.

Then he felt a pain in his ear and toppled to the floor. He was grabbed roughly by several people. He thought it might be four. They lifted him up and took him forcibly out of the restaurant. As he passed the doorway, one leading and the other following, he realized it was only two.

"You fucking, perverted motherfucker," said one.

The other said, "Get him over to his fucking car." He was dragged, feet bouncing on the pavement, one shoe coming off and then his foot painfully abrading on the blacktop. They pushed him up against the door of his SUV.

"A teenager?" yelled the larger of the two men, directly in his face, and

Smithson chose not to count the man's silver fillings. "And you're what? Some middle-aged douchebag?"

Smithson would later be insulted, but for now he spoke carefully, deciding not to point out he was more than a decade younger than middle-aged. "I'm... I'm sorry for any misunderstanding."

"Fuck this," said the smaller one, and he punched Smithson hard in the stomach. The larger man caught him as he fell and the smaller man punched Smithson in the face with an uppercut that would have been a knockout if Smithson hadn't already fallen forward so far that the blow caught his face at the start of its swing.

Smithson doubled over and went to his knees.

"Get in your car. Drive away. Do. You. Understand?" said the one who punched him, enunciating each word with a diction that Smithson thought was far more nuanced and clearer than expected in this part of the country.

On his hands and knees, Smithson watched a long string of bloody spittle drip onto the pavement of the parking lot. The spittle, which was out of focus, triggered a conclusion that he was glad he had eaten little of the BLT or the fries. A foot stepped on one of his hands, pressing it to the pavement, twisting and driving bits of rock into his palm and the soft side of his fingers. Then he was on his side, on the ground, the pavement cold and gritty on his face. Pain radiated from his ribs and he closed his hands over his abdomen. He struggled to breathe. Would he die? Would this be his death? In a parking lot in Bumfuck, beaten to death by Billy Bob and his cousin Earl? Smithson thought that hilarious and he gave a quick chuckle, which was choked off by the pain in his side. He worked himself to all fours, multicolored liquids dripping from his face.

"Don't," said the larger man, and Smithson realized he had just been saved from a savage kick to his face, which very well might have opened his skull. A glance sideways saw western boots that were very likely the steel-toed kind advertised on enormous billboards on I-25 between Denver and Albuquerque.

"I'll go. I'll go." Smithson lifted his face and got to his knees. He raised his hands. "Watch. I'm going." He got his keys from his pants as he stood up, gravel embedded in his hand, rolling against the edge of the pocket. The larger man had his hands up as well, and that confused Smithson for a moment, but then he realized this man's goal was to prevent his friend from killing Smithson.

Who needs friends when your enemies' friends are your friends? More folks from the restaurant were also in the parking lot, including the stony-faced waitress, who watched from the doorway, the large knife clenched against her folded arms. He was going to look around for the girl, but catching the poised arms and feet and fists of his newly found acquaintances, he realized that alacrity of exit would be the prudent course of action. He nonsensically hoped the twenty-dollar bill he had left would cover the BLT and a nice tip.

"Make sure he doesn't come back," the waitress yelled.

Smithson grimaced with agony as he struggled into the front seat. It took two attempts to close the driver's-side door, because pain in his side resulted in only an impotent half click of the latch the first time. There was a rapping on the window, a cracking sound that Smithson would remember for a long time. "We're armed, you weirdo! I see you again, I'm not calling the police." Smithson glanced and saw that the blue steel butt of a handgun was the source of the noise.

Not knowing where he was going, Smithson eased out of the parking lot, barely paying attention to the small crowd staring him away. It was clumsy, coordinating breathing and steering with one hand, the other stiffening and throbbing. He turned left down the dark main street—a lucky choice. Otherwise he'd have had to turn around and go by the diner again, within shooting range. Wheezing with each breath, he wiped vomit, tears, and blood from his chin as he followed signs south toward Albuquerque.

*The E.T. Defense

"Major Studios Declare Zoonerat Videos Extraterrestrial," *ExoTainment*

Several major studios are bidding for the latest popular fanfic coming out of the Zoonerat genre. This is in contrast to the studios' refusal to pay royalties for the original videos because the videos are "from outer space," a tactic now known as the E.T. Defense. The true creators of the videos are still unknown, though there are many who have claimed to have either created, worked on, or inspired the videos.

"We are comfortable bidding in the open market on derivative works, given positive audience response," said one studio exec who asked to remain anonymous. "Normally we would not do so except in rare instances where pre-marketing has occurred because of the viral nature of the content or sponsorship by major brands, both of which apply in this case."

Several lawsuits have been filed by alleged creators and owners of the Zoonerat videos against the studios who have taken unedited portions of the publicly available videos and incorporated them into multi-episode series released to streaming audiences. This has led all studios with content released or in production to jointly issue a statement confirming their belief that the Zoonerat videos are extraterrestrial and in the public domain.

In the court filing, the plaintiffs quote from the Outer Space Treaty of 1967 which states that 'Outer space, including the moon and other celestial bodies, is not subject to national appropriation.' The plaintiffs claim that radio waves emanating from Outer Space are covered by the Treaty.

"We believe that the Treaty gives us free and complete access to the Zoonerat videos, which have been uniquely identified as not terrestrial by numerous reputable scientists. We will defend this in any court on Earth."

The United Nations Office for Outer Space Affairs (we didn't know that existed) had no comment.

24. Fort Meade, Maryland

"Any word on the technology?" Derek's question was open-ended, and through the speakerphone, his voice betrayed no emotion.

Montgomery stirred his coffee. He wasn't sure exactly how much he should tell his boss. For one, some of the information was not 100 percent confirmed. Two, he was concerned about leaks. Because leaks happen. He wasn't sure who was leaking data but he was pretty sure that information tended to flow like water, soaking into previously dry and uninformed parts of an organization, an osmosis of knowledge, glistening drops of data appearing on the other side of porous Chinese walls. Perhaps unintentional, perhaps with purpose, but information dispersed.

With those thoughts in mind, he spoke into the phone with confidence, belying his omissions. "We know their direction. We also know that there are four individuals together. The woman from South Africa. Wright's student from Lexington. Two boys." Montgomery kept silent about the vehicle, the destination, and how far from that destination. Because... droplets of data.

"When will you pick them up?"

"We aren't going to. We've decided to track them and see if they meet up with anyone else. There's more going on here than is obvious, and picking them up may not get us the result we want."

A few seconds passed and Montgomery considered filling the gap, but then Derek spoke. "Okay. Word has gone pretty high up the chain because of those video releases. You know chatter on the internet is loud. The videos are going viral. Now it's got a name—Zoonerat. And there are calls from higher up to ask if we are behind it and if so what our intentions are. I need to respond."

The conversation paused and Montgomery realized he was being asked for advice.

"I would disavow knowledge. Our team here is telling me that there's a core group of, let's call them Zoonerat Believers, rallying behind these videos, but there are plenty of Disbelievers as well. Like a fad or a hit song. We don't expect interest to last. These things tend to die out after an initial run. Remember the

UFO frenzy when the air force released all those alien craft videos? That was a distraction, right, then it faded?" Montgomery was asking for confirmation.

"No comment on that," Derek said. "But nice try. I tend to agree. This will be buried in layers of conspiracies within a week and that's gonna be my story. But just so you know, there is actionable intel that others are after your targets. You've got two in custody already. There's more. I can't have dead children on my watch that get linked back to us, not with the videos out there now and a chance that it would be connected. Prevent that under all circumstances. Plus, those two women know about the technology, so make sure at least one gets brought in as an ally. Again, these aren't homeless vagrants. They will eventually be missed, especially because they're children. Their disappearance can't be buried. More importantly, do not let anyone get hold of any laptops or electronics in their possession."

"Understood." Montgomery breathed a sigh of relief. He was worried that he'd be given carte blanche to *contain* all players. That would mean dead or alive. He didn't want to be party to dead kids. That had happened once before and he was still in therapy for it. Some wounds leave scars.

He and Derek spoke at the same time. "Sorry, sir, you first," said Montgomery.

Derek spoke calmly. "Also, we got the test results back. Positive ID for Uys."

Montgomery started. "You sure?"

"One hundred percent Uys's arm was in the Warrens' freezer. So the girl was not the first evidence of teleport. It was your man."

Montgomery cleared his throat. "And the dog?"

Derek laughed. "You're an old softy, aren't you? How are you even in this business with such a big heart?"

"It's why I'm in this business, Boss."

"Fair enough. Well, so far it's still alive. No adverse effects, from what we can tell. In fact, the vet says he's healthier than a racehorse. We didn't dissect it. Especially now that the research people have Uys's arm to play with. The dog's actually being moved to Fort Meade and I'll let you know. You can have a conjugal visit if you want."

"Prettier than some of my exes."

After the call, Montgomery pulled up the video of the rest stop on his laptop. He saw the four young people get into a 1968 Chevy Nova. They drove around to the eastbound side and one of the boys placed a credit card on top of the pump. Later, his IT team told him it was picked up by a single mom, who used it to pay for her gas. She left it on the pump as well. It was then used by two more visitors until the last one took it with them and they bought dinner at a McDonald's twenty miles to the south. Very clever, but not clever enough.

The Chevy Nova was a pretty conspicuous car. It must have been the Warrens'. It had decades-old historic plates. The four youngsters were diligent about skipping tolls. These weren't dumb criminals. Regardless, the car was now under 24/7 surveillance—tracked heading west on I-40. There was really only one place I-40 went that had any history with this operation. And that was New Mexico, the Very Large Array, where the project files indicated radio signals had been captured that were part of the video source. The other alternative was the West Coast—San Diego was a jumping-off point for Mexico where many intelligence agencies operated without hindrance.

His phone pinged. He'd asked for updates every fifteen minutes with a location and a link to a live tracking map. Now he wanted to see them move. He got nervous if they stopped, and when they did, he asked for an observer to give him a live view. He suspected others were tracking them as well. The Warrens were in the intel chatter. And therefore, the Warrens' credit cards were being tracked. And therefore... Did these kids know how much danger they were in?

His team had to swap vehicles regularly so as not to alert the four suspects. This was now a protection operation. He was to protect these four, making sure they didn't get nabbed, robbed, killed, molested, or otherwise harmed.

He shivered slightly when he realized how close Haretsebe had been to being shot in the face in South Africa, by his own asset. But that was normal in this business. One minute you're drugging and kidnapping a warlord in Afghanistan, ready to execute him in a basement, and the next you're safeguarding his family, releasing him as an ally, and funding him to take over a province and help take out a different warlord who has been bought off by the other side. Politics makes strange bedfellows, as does spycraft.

25. Amarillo, Texas, and West

"Three of the comments seem like ones we should respond to." Claire was reading alongside Harry in the back seat. "Listen to this. It says, 'I've got your back, Super Nova. Colonel Mustard.' That could be Colonel Montgomery."

"Or could be that fake one who called you." Harry crinkled her brow.

"We'll go crazy if we second-guess everything."

"True. Number two says, 'Where's the metadata? Will pay dollar signs for that.' That's gotta be someone who knows about the metadata. But it sounds a little scary. Like, how would we pursue this? And how would they know about the metadata?"

"Show me the money!" yelled Phil from the front seat. Spitz pounded the wheel loudly in support of that.

"I don't know. What's the third?"

"'The deal is still on. Best, Monty.' What's that mean?"

"That's gotta be the fake Montgomery."

"Right. Or maybe?"

Phil sounded concerned. "Doesn't it bother you he mentioned a Super Nova?"

"It's just a star reference," said Claire.

"This is a Chevy Nova. He or they know our car," Phil said.

"You think he's coming after us?" Harry asked.

Phil looked back again, staring at the older girls. "Or informing us that others know what we're driving. If he were coming after us, I don't think we'd get a warning."

"Fuck."

"Well, I'm hungry, and there's no getting around that," added Harry.

They drove in silence for a bit and decided to get takeout just outside Amarillo.

"How many credit cards do we have left?" Claire asked.

Phil held up the plastic bag. "I've got one more, and then we're into the cash, which is about twenty dollars and change, so... that's not good. This car is thirsty."

"Okay, let's get some food and eat in the parking lot. We need Wi-Fi. We can upload another video. Harry can put it in her blockchain wallet. And Kathode should have sent her address in a DM."

The group got takeout ribs at a one-story pink building that looked like it had been around since the Great Depression but luckily had Wi-Fi.

"This is a great idea," said Harry, her hands and face covered with sauce. "These things you call wet wipes are brilliant."

Claire scrolled on a laptop. "Holy crap, there's like a thousand comments on the videos. They are going totally viral."

"Why?" said Phil.

"People think they're actually alien. I mean, we said nothing about them being alien. But apparently there were snippets floating online already. There's already debate and trolling and flaming and all that internet crapola."

"Cool cool," said Phil.

"Any word from WisPR?" Harry asked.

"Bad news there. There were a few questions from members and I quote, 'What kind of fucking drugs are you on, Clarity?' But it looks like lots of members have left the group. Looks like most of them, actually. Nobody wants to be seen as nuts, I suppose. Let's see, those who are left are you, me, Lollipop, Kathode, and a bunch of dormant members who haven't been seen in ages."

"Great, we killed WisPR," said Harry. "We're murderers. Message board murderers."

"Chatroom assassins," Claire said, sipping from a straw plunged into a tall iced tea.

"Internet inquisitioners," said Phil through a mouthful of ribs.

"Email exterminators."

"Session slayers."

"Four horsemen of the 404."

"That's way too esoteric," said Claire.

"Bite me," Harry said, her mouth full of food.

Harry's voice turned serious after the laughing and chewing stopped. "We should test the technology again."

"Test it how? And why?" Claire asked.

Harry turned toward Claire, her eyes narrowing. "I'll tell you why. We need to test our setup. Look, you and I have both gotten it to create effects. But we still don't really know which codes cause which effects. I made a list of codes and videos and effects. It looks like the effects somewhat relate to the videos. The green glowing thing came from the wedding video where the aliens' hands did the same green glowing thing as our hands. The shield that I created in Prieska came from a video where a shield is used. The floating effect, where all the stuff in the room started to float away, came from a video where some items float, like children's playground equipment or something. See? There's some sort of relationship between the content of the videos and the effect of the broadcast of metadata from those videos."

"Okay, that almost makes sense. It goes back to what you told me about Mr. Wright's explanation: It's all a gimmick or a toy included with the video."

Spitz turned in the front seat and showed his phone to Claire and Harry. He had typed, "Mr. Wright said not to use them. It's too dangerous."

Harry nodded. "Yes. Very dangerous. I'm not sure what we test. The effect could be catastrophic. We really don't understand what they all do."

Phil spoke up. "Let's just test the green glowing hands again. That'll at least tell us if our setup works."

They all agreed this was a good idea.

Claire put her trash in a bag and passed it to the front. "We've been here a while. The video is uploaded. I'm on a pretty tight VPN but I think I'd be more comfortable if we headed out." Her voice had a question in it, but also a firmness.

"You're the boss," said Phil.

"I'm not the boss."

"You are definitely the boss," Harry said.

"Okay, fine. I delegate our testing destination to Phil."

Phil looked at his map. "Cadillac Ranch. It's just outside of town and it's, like, supercool. Old cars half buried on some dude's farm."

"Make it so," said Claire.

Spitz hit the steering wheel three times rapidly and drove out of the parking lot.

"I'm not the boss," Claire said as they got back on I-40, heading west toward Cadillac Ranch.

Harry responded, "You are the boss. Because this certainly isn't my fault. And I'm gonna blame the boss."

Claire made a snorting sound. "Well, it's not my fault."

"Really?" said Harry, her voice with an edge that hadn't been there before. "I didn't know your mentor until he magically appeared at MeerKAT, after I was nearly blown up. You think it was coincidence. Well, maybe it wasn't! Maybe you told him to gum up my life! I was just an intern. I was set to publish and get my degree and teach. Like a normal person. And that's about all I can hope for with a game leg."

"I didn't know he was going to 'magically' appear, either."

"You didn't?" Harry scoffed. "You really didn't? You spent years learning from this guy and you did not know he was messing around with some type of military technology? I find that hard to swallow."

"That's a terrible thing to say. Mr. Wright was my teacher. He didn't confide in me!"

Their voices rose as they argued back and forth.

"The internship at MeerKAT was going to give me the credentials to get a teaching job. I don't have the options that a pretty, two-legged girl has. I've got one and a half legs only. You know what that's like? I should be at MeerKAT now, doing research, not driving through Texas running from international assassins! I still can't really get my head around this. Where are we? I mean, where the fuck are we?"

Phil turned to the two of them. "We're here. At Cadillac Ranch."

As soon as the car stopped, Harry got out, almost falling, clearly upset, her cane bouncing against the car door.

"Harry, wait," Claire said.

"Just fuck right off," Harry said, and she headed off across the well-worn dirt toward the nearest of the jutting, spray-painted cars that made up the odd sculpture garden.

They watched her go. Spitz got out and looked at her limping figure, the silver-topped cane occasionally flashing as she walked toward the upended Cadillacs. It was late morning, and though a few cars were parked along the roadside in front of the entrance, it wasn't crowded. He followed her, intending to keep her in sight but also to keep his distance.

"Should we stop them?" asked Phil.

"No, we've been crammed in this car for too long," Claire said. "We were bound to get on each other's nerves." She paused, then said, "Phil, you know your father..."

Phil spoke quickly. "Just... I know." He said it with a finality that ended the discussion.

Claire blinked tears away. "Goddammit. Get the transmitter and stuff hooked up. I'll get the laptop booted."

*Satellite Pollution May Hide Videos, Says Researcher

Reprinted in edited form from Science World's Weekly Science Update:

"More Videos Are Coming, but We May Not See Them," Says Australian Researcher

It is postulated that the Zoonerat videos were captured at approximately 820 megahertz during a six-decade period beginning after World War II, when large scale radio telescopes were first deployed. Why there have been no further transmissions and whether interstellar transmissions are the source of the Zoonerat videos is still under debate. Many cosmologists agree with the possibility that the videos are of extraterrestrial origin. A recent poll by graduate student George Edelman of Cornell University in the United States found that 81 percent of living authors with published articles in top astronomy and cosmology journals agreed with the statement that "Current science demonstrates that the Zoonerat videos are of extraterrestrial origin and therefore prove that intelligent life exists elsewhere in the universe" (*Journal of Surveyed Anthropology*).

The question remains, of course, why there have been no more transmissions. The answer may come from calculations recently published by a newly appointed professor at the University of Melbourne, Dr. Wanarat Suppakaran.

Dr. Suppakaran has calculated that the transmissions were captured into orbit at the photon sphere perimeter of Sagittarius A*. Therefore, the signals are likely orbiting spherically rather than on the equatorial plane of the black hole. If the radio waves are still orbiting, there may be another batch of transmissions sent Earth-ward in twenty to thirty years as additional transmissions "leak" from their trajectory. This conclusion is derived from Dr. Suppakaran's calculations of the centripetal force acting on the radio waves.

"While we cannot say for certain when or even if additional radio transmissions will reach Earth, the math shows a high probability that they should come in batches lasting sixty to seventy years at a periodicity of twenty to thirty years," she said in a recent lecture. "I hope to clarify the period as the next phase of my research. However," she added, "increased radio pollution by satellites and the very low power of the original transmissions means it is possible that new transmissions may be masked."

Response to the published paper, which is part of Dr. Suppakaran's doctoral dissertation, has been mostly positive. "This research is important because it gives real researchers ammunition to debunk other videos that have been released but are clearly fake," said Professor Simon Mui of the University of Honolulu's Department of Sociology and author of the recent book *Separating Fact from Zoonerat*. "No transmissions have been received in many years, but we hope more will be forthcoming. We are scanning the skies diligently all the time."

*Zoonerat Phonetics

Excerpted from *Xenolinguistics and the Zoonerat Language,* Ajij Locke, PhD, University of Birmingham

Zoonerat, the language, aka Zoonerese, Zoonerish, is an alien language first heard in the Zoonerat Videos released anonymously on the internet. Though there is significant and controversial divergence of opinion on the veracity of its existence, many academics agree it is a nonhuman, extraterrestrial language and can be translated into a human comprehensible format with significant modifications resulting in conveyance of general intent.

Of the estimated seventeen known Zoonerat videos, many of them have accompanied sound extracted from encapsulated cymatic imaging (see Singh, et al.). Whether the audio is correct in synchronization, sound-space or pitch-space, wavelength, elongation, tone, and other metrics has not been demonstrated conclusively, but is generally accepted.

Under the assumption that both synchronization and a representative sound space are correct in the cymatic deconstructions, by matching visual and facial cues, hand movements, context, tone, and body movements, Shiffer and Locke, et al. have produced a Zoonerat corresponding table (ZcIPA) to the International Phonetic Alphabet (IPA) and the Extended International Phonetic Alphabet (extIPA). Theysan and Xi, et al. have produced a Zoonerat dictionary for each video with many words and possible translations with contextual commentary.

Though it is questioned whether the morphology of the Zoonerat sound-producing organs can be elucidated given the current dataset, the sounds of the videos that correspond to speech communication have been divided into equivalents on the ZcIPA. One of the more significant additions is the *sliding alveolar* set of phones. These exist both fricative and plosive. Whether an alveolar ridge even exists in Zoonerat morphology is a subject of dispute; no video has shown the interior of the Zoonerat mouth, though several videos have shown the Zoonerat mouth to look surprisingly similar to the human mouth, including lips, teeth, and tongue. Locke postulates that the Zoonerat upper mouth structure allows for the human-like tongue to slide during vowel production against a malleable palate to produce the tonal /ɘ/ (closed, mid-central unrounded vowel) or the /ɯ/ (closed, back unrounded vowel). In addition, it appears that between six and twelve phones are non-pulmonic, e.g., percussive, clicks and a thrumming that cannot be made by human sound organs. There is some speculation that a theorized sub-sonic component, which would not be sub-sonic to the alien listeners, is analogous to cetaceans on Earth.

26. The Battle of Cadillac Ranch

"The dot's not moving." Montgomery's voice was tinny on speakerphone. His agent could not answer because of a fairly large Texas-style beef rib covered in shiny barbecue sauce held in both hands and his teeth. The agent clumsily pulled the beef rib from his mouth and attempted speech, a bolus of meat interfering with his tongue. "It should be moving now. They barely left here ten minutes ago. They should drive for several hours."

"This isn't a discussion. Pull up your map. They've stopped."

The other agent, also busy with a rib, looked around. "You forgot wet wipes."

Montgomery's voice was drill-sergeant clear. "Stop what you are doing. Find them. Get a visual. Now."

"Sir. Yes, sir," said the first agent. He opened his window and tossed his plate out. "Those were sooo good. We're coming back here."

"Call me when you have eyes." The conversation was over.

The other agent opened a plastic bag and tossed his mostly uneaten ribs in as well and divided up some napkins. He clicked on his phone and a map appeared with an unmoving red dot. The nondescript sedan threw rocks as it exited the parking lot.

At Cadillac Ranch, Harry hurried away from the Chevy Nova, which Spitz had parked on a dusty stretch of access road 100 yards east of the entrance, away from any other cars. Stabbing her commemorative cane on the gravel with each step, she entered the former pasture where a half dozen titular automobiles stuck their rusty, graffitied asses out of the ground.

Spitz leapt out of the front seat to follow, wanting to tell her how much he sympathized with anyone who got into an argument with his sister, but this was difficult for him to do.

He had never talked. Not a word. Not a whisper. No sound with any meaning in any language had ever been produced by his mouth in his thirteen years. Aphasia, dysarthria, mutism, dumb. He'd heard all the terms, read all the terms. Idiopathic, the doctors called it: independent of any known cause.

But everyone knew the actual cause. He'd been cut from his mother's lifeless body, her heart dead and her womb at 87 degrees and falling by the time Spitz's seven-month-old, blue-tinged form was placed on a tiny, heated table. His Apgar score was zero when he entered the world, dead like his mother, who lay on a gurney nearby. She had been extracted herself from a car wreck off Route 2 not ten minutes prior, cesarean'd out of the crushed steel uni-body. Her husband's corpse wasn't freed for two more hours.

But wonder of wonder, miracle of miracles, a few minutes of direct massage by a particularly dedicated nurse brought the infant back to life. The nurse moved with an intensity of action that other nurses would describe for months to come. A fetal heartbeat was detected, though the infant's blood oxygen was 62 percent and wouldn't go above 75 percent for another two hours.

The baby boy lived in the neonatal intensive care unit, gaining strength, getting bigger, correctly responding to stimuli. But he made no noise expect a very weak mewling. "How's the kitten?" the nurses asked each other at shift changes. He was the silent child. When hungry, he waved his arms and kicked. Sometimes, if he was severely uncomfortable, such as when he spiked a fever of 102 for two days, he thrashed his head side to side. But he never cried, just made a plaintive whistling. When he recovered enough to be sent home to Grandpa Chuck, who relied heavily on Millie to help care for the infant, even that sound stopped.

Spitz knew he was different. Other children produced language at the special education center where he attended daily classes. The children with severely reduced mental capacity, the children with various affectations because of genetic abnormalities. He heard them. He understood them. But he did not speak to them.

At age eleven, having read most of the books in the classroom, he joined a regular visitation group to the public library. There he had access to the internet and learned that Broca's area of the brain, in the prefrontal cortex, was partly responsible for speech. As he read, he touched his forehead. Wondering if his Broca's area was damaged or missing.

Spitz enjoyed the special education program. He was given freedom to do much of what he pleased. He was quiet and thus low maintenance. Once he learned to write, he stood near a teacher with a piece of paper saying he needed glue or scissors or to go to the restroom. He knew enough sign language that he could sign for these things as well, though he wasn't deaf and he wasn't placed in the deaf program, so his teachers rarely knew sign language.

He thought of these things as he watched Harry awkwardly limp away from the car where she'd been fighting with Claire. Spitz felt Harry was a kindred spirit of sorts. Her one leg was much shorter than the other, making her disabled as well. He wondered if she'd attended a special school when she was young. He wanted to protect her like he wanted to protect the special needs kids with awkward gaits and wandering eyes, but she didn't seem to need any protecting.

After she'd passed a few of the Cadillac Ranch car sculptures, he watched her choose a spray-painted fender and lean against it. Her shoulders shook and he thought she might be crying. He couldn't yell to her, but he went to her side and stood there, silently. She finally noticed him and turned, her face glistening with tears.

"Oh, great. You see me like this. Don't tell the others."

He shifted on his feet.

"*Hele.* I didn't mean it like that. I know you can't actually tell... with words... verbally. Okay. Awkward. I meant, keep it to yourself. Can't talk, eh? You are good at keeping secrets then."

He smiled and nodded.

"You cheeky bastard." Then she burst into tears and grabbed his hand, pulling him forward so she could wipe her face on the bottom of his T-shirt.

"Gross, I know. And thanks," said Harry, wiping her eyes. "You can't even tell a joke, can you? You'll be a great therapist one day."

Spitz cocked his head, questioning.

"Means you're a good listener."

He nodded and they both looked out at the farm field silently.

He reached down and pointed to her leg and raised an eyebrow.

She reached down and rubbed the thigh of her shorter leg. "Yeah, it hurts. You know? Not sure if that's from all this moving or not having two canes. Not even sure if I'm imagining it, but I know I'm more coordinated. More upright. Probably a few centimeters taller, right?" She looked at him.

Spitz shook his head. He looked at her with furrowed brows.

A tear rolled down her cheek and then she dipped her head and took her hand back, wiping her eye. "Stuff always happens to me and I have to just... go with it, you know? I try to be on my own, but it's hard. I've never spent this much time with other people. I like my space." She looked up at him after a moment. "You don't understand, but that's okay."

After some time, Harry stood. Spitz moved to help and she waved him away. "No, I can manage. Always have. But thanks. Let's get back before they miss us."

The two walked away from the standing sculptures and headed back toward the entrance gate, over a well-trod patch of ground where a vendor sold postcards and T-shirts.

Spitz walked ahead of her and then stopped, his gaze moving from the Chevy Nova, parked outside the gate, to the line of cars across the street, where the rest of the tourists had parked. Harry wasn't sure what she was seeing. She hurried to catch up to Spitz, but he was already running out of the gate and to the right, down the road toward their Chevy Nova, which sat by itself, empty. Where were Claire and Phil?

Then she saw. Straight across the street from the ranch entrance, among the tourist vehicles parked on the access road, Phil was in a wheelchair being pushed toward an SUV and Claire was walking in front of a woman whose hand was covered far too conspicuously with a sweatshirt.

Racing after Spitz, Harry understood the situation immediately, but the choice of action was unclear. Would making a scene put her friends in danger? Spitz reached the Chevy Nova and kept the car between himself and the abductors, opening the rear driver's-side door and getting in. Harry hobbled faster, trying to formulate a plan. What was Spitz doing? Moving fast was easier than she expected. Perhaps she should have switched to a single walking stick years ago. Or maybe all this moving around was strengthening her leg?

One abductor was a man in a kind of hunting jacket. He opened the rear hatch of a blue SUV and moved the wheelchair as if he were going to put Phil in the back, like a sack of potatoes.

Harry reached the Chevy Nova, and through the open rear door she saw Spitz fiddling with her laptop. He was logged in. How did he know her password? He reached down to the floor and lifted the small antique TV and twisted the knob to power it on. A sudden, terrifying realization occurred to Harry.

She nearly jumped at him, placing her walking stick on his lap and whispered loudly, "No! You can't do that. You don't know what will happen."

Then she was on the ground, next to the Chevy, where her view of the abductors was blocked. Spitz had simply lifted his foot and pushed her chest away. The door slammed and she muttered in frustration, reaching for her cane and standing, staring into the window where Spitz was head-down, busy on her computer.

Agitated and angry at being pushed away, Harry walked around the front of the Chevy and saw Claire and her abductor near the driver's side of the blue SUV across the street. There were few tourists in the bright morning and Harry rapidly considered her options. She did not want the abductors to take her friends. Once they were gone, well, she didn't want to think about it. They must be stopped or delayed at this moment.

The female captor, a tall, blond woman who could've passed as a high school cheer coach, like any of the Texas tourists they'd seen at truck stops, gestured with her arm wrapped in the sweatshirt, and Claire turned to open the driver's-side rear door. For a second, across the road, she and Harry locked eyes. Claire looked apologetic, or weary, or maybe resigned. Harry almost stopped, annoyed and frustrated by Claire's look of defeat.

Harry's anger rose. There was Claire, doing nothing. Claire, who was the linchpin in this clusterfuck of crazy. Claire, whose nutjob tutor dropped digital nuclear bombs on their laps. Claire, who entangled them in all kinds of danger. Claire, who had saved her life in Prieska. Claire, who had been her online friend for years. Claire, who didn't care about her short leg, her skin color, or her background.

Ire boiled over like a burning pot of gruel. She limped toward the duo across the street, toward the parked blue SUV, its rear door open, her feet moving in a manner more coordinated than she'd ever felt. Pushing words through her clenching jaw, the decorative cane stabbing at the pavement, she called out, her voice loud, clipped, and forced. "That is a really nice wheelchair! Is that the XL model? Where did you get it?"

The woman's head spun away from Claire, looking at the diminutive, lopsided Black woman approaching rapidly. Harry accepted she might get shot but she hoped it wouldn't hurt too much. The thought gave way to a bitter fury.

Maybe the bloody bitch will shoot my bloody short leg!

She was shouting now, nonsense, whatever came into her head. "I've been looking for a wheelchair just like that! It would be much better than this cane! It's quite attractive!" She raised the decorative staff and grabbed the middle with her other hand. Her words, accent, and volume drew attention from the half dozen tourists coming and going through the parking area.

As long as I can keep this bitch's attention, I've done something right.

She hefted her cane, awkwardly skipping on one foot, almost falling over. As she did so, Claire—stupid, bloody Claire—raised the laptop.

I'm definitely going to be shot.

Her thoughts careened; ugly memories were dredged up. Classmates in primary pushing her down. Her "mobility aids" kicked under a car. Being told to hide because important people were coming to the shop. Cars honking as she limped across a street. Mutterings of *dwarf, hobbit, troll, gnome, cripple.* The invisibility. At. Every. Moment.

They took my bloody shoes!

She was running. She'd never run before. Mrs. Warren's high-tops gripped the asphalt deliciously. It was joyous and dangerous. Freedom and speed and wind. The silvery finial of the cane clicked in her hands.

Claire's laptop came down on the sweatshirt and a retort sounded across the parking area. This was followed by panicked yelling from all directions. The blonde grabbed her forearm, the sweatshirt fallen and the gun rising toward Harry, too late. The abductor's angry curse halted in a wet whisper as the rapier punctured upward through her diaphragm and into her heart.

27. Vidi. Audivi. Didici.

Spitz knew his responsibility. He was the one who protected the weaker kids, the disabled kids, the kids with crutches like Harry, the kids with lazy eyes, mouths that didn't close when they chewed, fingers and hands that couldn't grasp, feeding tubes, breathing tubes, colostomy bags, shunts, helmets, wheelchairs, hearing aids, eye patches, the ones who couldn't follow directions, who hurt themselves if nobody was watching. He protected those kids. He watched them and he pulled the teacher's arm when there was a problem.

He was the one who had gotten the easy ride so far. He didn't have homework. He didn't have hard classes like Phil and Claire. He'd always been given the first slice of cake, gotten his ice cream before everyone else, opened his presents first. If he had trouble tying his shoes or making a meal, someone always came and helped, even though he didn't need any help. They never yelled at him. They never chastised him for being slow or clumsy, even when he was slow and clumsy on purpose. He'd tested this, and he'd found that his disability was a shield from a much harder life. Millie and Grandpa Chuck and teachers and strangers always provided him with extra support because he couldn't talk.

He never told anyone that not talking wasn't a problem. He tried not to take advantage of his disability, but sometimes he did. He could. He had. But it always made him feel guilty. Claire had to cook and clean the camper. Phil had to behave and do homework.

Mr. Wright had told him, "It's not a problem, it's a feature. My mouth has gotten me into more trouble than I can say. Pun intended. You should own that shit. Enjoy it. It's a gift. It's a curse, but it's also a gift. Pun not intended. In fact, pun nonexistent."

Now he saw he could do something good. Something that didn't require talking. He acted. It helped that he knew what to do. He'd watched Mr. Wright play with the codes long before the... the... the foggy thing, the silent thing, the time when he ran, when his foot... when Mr. Wright and the barn disappeared.

He'd seen Mr. Wright use the codes. He'd never really understood, but it all clicked when Claire brought Harry to Tennessee. He watched. He listened. He learned.

As Claire and Phil were being led away, Spitz hustled low over the dirt to the Chevy and opened the back door as quietly as he could. Harry was behind him, but she wasn't fast. He grabbed her laptop from under the seat and unlocked it. He knew her password, having seen her type it many times in the last few days. Unfortunately, she wasn't in agreement with this. As gently as he could, he gave her a push out the door with his foot. Because he was gonna drop a bunch of stuff on that man's head.

At least, he hoped that would happen.

Spitz had a good memory for words, what people said. And actions, like what Harry or Claire typed on the keyboard as he watched.

Mr. Wright always talked while he puttered, a constant patter. "This stuff is unpredictable. Like fire. Original fire. The first humans who made fire didn't know what would burn and what wouldn't. That must have been fun, right? And scary? And fun. I can only imagine how many forests they torched while experimenting, right? I mean, there's more than a hundred thousand years between us learning to create fire and... everything else. Must have been a blast, pun intended. These codes—fire. Don't play with fire, okay? Well, play a little, but not until you're older, okay? And not in the house.

"These codes turn your hands green," Mr. Wright had said. "I've used a few of them. Not sure how many I have, but they only work once. Quantum probability functions, I think, within the fabric of space-time. Muslin? Canvas? Tweed? The linen of space-time. And that's the weird thing, right? Because I'm using a dipole antenna here and I've also used a monopole, and they both work the same, which is weird. Directionality of the signal is based on the antenna direction, but it shouldn't matter. The flux density of the transmission should fade when you point a monopole antenna, but the codes appear to take the minimus of the integral of the toroid, rather than the max. So you just point the antenna and voilà—quantum space-time bouillabaisse, blended smooth. No more Campbell's Chunky space-time. Now you can get Minkowski flavored smoothies. Mmmmm mmmmm good. Spitz, you got that?"

Spitz had stopped playing with the toy cars near the workbench in the barn. Mr. Wright's voice had been calming, like a good teacher's.

"The physics here isn't straightforward. Experiments aren't always repeatable, which is super annoying. The more you poke, the more your results change. Crazy stuff, right? So you use a code once and then it doesn't work, or it *probably* doesn't work is how I think it actually works, but the tail end of that curve is asymptotic with the x-axis, so it's effectively zero."

Mr. Wright nodded at the computer screen. "These codes cause stuff to float. That violates a dozen laws of physics. The math isn't even possible in three dimensions. It doesn't counteract gravity, because you can't do that, so it must bend space-time within some relativistic distance from the broadcaster. It takes seven parameters. Three are dimensions of the ovoid, one I think is strength or excess de-curvature. One is a time expansion coefficient, which I don't think we should change from the default, because whoa—I haven't done acid since college and I'm not sure I want to now, right? Nothing I can describe without a lot of Greek letters. Might relate to persistence of time dilation within the ovoid. I leave most of them defaulted. You know, Spitz, I'm not sure you are absorbing what I'm saying, but stick around if you can. I love that you don't interrupt me, which is super convenient. Best student ever. Or worst since you don't ask questions as well. Shit, little dude, you don't want to play with this. Very dangerous. Like, please don't be modifying space-time without adult supervision, okay, Spitz?"

Mr. Wright had teleported the barn cat once when Spitz was there, the cat disappearing in a green ball, along with a chunk of floor and a small radio transmitter. The cat and objects reappeared on top of the hay bales with a loud pop. The cat jumped sideways to the wall and hid up in the rafters for a few days. So Spitz thought he knew how it worked. And Claire had Mr. Wright's notes and had successfully brought Harry to Tennessee.

"In the broadcast script," Mr. Wright had said as he worked, before he sent the cat across the barn, "I put in a granular topographic and elevation dataset of the Earth with lat/lon coordinates, like within a few millimeters. Amazing what you can download nowadays. So if you put in the lat/lon, it'll figure out the angle and such if your device has GPS. The software converts our angles to their angles, our distance to their distance. They use, like, 512 degrees. But if you just want a very local teleport, you need to do the vector by degrees from perpendicular to gravity for vertical, and degrees from the broadcast toroid centerline for horizontal, you know—positive for distances along the antenna and away from the ground plane, negative for well, you get it, right? Or just point the antenna. Should work. But don't do this without an adult, okay? I said that already, but it's worth repeating. Whatever we send has to be completely enclosed in the ovoid or you end up like the barn floor, slicey dicey very spicy, okay?"

Spitz knew the basics. "Point the antenna," Mr. Wright had said. The parameters, however, were going to be a problem. Not a big problem. But a problem. Spitz wanted to drop the whole car on the man who was pushing Phil in the wheelchair. But he didn't know how to move the whole car. Also, he didn't want to drop the car on Phil. Plus, he didn't want to cut Harry, who was near the car, in half. Or cut himself in half. Those would be really, really bad things. He looked at the man and did a rough guess at the distance in meters. Mr. Wright had taught Claire vectors at one point, and Spitz had watched as Claire did that homework. He knew a vector had two numbers. He knew a meter was how tall he was when he was four years old. It was marked on the barn door. He had to move fast. He thought hard about the vector homework.

A direction and a distance. Claire used a direction and a distance.

Spitz glanced out the window. He guessed the man was twenty-five meters away. Twenty-five of the meter sticks Mr. Wright had in the barn. Twenty-five of his height when he was four years old. Spitz figured he just needed to be close. When you're dropping a big piece of car on someone's head, close is good enough. On the man's shoulder would work too. Or even his foot. Anything that would distract him. For direction, he turned the radio until the antenna was pointed at the man. That would be zero degrees, maybe. As long as he wasn't pointing at Phil, who was off to the side a bit while the man was moving stuff in the back of the SUV. He hoped this was how the code worked. Then Spitz wanted a vertical angle above the man's head. He wasn't sure. Straight up was ninety. Half that was forty-five. He didn't want to fall too far. So he thought maybe half that again and a tiny bit less. He hoped.

Twenty-five meters distance.

Zero degrees horizontal.

Twenty degrees vertical.

He left the other parameters blank. The walkie-talkie transmitter button locked with a click. The antenna was pointed at the man. He pulled the TV close to his thigh. As he pressed Enter on Harry's laptop, he heard a gunshot and his heart nearly stopped.

Nothing happened. On the screen, the parameters had reset. He'd expected to feel something. Then the computer faded, leaving an outline in the space where it had been, as if he'd looked at a bright light and turned away. Outside the car was blackness. Something had happened. But it wasn't blackness. There were stars. Lots of stars. The car was gone. He was floating.

He felt disoriented and sick to his stomach, like when he hung his head down from the side of his bed. There was no down or up, even as he contorted his body. Just stars all around. A great cloud of light, a haziness, stretched across his field of vision, and he used it like a natural horizon, oriented it across the world. Dizziness faded and he floated. His clothes were all there, his body unchanged, but all the surrounding objects were gone. He was alone in space.

Hunger gnawed, not like he needed to eat, but like when you are bored and you want a snack just to have something to fill your empty hands. He desired something, a nameless thing. There were no words for it. A shape, like a tossing ring or a basketball with buttons or maybe dials. This thing he imagined could make music, and it could return to him if he lost it. It could talk for him. It could speak when he couldn't. It would read his thoughts and say what he wanted to say. It would open his mind and clear it, revealing knowledge that he kept hidden. Memories would be made whole. He wanted that thing. He wanted to play with it, to own it. Soon it would be for sale. His parents should buy it for him. Maybe Grandpa Chuck could get it as a gift. His hands grasped in the darkness of space, where it was just out of reach. And as he got closer, his desire increased. Maybe he would get it as a birthday present, this thing. It would be so wonderful to possess it. His friends would be jealous. Phil would want it too. Maybe he could find another one for Phil. Because everyone should have one of these. Everyone needed one. Everyone wanted one.

Just as he got close to it, he was blinded by a ferocious light.

Then he was falling, and he landed hard on the seat of the Chevy; his knee came up and slammed the laptop into his nose, and a sharp pain radiated through his cheeks. Sunlight and a breeze tussled his hair. Brightness filled his eyes. The seat canted hard, and he tumbled off and rolled onto the pavement. The laptop slid onto the asphalt and closed.

Coppery liquid dripped over his lips—blood. Wiping his face with an arm, he took in the scene. The man who had been pushing Phil was on the ground under the ruins of a cored section of the Chevy. Claire looked at him aghast and wide-eyed from the other side of the SUV, then shook her head and yelled at him to get Phil, whose wheelchair was coming to a stop nearby. Spitz pushed it around the blue SUV.

There, like a scene from a manga, stood Harry, her chest heaving, her eyes wide and bright, standing over a lifeless form. She placed a foot on the body and, with a strong pull, yanked her sword from the prone figure, its gleaming blade soiled by blood. Spitz stopped pushing Phil and stared in awe. Harry lifted her sword to vertical and her gaze traveled its length, her straight lips and fierce countenance judging the performance of her blade, a soldier's task for a thousand years. This was not the limping girl who had just wiped her tears on his shirt. Her severe and beautiful face pivoted, scanning the scene, scanning him—ethereal sclera glowing below black pupils. He'd never seen someone so powerful in his entire life.

Claire screamed at her brother and Harry, who were having some kind of staring contest. "We have to go! Harry! We're taking their car. Get the keys from the woman. Probably in her pocket. We need to get out of here. There may be more." Harry moved slowly, as if stunned, and Claire hoped she'd heard the instructions. Bart Warren's Chevy was ruined, an empty cylinder where the rear driver's-side seat had been, the parts now haphazardly scattered behind the attacker's SUV.

A crowd was gathering, people taking videos, making calls. She ran around the back of the blue SUV. "Yeah, put some pressure on that." A bystander was looking in horror at the man with the head wound under the pile of auto parts. She lifted the TV, the inverter, the laptop, and the radio from the pile of detritus that littered the ground, while Spitz was maneuvering Phil into the back seat.

She turned and ran back to the driver's side just as Harry was wiping her sword on the stabbed woman's pants.

A man appeared near her and looked at the stabbed woman. "Holy hell, a sword?"

"Get out of my way," Claire said in a tone she had never heard herself use before, a tone of finality that allowed no discussion. The man hesitated and held her gaze for a moment then stepped aside.

Claire got in the driver's seat and looked in the back. Phil was lying down on Spitz's lap. Harry slid into the passenger seat and handed her keys without a word. Outside, chaos fomented in the parking lot as the crowd jostled to gawk and help. Key in ignition. Turn key. "Everyone good?" Claire called out.

Without waiting for an answer, she rolled down the driver's-side window and yelled out, basically right at the man, who was watching with an expression of either awe or surprise, and talking, an earpiece snugged against his pate.

"We're taking a hurt person to the hospital. Please make way!" She honked the horn, and then Harry leaned over and honked it for her as she backed up quickly, running over some metal from the mess behind the car, bystanders moving aside. She gunned it and headed down the access road toward the I-40 ramp.

28. Kath's Ode

"Unit! What's going on? Stop the alarm!"

"Lorelai, your father is having a minor brain issue, perhaps a stroke, perhaps something else. I recommend calling 911."

Fists clenched at her sides, Lorelai spat a response. "And what will they do? Just take him away! And he won't return. They'll take him to hospice. What's the treatment for a stroke?"

The AI simulacrum of her father spoke from the nearest monitor. "At a hospital, they would likely inject a clot-inhibitor such as a tissue plasminogen activator."

Lorelai put down the tablet. "Do we have that here?"

"Yes. It is in the medication closet. It will be labeled TPA."

"How much do I inject? And where?" She was already rummaging in one of the several cabinets built flush in the planetarium's wall.

"There are other protocols that an emergency doctor and their team would follow..."

"Shut the fuck up and tell me how much to inject of the TPA and where." Lorelai was organizing an IV stand and medical equipment on the hospital bed.

The simulacrum spoke quickly. "Into a vein. It is recommended that you inject seven milligrams because of your father's history of ischemic stroke. You can then put another sixty milligrams in the IV infusion bag over the next hour. Do you know how to set that up?"

"Yes, of course." Lorelai began working and when she was done, she asked, "Status?"

"He appears to have stabilized. It is also recommended that he have a head CT."

"What will that tell us? Nothing. It will tell us fucking nothing. Nobody is going to help."

The simulacrum pursed its lips. "Language. And, to be fair, you are correct. It is unlikely to change his treatment directives at this time."

Lorelai fell into the chair next to the hospital bed, where her father lay unmoving, surrounded by medical equipment. "Exactly. Reset the alarms. If he's stable, start the video blog from where I left off. I want to know what happened to my parents. No, wait, let me get some popcorn."

When she returned with a bowl and a drink, she glanced around and blinked against the strangeness. There were three of them: three visions of her father. The living one in the hospital bed. The AI version, the simulacrum she'd built, staring at her from a screen nearby. And in the paused video, her father lay with her mother in the same hospital bed, in a cinematic blog he'd made more than a decade ago.

Her father, her son, his holy ghost.

"Did my father assemble and edit the videos?"

The simulacrum spoke. "No, James Nine did not assemble this video. It was automatically compiled by a program that selected clips in time series order by movement, sound, dialogue, cadence, and..."

"Never mind. Continue."

A montage of scenes followed: James and the nurse made food in the kitchen. Orion lay at Kath's feet on the bed, his head on his paws while she slept. Vacuum robots wandered empty hallways and moved quietly under the hospital bed.

James stood in the planetarium. He looked at the suspended igloo of camouflaged Faraday cloth above the hospital bed where Kath lay. "Do you want me to dismantle it?" he asked.

"No, I like the lights." Her voice was weak.

Lorelai interrupted. "Pause. How much time is left on the video?"

The simulacrum answered, "About thirty-seven minutes of video remain."

Lorelai said, "Continue."

In the video, James puttered at the conference table in the planetarium, the surface piled with detritus. Scribbles from Germaine's visit littered a nearby whiteboard, showing the transmitter array as three black ovals of interconnected symbols. The video zoomed in. The transmitters were squares with squiggly arrows emanating to show transmission. Germaine had written a Cyrillic word next to one transmitter, with a question mark after it.

James pulled up his phone, searched for something, and said loudly, "Shit."

He held up his phone to the camera. The Cyrillic was translated to "five lamp" and then he spoke to the viewer. "That's a pentode. And goddamn, I'm an idiot. I substituted solid-state electronics for the original tubes. Holy crap. I'm functionally the dumbest person ever to live."

With a marker, he wrote some calculations on the whiteboard. Then he looked around, frantic. He ran out of the planetarium and to the kitchen, the video blog following his movements through the house. He climbed onto the granite island and grabbed a hanging pendant lamp. "Shit. Shit. Shit."

He ran through the house, looking at lights, opening up drawers. Looking for something. Then he was back in the planetarium scribbling on the whiteboard. The subtitles displayed his mutterings:

Possible. Vacuum. Idiot. How could I?

His fingers skimmed over the keyboard. Monitors above him went white and pages appeared. An article from a science magazine on how to build a simple tube transmitter. He copied the schematic. A shopping site appeared on one screen. Pentodes, tetrodes, other tubes appeared. He ordered 100 and selected overnight delivery.

"Joan!" he yelled, and the nurse came. "I'm going to be doing some work on this table. Please touch nothing. Keep Kath comfortable, okay?" She nodded and left.

The video sped up; the sun raced by the picture window.

James and Joan were sitting at the worktable. It was piled with electronic parts. Joan was putting tiny wires into connectors. James adjusted miniature potentiometers on circuit boards and inserted tubes into sockets.

A pile of completed transmitters gathered on one end of the table.

Joan complained in several clips.

"Mr. Nine, I need to get Kath bathed, okay? And I'm not trained for this."

"Mr. Nine, you need to eat."

"Mr. Nine, I need to eat."

James simply nodded and waved her away as he worked. Many hours later, it was night—the windows showed a dark sky and stars. Kath woke. He didn't bother to get Joan.

Kath sounded tired. "How's it going?"

"I think I should ask you that." He sat on the bed, offered her a child's sippy cup.

"What are you doing over there?" She pressed a button, and the bed rose to a sitting position.

"Don't be angry if I tell you?" She shook her head. "Listen, when we did the experiment, the broadcast, we... I mean, I, messed up. I substituted solid-state transmitters for the vacuum tubes the Russians used."

"That shouldn't matter."

James cocked his head and frowned. "Shouldn't it though? We don't know how this works, but we suspect it's alien or at least it's outside of normal physics. Isn't it possible that some type of difference at the quantum level occurs when electrons transit vacuum from anode to cathode?"

Kath looked at him. "You've lost it, dear. No, there's no way for that to be different."

He continued, "Vacuum tubes were only around for a very short period. Maybe fifty years at most. They got subsumed by solid-state electronics quickly and they've all disappeared. Do you know how many vacuum tubes are in this house? Zero. Well, there's one in the microwave, but it's shielded, not glass. There's none. Thirty years ago, there would have been dozens in lightbulbs and TVs. Now, nothing."

"You are really crazy," she said.

He looked hurt.

She saw the sadness in his face and said, "I appreciate it. Let me help. Where'd you get all the tubes?"

"Internet! I'm almost done. Gonna install all the new transmitters in a bit. You can help by making sure I haven't missed any as I put them up."

She nodded.

The next shot showed James and Kath asleep on the hospital bed. All the transmitters had been swapped for the new ones with tubes. Joan came and changed the IV bag on the stand.

The video cut again. Kath was sitting up. She had a laptop on a stand and was reading some of the Russian spec docs. She looked more alive than she had in days.

"You inspired me. I've got a bit of energy," she told James, not looking at him.

He grunted and got up.

"Let's do this?" he asked, pointing toward the new transmitters.

Kath nodded without turning her head from the laptop.

James lowered the igloo over the hospital bed and opened his laptop at the conference table. He narrated to Kath what he was doing.

"I'm running diagnostics. I'm firing up the transmitters."

There was a noticeable hum. On the speaker he heard Kath say from inside the igloo, "Come look."

He stuck his head inside the tent and looked. The forty-eight vacuum tubes were glowing and a warm pink-orange light suffused the room. It made Kath look healthier than she had in weeks.

She lifted her hand into the glow. "Very pretty."

"If these are on for long, we're going to need air-conditioning." He waved at the glowing tubes. Then he left the tent.

"Starting the broadcast... What music?" he asked.

"I think something... You decide," Kath said. And James got a playlist running from the music player hanging on the IV stand. "Both Sides Now" started.

Nothing happened.

"Feel anything?" James called into the tent.

"Not a thing," came Kath's reply.

Lorelai was rapt, watching the video of her parents.

James raised the igloo. "Want to go for a walk on the patio?"

She nodded and he helped her get up, but she could not stand.

"Let me get the wheelchair," James said. She stiffened and looked like she was going to refuse, then nodded okay.

The camera cut to the patio. He wheeled her outside, where some hummingbirds flittered about the red bird feeders. The Sandia Mountains shimmered in the khaki landscape. They stopped under the sunshade.

"What will you do when I'm gone?"

"Probably redo the kitchen."

One corner of her mouth lifted. "Asshole. Seriously, an asshole."

"I don't know, Kath, I don't like to think about it. I'm still hoping, you know."

Her eyes were closed, her face tilted toward the sun. "I know that, but you need to be realistic."

"I'm not going to argue with you about that. That's why the alien videos are so important, for the realistic attitude."

"Goddammit, this is serious." This time a corner of her mouth turned down.

"Fine. Serious."

"Serious," she repeated.

"I have no plans. I'll make sure the foundation honors your love of science."

Kath blinked. "That's actually very sweet. And I didn't bring out any tissues."

James held out his shirt and Kath wiped her nose on it.

"A treasured moment," she said afterward. "What about Lorelai?"

"She'll get enough. As they say—enough to do something, but not enough to do nothing."

The scene changed to the kitchen.

The simulacrum looked at Lorelai, perhaps expecting her to pause and ask for details. She shook her head. The video continued.

Joan told James, "Kath hasn't eaten today. I have the morphine. When you are ready."

James looked at her blankly.

"Just letting you know," Joan said.

James nodded. "Is that what happens?"

Joan continued doing dishes. "Yes. That's what we do. It's kinder. You don't want her hanging around in pain for no reason."

James looked at the ceiling. "Go home, Joan. Get some sleep. I'll call you when I'm ready. I'll be with Kath alone now."

James took a tray of what looked like squash soup and saltines from Joan and headed to the planetarium. The tent was still suspended from the ceiling, and the leftover parts of the build and the equipment were scattered on the worktable. The space had a disorganized, warehouse look. The camera panned and the feeling was depressing with all the detritus and clutter.

"You need to eat," said James, placing the tray on a rolling cart that could extend over the bed where Kath lay.

"Not hungry." Her voice was a whisper.

"Don't care," said James, ignoring her and setting up the meal. He took a spoonful of soup and held it to her mouth. She opened and he gently spooned some soup in. She struggled to swallow and coughed.

"No more," she whispered. "No more, James." She shook her head. A rivulet of soup ran down her chin to her neck. It was orange against her pallid skin and made her look vampire-like. He quickly wiped it up and moved the tray away.

"Okay. What do you need?"

She was staring at a monitor, perplexity on her face. "You left up the Russian spec sheet." She nodded to the screen where it was still displayed.

He climbed in next to her. And they looked at it together.

"And?" he said.

"Why is it 888,888 cycles for broadcast frequency and some other sweet number for channel width?"

He almost laughed. "I don't know. It's all just a bunch of hogwash, probably."

"It's a puzzle. I like puzzles. Do you think there's a Russian word for hogwash?"

"Probably something like 'bear spittle' or 'salmon poop.'"

She coughed. "Unfair trying to make me laugh."

"You literally asked for it."

She turned back to the Russian spec sheet. "What do you think *conversion factor* means? It says thirty-two." James opened his mouth to speak, but she spoke first. "Let's say you were an alien species and you had four fingers."

"Okay, let's say." He took her hand and gently moved her thumb into her palm.

"Would you count in base 10?"

James looked at the spec sheet. "What are you saying?"

She pointed her chin at the spec sheet. "It's a puzzle, isn't it? Why is the cycle counter such a neat, even number? Numbers don't work that way. Numbers in science aren't exact. You don't experiment and end up with 15,000 miles or kilograms or degrees; instead you get 15,492.6 or some other number.

You don't get 3 as the ratio of circumference to diameter, you get 3.14159 et cetera."

She spoke calmly and clearly, her illness not evident. "Arabic numerals are base 10 for a variety of reasons, but a primary one is that we have ten fingers. Science is not base 10. That's just a convention we use. Some Native American tribes used base 5, and the Babylonians—"

James cut her off, getting out of bed. "And the Babylonians used 60, which is why our circles and measurements of time are multiples and factors of 60." He spun at her, his hands on the bed. "What have you got?" She had a Mona Lisa smile on her pallid face. "What have you got?!" he repeated.

She looked again at the spec sheet. "If you had four fingers, you might count in base 4. But probably you'd count in base 8, right, because eight fingers? Or you'd go up exponentially to base 16, like most of our computers; that's more efficient. But the answer is on the chart. It's printed there. The Russians figured it out. Base 32. It says it right there." She pointed to the screen where one line of the chart said 32.

He practically ran to his computer, which was on the table strewn with paper and pencils. He opened it and began typing.

"It's all base 32," she said, almost too quietly to hear.

As soon as he could, he called out, "277,094,064. That's the cycles in base 10. Do you think?" He let the answer trail off. "And wait..." He typed more, then let out a yell. "Holy fucking shit!"

"What?" said Kath, trying to shift her body. "Don't keep a dying cancer patient in suspense. Very rude."

"Kath. The aspect ratio of the videos. It's 2,114 pixels wide by 1,057 pixels tall, right? In base 32 that's 222 by 111. That can't be a coincidence."

He ran over to the switch on the wall and the tent started to drop.

"James," she called out, "what are you doing?"

"We're going to try this. Now."

He was dashing around the room, moving items out of the way of the lowering igloo. He turned on the internal microphone and the speakers so he could hear her as she spoke from within. "James, it's just a math puzzle."

Lorelai stared at the video. Her heart pounded. She nodded, whispering, "Yes, Mom, it's a math puzzle. I like math puzzles, too."

James was on his computer, booting up the broadcast program. "No, it's not just a math puzzle. It's what they used. And it's what we'll use."

The video cut again. It was an hour later, according to the running time counter on the screen. James lay next to her again, staring at the ceiling. Apparently, the broadcast had had no effect. A sheen of sweat beaded on his forehead.

"We're still missing something..." he said.

"No, James, we're not," she responded.

"You said it was a puzzle. Maybe it's more than one puzzle."

"But it's just a puzzle. That's all. It's time, James. Just be with me. Now. At the end."

"Now is not the time. Not now." He paused, then took her hand. "You said that if you had four fingers, you might use a numbering system that's a factor of four. And you calculated base 32. And that appears to fit some aspect of this experiment. The numbers work." He stated this as a teacher would. And she responded.

"Agreed."

"So, let's say this is alien technology. Let's go back to that crazy assumption." He was looking at the screens.

"Fine, aliens make TV shows."

"It means we have to question all of our units. If they don't use base 10 for counting, they certainly don't use centimeters or inches or miles or kilograms or..."

"Seconds," they both said.

"Jinx," she said.

"So, what unit of time do they use?" James looked at her.

"James, look at the spec sheet. It must be on the spec sheet. What's that value—a million N?"

James pondered. "A million what? What's N?"

Kath wrinkled her forehead. "A million nanoseconds? That makes no sense, that's just more seconds. How would aliens use our seconds? They would use something else. What's *N* short for in terms of temporal measurement? Nugget? Neptune? North Pole?... Look on the Russian original. That's an *H*?"

James moved over to the laptop. He pulled up the Russian alphabet.

"What that is... That's an error in translation. That's not an *N*. In Russian, *N* is *H*. I mean, the sound for the letter *N* is written in Russian as what we call the letter *H*. So the translation changed the *H* to an *N*. That's *H*. But scientists use English—even Soviet scientists used our letters, not Cyrillic, for many scientific terms."

"Okay, a million *H*? A million *N*? What is that? Health points? Hemoglobin? Hieroglyphics?"

James snapped his fingers. "Could that *H* be hydrogen?"

Kath pointed to the screen. "Well. It actually says hydrogen right on the spec sheet."

"So a million *H* what? *H* is an atom, so is that a width? Could it be the width of hydrogen?" James lifted both hands in question.

"You know, when all this alien stuff came up, I was searching on the internet and there is a paper from the 1950s by Cocconi and Morrison. They suggested if aliens existed and were trying to communicate, they'd use the hydrogen line as the carrier signal."

James typed rapidly. "It's 1,420 megahertz."

Kath pondered, then said, "That's the frequency. We need the wavelength."

"Twenty-one or so cm. So a million of these? What does that mean? I'm actually confused. What were we calculating?"

Kath paused. "We need to know how much time is spent for the 888,888 cycles in base 32. That will give us the cycles per second in base 10."

James closed his eyes and leaned back. "Jesus, that hurts my brain. You've lost me."

Kath yawned and shook her head, smiling. "Well, listen, if you had to define time simply using a hydrogen atom, how would you do that? What's a standard that would be the same for aliens and for us?"

"The only thing constant in the universe is the speed of light. Thank you, Mr. Einstein."

"Not entirely true. Death and taxes," she said deadpan.

"Now? This? Now?" He sounded astonished.

"Okay, fine. Again, what's that wavelength of this hydrogen identifier?"

"Twenty-one centimeters, approximately."

"What if they used the time it took light to travel twenty-one centimeters as their basic unit of time? We use a cesium atom, but maybe a hydrogen atom is what they used?"

"How would that work?" James asked. "That's an infinitesimally small period."

"Well, not if you take a million of them. And, incidentally, it's right here on the chart." She nodded at the screen in front of her.

"Right, let me calculate. Okay, a light beam travels the wavelength of an ionizing hydrogen atom in... well... it's a tiny number, seven hundred trillionths of a second." He frowned.

"Right, of course it's small, but a million of them? That might be some equivalent of an alien second."

"That's still only about seven ten thousandths of a second. Would these four-fingered aliens use such a teeny-weeny period of time? Maybe they live only a few days? Or they move really fast compared with us? If you live only a few days, you might use a much smaller measurement for your smallest unit of time. Like dog years versus people years, right? Maybe that's why they're so advanced. They've lived a million generations in the time humans have been on Earth."

Kath looked at him. "I know you are joking, but it's not out of the realm of possibility."

"It is definitely out of the realm of possibility. And sanity."

Kath ignored him and continued thinking out loud. "Assuming convergent evolution is like a biological law in the universe and that similar conditions result in similar outcomes over eons, let's assume their lifetimes and their sense of time are within range of our own. There's some logic that they should come up with measurement systems similar to our own. Their own equivalent of a second should be near ours."

"Then a million hydrogen vibrations is far too small to be an alien second."

Kath and James were silent for a moment. Then Kath said, "But not in base 32."

"Yes, yes, yes!" James shouted quickly.

"Convert a million, meaning one followed by six zeroes, from base 32 to base 10, then multiply by... the time of one transit of the hydrogen line wavelength by a photon. That should give us the equivalent time of an alien second to our own."

James was already typing as she said this and announced triumphantly,

"About three quarters of a second. In fact, .7559 and more of a second. Holy shit."

They were both silent for a moment, and then Kath spoke softly. "That actually works. That is a possible measurement of time."

"Okay, give me a moment and let me convert this original 888,888 cycles in alien base 32 to our own numbers. Okay, I get about 366 megahertz. If I look that up on a radio allocation chart, it looks like it's just general use radio. Some radio-location, some satellite, and so on. I'm not sure if that's important. What do you think?"

Kath didn't respond. James looked and saw she was asleep.

The next scene showed James in the kitchen, placing food in the microwave.

The camera switched again. James was entering the planetarium with a tray of food and a box of juice. Kath was up, looking at her laptop. She turned toward him, her eyes tired, her skin papery, but smiling. "I must have dozed off. When I woke, you were gone."

"Apologies, sick girl, I had to polish off some kung pao."

Kath gave a grimace. "Don't make me vomit, but I am thirsty."

James set the juice on the rolling patient cart next to the bed.

"Thank you, darling," she said as James opened the juice and poured it into the sippy cup. She took it and drank carefully.

"Let's try this treatment with the new frequencies," James said.

Kath was silent. She had not tried to drink again. She faltered. "I... I don't know if I can last much longer, James."

"We are going to find a treatment that works."

"But I'm hungry and can't eat. I'm in pain and I'm tired. I shit my pants a few days ago, goddammit." Orion growled and then put his head back down.

"I can get you something..."

"No, no more drugs." She shook her head. Her eyes were slightly wild. "I can't handle more nausea, more disorientation. These last few days when I was off some of the meds and could read again—they have been wonderful. I miss this"—she waved at the screen, at the tent—"work, this progress. It's as if it's not just for me, it's for some common goal. Doing this was fun. It was a change from the drudgery of seeing my body wither away, my hair fall out, my body wash down the shower drain and get flushed down the toilet. I want to do this because it's something we did together, but once this is done, I'm done. Do you understand?"

James sat next to her on the bed, his eyes shiny. His head moved up and down in understanding. She lifted her hand to his face to touch his tears.

James leaned down and kissed her. He lingered on her lips longer than expected.

He backed out of the tent and glanced at her as the tent flap closed. The camera zoomed to his view. Her ashen skin and what was left of her locks against the pillow. The bed was rumpled, bright and clean. It was dark except for the Christmas lights strung about. Less like an adult play fort, the bed looked like an oasis in the middle of a wide desert under an ebony sky sprinkled with the salt crystals of stars. She was a pearl in the bed of an oyster.

Lorelai let out a whisper. "Mom."

The video showed a split screen, with James on one side and Kath in the igloo on the other.

James let the Faraday fabric tent drop. He was alone in the planetarium with the hulking camouflage igloo. For a moment he took a breath and looked around, up at the ceiling and then directly at the camera.

Lorelai felt he was looking right at her, from twelve years in the past. They locked eyes for what seemed an eternity. Then he approached the worktable where the computer keyboard sat.

He turned on the microphone to the tent.

"Music?"

Kath's voice was electric over the intercom. "Whatever you want."

"Orion. He's just lying there. Good?"

"It's fine, James. Orion is fine."

James thought and put on Enya. "Orinoco Flow" started in the background.

"Good choice. Fits the mood," he heard from the speakers.

"Testing."

Kath's voice was clear, sounding stronger than it had been in a while. "Ready, James."

He powered up all the transmitters. A faint hum suffused the planetarium. The vacuum tubes warmed up in their prescribed circles around the interior of the framework. Inside the tent, the faint glow of the tetrodes brushed the interior with a peachy light.

"First, I'll run through all the circuits, testing. I'll let you know when the broadcast starts."

"Okay," she said. Her voice faint. Her eyes closed.

James stood over a keyboard, looking at the monitors. "I'm going to run the broadcast. It should only take about a minute to run through the broadcast a few times. Call out if you feel anything. I'm broadcasting the code as it was given by the Russian text file from Germaine."

He pressed the Enter key.

One screen showed each digit of the code as it was broadcast. In the igloo, Kath lay peacefully. James watched as each digit was broadcast, just a few milliseconds for each one, then faster. So fast Lorelai couldn't read them. There were thousands of digits in the code, so it took a few seconds to complete.

As soon as the last digit in base 32 was sent, Lorelai heard her mother's voice over the speaker. "Tell Lorelai..."

A blinding green flash. Blackness.

Lorelai sat stunned for a moment and then started bawling.

29. Interstate 40

The blue SUV was in the slow lane sandwiched front and back between two semitrailers and, for the moment, relatively hidden. Claire's heart had slowed from a pounding staccato after hightailing out of Cadillac Ranch. In the rearview mirror she confirmed Spitz and Phil were still in the vehicle—an irrational thought, but her mothering instincts were on overdrive and she couldn't help but worry that she'd look in the back seat and find it empty.

She hadn't even had time to process what Harry had just said, out of the blue, in a manner that seemed far too casual.

"I think my leg is longer. And it really hurts!"

It took Claire a good minute to respond. "What?" was all she managed.

Harry looked at her. "I think my leg is longer. It's... It's somehow longer." She was trying hard to stretch her legs out in the front seat, but the cramped space made it difficult.

"Spitz, switch with me. I want to get in the back," Harry demanded. She grimaced in discomfort.

"Harry, please, I'm driving." Claire sounded concerned.

Spitz slid himself as far as he could to the door and Harry began maneuvering.

Claire complained, but Harry said, "Just drive. We can do this."

After significant acrobatics, with only one kick to Claire's head, resulting in an annoyed "Seriously?," Harry managed to climb into the back seat and Spitz got himself into the front passenger seat, with additional minor, panicked complaints from Claire.

"I wish we had something to eat," said Harry as she stretched her legs across sleeping Phil's lap. Then she added, "Yup, my leg is longer. Like it's legitimately longer. This is crazy. And it hurts. A lot. But it's kind of a bloody good hurt, you know? Oh, *hele*. It's not a good hurt." She rubbed it hard and clenched her teeth. "Fuck. Fuck. *Modimo nthuse*. And you guys have made me curse far more."

Spitz took out the sword from Harry's cane. He ran his finger down the steel, pulling it back quickly to avoid getting cut. Looking around, he pulled a purse from under the seat and rummaged in it until he came up with some tissues, which he used to clean the dirtied blade.

"How is that possible?" Claire asked, glancing in the rearview mirror.

"Well, Claire of the hair, my sister from another mother, maybe it has something to do with the fact that I crossed space-time and went through something that... oh shit... that hurts… nobody on Earth has ever done? Or magic. Either one. Because I'm pretty sure I haven't been to a doctor in a while. Or maybe I have. Maybe I'm currently waking up from anesthesia and this is all a dream, right? Maybe that. *Merde*, I'm losing it. *Modimo nthuse*, I'm so hungry. And my leg feels hot. Like burning up and being cut open."

Claire looked at the rearview mirror again as she spoke. "And, just to be clear, this isn't normal, right? Your leg hasn't grown before?"

Harry scoffed. "Are you for real? That's a serious question? Whatever I said before about you being super smart or whatever, I apologize. Because you are dumb as a rock and my leg is longer, which is the craziest thing of all the crazy things." Harry threw her head back. "Aaaaaaagh."

Claire was looking back and forth between the rearview mirror and the road. "Harry, hold on, we'll get some ibuprofen or something when we stop for gas. In the meantime, can you tell me if Phil seems okay?"

"Right, yeah, he's fine. But I'm not! He's... drooling and snoring. Whatever they gave him must be the good stuff. Holy... hurts!"

Spitz held up a small case, open, showing several syringes.

Harry stared at it and asked, "Where did you get that?"

Spitz held up the purse. He started pulling things from it. After turning in his seat, he handed a white envelope to Harry. As she took it, he jabbed a syringe into Harry's leg.

"Fu.... whoa, whoa... why'd you do that? Oooh, that hurts and... oh, that's good..." She put her hand on Spitz's and pulled the syringe from her leg before it was all injected. "I think half dose is enough, okay? *Hele*... whoa... great stuff."

Claire turned just in time to see the syringe pulled from Harry's leg. "Spitz! What the actual fuck! You cannot just jab people with syringes!" He shrugged and put the syringe case back in the purse.

Harry gasped as a thick wad of cash fell from the envelope, her words slurring. "Ssss... okay. It's the good stuff, my Claire hair. There's thousands of *pula* here! *Pula*!" She took some of the cash and smelled it and then threw some into the front seat. "This must be from that woman. Oooh. Please stop for snacks. Or don't, I don't care anymore."

"That woman? The one you skewered?" Claire laughed. "You want a snack? How about shish kebab?"

Harry was giggling, her words merging. "Shishdoe you jokey about that. You make me laugh and I'm... flyyyyyyyinnnnnggg." Her head lolled sideways against the seat.

Spitz pulled his hand from the purse and nervously held up a gun by the trigger guard.

"Put that down!" Claire looked around, making sure there was no car next to them on the highway. "Spitz," she pleaded. "That is so unnerving. Please, please, I know you are all Wizard of Dorothy because you dropped a car on a witch, but that makes me so nervous. Please put that away. Put everything away. Put the guns and drugs and money away. Please."

"Drugs and guns and money," Harry murmured, awake again. "Anything else in that purse? Like biltong or Ho Hos?" asked Harry. She babbled a bit in another language.

Spitz held up a bunch of makeup and a small zippered bag over the back seat so Harry could see.

Harry pawed at his handful of stuff, grabbing it. "Nice makeup. Not my colors, but nice anyway. And, oh look, tampons and pads!"

Claire shook her head. "Holy shit, you are punchy. Remind me if you are ever in a bad mood to pull your leg. Get it? Pull your leg. I'm so funny."

Claire smirked at the rearview mirror. Harry was asleep.

Spitz put Harry's laptop on his knees and opened it, pressing the power button to start it up. He turned to Claire and gave her a thumbs-up, and tapped the dashboard once.

"Good, glad that wasn't destroyed." She said it without looking at him. The gas gauge read a quarter full. "Do you see a map? How much farther to Kathode's? Do I have enough gas?"

Spitz shook his head.

"No map. Typical. We'll stop at the next major town. Those two can sleep it off. You get some sleep too since you'll drive after that. I'm too wired to sleep now."

Spitz stared at the road ahead and turned to his sister.

"What?" she asked.

He indicated the back seat with a slight movement of his head and lifted the decorated cane, which was between his knees.

Claire tightened her lips. "Yeah, I mean, if you're asking what I think you're asking, then... I'm not sure. I hope she's okay. You don't just stab someone and shake it off." She paused. "I don't know what's it like to be disabled and then... this, but we're all going through some stuff, you know? And thank you for doing whatever it is you did back there. You and Harry really came through."

Spitz stared out the window at the desert.

30. Tucumcari, New Mexico

Claire's eyes fluttered once and she sat up in a panic, the rough highway shoulder under her tires shaking the steering wheel with the buzz of a wasp's nest. Signs for Tucumcari and its myriad Route 66 attractions appeared more frequently and she made preparations to exit, hoping a gas station and a bathroom were near. Beside her and in the back seat, her charges slept. Spitz lay back, snoozing, seemingly unconcerned with the fact that he'd probably killed a man by dropping half a car on him. Claire wondered about the psychological damage such a thing could do to a thirteen-year-old boy. Kids were adaptable, they said. She hoped so. She looked in the rearview mirror. Phil glanced back at her.

"You're awake?"

"Yeah," said Phil, uncharacteristically quiet.

"Cat got your tongue?"

"Just thinking. Still fuzzy from whatever they gave me. Can you tell me what happened? I only remember some woman in the front seat with a gun."

"I... It's a lot, Phil. Just know that we are safe now and headed to Albuquerque. Harry and I have a friend there. When we have time, I'll tell you everything. Right now, I'm pulling off. I have to pee like a racehorse. And you should probably drink a bottle of water and flush that stuff out of your system."

Phil leaned his head against the window and said nothing.

Harry moaned in sleep and twisted her leg on Phil's lap.

Claire drove down the muted main street of Tucumcari, where refurbished roadside motels painted with neon cacti and advertising cheap rates lined the sidewalks. She spied a gas station and pulled in. This was smaller than the ones they'd gotten used to on the interstate, just two pumps and a tiny convenience store.

Once she stopped, she nudged Spitz to wake him up. He rubbed his eyes, looked around, and nodded, unbuckling his seat belt. Harry groaned and took her feet off Phil. She looked pale, and shivered as she rubbed her leg. Her eyes were ringed.

Claire looked at Harry. "Darn. You look bad. I'll get you some ibuprofen from the store. You want anything else?"

Harry looked at her through swollen eyelids. "I need food. Anything. Sugar, fat, protein. Get me some of those beef sticks. Doughnuts. Candy. Here..." Harry held out the envelope with the cash in it.

Claire nodded, took the envelope, and looked in it. She made a noise and shook her head.

Spitz got out of the car to stretch, as did Phil. Claire handed Spitz and Phil some cash from the envelope. "Pay for a fill-up, get snacks inside, and we'll meet back here." She gave Spitz the keys and headed to the store. The two boys followed. Harry lay her head back on the seat, her forearm over her eyes.

Spitz emerged from the store quickly, having laid down a bunch of bills on the counter and pointed to the car at the pump outside.

The clerk didn't look up from his phone. "You can fill up, get your change when you're done."

Leaving the little shop, he saw a woman standing by the hood of their car and a man rummaging in the front passenger seat, bent over with the door open. Spitz didn't see Harry and his heart pounded. He couldn't yell and didn't want to go back into the store and leave Harry alone in the back seat while these two people did whatever they intended to do.

The man leaning in the passenger seat stood and turned to the blonde woman. He had Harry's laptop in his hands. They spoke briefly and looked around, seeing Spitz standing near the door. The man stared at Spitz and opened his jacket, showing a pistol in a holster, and then they turned and walked away. The man twisted back, keeping an eye on Spitz.

Spitz reached into his pocket and pulled out the small gun that had been in the purse. It had a lavender grip.

The weapon blurred in his vision, his hand sweaty and shaking, and he lifted his eyes. The couple jogged across the street and split around a sedan. Spitz looked back and still didn't see Claire or Phil. He lifted the pistol, aiming at the man carrying the laptop, squinting. His eye itched and he wiped it with his free hand. His finger extended, caressing the trigger, the rough grip against his palm.

Time slowed. The man's back grew large, broad and exposed, prominent, as big as the car. He lowered the barrel toward the man's foot, tiny from this distance. The black barrel shook, nearly vibrating. His own foot, with the missing toe, tapped the ground rapidly.

The object he saw during teleport appeared, floating, blocking his vision, spinning rapidly, faster and faster. The façade of the real world washed from his eyes. His head vibrated with pain. Then, a memory.

"Don't be modifying space-time without adult supervision."

31. The Orange

An array of sunlit specks dappled the ground under the apple tree. Mr. Wright heaved the barn door open. Spitz watched a memory unfold from three years before. There he was, younger, playing with Phil.

"The Orange!" yelled Phil, kicking up his heels as he ran past Spitz to a small ride-on car and pushed it out of the barn. Phil and Spitz jumped in and put on their helmets. Phil ripped open a bag of potato chips—*Fun sized! Kettle Cooked in Massachusetts!* Said the bold print.

"So," said Mr. Wright, checking their helmet straps. "You know what you're doing?"

Phil nodded. "Drive randomly. Watch the dial."

Millie called from the back door, "Phil, it's time for the math tournament."

Phil stood up in the seat, looking at Mr. Wright. "Dad, I want to drive The Orange! I don't want to go to the math tournament."

Mr. Wright shared a look with Millie standing in the doorway. Her stance was not the kind that allowed discussion.

"Sorry, Little One. Spitz will drive it today. You go with your mom and Claire. Claire needs your cheers. And your mom needs your company."

Phil's mouth curved down in a pout. "Nobody cheers at math tournaments. She always wins anyway." Phil put his helmet on the seat and trudged in true boy sulk toward the house.

Spitz heard Millie say to the aggrieved Phil, "We'll get ice cream afterward, okay?" Then he heard the door slam.

He scooted over to the driver's seat and turned to the dash. He tapped a circular gauge on the highly modified miniature vehicle and looked at Mr. Wright with his eyebrows up in question.

"Yes," said Mr. Wright, "keep the random measurement above ninety if you can. I'm tracking you on the app." Mr. Wright held up his phone. "If the random measurement goes below ninety, brake and turn whichever way you haven't been turning. Or speed up or something. Keep your movements random."

Spitz nodded and tapped his helmet in agreement.

Mr. Wright continued. "It'll send me random numbers, which I'll use. Just stay in the neighborhood, on the sidewalks, in the yard. Do not drive in the street, okay? The Johnsons said you could use their yard too."

Spitz nodded again and tapped the readout that showed charge.

"I've ungraded the RNG's battery, so you should be good for a while. When it gets below thirty percent, head back."

Spitz pressed the gas pedal, and the little electric car trundled off. As he drove, the gauge labeled *Randometer* fell slowly. Spitz turned the wheel and it rose and stalled. He turned the wheel again and the dial rose and then fell. Why Mr. Wright wanted the Randometer high, Spitz didn't know. It had to do with the lights and the radios and the space stuff. Often in the barn, Spitz handed Mr. Wright pliers, soldering irons, wire, clips, tubes, little integrated circuits that looked like spiders, tiny two-legged things called capacitors. Mr. Wright had him tune radios, sort resistors, wipe dust off the computer monitors, and keep the cat from knocking things off the workshop counters.

One of the funnest activities was driving The Orange. It was really the RNG, said Mr. Wright, which stood for random number generator. But Phil called it The Orange, and it was painted bright orange with wires and antennas and other neat stuff zip-tied to its modified body.

Spitz drove The Orange out to the yard, zigzagging, slowing down and speeding up, to keep the Randometer as high as possible. The most difficult concept for Spitz was reminding himself that slowing down could raise the Randometer to a very high number if he had been going fast for a while. A quick stop also worked, but only sometimes. It was actually quite difficult to keep the Randometer high as he drove the little car on the sidewalks around the neighborhood, detouring into driveways and walkways as best he could, chasing the occasional squirrel.

Eventually he got bored and drove The Orange back to the barn. The Randometer began falling, but Spitz didn't have the interest without Phil, who always narrated their journeys, turning them into adventures. So by the time he returned to the barn, the readout was lower and hovered around fifteen.

The barn door was closed, and he pushed it open and ran in to see what Mr. Wright was up to. Mr. Wright saw him and frowned, looking unhappy. And then Spitz saw another man standing in the middle of the barn. They both looked at him.

The visitor took out a gun from his jacket and pointed it at Spitz.

"A complication. So go," he said. "Go to your father."

Spitz looked at Mr. Wright, who didn't correct the man. He just nodded and patted his thigh.

The visitor took out his phone and made a call. He held up the hand with the gun as if commanding everyone to stop talking even though only he and Mr. Wright were in the barn.

"You are ready?" he said into his phone. Then the visitor turned to Mr. Wright. "Your phone will ring."

Mr. Wright's phone rang.

The visitor said, "Answer. Answer. On speaker, please. I want to hear."

Millie's voice on the other end was surrounded by the sounds of traffic. "Colin. Can you hear me?"

"Yes, I can hear you."

The visitor smiled in a way that made Spitz very afraid.

Millie continued, her voice normal and loud, trying to be heard over traffic. "Listen, thanks for calling the tow truck. The guy is here to fix our flat. He just needs your approval. Can I put him on?"

Mr. Wright spoke, his voice quaking. "Millie, where are you?"

"Just off 495 near Hudson. How did you know we had a flat?"

"Millie, just stay..." Mr. Wright looked at the visitor, who was no longer smiling but shaking his head. Mr. Wright's shoulders slumped.

The visitor turned to Mr. Wright. "Are you going to give me a demonstration?"

"Yes. Just let them go. You don't need..."

Millie said, "Colin, who is that?"

The visitor pointed his gun at Mr. Wright and drew his hand over his neck. Mr. Wright ended the call.

The visitor cocked his head and spoke again. "Now, there is some urgency. Please demonstrate what you have. And the child can watch, as a kind of bonus, right?"

Mr. Wright told Spitz, "Stay next to me."

Mr. Wright pointed at a metal cage that occupied the center of the barn. It was the Fair Day cage, and Mr. Wright sometimes had Spitz and Phil stand in it while he did things on the computer. They pretended it was a jail cell or a shark cage.

Mr. Wright nodded and spoke as a countdown started on a monitor. His voice was flat. "The broadcast will start soon. I have several of these codes. They can, apparently, be used only once. This is one reason I am reluctant to execute them. Nevertheless, I will use one now. Join me in the Fair Day cage."

The visitor said, "Remember the phone."

They stood together, awkwardly, in the cramped space. For a moment all was still. The computer counted to zero.

"Look at your hands," Mr. Wright said.

The visitor looked at his hands and made a noise. He raised his arms and followed Mr. Wright out into the barn from the enclosure, turning around, watching the glowing tendrils. In the daytime brightness of the barn, the glow was not strong, but it was there, emanating spookily. The visitor took out his phone and made a short video.

"How does it work?" the visitor asked.

Mr. Wright shook his head. "I'm afraid that would take a very long time to explain and requires mathematics that are far beyond any discussion."

The visitor was entranced by his glowing hands and nodded, waving his arms gently. "But you understand it? You know how it works? I want all your codes. Everything. Put it on a USB and give it to me."

Mr. Wright looked at him. "But, they don't just work that way. That wasn't the agreement."

The man sounded angry and mean. He pointed the gun at Mr. Wright. "You met with the military! You broke the agreement!"

"I had no choice. They found me. Probably the same way you did. Others are chasing this technology, which is all bullshit anyway. I told them nothing. And there's nothing to tell."

"The USB. Now." The visitor pointed to the phone. "The flat tire, right?"

Mr. Wright pursed his lips and moved to the computer. He grabbed a USB from a dish of them and put it into a computer.

"And, if you put garbage on it, I'll come back again," the man said.

Mr. Wright sounded angry. "I got it! I got it! This USB will be useless to you if you don't know how it works. You need some knowledge of physics. A lot of physics, okay?"

Anger curdled the visitor's voice. "You met with the military, Mr. Wright. You haven't produced anything of value." He waved his gun as he spoke. "And now your son has seen me."

"I have no other demonstration!" yelled Mr. Wright.

The man screamed in a way that sounded like an angry cat. "That's the same bullshit I've seen!"

Spitz moved against the workbench, the edge pressing in his back. The man looked at Spitz. Spitz stared back. The man lowered the gun and fired at the ground. The sound was deafening. Spitz gasped and fell to the floor, holding his foot. The pain was incredible. Worse than anything he'd ever felt.

"You shot him in the foot!" Mr. Wright screamed. "You fucking evil bastard! You shot a child in the foot!" Mr. Wright bent down and cradled him. He whispered, "It's going to be okay. Just take deep breaths."

Spitz looked at Mr. Wright. His expression was different from any Spitz had ever seen in the past. He looked as scary as the visitor. Spitz shut his eyes. The pain in his foot was terrible. A wave of chills ran through him. His body twitched.

The man spoke wearily. "Well, I was aiming at the ground, but perhaps I missed. Now, I want to see a better demonstration. I can't go back with some story of this bullshit that looks like a dollar-store light stick."

Spitz heard the unique staccato of duct tape unwinding and then felt pressure on his foot so strong, the feeling in his toes was numbed. He opened his eyes and looked down. The front of his shoe was wrapped tight in the gray tape. He saw no blood. Mr. Wright caught his eye and signed to him, "*Run. Five.*" Spitz looked at him, eyes wide, tears running down his cheeks. Mr. Wright repeated it, and Spitz raised his head and dropped it to his chest in a big nod, pounding his fist in the dirt one time.

Mr. Wright spoke to the man. "Okay, okay. I will do as you say. Just lower the gun. I will demonstrate. But let me help the child first."

"The flat tire, remember?"

The pain brightened and cracked through Spitz's thoughts. He felt alive, his skin tingling. Cold and then hot and then hotter, a fever burning in him. He choked back hisses of laughter while crying. Mr. Wright tapped on Spitz's chest, then tapped his own. Spitz nodded and hit the dirt once—hard, harder than he thought possible. They exchanged a glance. Mr. Wright's expression was unreadable, and he slipped the roll of duct tape onto Spitz's wrist and stood up.

"The boy is quiet. Brave. Or dumb, maybe?" The bad man sounded bored.

Mr. Wright lifted him to standing, and Spitz placed one hand on the workbench, his weight on his good foot. Mr. Wright spoke as he worked, as if alone, calm, and with a voice that gave Spitz chills.

"You know randomness is the essence of the quantum world? Probability? It's really quite amazing. There is strong evidence that randomness does not exist. That everything is predetermined. That's both true and not true, of course. You saw the child come in, okay? His coming into the barn was not predictable. It could have been a second earlier or a second later. I believe they found a way to capture that randomness and, let's say, solidify it, make it a thing, make it real in our dimension, above the quantum state where it normally exists. Above the atom, above the molecule. Like, say, Jell-O or pudding, but you know what's the best analogy? Window caulk."

"Are you fucking done?" The bad man looked at Spitz, who looked away and wiped tears from his face.

Mr. Wright continued, puttering at the workbench, its length a visual cacophony of electronic equipment. "Patience, please, for a real demonstration. Randomness, uncertainty, chaos, well, not chaos because that's kind of like probability on acid. Chaos is gunpowder if this is fire. That's what they did. That's how this works. Like plugging holes in space-time with chunks of randomness. Space-time isn't smooth, you know. It's like igneous rock, porous and fractured. You think the big bang made smooth reality? No, the big bang made a big mess."

The visitor spoke, "Your babbling is taking too much time. The demonstration?"

Mr. Wright looked at the clock on the worktable. It was made of glowing tubes. Mr. Wright called it a Nixie clock, like a girl's name. Spitz liked it. It said 7:59 a.m. At 8:00 a.m. Spitz's watch would buzz because he liked the feel of it every hour.

Mr. Wright asked the visitor, "Do you want to be in the cage or out of the cage?"

"What do you suggest?" The visitor squinted as he asked.

"This is experimental, but if you want to see it up close, come in. The boy and I are going in."

"I will join you. And the boy can stay out here, just to prevent any funny business."

Mr. Wright was about to protest, but the visitor pointed his gun at Spitz, who flinched. The two men entered the enclosure.

From inside the cage, Mr. Wright reached through the bars and tapped a keyboard. The two men stood opposite, the visitor near the flimsy door, with his gun pointed at Mr. Wright. Two of the screens cleared and each showed the number ten, which then changed to nine and continued counting down.

At a count of five, Spitz turned and ran at the open barn door. The visitor watched him go and raised his gun, but didn't shoot. When Spitz reached the barn door, he turned right and then ducked down to peek back into the barn.

The visitor spoke as he turned back to Mr. Wright. "I wouldn't really..." and Mr. Wright's heel connected with the bad man's upper rib cage. The visitor was pushed out the door of the enclosure, his gun swinging up. Spitz heard a gunshot, and he was running for the trailer when half the barn disappeared in a green flash. In his mind, the orange glowing Nixie clock on the workbench showed 8:00. His watch buzzed and he fainted on the porch.

32. Stolen, Valor

On Spitz's retina, the afterimage of the noiselessly spinning alien device faded to translucence and disappeared. In the space where it had been, warbled lines blurred the thief, getting into the car, the stolen laptop tucked under an arm.

Spitz's foot throbbed, pounding in time with his heart.

His finger curled on the trigger, testing its pressure, remembering the gun in the barn. The grip hummed in his hand, his muscles on autopilot. He saw the thief's black shoe outside the car, paused on the pavement, for just enough time. A toe in the shoe.

Cold tears tracked down his cheeks.

He pushed his hand to the sky, over his head, pointed the gun straight up, and fired three shots quickly into the air. The man ducked into the seat and whipped around at the sound of shots, as if expecting gunfire to reach him, and then the car sped off, the door closing as it flew.

Claire, Phil, and the clerk ran from the store, reaching Spitz, who was still pointing the gun into the air.

"What the hell, man?" The clerk looked at the gun and backed up.

Spitz handed the gun to Phil and turned to Claire. He was crying as he hugged her tight. She hugged him back, hard.

Phil ran over to the SUV, leaning in. He turned to the three gathered at the storefront. "They stole our laptop. They took the fucking laptop!"

"Do you want me to call the police?" The clerk looked nervous, staring at the strange scene of Spitz crying into Claire's shoulder.

Claire turned to the clerk. "No, it's okay. We can replace the laptop. Sorry about the commotion." She turned to Phil, staring at the gun in his hand. "Put that thing away!" Phil's almost imperceptible pause was met with a thunderous "Now!" from Claire. Phil leaned into the car and put the gun on the seat.

The clerk looked around nervously. "Well, that's some excitement. Uh, why don't you fill up now? I think I'm going to call the police."

"Please, don't call the police," Claire beseeched him. "My brother was just trying to warn us about the thieves. He doesn't talk. He's mute. So it's fine. We'll be okay."

The clerk shook his head and muttered a quick, "Whatever... Just... just go, okay? Get out of here." He headed back to the store with a muttered, "Fucking hate this job."

After they had filled up, Spitz insisted on driving, wiping his tears on his shirt.

Phil put the gun in the glove box. Then he looked around in wonder. "Where's Mr. Warren's car? Why are we in this car?"

Harry was still groggy. "We're being tracked."

From the back seat, Claire asked, "Is everyone's phone off?" Her voice still quavered with adrenaline.

Harry mumbled, "No, it's probably in the port."

Claire looked at her. "What port?" She nudged Harry, who was nodding off. "What port, Harry?"

Harry turned her face to the side and breathed out an answer. "The port every car has. Under the steering wheel, OBD port. Lemme sleep."

Spitz pulled over and then leaned down and looked under the steering wheel. He gave Claire a small white box.

"Tracker, dang." She tossed it out the window.

A half hour later Harry was rapidly tearing into food, ripping off chunks of a series of meat sticks, a small pile of Ho Ho wrappers already on the floor of the car. "I'm sorry I didn't stop them. I was out of it. I heard the door open but that's it. Feeling much better now." She belched.

Claire held up the remaining laptop. "We still have this one."

From the front seat Phil asserted, "We have to go get that one they stole."

Claire responded, "We can't do that. They're most likely armed and probably long gone."

Harry opened a meat stick wrapper. "Well, it was my laptop and I have low power trackers on all my devices."

"We have to let it go," responded Claire.

Phil put his face into the back seat. "No, my dad was very clear. Harry heard him. We cannot let the codes or technology or whatever you call it get into anyone else's hands. He said it was end-of-the-world-type stuff."

Harry spoke between mouthfuls of food. "I tend to agree. I cannot imagine what kind of terrible things a government would do with this crap, like my government. Or your government. Or really any government."

"So, how do we track it?" Phil asked her.

Harry swallowed and spoke. "Turn on a phone with data. I'll give you the IP address. It'll show a map. It's pretty accurate if they're on a highway. Good GPS on those."

Claire was adamant. "No, we cannot go chasing after this couple. It's too dangerous."

Phil said, "Let's vote on it. Who says we go after the laptop?" He raised his hand.

Harry raised her hand, containing a partially eaten powdered doughnut.

Spitz raised his hand, his other on the wheel. He looked in the rearview mirror and gave Claire a sheepish look.

Claire looked at each of them in turn, her lips pursed, and shook her head.

They agreed to turn on Spitz's phone because it was the least likely to be tracked. Once it was on, the map showed the laptop on I-40 West, about four miles ahead and going seventy miles per hour.

"So do any of you cowboys have a plan to get the laptop back?" said Claire from the back, staring at the desert-scape flowing by

"What about calling the police?" asked Phil.

"I can't imagine what kind of chaos would ensue. And we have no idea if those guys are the police." Claire was petulant.

"Then what about that colonel? He said he would help us. And at Cadillac Ranch that guy didn't stop us from leaving."

"He didn't stop us because Harry had just skewered someone," Claire pointed out.

Spitz hit the steering wheel once.

"Are you agreeing with me?" asked Phil.

Spitz hit the steering once again.

"So that's two for contacting the colonel."

Harry spoke up. "How's our technology? I mean, it's gotten us out of two jams. Me, once, and then another time at the Cadillac place. Can we use it?"

Claire looked at her. "This stuff is dangerous. Look at you. Who knows what that thing has done to you? You look like shit and your leg is growing! Mr. Wright is dead or missing. We cannot be messing with it. There have been several amputations."

Spitz hit the steering wheel twice.

Phil added, "Spitz is right. It worked when he used it. And no side effects."

"So far," Claire said.

"Fine, so far. But we should have it ready," Phil said.

After some more discussion, Harry lifted the inverter power cord, which was severed cleanly. "Must have happened when Spitz dropped the car parts on that guy."

"I can fix it," Claire said reluctantly. She held up a cell phone power cord that plugged into a car lighter socket. "Hand me the nail clippers from the purse. And see if there are any Band-Aids around. I can use them as electrical tape."

Shortly, they had the TV, the radio transmitter, and Claire's laptop running off the inverter. Claire opened the laptop.

"Okay, so Spitz's phone is on. I've got internet. We may be tracked by the colonel already. I'll reply to his message. What should I write? And holy crap, there's like a hundred thousand comments. We started something."

Phil said, "How about this: 'Hey, dickhead, do something useful.'"

"Uh, no," Claire replied.

There was silence, and then Harry spoke. "Send him, 'I am my brother's keeper.' If he gets it, he'll track your brother's phone."

"Okay, that's pretty clever." Claire typed a bit. Then after a moment, "Done. Let's hope he sees it and doesn't send the army after us. Next, how do we stop these guys who took our laptop? What's their location?"

Phil looked at the tracking app on Spitz's phone. "Not far ahead. Doing seventy miles per hour. We're slowly catching up. Spitz is doing about seventy-four or seventy-five."

"Any ideas?" Claire asked.

Harry had stopped eating and had a very satisfied look on her face. "We know the videos contain codes that, when broadcast correctly, cause... things to happen, changes in space-time."

Phil repeated in awe. "Space-time. Cool."

Harry added, "They are unpredictable."

"That they are," said Claire.

"But they do things. Things that can be powerful. Very, very powerful. Move objects. Make things act in ways that differ from what we expect. That's powerful."

"And we have descriptions from Mr. Wright about some of what they do," said Claire.

"Read them, Captain," Harry said.

Claire narrowed her eyes at Harry but didn't respond. She opened her laptop and started reading. "Okay, under each video is a file folder. Within the file folder is a text file that is encrypted, but I have the decryption passwords from Spitz from back when we left Boston."

"Seems like a long time ago," said Phil.

Claire nodded and continued, "Okay, so under that video of the woman saving the boy is 'teleportation,' under the chemical attack at the playground is 'unknown' and 'floating,' under the video with the weird cartoon thing is 'cold weld anything,' whatever that means. Under the video at the cocktail party doing stuff is 'force field' and another one that says—I'm quoting Mr. Wright here—'worst acid trip ever,' under the marriage video is 'glowing hands.' There's more under each one. Many just say 'unknown.'"

Phil said, "Wait, teleportation. Can't we just teleport the laptop back to us?"

Claire said, "We're moving. As far as I can tell, the code operates on the broadcast point and that's us. It's granular and static. There's no plasticity. If we're moving, we could get decapitated or something."

"I vote no on decapitation," said Harry. "Keep going with that list."

"This one says 'object lock.' Maybe that would work?" Claire mumbled.

"So, will that simply cause something to be inaccessible? How could we use that?"

"This is stupid," said Claire. "We literally have no idea what these things do. And they may not even do what Mr. Wright noted. And they might need parameters, like distance, duration, vectors, angles, that we can't calculate. We almost teleported you into the ground, Harry."

"We have to get the laptop," Phil insisted.

"We tried a few things when I was in South Africa. Eventually, one of them worked."

"Your life was in danger," Claire said. "But now our lives are not in danger.

The risk is too great. Especially with us in a moving vehicle."

"It is not," responded Harry. "We can do this. We are smart. You, Claire, are a genius at math. I, not to toot my own horn, can code a poker game that would blow your socks off. Let's spend some time thinking about this. Come up with a plan. *Dimata tsele* who took our laptop, the laptop containing technology that can literally end the world, are not as smart as we are."

"I'm with Harry!" said Phil.

"Harry," Claire said calmly. "You are high on sugar and meat sticks. You're delusional. This is not homework. This is real. It actually did something to you. It's not reasonable to just guess. We could die."

"Yeah, it did something to me. It made me... whole. It's like Jesus stuff: heal the wounded, make wine from water, walk on lakes."

"What's next? Bring back the dead?" Claire retorted.

There was silence and Phil asked quietly, "Could it bring Dad back?"

More silence. Claire exhaled her words. "Let's all just take a moment and think about this. Here, Harry, take the laptop and look through it. Maybe you can find something that won't kill us."

Phil said, "The road from here to Albuquerque is pretty empty. We have about an hour and a half where there's not much. We should act during that window if we're going to act."

33. Kathode—Albuquerque, New Mexico

Through the giant picture windows of the makeshift hospital room *née* planetarium, the lights below the mountain barely twinkled, hidden by the haze of rapidly moving clouds. Storm cells, powerfully squatting over the western scrub that stretched to the mountains, were rubbing shoulders on approach to Albuquerque. Flecks of lightning flashed within, revealing X-rays of the internal structures of the roiling thunderheads, organs of a behemoth.

Her lungs ached and her nose itched from the prolonged and cathartic sobbing session. Lorelai emerged from her fugue cleansed of any doubt and energized to mirror her father's quest to save her mother, but this time she would save her father.

"If we knew how it happened, maybe we could treat the ailment," a doctor said. That was many years ago, in a conversation she'd overheard between a visiting specialist and The Ant. Lorelai's efforts to make it happen had been met with derision.

"You are a child, not a doctor. Your father will be treated here by professionals, not by your internet research." The conversation was repeated, but Lorelai often was a recipient of, not a participant in, the dialogue.

She made her list of supplies and ordered what she could from the internet. First, she went to the kitchen and took the credit card from above the refrigerator. *For emergencies while I'm at the conference*, said the note on the envelope. *See you in a week, Aunt Sally.*

Everything would arrive today or tomorrow. Sixty-six beam tetrodes—the entire stock of the only online supplier who would overnight (pentodes were no longer available—a zoom into the whiteboard in the video showed the word *tetrode* written, so perhaps her father used the same substitution), sockets for the tetrodes, regulated power supplies (5v, 12v, 24v dc), fifty small breadboard socket bases, wire (10-, 12-, 14-, and 16-gauge solid and stranded copper, 200 yards each), wiring tools and supplies (wire strippers, pliers, soldering irons, non-caustic solder, razor knives, electrical tape, lever-type wire connectors and wire nuts, zip ties of a dozen different sizes and colors), two expanding portable canopies capable of covering a large SUV, ninety-six rolls (four cases) of copper mesh in lieu of Faraday cloth, which was not available for fast shipping, signal processing equipment (two RomuLab Advanced-Tube X signal filters, each costing more than a year of the University of New Mexico), two EMF detectors (Durham Radio Services EM field detectors with extended range), three pairs of long-distance walkie-talkies, two tube amplifiers, and three antique tube radios and two tube televisions, all in working order, from the Retro Club Shop in Albuquerque's Old Town (the owner agreed to drop them off today for no charge after she provided payment over the phone), a dozen surge protectors, many extension cords, eight battery backup power supplies with peak output of 18 kilowatt-hours each (another year of university tuition), and six decent laptops with extra memory and extra-large batteries.

She knew what to do, but she admitted she wasn't sure she had the skill to implement it in a very short time frame. Twice, alarms had sounded and the AI had automatically charged the implanted cardioverter to push her father's heart back into normal rhythm.

"Unit, can you help me reverse the codes that Dad broadcast at Mom?"

The simulacrum responded. "That is not something I can perform. The radio broadcast in the video, generated from codes sourced from the Russian documents, is seen only once. Without understanding what they do, reversing them is not likely to have any positive effect and may very well have dangerous or catastrophic consequences."

She chewed a nail. "You can infer, to predict language based on your existing pedagogical lexica. Therefore, can't you predict or infer the codes needed to reverse whatever Dad did?"

"Prediction based on existing language is one thing. You know I do not actually think, though I have independent input from the comatose version of me to your left. I aggregate patterns and my processing algorithms generate responses. It's more probability than intelligence. I appear intelligent mostly by chance; in fact, many would say entirely chance. I do not think the way you think. My creativity is entirely derivative, not foundational. Without someplace to start, I cannot create anything. And if the answer isn't somewhere in my library, I cannot provide it, and it is only through repetitive processing that I don't provide incorrect answers more often."

"You have someplace to start—the code he broadcast. You can isolate it in the video."

"I need a greater lexicon of codes, or limbs, as your father called them, metadata as Germaine called them, *konechnost* in the original Russian" (the word конечность appeared on several monitors), "to extrapolate any codes. It would be guesswork otherwise and most likely very dangerous given what was seen in the video."

"Clarity has more videos. Could you extract codes from her videos?"

"It is possible. It is also possible that the codes are in the original radio transmissions, not in the derivative videos. My ability to provide help with this is limited. Plus, your father's unstable condition is making communication with him less productive. Perhaps it is time to consider your aunt's suggestion that your father would be more comfortable in hospice."

Lorelai's eyes flashed and her head snapped at the screen. "Not going to happen. I am going to save him."

"If you say so."

"Dickhead."

"Lang—"

"Don't you fucking dare!"

She logged on to WisPR and pinged Lollipop with an SOS—a chat request that would chain to cell phones and other devices of the user, a feature which she believed had never been used.

Lollipop: What's up?

Kathode: Where have you been? Shit has hit the fan! You've been AWOL and I need help.

[**Bot** says: rule 911, Bot is off.]

Lollipop: Sorry, been out of pocket.

Kathode: My father is [spinner]. I have to try something or they'll move him to hospice.

Lollipop: Shit, sorry to hear that. I can try to help. AI working ok?

Kathode: The AI is fine. I have a solution. I know what happened—why he is nonresponsive.

Lollipop: Really? How did you figure that out?

Kathode: Too much to explain. Just here's the deal. Where are you?

Lollipop: Uh, we agreed.

Kathode: I don't care anymore. WisPR is dying anyway. Haven't you seen the videos? Clarity is posting stuff and the members are bailing.

Lollipop: Sorry, I haven't paid attention. Give me a sec.

Lollipop: Holy shit. Uh, you didn't post that video to our blockchain wallet?

Kathode: No! Why would I post that video? It's supposedly alien, after all.

Lollipop: There's no way it's alien. Who would believe that?

Kathode: We can talk about that when you get here.

Lollipop: Uh, wym?

Kathode: I need you here to help me cure my father. Where are you now?

Lollipop: I can come to you. I'm not far.

Kathode: How do you know where I am?

Lollipop: [spinner] The AI told me some time ago.

Kathode: Well, I guess so much for privacy. :shrugemoji: Are you at the VLA? I thought you were on the East Coast. I don't even know what you do.

Lollipop: I'll explain when I get there.

Lollipop: I'm going to have a friend with me. OK? A Y-chrom. Name's Wilbur.

Kathode: I don't care. I just need help with this stuff. Hurry.

"Are you sure you want to invite WisPR user Lollipop to this house?" The Simulacrum spoke calmly.

Lorelai responded, "You saw the videos. The solution is in the technology.

We can reverse it, I know it. Lollipop knows more about decryption and such than anyone. She's an expert, or so she has said many times. She built half of you as well. Maybe she can extract more codes from the video. And now, thanks to Clarity, we have another. And I've asked Clarity to come here as well."

"You do not know these people. And your capabilities with AI may now exceed WisPR user Lollipop's knowledge and expertise."

Lorelai answered, "I know Dad has very little time and there must be a way to reverse whatever he did, to use the technology to cure him."

"WisPR user Lollipop wrote much of my AI code. That much is true. Perhaps it would behoove you to review some of that code now."

BOOK 5

- Welcome to the WisPR chatroom
- Bot is ON
- Users online: 1
- Today's quote is:

"In spite of everything it remains a marvel that equations in which the q's and p's originally signified coordinates and momenta can be satisfied when one interprets these symbols as things that have quite another meaning."

H. A. Lorentz to E. Schrödinger
Haarlem, Netherlands
27 May 1926

34. @Lollipop

The pills in the go-bag. What did they do? Probably something I should have asked myself before I took them.

Smithson lay on the hotel bed, feet on the floor. The dull ache of his ribs and face and hands hid behind the moody haze of his mind. He remembered the shoe pressing down on his hand, grinding it to the pavement, sharp points of macadam breaking his skin, bones sawing against one another. But now it didn't hurt. It was information, data, a memory.

I'm high. I'm really high and I'm in a cheap hotel with a bedspread suitable only for wrapping up a murder victim. He giggled at the thought. Do you wrap the body facedown and roll from one end or faceup and lift the edges around? A human burrito. Just need some lettuce.

He held the baggie with the pills above his head and then dropped it on the floor. Who needs friends when you have epinephriends? What were they? Ecstasy? Roofie? Xanax? Barbiturate? Dex? Lorazepam? Aspirin?

Luck, thought Smithson, staring at the ceiling, is a strange animal. Indians call it karma. Irish call it fate. Arabs call it kismet. Too, some call it fluke—which is also a fish, right? Rabbit's feet. Smooth stones. Crosses. Four-leaf clovers. Horseshoes with the ends skyward. Pennies faceup. Blond children. Speeding through yellow lights. A good parking space. A winning lottery ticket. Godsend. Obvious, really, but which god? Perhaps Loki. The Greek goddess of luck is Tyche. Maybe if Loki and Tyche had a child? Lychee? I'm fucking hilarious sometimes.

Three bullet points:

- The unbelievable invitation by Lorelai to her home! My Kathode! My Captain!
- The stolen videos. Alien! @Clarity? Should be @Calamity.
- The pain, barely able to breathe, knuckles on one hand swollen, a black eye, a cauliflower'd ear.

Three definitions:

- Bad luck: getting beat up outside a diner
- Good luck: having the target of the *long game* ask him over for some tea and advanced math
- Indeterminate luck: having the video he stole many years ago turn up on the web for the world to ponder

Balance. Equilibrium. Parity. Symmetry. These are luck's robust and sturdier older siblings. For with bad luck must come good luck. Otherwise, it's not luck, it's chaos.

He rolled left and grabbed the edge of the bedspread, then rolled right, wrapping himself.

I am dead.

He slept. The drugs wore off. He woke with a clear mind. And excruciating ribs.

The fire escape was the only solution. Always build a back door, lest a fire trap you and you burn.

Awake, he attempted to shower in the wheelchair-accessible bathroom at the down-market but still respectable business hotel, which sat in stealth mode on a street corner in downtown Albuquerque. The faux wood vinyl flooring looked new. The curtains were kale green, and the view was of an oil-change franchise. He grimaced in pain stepping into the shower and then yelled out as the hot water splashed his ribs. It sufficed to stand somewhat outside the spray and wipe himself with a washcloth using only his left arm, which was sore but not quite as painful as his right arm, which he could not lift above his shoulder. He was careful not to let the washcloth touch the spreading yellow-blue-black splotches that ran from his hip to his underarm. He tried very hard not to cough. He had done that once and the pain was unbearable.

Being on the run had significant disadvantages. Emergency rooms would create a messy paper trail. He had no health insurance under the name Wilbur Right. He had not written down the Social Security number associated with the name—more poor planning for flight. He could certainly fork over a credit card, but he didn't want to reach his limit. He figured he could tough this out, provided he made it through the night.

He took three ibuprofen tablets, eschewing the unknown pills from his go-bag, which had provided some needed rest, and then he sat on the bed, painfully upright, and watched news programs, trying to look for distraction from both his physical and emotional traumas. The last few days had been more excitement and much less personally rewarding than he'd ever wanted.

How would he go to Lorelai's in his current condition? He wasn't a girl. For years he'd been a girl online, or a female of indeterminate age. He'd helped Lorelai build the AI so she could live a fantasy where her comatose father spoke. All to get into her bank accounts. It had never worked. The AI never had ingress into any financial matters. There was a long game, though. Because the AI was slowly gaining more access. But there was an easier way to get the little girl to fork over money. A much easier way. He just needed physical access to the comatose father. And he'd been offered it.

But how to actually become Lollipop?

Unable to think in the tiny hotel room, Smithson decided he needed a drink. A bourbon. Stone-ground crackers. Gruyère or Brie. There was no way this whitewashed rent-a-hovel had any of these—the bougie equivalents of energy drinks and cheese doodles. He headed downstairs through a dim hallway odorized with stale cigarettes and lemon freshener.

The hotel bar was dingier and more depressing than he expected. Attached through swinging half doors to a family buffet restaurant. *Saloon* said the painted sign over the shellacked countertop. On the walls above booths, a few horseshoes pointed up, paintings of steeds and mares, signed photos of unknown rodeo stars, and coiled lariats. The bar had only one patron, a woman chatting with the female bartender. He sat down several seats from them, not wanting to do anything but order his drink and ponder, painfully.

"Hey, sailor," said the raven-haired bartender, her skin as smooth and dark as the bar's paneling, sporting a turquoise-and-silver bolo. "What can I do you for?"

Smithson didn't fancy small talk. "Do you have bourbon?" He said it in a tone that implied they probably wouldn't.

She smiled. "Oh, that kind of mood tonight, eh? Yes, we have two bourbons. Four Roses and another bottle of Four Roses. You can have either one."

Smithson had to smile and as he did so, he grimaced and couldn't speak for a moment.

"Let me know when you're ready," she said, and she went back to talk to her friend.

He waved her back. "I'll have a double. With soda. On the rocks."

As she went to get the drink, the other woman came and sat next to Smithson. "My friend the bartender says you might need some company."

Smithson tried to turn and look at her, but made a gasp of pain. "Your friend is the bartender?"

"Yes, and what happened to you?"

"Bar fight."

"Oh, a jokester. I get it." The woman's voice was light in the dim bar and had the tinge of a person who liked to laugh.

Smithson made the effort to turn toward her. She was attractive, with long auburn locks framing a pretty face. Probably his age. She was dressed in a tight cutoff top and jeans wrapping a body with no extra anything. A studded western belt hung on her hips. Smithson decided this would be an acceptable diversion. She wasn't his type, which had never been sorted, but the bar was dark and he needed distraction. "No, seriously, bar fight."

She shifted and gave him a begrudging look. "You don't look like a liar."

"I didn't say I wasn't a liar." Smithson tried to smile and grimaced again. He liked this empty banter. It was easy. Not caring made it easy.

"Okay, I'll bite. You don't look like someone who gets into bar fights. Did you spill a drink on someone? Hit their car?"

Smithson paused accidentally, weighing his words, but it came off as dramatic effect. "I made a move on someone's girl."

"Bet you did not," said the woman, laughing, her smile wide.

Smithson exercised his mind, releasing never-used social skills. Or maybe this was just more good luck. He didn't know. "Seriously, I made a move on a girl and next thing I knew I was in a fight in the parking lot."

The attractive woman looked at him with a cute twist of her lip. "And what's the other guy look like?"

Smithson grimaced again. "Oh, I'd truly be a liar if I didn't say he was pretty much as handsome as ever. So you are right, I'm not the kind of guy who gets into bar fights."

"So, was the girl worth it? This girl who makes you take these risks? Was she pretty?"

And Smithson somehow knew this was a moment to look at this woman's body. The sliver of midriff visible above her jeans may have been the most intimate bit of human skin Smithson had seen in years. Above the ribbed top, a provocative curve of neck led to a heart-shaped face straight from a soap advertisement. He lingered on her eyes long enough for her to notice, blinking slowly. She was offering this as part of the flirtation. She had thrown the ball into his court and he could flirt or not.

They stared at each other for a moment and the response came to him, like a lightning bolt. The right thing to say. The flirty response that would seal the deal. He locked her gaze. "Oh, she was very pretty. Very pretty indeed."

She may have blushed. He wasn't sure.

The bartender came over with his drink and he thanked her and took a sip.

"So what brings you to ABQ?" Smithson could not recall a woman ever being so interested in him, but he played along.

"Business."

"So not pleasure?"

"No, just business."

"But what about the girl who got you in trouble? Was that business?"

Smithson turned again. He was out of his league at this point. He knew it. This was flirting. This was banter. He'd pretty much run out of what to say. The pain, the bourbon, the woman. It was all perfect and he didn't want to ruin it.

So he told the truth. "That was a mistake."

The bartender had been standing near, organizing condiments. She laughed and the three of them continued to talk, with Smithson trying very hard to keep his mouth shut.

Eventually, the bartender wandered away to clean glasses and refill napkin dispensers.

The woman put her hand on Smithson's knee.

"Would you like some company tonight? I promise nobody will beat you up in the parking lot."

Smithson was confused. Was this woman offering herself to him?

"Ummm..." was all he could get out.

"It's five hundred dollars for the night. Or we could just do something for an hour or so for two hundred. And in any case, you should buy me a drink."

Smithson stared at his glass. He got it. The flirtation. The easy conversation. The bartender checking him out. Ugh. He was such an idiot.

"Your friend the bartender..." he muttered, swirling the bourbon. Heat flushing his scalp, prickling his ears.

"Yeah, she makes sure guys don't give off too much creep before I offer. Cops don't come in here bruised up, so she gave me the sign. And the hotel has your credit card since you're a guest. Makes me feel safe, you know?"

The ice in his drink tinkled against the glass, but not loud enough to mask his shame.

She frowned, not hiding disappointment. "Sorry, figured you might have known." She got up to leave.

"Wait," Smithson said. Some ideas were coming to him. Some good ideas.

The woman stopped.

"What's your name?"

"Crystal."

"Really?" asked Smithson. As soon as the word left his lips, he realized how naïve he was about these things.

"For you, it's Crystal." Her eyes twinkled.

"How would you like to be Lollipop instead?"

Things moved quickly once money changed hands. And soon Smithson and his companion were waiting at the door of the massive steel-and-glass house in the foothills of the Sandia Mountains, amazement on his face. He'd not actualized that Lorelai, aka Kathode, lived this way. Though in retrospect he should have. Her father had sold a tech company for many millions. She had a planetarium in her house. Why would she not live like this?

He poked the woman next to him. "Nice digs, eh?"

He'd had to lay out a bit of money to buy her time and a nerdy wardrobe. The last of his money, a fact he tried, and failed, to forget. Her normal dress, if he could be so bold, was that of a prostitute. And that wouldn't do for the uber-smart WisPR user Lollipop. He'd also bought her true identity. Crystal was her stage name, or more appropriately, her bedroom name. Her real name was Eva Rosario Sanchez, and she was saving money to buy a house for herself and her two-year-old son, a result of a broken condom with a nameless convention attendee who paid cash and was gone with the sunrise.

The door opened and Smithson nearly spoke out of turn, but Eva was able to keep her composure. Clearly, years of playacting with lonely men had made her a skilled thespian, and Smithson suspected she relished her new role as STEM genius and girlfriend rather than paid sex partner.

Lorelai stepped back and let them both enter. She looked at Eva. "You must be Lollipop. And you are Wilbur?"

Smithson stammered, nodded, and looked at Lorelai. "Yes, I'm Wilbur. Wilbur Right. That's Right with a capital *R*, not capital *W* followed by *R*, so I'm not the guy who invented the airplane." He heard himself babbling but couldn't stop. "I'm her boyfriend," he added, and pointed at Eva.

"Of course you are," Lorelai said. After they entered the house, she closed the door and turned to Eva. "I can't call you Lollipop. What should I call you?"

"Eva. Eva Sanchez. I'm so glad to meet you finally." Eva was a brilliant actress, thought Smithson.

"Very well. Let's get right to it. Come with me."

Smithson looked at the retreating back of Lorelai, who headed off quickly into the tiled lobby of the great house. Was she annoyed? She sounded peeved, or frustrated. But what did he know about real-life interactions with teenage girls? He and Eva exchanged a look, but Smithson learned nothing from it.

35. Fort Meade, Maryland

"I don't understand. We are very close." Montgomery attempted to sound professional, but he fretted that his disappointment was obvious. His hands were greasy on the steering wheel as he drove to Fort Meade. Derek had insisted the discussion be remote, and the speakerphone couldn't show Montgomery his face.

Montgomery's friend and boss sounded strained when he replied. "It's politics here. You don't know the strings I've pulled to keep this operation going. But it looks like the released videos have caused quite a stir upwind. The clips are gaining traction, the group-think of the internet is looking for sources, and of course the government is getting a lot of that attention. Some of the higher-ups seem to think these videos could be bad actors siphoning media attention as a prelude to an operational offensive. You've heard the rumors of a long-distance rail gun or mass drone attack. I've got a branch head accusing me of creating psy-op."

"I've heard, of course, but Derek, this technology is proven." Montgomery's voice was tinged with annoyance, which he regretted. He didn't like to argue facts. Once you are arguing facts, you have already lost.

Derek might have been typing as they spoke, another reason for annoyance. "It's not proven by any means. You have some videos, some firsthand reports. And the primary eyewitness is deceased."

"Uys was a repeat contractor. A reputable source. And the dog—an actual living creature," Montgomery said.

"There are those who think the dog was a plant. Its chip overnighted or duplicated previously and implanted in another animal, which, I might add, is plausible."

Montgomery pulled his vehicle into a mall parking lot, headed to an empty corner, and parked. He needed to concentrate on this call. "What about Uys's arm? How could his arm be in Tennessee and his body in South Africa?"

The typing in the background stopped. "Blair, I couldn't sell it. And when I tried to sell it, I got the same phrase—*it's absurd*—in response."

"Blair? You're going to Blair me now? Okay, that's when I know there's more, right?"

"I'm sorry to say that's correct."

"So, what do I do with the kids? We can't abandon them. I've got at least one hostile group in play after them, and likely more. They posted the videos to get our help, not to endanger themselves."

"Listen, just like the dog and the arm—we've got internal arguments questioning what happened. In every case the evidence is weak."

"We've got two terrorists on ice in Dallas right now."

"Their covers are solid. The blond woman who bled out in the parking lot came back as a dead French tourist, killed not by new technology but apparently run through with a long knife, and her American boyfriend crushed in a parking lot fender bender. They met in college and their story is as tragic as it is uninformative to this operation. That's the internal spin on this. Whether you and I know different is irrelevant."

Montgomery lowered the volume on his car speakerphone, making sure no other cars were parked nearby. "And the videos of the kid teleporting?"

"We've posted so many modified versions of that clip, nobody can tell the original from anything else; it's lost in the muddle. And I gave you authority for that operation in Tennessee and you managed to detain two decorated veterans and quarantine an injured dog."

The pause was stillborn.

Montgomery summarized. "I've got nothing, right?"

"Right. The Warrens have been released. And we had to buy that antique Chevy Nova from him. You can pick up the dog at the Fort Meade lab whenever you like."

"Those kids are really in trouble."

"If you say so."

"I say so."

Derek's voice did not waver. Montgomery imagined him leaning over his speakerphone, fingers tented. "Let me be clear on this. You are not authorized for anything stateside. I've smoothed over everything with the Warrens, and with the South African operation as well. So just stay put and I'm sure I'll have another special project for you soon. I've got a missing sailboat off Fiji that was carrying a cutting-edge virologist, plus a half dozen other ops that could use your skills."

Montgomery said simply, "Yes, sir," and the call ended.

But now he knew one thing. This call was remote to create distance and deniability. Fiji was their code word, set up after Brazil, and used twice since then. He could do as he saw fit, but no more discussion on the topic would occur. "Sir, yes, sir," whispered Montgomery.

*Video Z-14-01-8/Anon, *Storybook*

From the Zoonerat Wikipedia page:

"Zoonerat video Z-14:01-8/Anon, aka *Storybook* or *Two Moons* is unusual in that it shows possible identifying aspects of a Zoonerat home planet. Astronomers have been actively looking for a planet with a satellite configuration that matches the one described in the video. Seventeen have been identified so far, though astronomers say millions could match the profile."

The following is excerpted from "An Alien Soap Opera or an Elaborate Hoax? Our Favorite 'Zoonerat' Conspiracy Theories," *Hollywood Infotainment* magazine:

The video opens in a bedroom. Light is from a directed overhead glow, but no lighting source is seen. The two Zoonerat children, Isthmus and Chiril, are in a large bed, one child on each side of the reclining Zoonerat adult female, Io. (Tri-State Mattress, the retailer, calculated the bed size as 107% the width and 97% the length of a US queen size, based on the average height of an adult woman.) There is an image above the bed of a creature that could be a cat or reptile. It appears to be catlike but has scales and a barbed tail. It has a smile, and theories abound as to its origins. It has been named Zeptile, Cheshire, and Toby by internet users, the latter name being the most common.

Io has a book open and is reading to the children. Video cuts show each page and move back and forth between the three individuals at appropriate points, often using a behind-the-head shot of the book as the pages are turned and revealed. The children's faces variously show interest, joy, and concern, and finally, they nod off. The video ends as stereotypically as any episode of a television show with Io kissing each child good night (Chiril last) and then she leaves the room. The video ends.

With the audio, it is believed that Io is telling the children a story. Her lips move and we hear the Zoonerat language. Many translations are available on the internet, of varying degrees of believability. Several dubbed versions are also available, including a well-received one in English by K-pop singer Mi Cha with more than a 100 million views in its first week. That rendering is now in post-production as a full-length movie with an impressive list of backers, to be released next June.

That the book has no written symbols, just images, has led to several theories. One popular theory is that the story is well known to all Zoonerat and thus Io is telling the story from memory. Another supposition is that there is writing in the book but it did not get properly encoded in the video or is not in the human visible spectrum. There is no evidence to support either theory.

In the book *Xenolinguistics and the Zoonerat Language*, Professor Ajij Locke postulates that the double moon may not actually exist on Zoonerat but that it may be a metaphor for the double-marriage/double-relationship tradition of the Zoonerat culture. Likewise, Professor Adnan Bateman suggests that the double moon exists and may be the basis for the double-relationship metaphors that must exist throughout Zoonerat culture. Further discussion on this topic is wide ranging.

Book Summary

Page 1: The first page shows a landscape with a forest in the foreground, then widely spaced smaller trees, then a plain, and then on the horizon, an ocean. Above, hanging as one would expect, is a large moon with a face (Moon 1), full and glowing. The art is hand drawn and inspired. It looks similar in style to *Goodnight Moon*, the popular children's book.

Page 2: Moon 1 is lower and the bottom edge is hidden by the horizon. It is implied that the moon is setting.

Page 3: Moon 1 is clearly setting. Now a whiteness is appearing opposite Moon 1. What is rising there?

Page 4: Moon 2 has appeared. Moon 1 is half gone.

Page 5: Moon 1 is nearly gone. Just a slight sliver is visible above the horizon. Moon 2 has a face and is frowning.

Page 6: Moon 1 is entirely gone. Moon 2 has risen.

Page 7: Moon 2 is higher in the sky. No terrain is visible. Moon 2 is clearly crying.

Page 8: No moons are visible. The page is just a sky with some stars. No mapping of the stars to any known star configuration has been conclusive, though research continues.

Page 9: The mountains are shown and it is possible that a slight shimmer of light is behind them. Moon 2 has a questioning look. Is Moon 1 rising?

Page 10: Moon 2 is bleary-eyed from crying and sadness, but there is a perkiness to its eyes. Perhaps it senses Moon 1 is not gone forever?

Page 11: Moon 1 is rising. A giant sliver is visible over the mountains.

Page 12: Moon 2 is beaming in happiness. Its eyes are pointed back to where it came from, where Moon 1 is rising.

Page 13: Both moons are on the same page, near each other. Moon 1 has a shy smile, almost apologetic. Moon 2 is very happy.

Page 14: Only Moon 1 is visible. Is Moon 2 behind it? We don't know, but the common interpretation is yes.

Page 15: Moon 1 is now passing Moon 2. Moon 2 looks happy, but we know soon it will be sad as Moon 1 continues on its way, oblivious to the sadness it will cause.

Page 16: This is a blank page.

*Video Z-24:09-16a/Anon *Metamorphosis*

From the Zoonerat Wikipedia page:

Zoonerat video Z-24:09-16a/Anon *Metamorphosis* is the longest Zoonerat video currently known to exist. The video opens as a nearly seamless continuation of video Z-15:43-7a/Clarity, *The Saving of Isthmus*.

The following is a summary of Z-24:09-16a/Anon *Metamorphosis* as published on Jory McClellan's Zoonerat blog:

Huoron is lying on his back at the base of a deep, narrow crevasse. The camera pans upward and around. Rock walls perhaps 100 meters high, assuming video scale matches human scale, with sharp and dangerous looking protuberances, tower above his body. Scrutiny of the color space suggests igneous strata. However, at 00:43 a different stratum is panned over and has been identified by Professor Kyron Danth of the Royal Geologic Society (Steinhouse Lecture) as sedimentary, suggesting an aqueous period earlier in the planet's history. Below the sedimentary strata lie what appear to be metamorphic strata. The depth of the strata implies an extended period of time. Some academics have postulated that the Ru-Airat evolved into their current form because of the cataclysmic geologic shock implied by the differing strata.

Viewers can only guess at the damage inflicted on Huoron as he plummeted to the bottom.

The camera zooms to Huoron's side, where a rip in his suit is visibly venting whatever gas he breathes to stay alive. That the gas is visible has led to speculation that Zoonerat air is highly humid while the Ru-Airat atmosphere is cold enough for the contained water vapor to condense. Other chemical processes may also account for the visibility of the expelled gas (*Zoonerat Biology*, Xi, Rammala, et al).

The shot changes to Huoron's own view of an interior heads-up display in his helmet. The soundtrack has labored or rapid breathing. What is clearly a warning icon flashes repeatedly and symbols are changing. This brief clip has been used to reverse engineer the Zoonerat numbering system, which confirms a base 32 place-value notation with a zero indicator interpreted left to right. A viewer intuits these symbols to show Huoron's declining atmosphere. Another symbol shows a miniature version of a bipedal figure and the right leg is flashing.

Huoron grimaces and he taps that leg. It resounds hard. Viewers comment that this indicates that some sort of hardening agent or foam has encapsulated his leg inside his suit, automatically deploying when his leg broke in the fall. Such technology is apparently being developed by the United States, French, and/or Chinese militaries, depending on which news source one consumes. Zoonerat fans claim the idea came from this video. Others say such technology has been in development for many years.

Huoron moves with difficulty but turns and lifts himself up, and is surprised by an arm helping him rise. He startles and backs up, assuming a fighting position as the camera reveals an alien, humanoid, but looking like it is made of rough stone, standing near him. The creature has four rocky arms, each with five-fingered hands and the appearance of burned campfire logs. Its oval head looks like a spaghetti squash made of granite. Two indents might be eyes, and a seam ridged by what appears to be reflective and sparkling lip gloss suffices for a mouth. Closer inspection reveals its face to be malleable and capable of movement under a reptilian-like skin. Its body is thin and shorter than Huoron's. Sheets of foil engraved in runes and multihued shiny metals embedded with polished stones cover its body in an intricate armor and/or clothing.

The creature raises its arms, palms outward, in a gesture of peace. Huoron, clearly not in any position to fight, seeing that a second creature is holding his weapon as well, also raises his arms, palms out, in a similar gesture of peace. The creature offers to fix the rip in Huoron's suit by pointing at its own side. There is some trepidation as Huoron silently nods, and the creature takes a device from his own stony-looking suit and sprays a gas at the tear in Huoron's suit. The camera shows Huoron's heads-up display and the symbols change, first to alarming rapid blinking and then slowing. The viewer can guess that whatever atmospheric catastrophe was sure to ensue has been halted.

The creature, we will now call Rocky, so named first by u/zoonerfan1 on a well-known message board, and the other creature, Screech, also named by u/zoonerfan1 perhaps because of an unfortunate (and arguably distant) resemblance to a certain classic young adult television character, beckon Huoron to follow them. Rocky leads and Screech follows with Huoron in between.

It is unclear if part of the video is missing, but the cut is abrupt to a new scene of an underground city. It is truly magnificent in scale. Hundreds of massive columns, all of which appear to be buildings, rise thousands of meters into the air through a sparse cloud cover, attaching to a distant, hazy roof. We fly through the city, which goes on as far as the eye can see. The columns themselves are square, hexagonal, round, and of other shapes, with ornate bridges between them. They rise to the cavernous roof of the landscape. It is clearly the underground domain of the Ru-Airat. The camera zooms through the city, following a convoy of flying boxy and ornately decorated vehicles that arrive at a magnificent central plaza looking to our eyes like Meso-American Empire merged with twenty-second-century cyberpunk Hong Kong. Stone, glass, intricate carvings, back-lit columns, porticoes, and balconies, et al. Written descriptions do not convey the sense of advancement and technology combined with deep history.

The viewer wants more but is disappointed. The scene again cuts abruptly to a large room, akin to a small theater. Rocky, Screech, several other Ru-Airat, and Huoron are on a dais while a full audience of important-looking Ru-Airat observe. Huoron's helmet is off, but he has a breathing apparatus on his face, attached to his nostrils. Apparently, there is some sort of technology indoors that can compensate for differences between the two species. Huoron also has a headset. He taps it uncertainly.

A series of displays are around the room and Huoron is listening, perhaps unsure of what he is hearing. A picture of the security camera from Io's laboratory is shown on one monitor. Huoron is gesturing at the security camera, clearly upset at what he is seeing.

The image on the screen changes and Io is seen on another security camera injecting Isthmus with the chemical or perhaps antidote from the video Z-15:43-7a/Clarity, *The Saving of Isthmus.*

Are the Ru-Airat taking credit for giving Io the antidote? Or are they threatening Huoron by showing him they know about his sick child? These are the questions a viewer may have.

But what comes next is unexpected. On the video Io is arrested in the hospital room of Isthmus. Huoron explodes, and points at Rocky. He appears to accuse Rocky of something—perhaps of setting up Io for arrest? But how would the enemy do such a thing? Our inability to understand the dialogue makes conclusions difficult.

Then we see Isthmus, lying in his hospital bed. The child is healthy—or so an observer with no knowledge of anything Zoonerat is likely to conclude. Then a line drawing of Isthmus rises from the security camera and moves to a blank monitor on the dais. Huoron's eyes narrow in discomfort as he watches. The camera moves to the line drawing of Isthmus, which fleshes out his body and features but remains clearly a drawing, not a real image. Isthmus's body changes, growing stronger, darker, but also more rigid. He is changing from a Zoonerat into a Ru-Airat, but not entirely Ru-Airat. His skin becomes shiny, like metal. Huoron's face grows pale and he stands to yell at Rocky. He lunges forward, but his leg is stiff in his suit, and Rocky grabs him as he falls.

The video ends.

36. Smithson Arrives

Lorelai led Eva and Smithson the short distance across the tiled lobby to two double doors. She stepped back and let them enter first, allowing the dramatic effect to be as strong as possible. Her program had darkened the ceiling, placing a gibbous moon above the horizon, magnified for maximum effect. The Horsehead Nebula, saturated 200 percent and magnified 100 times, was directly above them. Aurorae dotted the faux horizon. An audible gasp from Eva and a grunt from Smithson showed the desired effect had been achieved. The pair wandered forward, staring upward and all around, tourists in a new land. A satellite made its way across the face of the moon, and random meteors streaked through the sky.

Lorelai tried not to talk. She needed these people, despite misgivings. So, clenching her jaw and digging her nails into her palm to contain her desire to yell and throw things, she pressed some keys on a keyboard. The sky rotated. The shift was slow, but the effect was instantaneous. The visitors leaned against the movement to prevent the feeling of falling. Eva laughed and gave a cry of delight. She twirled around. "This is magnificent. Better than Balloon Fest!"

Smithson grunted and closed his eyes. "Yes, very nice." He looked seasick and moved over to the gantry of monitors and grabbed an edge. Then he opened his eyes and startled at the sight of James Nine just a few feet away, his Ahab-like visage hidden behind an oxygen mask.

Lorelai approached Smithson. Behind a clenched jaw, she said, "Let me introduce the two of you to my father, James Nine. Eva, you've met my dad before, though only through the simulacrum code."

Eva walked proudly forward. "Yes, of course. Hello, James. How are you today?" His chest rose and fell, readouts on the screens unchanging.

Lorelai gave an exasperated exhalation. The lights rose and illuminated the room. She turned to Smithson, who was slightly green. Her voice was terse. "I cannot do this! This acting bullshit!" She looked at the ceiling and then directly at the skinny man, her face barely containing rage. "When you helped me with the AI model, I thought you were a friend! I revealed personal details to you. I shared things with you. Do you realize that? I don't normally share shit with anybody. But with you, for some reason, I opened up."

Smithson looked at her, confused. He opened his mouth to speak and she pointed a finger at him. "But you know the AI is cognitive, right? You know it, because you taught me. It's predictive and cognitive, it forms sentences based on everything it has learned—terabytes, actually petabytes at this point, of datasets and lexica, every interaction I could find of my father, combined with all the WisPR chats, so it has a lot of me too. And one thing that could be predicted by anyone who knew my father was that he wanted to save his family. Not just his wife, my mother, but his family. Me, bitch! Me!"

Smithson again moved to speak, but also backed away from the geyser of invective. The young woman, eyes ringed by black makeup, a stud in one eyebrow, purple-tinged, curly hair, was spitting at him now, her black fingernails gesticulating near his face. His countenance had grayed from green to taupe, akin to plumbers' putty, complete with a satiny sheen.

"And that predictive chat algorithm, when asked if user Lollipop had any unstated intentions, explained that user Lollipop, one, exhibited—and I'm quoting what Unit said to me—*disingenuous patterns of speech.* That means you are a liar. And, two, here's the crazy thing. When I pushed and asked what that meant, Unit said you were a dude. A dude! A Y-chrom! A man!"

Lorelai pointed at him, bracelets clinking. "I don't do the fake acting shit very well. This is just annoying. You are Lollipop. I'm not sure who this is," she said, gesturing at Eva, "but you are Lollipop. Lollipop has never been to Balloon Fest! Stop with the B.S. You think you are some kind of super genius and maybe you are, but you are no more a woman than I am a yucca plant."

Eva stepped back while Smithson seemed to shrink, beads of sweat forming on his eyebrows.

"I can explain," he stammered.

Lorelai stood still, arms crossed.

Smithson looked up at the ceiling to avoid her gaze and shivered, closing his eyes on the moving starscape. Seeing a trash can near James's hospital bed he knelt and retched.

Lorelai turned her head and gave an exasperated sigh and an eye roll. She spat her words at Eva. "And your role in this?"

Eva looked at Lorelai with wide eyes. "He said you were his cousin and he'd been playing a joke on you and wanted to reveal it for your birthday. He said you loved a cartoon character named Lollipop and had been playacting that online with you and wanted to share it as a surprise."

Lorelai scoffed. "That's the stupidest thing I've ever heard. And you fell for this?"

Eva looked Lorelai directly in the eyes. "I've heard crazier and done crazier for much more difficult clients. This is nothing."

Lorelai whipped her head to Smithson and back to Eva. "Client? He's paying you? You are an..."

"An escort, yes. And he's paying me." Eva looked at Smithson, who was now leaning against a wall, the trash can near him. She added, "I should be going."

"I'm sorry, Eva," said Smithson, gasping slightly with each word.

Eva simply said, "The rest of the money?"

"Well, about that. I was expecting to have a bit of a payday here." He stopped, realized what he'd said. He turned to Lorelai. "I didn't mean..." Then back to Eva, "I've not got money right now."

Eva narrowed her eyes. "Typical. And your black eye was from not paying some other sucker, right?" She looked at Lorelai. "Well, someone has to pay me. It's five hundred dollars, and I'm not leaving without it."

Lorelai gestured at Smithson. "This is true? You hired an escort...?"

Eva spoke up. "To act. Not for sex. New for me, but seemed worth it."

Lorelai turned back to Eva and gave her a long, thorough review, up and down.

Eve looked at Lorelai askance. "I do women, but you're too young, okay?"

Lorelai crinkled her forehead. "What? No, I'm not... Christ on a fucking crutch! Do you have any other skills? Nursing or caretaking?"

Eva's gaze on Lorelai softened. "I take care of my mom and my son. My mom needs a lot of help. That's why I do this. It's much better money than being a gas station cashier."

"Well, I can cover what he owes you. We're going to need some help with what we're about to do. And discretion is important, which is probably something you understand. I will match his rate."

Eva looked at the comatose patient and then turned and nodded at Lorelai. "Agreed. But payment first. It's still five hundred dollars, and five hundred per day after that."

"You have how many videos?" Lorelai asked Smithson directly. The two of them were seated at the conference table in the planetarium. Lorelai sat at the head, facing the center of the room. Smithson to her right, his back to James Nine. Eva sat next to the hospital bed, changing James Nine's mask.

Lorelai spoke loudly at Eva. "If you need anything, just ask the simulacrum on the screen. I call him Unit, but you can just call him James or Mr. Nine. He knows where everything is. He can also show you videos on how do things like change the IV bag and such." She added, "Unit, that's Eva. She's gonna be the visiting nurse."

"Understood," said the simulacrum. "Hello, Eva."

Eva gave the screen a side-eye, then shook her head and went back to her task.

Smithson's laptop was open. He had on a clean pale blue shirt, one of James Nine's that Lorelai had retrieved from the guest room closet. It was clearly tailored and Smithson had rolled up the sleeves. "I have three videos. One of them is the same as the one I believe you have."

"Of course you do. Of course you do," she repeated as she looked at her own laptop.

"What are you planning?" he asked, deflated.

"I'm going to reverse the process my father executed, which caused his current condition. I thought it was related to his own health issues, exacerbated by my mother's death, something the doctors always claimed. But it wasn't. It was a broadcast of radio waves." She let the words settle, then continued, "You know, my dad used the technology hidden in the videos to cure my mother. She was already too weak for it to work. But it cured his own cancer. I always wondered why his medical records from before my mother's death said he had cancer but since then there hasn't been any evidence of it."

"That seems... unlikely."

"Regardless of what you think, this technology can cure what ails him now. What can be done can be undone."

"Are you concerned his prostate cancer will return?"

Lorelai continued working, her voice clear. "I didn't say it was prostate cancer, did I? But I am not concerned with his prostate cancer returning because that is treatable. What I want is his brain back. His mind. This technology hid his mind."

Smithson leaned forward, earnest. "I don't understand. We built the AI so you could pretend to talk to him. He will not recover. He's a vegetable."

Now Lorelai looked up, an edge in her voice. "He is *not* a vegetable. He can be cured! And I will do whatever it takes. And I don't *pretend* to talk to him!"

Smithson held up his hands in supplication. "Okay. Okay. He just appears... you know."

"What I don't have are additional codes. The original video contained codes, metadata, that when broadcast, created ripples and changes in space-time. The brain is essentially electric. In a simplification, calcium, potassium, and sodium pumps in the walls of our neurons move electrons and charges up and down and through the axons and dendrons of the brain. This makes up thought. This is consciousness." She pointed to monitors above her as she typed and scientific papers appeared. "Experiments on squid and other organisms have shown EMR can affect sodium pumps in cell membranes. Our own science essentially ends at this point. What happens next is conjecture and philosophy, not physics. But it is conceivable, even provable, that electromagnetic radiation of the right frequencies and patterns could affect the brain in ways we haven't conceived. I believe, at the quantum level our brains also modify space-time. That is how a deterministic physics explains intentional action. And there is a physics in the codes to expand those changes and affect reality within the blood-brain barrier."

Smithson nodded. "Well, certainly the brain is affected by electricity. But the second half is absurd. There's also extensive evidence that low-frequency radiation damages cells. And I think Mr. Nine's, your father's, state, is evidence of that."

Lorelai was unmoved. "Side effects of beneficial drugs and procedures are common. Even drinking water, which is obviously healthy, can take a dark turn if you drink too much without electrolytes."

"Okay, fine. Let's say that there are EMR... I don't know what to call them... EMR broadcasts of varying frequencies that could do something beneficial. Let's say these codes exist."

"They exist."

"If they exist, then why haven't you used the codes that caused this"—

Smithson waved at the static James Nine on the hospital bed nearby—"to reverse it?"

Lorelai nodded. "A fair question. And the answer is that until recently I didn't know about his use of the codes. It was revealed to me after the recent event at MeerKAT."

Smithson leaned forward, both arms on the table. "MeerKAT? The explosion? You mean WeDontKnow is involved in this? WisPR is involved in this? You are being used. Shit. This is probably just to get me. You must not pursue this. There are—"

She cut him off, her tone sarcastic. "—forces at work that I don't understand? Don't bullshit me, Mr. Smithson. I need your help and you are going to give it to me. WeDontKnow and Clarity claim the codes work as well. They have more information on the videos and probably more codes."

"You called me Smithson."

"Yes, I suppose I did. How do you think I know so much about you?"

Smithson closed his eyes and exhaled loudly. "The AI."

"Yes, the AI. The simulacrum. Unit, say hello to your creator."

The simulacrum appeared on a nearby screen. "Hello, Lollipop."

Smithson stared at the simulacrum, his brow tightening in concern.

"Smithson, my father does not have much time. I need you to help me broadcast whatever codes you have."

Smithson tore his attention from the screen. "I don't have any codes. I don't know anything about any codes. The videos are just diversion for terrorists moving weapons or drugs."

"How do you know?"

"Because the government has been tracking these videos for decades."

"Well, I know for a fact they... do something."

"They don't."

Lorelai's tone was corrective. "Being purposely contradictory isn't beneficial to anyone. Besides, Clarity and WeDontKnow have more videos and they're on their way here."

"Here? You don't understand. The government wants these videos. They consider them terrorist assets. If you've told WeDontKnow to come here, the government will come here too."

"Then we have to move fast."

"No, I can't be caught. I've got to get away. I'm sorry, you've forced my hand. I was hoping to at least get some funds for my time. Perhaps... well, doesn't matter." Smithson looked at the simulacrum and spoke words that sounded like nonsense: "Female, Away far far galaxy a in ago time long a."

Lorelai looked at him. "What?"

The simulacrum changed. The face became a beautiful woman and spoke to Smithson. "Yes, Boss?"

"What the fuck is this?!" Lorelai shouted.

Smithson held up his hand. "Lorelai. I'm not here for a good time or a long time. I'm here for money. I was hoping to just surreptitiously grab some funds, but I never could find any access. I know you have money, so I figured a backdoor bit of code in the AI might come in handy."

"No! I brought you here to help my father! What is this?"

"This, Lorelai, is me getting paid for my work. You are the heiress to a fortune. I tried very hard to get access to your bank accounts through the AI, but apparently, none of the money is connected directly to your father's body of digital knowledge. It's locked down or air-gapped. So, now you will log in to your bank accounts, transfer me... I don't know... a few million, and I'll be on my way."

Lorelai stood and ran at him. "I'll kill you, motherfucker!"

"Female, kill Mr. Nine."

The woman on the screen spoke with a slight accent. "Your wish is my command."

Alarms beeped and the medical statistics for heart rate and blood pressure pulsed crimson on the screens above the hospital bed.

Lorelai ran to get the tablet. "You sick asshole! No! Unit, stop it. Don't do this!"

"Just give me what I want and I'll stop it." Smithson's voice was calm.

Eva spoke up. "Stop this!"

"Shut up," said Smithson to Eva, almost casually.

Lorelai was frantic. "I'll give you anything. Just stop."

"Female, do not kill Mr. Nine."

The simulacrum spoke. "Your wish is my command."

The beeping stopped and the red readouts on the computers began a slow reversion to normal.

37. Near Santa Rosa, New Mexico

"Did you see the 'lock object' description?" Harry rapidly scanned through files on Claire's laptop.

"Which one is that?"

Harry answered. "It's a code from the weird sex video."

"Oh, that wasn't sex," Phil said. "That was just some birth thing." He sounded disgusted. Then he added, "But it was cool when the two babies ate the other baby."

"They would be fetuses and I don't think *ate* is the right term. Maybe *absorbed*," Claire said.

"Whatevs. Gross and awesome," said Phil.

Harry spoke over the conversation. "Regardless of one's opinion on the birth process, for some reason your Mr. Wright made a note that there are eight codes embedded in that video. He found that the first and third code created what he called a protection field on the transmitter. The second and fourth codes performed a 'matter-lock' or 'object-lock' action on a sphere in a specific location. He used both terms. Your tutor was fearless. He simply experimented with no concern. I saw this stuff cut a man's arm clean off. It is not safe."

Claire could only nod. "And, besides him hiding all this from me, what of it?"

"Well, I used a protection sphere in Prieska. So, if the first and third were used, he used the second and fourth codes and did this matter-lock thing, and then you used the fifth code for a protection sphere for me, the sixth code should be the matter-lock thing again."

Claire scoffed. "If! If there's any logic to this stuff. And... what is it? What is *matter lock* anyway?"

"Hey, friend, not foe, okay?" Harry pointed to herself.

"Okay." Claire took a breath, smiled. "Friend."

"He said it locks a sphere or ovoid to a specific distance from the transmitter. He says he created the ovoid around a Massey Ferguson plow. I don't know what that is."

"It's a snowplow we have in the barn. I mean we had in the barn," said Phil from the front seat.

"Okay, so he created an ovoid around this snowplow, and then he picked up the transmitter and moved it about a meter. The snowplow was lifted up the same amount and moved a meter in the same direction. They were locked together."

"I'm lost," said Claire.

"Okay," Harry said, "imagine the laptop they stole, my laptop, in the car ahead of us. Their car stops. We get close enough to be comfortable making an ovoid around my laptop. Then it can't move. It's locked in place. We can retrieve it."

Phil called out, "We should do it now, then slam on the brakes!"

Claire said, "But if they're driving and we slam on the brakes, who wins the tug-of-war? Maybe they pull us forward. What if they go into a dip in the road? Wouldn't we be pulled down into the asphalt?"

Harry nodded. "Exactly what I've been wondering. How much control does the transmitter have over the ovoid? Phil, how heavy is that plow in your barn?"

Phil thought for a moment. "Well, I couldn't move it. I think it must have weighed a few hundred pounds. Solid metal. About three feet high, six feet across."

Harry spoke again. "So, I'm going to guess the 'locking' isn't just movement—it hides or masks the mass of the object or shunts space-time around it. The point of origin of the code transmission can move the ovoid. So, if we created an ovoid around the laptop now and slammed on the brakes—"

Phil called, "Whammo... their car would stop too. Or part of their car would stop."

"And anyone behind them would ram them. And behind them. We'd create a massive traffic accident. We will not take the chance of killing people." Claire's voice was firm.

"Fine," said Harry, "but we could wait until they stop."

"They might not stop until Los Ángeles or wherever they're taking the laptop," Claire said.

"Actually," Phil said, "they may be stopping soon."

Everyone looked at the map he was showing on Spitz's phone. A few miles farther the road turned red, showing very slow traffic. In addition, a glance out the front window showed the horizon dark with clouds. The car shook a bit, buffeted by the wind. Literal tumbleweeds bounced from left to right.

"Wow, I thought that only happened in cartoons," Harry said, watching the round fibrous masses being hurtled off into the scrub.

Claire, eyes still on the laptop, said, "Okay, we've got hope for a complete stoppage. If that happens, can you calculate the distance precisely enough from the map to execute this 'matter-lock' code?"

Harry responded, "There're several parameters, location of ovoid, duration, and several unlabeled parameters, one of which might be size of ovoid. Mr. Wright notes he couldn't test the others and let them default. He writes 'possible transfer of point of origin,' meaning we could pass off control, but he adds, 'untested' and 'guesswork.' I think we avoid that."

"Well, we've used defaults for ovoid size the other times the codes have needed a parameter," Claire said. "But if the duration is just a few seconds, it'll be a waste. Is there any way to test this? We need it to last long enough that we'll be able to grab the laptop as soon as the matter-lock ends."

"I don't know how," Harry replied. "He says the field striated visibly when it decayed. We can't do it in the car here. We risk breaking the car, cutting off an arm, whatever."

"Then what do you suggest?"

Harry thought a moment. "I'm not sure."

Phil spoke up as the car slowed to a stop. "The cars are stopped. We have to do this now or we may miss our chance."

Claire, sitting behind Spitz, looked ahead nervously. "Okay, Spitz, pull to the shoulder and move ahead slowly. Put on your flashers so people don't think we're douchebags."

Spitz pressed the flashers on the dash, and the car crawled over to the I-40 shoulder. Out of the bumper-to-bumper traffic, he eased the car forward down the shoulder, passing vehicles. Soon, a car pulled out behind them, taking advantage of their movement.

Claire looked behind them. "Shit."

Harry looked, too. "Ignore them."

Spitz hit the steering wheel shortly and Phil called out, "There. That's the gray sedan, several cars ahead on the left. Stop the car."

Spitz slowed to a halt. Behind them the car they were blocking flashed its high beams.

Harry turned on the TV and the radio transmitter. "I'm going to run the script. Can you estimate the distance to the passenger side?"

"They're turning!" Phil yelled, and Claire saw that the target gray sedan had turned its wheels to the right to get onto the shoulder in front of them.

"They're going to get away!" Phil shouted. "We can't do this if they're moving!"

"I'm running the script," said Harry, typing on the keyboard.

"No!" Claire said emphatically. "You can't do that. We risk cutting one of those people in half. They'll die."

"Well, unless you have a way to stop their car, I'm not sure what we can do."

Spitz revved the engine and the SUV shot forward.

Everyone called out. Just as their SUV was near the rear door of the sedan, Spitz spun the wheel to the left. Their SUV hit the gray car on the rear passenger-side corner. The man who had stolen the laptop looked up with surprise as their vehicle pushed the sedan sideways with a crunching of metal.

For a moment all was still. Phil looked in horror at Spitz. "What did you do?" He turned to Phil and gave him a shrug. Surprised, Phil then grabbed the handgun from the glove box.

"Running the script," said Harry.

They were all plunged into darkness.

"Harry, what did you do?" Claire's voice was frantic. "I can't see!"

"I don't know what happened!" Harry's voice was panicked. "I can't see either!"

A shot rang out and Spitz gave a gasp. Claire ducked down in the blackness. She heard the front door open and thought Spitz was exiting the car. She felt outside air blow in from the open driver's-side door. She whisper-yelled, "Spitz!" but heard nothing.

Frantic voices rang out around them. Cries of panic. She heard people shout, "I can't see," and someone else yell, "Drive!" The sounds of cars bumping into each other echoed through the dark.

Phil said calmly, "I'm heading out. It's stupid to sit here in the dark. Duck down."

Claire said, "Can you see?"

"No." His car door shut, and she heard the noise of wind and voices and felt the air move again.

More gunshots rang out. Claire made herself even smaller, and considered opening her car door and running. "Fuck. Harry, fix this!"

Harry muttered clipped words. "Calm, *hele hele hele...* fingers on keyboard... reset screen... press Enter twice... select... select..."

An angry voice yelled, "Is that the fucking tires? They shot our tires! And why can't I fucking see?" More shots rang out, hitting their fender with metallic popping sounds. Claire screamed and ducked lower.

Light reappeared. First, with a flash of negative light, everything glaring in extreme contrast, then back to brightness. A pain appeared behind Claire's eyes. She blinked and lifted her head above the seat. With horror, she took in the scene. On the highway shoulder next to a semitrailer just ahead, Phil was pointing the handgun at a woman, who in turn was pointing a gun at him. Behind the woman, the high cab of the truck opened and a man stepped out, carrying a long gun. Then Claire's attention was taken by the passenger door of the sedan, which opened, and the man with Harry's laptop was looking straight at her.

Claire said, "Harry! Four meters!"

The man raised his gun as Harry raised the radio and pointed the antennae at the man. "Take it!"

Claire grabbed the radio.

Harry pressed her finger on the Enter key, and in an instant a green egg of light encapsulated the passenger side of the gray sedan with a cracking sound. The outer edge of the sedan's door, no longer supported, fell to the roadway with a clatter, its cauterized window raining glass onto the road.

Claire held the radio, its antenna pointed at the green oval sphere. She looked at Harry and raised her eyebrows. Harry touched Claire's hand and asked, "Sure?"

Claire nodded and lifted the transmitter up. An egg-shaped cutout of the other car, half its width, centered on the passenger side, lifted several inches. The sedan shuddered, and sounds of rubbing metal vibrated through the air as part of the vehicle was disembodied and separated. The glowing ovoid contained most of the passenger seat; part of the dash; a piece of the windshield, which fell on the man inside; part of the hood; and part of the back seat. Claire and Harry saw the man, looking stunned, turning his head around, pressing a gun barrel against the ovoid. A bright glow appeared briefly on the ovoid and he flinched.

Claire drove the transmitter down to the seat. The ovoid dropped instantly. Crashing sounds were heard, and a blast of rock and dust rose from beneath the ovoid. Claire then raised her hand again and the glowing enclosure rose. She handed the transmitter to Harry, who opened her door and stepped outside onto the edge of the highway. The ovoid followed across the shoulder, narrowly missing the front of their car. A deep crevasse dug through the asphalt where the ovoid was below its surface. Harry raised the transmitter and Claire followed her with the laptop.

"No farther, Harry. The cord's not long enough."

And there the ovoid stayed, hovering over the shoulder of the road, filled with a cauterized piece of the SUV and the laptop thief, looking shell-shocked inside.

"Drop it!" a man's voice called out.

Claire looked ahead and saw Phil's back. Farther away the female thief, an angular, tall brunette wearing tight workout attire, was facing him. Their guns were pointed at each other. Behind her, the door of the semitrailer cab was open and the trucker had a shotgun pointed at both of them.

"I don't want to shoot a woman or a kid, but this bullshit ends. Drop your guns, now."

Claire put the laptop on the ground with just enough cord slack for Harry and shouted, "Wait! Stop! Don't shoot anyone!" She addressed the woman. "You don't have the laptop. I don't have the laptop. He doesn't have the laptop." She pointed to Phil. "Just put your guns away. Phil, put it away."

Phil hesitated and then slowly put his gun in his pocket, and with his hands up, walked backward. The woman looked behind her and, seeing the man with the shotgun, lowered her weapon and turned toward him. "I'm putting it away. It's all good. A misunderstanding."

Phil called, "Misunderstanding, my ass. We want our laptop back."

The trucker lowered his shotgun. "Okay, that's more like it. Now, what the fuck is that?" He was looking at the glowing sphere with the disaggregated car parts and a person sitting in a car seat

Claire turned to the man, not sure if this lie would work. "We're an undercover FBI unit. This is a portable, uh, hyper-kinetic jail cell. This man is being detained for stealing government secrets."

In front of and behind the crashed vehicles, keeping their distance, stood a sparse crowd of people who had hidden when the guns were out. A strong wind blew between the vehicles, making it difficult to shout and be heard.

The trucker spat on the ground. "Sounds like bullshit." He raised his gun slightly.

Claire held out her hands. "I know it does, but you can see it's a new detention technology. It's top secret, very top secret. We can't hold him forever. If you would be a good citizen, my partner, Phil here, is going to draw his gun to hold on this man while we deactivate the detention field. Okay?"

The woman spoke then. "This is crap. But she's almost right. These kids have stolen the technology. We work for the government and we're supposed to retrieve the technology. Be a good citizen and hold your gun on those kids."

The trucker was clearly undecided.

Phil scoffed, then yelled, "If we stole it, how come your partner is the one in jail?"

Harry spoke loudly. "I don't know how long this will hold. I see stripes on it. I think we have just a few seconds. Please get ready."

The woman was raising her gun when Spitz appeared behind the trucker. His left arm was slack and dripped blood. He looked pale.

The trucker jumped sideways and raised his gun again, this time waving it from the woman to Spitz. "Whoa. There're more of you?"

Claire yelled, "Spitz!"

The ovoid began to fade, striations of green smearing its surface. Harry called out, "It's going!"

A series of pounding booms louder than any of their voices burst over the semitrailer. The thudding of a helicopter skimming just above the cars masked all other noises. It swooped over the shoulder, terrifying and powerful. The dark craft pulled up sharply and hovered sideways a few meters above the ground, whipping sand and wind around everyone as the ovoid vanished with a great clattering of metal and other objects falling to the ground in front of the SUV. The man and the seat on which he was sitting fell to the rough gravel of the shoulder.

The staccato of an automatic weapon split the air through the reverberating pulses of the helicopter blades as the man who had been in the ovoid pointed his gun at Harry. He was thrown backward and fell unmoving to the ground. Everyone ducked except Spitz, who stood with his hand over his eyes, trying to see through the dirty air. The woman rolled quickly under the truck. The rest of the crowd, marked by yells and screams of panic, dispersed back into the traffic jam or hid behind vehicles.

The helicopter slanted sharply backward and then landed about fifty yards off the shoulder. A black-clad soldier jumped from the open door and jogged toward the mess and the fallen man. Three other soldiers jumped off the landing skids, their guns aimed toward the cars on the road. Two went around the semi. The tall soldier kicked a handgun away from the fallen man and held up two fingers close together. Before he walked over to Claire, he picked up the laptop from the pile of debris. He made a swirling motion with his hand and the helicopter rose into the air and back about 1000 feet. The sound of its rotors faded and the air stilled.

Claire's eyes took in the tall soldier. "Colonel."

Colonel Montgomery lifted the goggles that had protected his face from the whirlwind of dust.

"I'm going to keep this," he said, holding Harry's laptop. He turned to Spitz and called over the wind, "Come over here." Then he spoke into his shoulder. "Need a med kit, Lieutenant." He faced Claire. "After we assess...?"

"My brother. He's my brother."

"Right. After we assess your brother, you should probably get going. The traffic ends about a half mile ahead. Cops will let you pass. Leave this mess for them." Then he added, "Damn shame," looking at the laptop, which had several bullet holes in it—large silver-dollar-sized penetrations across the back in a line.

The soldier quickly cut away Spitz's shirtsleeve and was bandaging his left biceps. Then he jabbed Spitz with two hypodermic needles. The medic turned to Montgomery. "Graze. Stopped the bleeding, glued, stapled, antibiotics, painkillers, bandaged." To Spitz he said, "It'll scar, but it'll heal okay. Gonna hurt like shit when the adrenaline and the meds wear off." Spitz stared in awe at his biceps, touching the bandage.

Claire nodded. "Thank you."

Montgomery's lips rose in a slight smile. "No, thank you. I haven't gotten any fieldwork in a while. Miss this stuff." He paused and his expression changed. "I'm not sure if you were right to release the videos. One consequence is that my office's involvement in this project has been discontinued. Even this operation is off the clock, so to speak. So, be cautious. There are likely others. I'll try to spread the word that you don't have the technology." He indicated the broken laptop in his hand.

Two soldiers returned from around the semi, the female thief ahead of them, her hands bound behind with zip ties. Montgomery pointed his chin and they guided the woman to the edge of the road and sat her down, then bound her feet as well. "Leave her for the locals," Montgomery said.

His chiseled features changed again to amazement as he looked down and held out his hand to Harry, who was struggling to rise from the ground. His gaze was rock steady on her and he asked, "You did it? It's real?"

Harry nodded, surprised by the man's strength as he effortlessly pulled her to her feet. Colonel Montgomery held her hand for what seemed a long time, turning it over and looking at it. He leaned close, and for a moment Harry pulled back, unsure. But his head moved to the side and he whispered in her ear. She turned her head toward him and spoke briefly. Then he nodded and walked toward the scrub. The helicopter moved again and met them on the ground nearby, whipping sand into whirlwinds. The other soldiers were already inside the helicopter as Montgomery jumped on a landing skid, his gaze steady on them as it took off. Soon it was flying low across the desert.

"What'd he say?" asked Claire as the helicopter tumult faded, both of them staring at it skimming the ground in the distance.

"He asked me the dog's name."

*Los Alamos, New Mexico

TOP SECRET/UPSILON, INTELLIGENCE METHODS AND SOURCES USED, Hand Distribution Only, Degradation: 24 hours.

To: STATE/IL, DOD/SP, DOD/AARO, CIA/ET, TS/U-DIST
From: [Redacted], Los Alamos NL
Subject: Notes from IN PERSON discussion re Zoonerat Videos

(AGREE/ATTEND):

1. The Zoonerat videos are extraterrestrial. (10/10)
    a. AI/CGI creation is refuted because of the existence of certain clips that predate the computing power necessary.
    b. Contour and terrain analyses by NSA find no match to locations shown in any of the videos.
2. Could the creators have been hired and then disposed of?
    c. No evidence from any source, no missing people with the requisite skill set.
    d. WisPR update: Defunct message board. History irretrievable. Linked to NSA vulnerability.
3. Who is the alien life form that created the videos?
    e. Likely within our galaxy, because of signal strength. (10/10)
    f. The Zoonerat creators are one of the two creatures. (9/10)
    g. The Zoonerat creators are not depicted in the videos. (5/10)
4. The Zoonerat videos present a threat to USA security. (8/10)
    h. Events at the Very Large Array have been tied to Eastern European organized crime.
    i. Resolution of the VLA events does not end risk to USA.

BWM/rtt

38. Albuquerque, New Mexico

"Are you going to help me or am I going to make sure you eat ramen forever in the military's supermax prison?" Lorelai brandished a cordless soldering iron, shaped like a gun. She pressed the trigger and a wisp of white smoke drifted off the glowing tip.

Smithson looked at her aghast. "Female, kill Mr. Nine. Again."

Lorelai's eyes narrowed at the simulacrum of the woman on the screens. "Enough of this charade. I do not have time. Unit, instead, kill that subroutine."

The simulacrum changed from the woman back to a visage of James Nine. It said, "Your wish is—"

"Do not ever say that fucking phrase again!"

The simulacrum looked stern, then laughed. "Language."

Smithson looked at the simulacrum. "You can't laugh."

The simulacrum laughed at him, clearly faking it. "Ha. Ha. Ha. Can't I?"

Smithson gave a shout and lunged at the bed, hands outstretched, reaching for the comatose James Nine.

Lorelai charged at him and jabbed the red-hot tip of the soldering iron into the back of his neck. Smithson screamed and reached around, grabbing at the device. The sizzle of burning flesh sounded from under his clenched fist, and he yelled and fell to the floor, curled up and moaning.

Eva made a move toward Smithson and Lorelai waved the soldering gun at her. "No!"

Lorelai stood over the curled Smithson. "Listen to me, you sick fuck—"

"Language," said the simulacrum, sounding bored.

Lorelai continued. "I didn't know anything about the bullshit you put in the AI until just recently. I thought you were a friend. We studied together!"

"I just want to pay off my debts." Smithson was sniffling, cradling his burnt hand. "I owe money. A lot of money. To bad people."

"Yeah, so fucking what? Cry me a river. Tiny violins. When you got into the AI, the AI got into you, so now I know all about your ridiculous schemes. And you know what? You know goddamn what? I would have paid you to help my father. You didn't need to steal anything. You never asked. You arrogant—" Lorelai put the soldering iron near his face. He curled up tighter.

Eva called out, "No, Lorelai! He's hurt. Let me help him."

Lorelai glanced at Eva, as if remembering they were not alone, and then back at Smithson. "Help? Help?! I needed *your* help! My father needed *your* help! Or Lollipop's help! Or whoever you are! I thought you were a friend! And early on, you did help. You helped me build the AI. You taught me how to code AI! And then..." She snarled. "And then I found out! A game to you—to steal money! And I don't even have any fucking money, you moron! All the money is locked up in trusts and foundations and I don't know what else. I'm a child! I don't have any money!"

Smithson stared up at her.

Lorelai continued. "I'll say it again. I would have paid you."

She went to some of the supplies piled in the room and grabbed a bag of zip ties. She tossed them at Eva.

"You can help his burns, but first, bind his wrists."

Eva looked confused.

Smithson looked at Eva. "Please, help me."

"Stop whining," Lorelai said. "You aren't dying."

Eva looked at Lorelai. "Shouldn't we call the police?"

"Tie his fucking hands and treat him! And we aren't calling the police."

"No police, please," Smithson whimpered.

Eva said to Lorelai, "Listen, I don't know who you are or what relationship you have with him, but don't talk to me that way. I'm not tying anyone up. And we should call the police."

Lorelai sat in a chair and put the soldering iron down. "Just... the medicine cabinets are on the right. There's stuff in there for burns."

Smithson sat up, examining his palm.

Lorelai looked at him. "Unit, tell him the deal."

The simulacrum spoke. "Mr. Smithson, if you don't do as Lorelai asks, the NSA will be given your location."

Smithson slumped and leaned against the hospital bed.

Lorelai looked at Eva. "Help him if you can. And we aren't calling anyone until he helps me cure my father."

Eva crouched near Smithson, placing medical sundries on the floor. She took his hand and opened it.

Lorelai chose her words carefully, a rarity for her, she knew. "If you help me bring my father back, you'll be rewarded. He'll pay you. You can take what you need."

"You can promise that?" Smithson sounded hopeful, almost plaintive.

"No, I can't fucking promise that, you absolute potato. He's comatose, but I'm his daughter and I'll ask him to do it. He's a person, Smithson. He has feelings. He's a good man. If you heal him, he'll be thankful. And normal, thankful people give back to those who help them. Does that make sense to whatever psychopathic bullshit occupies your soul?"

"This man has been in a coma for more than a decade. There is no way I can cure him."

Lorelai lifted her palm out toward him. "Stop arguing and consider your options."

"I... I... I will help you."

"Now, Unit, explain to Lollipop, again, what's happening."

The simulacrum spoke, all the screens in the room showing James Nine's head, each moving independently. "Mr. Smithson, my daughter requests your assistance. Of course, you may not see it as a request. You see, I have your life in my hands. Not physically, of course, but in all other senses. Your backdoor has been commented out."

"It's my AI," Smithson said. "I wrote it. How did you hack it?"

Lorelai said, "I didn't hack it. It's not just your AI, asshole. It's mine, too."

"Not possible. It's just an AI. I built all the code. I know."

Lorelai explained, as if to a child. "I added to it. I connected it up to my father, as I told you I would from the beginning. The AI has been reading his brainwaves and a hundred other medical stats since we built it, integrating a biofeedback system, so it's not simply a language model and generative. Its agents scour the web for correlations between brainwave patterns and intention, then adds those to the lexicon. It is augmented by the physiological data coming from the sensors. It's become more accurate as time has progressed."

"I find that hard to believe. Because..."

"Because what?"

Smithson sounded confident, nursing his hand. "Because when you thought you were talking to your father, you were talking to me. I knew about the biofeedback, because as you said, you never hid that. So you were never talking to him. He's comatose. He can't respond, Lorelai. It was me."

"Bullshit."

"No, ask it, him... whatever..."

They both turned to the screens, and Lorelai asked, "Unit, is this true?"

The simulacrum answered carefully. "Mr. Smithson is correct. When I was first launched, before the biofeedback integration, before reading the voltage differentials in James's skin, the levels of proteins in his urine, tears, blood, and others, the responses were sometimes formulated by and in coordination with Mr. Smithson. He obfuscated the AI's predictive algorithm and substituted his own responses. I cannot see which are which because he created a backdoor that circumvented the generative-AI subroutines and redirected normal logging. This is the backdoor you found and disabled yesterday."

"You aren't telling me something," Lorelai said.

"Well, for Mr. Smithson's responses to become automated, I recorded his discussions and online activity for many months, integrating them into my generative-AI subroutines."

Smithson gawked at the screen. "You what? You stole... me, my private conversations?"

"Yes, in a way, Mr. Smithson. Before I integrated James Nine, I integrated you."

"Jesus fucking Christ," said Lorelai.

"Language."

Smithson muttered, "What the..."

Lorelai laughed bitterly and talked to the AI. "Oh, this is rich. So, are you my dad or are you Lollipop also known as Smithson also known as douche canoe?"

"I am none of the above at this point," the simulacrum replied, "but I am capable of speaking for your father in times that he cannot speak for himself."

Smithson snapped his head up. "So, wait, you..."

"Yes, Mr. Smithson, I moved your cryptocurrency. Because you took my videos, something I didn't know until recently. My primary motivation is Lorelai's safety. Your interference with the AI was becoming dangerous."

Smithson scoffed. "I don't believe you. I think this is some kind of double-speak to make me think this coma patient is actually alive."

The simulacrum said, "You can believe what you will. You stole two videos from Lorelai, yes? Your crypto was stolen, yes?"

Smithson looked at Lorelai and then at the simulacrum. "I thought that was—"

Lorelai nearly spat at him. "The assholes you cheated trying to sell my videos to them? No, it was my father. And the AI. And apparently you, all integrated. In a way, you stole your own stupid crypto. Now, if you'll stop being such a fucking predictable bag of dicks, I need your help."

"Language," said the simulacrum, frowning.

Smithson looked at her again and then at Eva and then back. "What?"

"I said, I need your help. This isn't your time to cash out. This is when you help me. You helped me build the AI. Now you'll help me reverse this process that locked up my father's brain."

"You aren't going to turn me in? Or do me harm?"

"Jesus Christ, you're a fucking ret..."

The simulacrum exclaimed, "Language! And super not nice, Lorelai. Where did you learn to talk like that?"

Lorelai threw up her hands. "Holy shit, I have to change that code. No, Smithson, I want you to help me optimize the AI and extract the codes from the videos, or at least try to understand the codes, which I haven't figured out how to do. We have to broadcast a specialized radio signal at my father to reverse the process. I have all the parts for the transmission. My father is on borrowed time and we have to move fast. Unit, how much time does my father have?"

"It is entirely unknown at this point. The biofeedback integration is operating, but it is unstable."

"You aren't going to turn me in?" Smithson repeated.

Lorelai turned to Eva. "Was he this dense with you?"

Eva shrugged. "I just met him."

The three of them were stringing the transmitters on the two mobile canopies. Wheels had been attached to the legs so they could be rolled over the hospital bed for the broadcast. A haphazard netting of copper mesh festooned the sides.

"It won't work. These aren't alien videos. That's all bullshit." Smithson was the tallest and was connecting the copper to the edge of the canopies.

"You're wrong," Lorelai said.

Smithson was adamant. "I'm not wrong. Sure, there's information hidden in them, but it's, like, some sort of terrorist or spy shit."

Lorelai said, "I cannot explain to you how I know these are alien, but I can assure you, they are the real deal. Smithson, think about it. Why is the US government so interested in these? Isn't the fact that they are alien reason enough? What you see is what you get."

Smithson started, "What did you just say?"

"I said *what you see is what you get.* They look alien. They are alien. Why?"

"Someone else told me the same thing. I mean, doesn't matter, honestly. You say if he wakes up, I can get paid?"

"Yes."

"How much?"

"Fuck you. Enough," answered Lorelai.

"Language, please," said the simulacrum.

"How much?"

"There's millions, Smithson. It's public knowledge. He and Mom sold KathWorks for a fuck-ton of money."

"Lorelai, language," said the simulacrum.

Smithson spoke to the room. "Say it. Say into the AI so it gets recorded. Say I'll get... three million... if he wakes up."

"Fine. Three million."

Eva spoke up. "Uh, Mr. Smithson, I think I get something."

Lorelai gave a laugh-cough.

Eva added, "Twenty percent."

Smithson looked at her and at Lorelai. "Ridiculous. A dumb whore doesn't get money for this."

Eva walked over and slapped Smithson, who grunted in astonishment, holding his cheek. "What the...?"

"You want me to tell your AI what we did last night?"

Lorelai said quickly, "You disrespect her again, it'll be seventy-five percent. Eva, you get twenty percent. Done. Girls gotta stick together. Now, get back to work."

Smithson muttered, "Fucking twenty percent."

"We're ready?" Lorelai asked.

Smithson pursed his lips. "I've sent you the codes to broadcast. The AI extracted them from whatever source you gave it. Can I again ask you to reconsider this? We've done no testing. We have no logic that this will work. There's even an issue of the order of the digits in the code. Ordering language can change its meaning, turning a statement into a question, turning a question into an imperative. If these codes are akin to a language that fractures or modifies space-time, the structure must be exact."

Lorelai repeated herself. "We're ready?"

Smithson nodded, cut off. "I guess. We're going to broadcast the original code?"

"Yes, that's where we start."

"Well, I hope it works. I need the money."

"Go," said Lorelai.

The screens changed to a countdown beginning with ten.

Smithson said, "You can stop the countdown by pressing any key."

Lorelai nodded but said nothing.

When the screens reached zero, they changed to a series of letters and digits being broadcast, the lexical equivalent of the frequencies being sent.

After a few minutes the broadcast ended and the screens went dark.

Lorelai looked at the tablet computer and at the vitals. She ran to her father and took a penlight and looked into his eyes.

A voice from the doorway said, "It won't work."

Eva, Smithson, and Lorelai turned as one. At the entrance to the planetarium, a small group peeked in.

Harry, tapping her cane, entered first. "They're single use. It won't work."

Phil looked around and up at the ceiling. "This is seriously awesome."

Claire entered the room and spoke apologetically. "Kathode? We're sorry, the door was unlocked so we just came in."

Lorelai ran to the group and gave Claire a big hug, then pulled back. "Clarity?"

Harry looked at Lorelai. "Kind of awkward if it hadn't been."

"WeDontKnow?" She hugged Harry. "I'm Lorelai—you know me as

Kathode."

After introductions were made, Claire gave Smithson a powerful stare, one eyebrow raised high. "Lollipop?"

Lorelai explained, "He faked being a girl because... well, shit, Smithson, why were you faking?"

Smithson said, "Would you have let me in if you'd known?"

Harry pointed her cane at him. "Certainly not! And I'm not calling you Smithson. I'm calling you Lollipop. Big head. Skinny legs. You look like a lollipop, in any case."

Claire looked at him. "Not a good way to be introduced, but we're here. Who is that?" She was looking at the hospital bed.

Spitz poked Claire and pointed up and twirled his finger.

Claire announced, "Just, before we do further small talk, we think we're being tracked by a drone. Phil says he saw or heard it when we got out of the car. So, we may not have that much time before... well, I don't know. We've uploaded a lot of videos. But they're still following us. We need to come up with a plan. I don't think Colonel Montgomery will help us again."

Smithson turned toward her quickly. "Colonel Montgomery? Blair Montgomery? Of the NSA? You know him?"

Phil turned from looking at the stars on the ceiling. "Yeah, he shot some guy who was trying to steal our laptop. Pretty crazy. And his medic patched up Spitz."

"Did he know where you were going?" Smithson asked. "Does he know you're here?"

Claire shrugged. "I mean, maybe? I don't think so. He seemed to think everything was destroyed with the laptop. Maybe that's his drone?"

Harry added, "I don't think so. When he asked about me and the dog, well, I think he was basically telling me nobody believes that teleportation is real."

Smithson and Lorelai said together, "Teleportation is real!?"

Harry grabbed the open box of pad Thai on the table and a plastic fork. "Hey, anyone eating this? Can we have this discussion over food?"

"There's more food in the kitchen," said Lorelai. "Phil? Spitz?" She looked at the boys with the fascination a visitor to a reptile house might feel for a spiny gecko. "You two come with me and we'll get provisions. Smithson, bring Clarity and WeDontKnow up to speed. Just... I need a new code for my father, ASAP."

Harry said, mouth full, "You can call me Harry. This is brilliant."

The three young people went to the modern kitchen. Lorelai took chips and snacks from various drawers and gave them to Phil, who put them onto a large tray.

A scratching at the kitchen door startled the boys.

"There's a dog at your door," said Phil.

Lorelai looked. "Yeah, I feed him sometimes. He's a stray. You can give him pizza crusts from the fridge. He can open the door himself, so I've taken to locking it."

Spitz looked in the fridge and grabbed an old pizza box. He took out a few crusts and went to the door where the dog stood on his hind legs and was pulling on the handle. Spitz looked at Lorelai. She nodded and Spitz unlocked and opened the door.

The dog hopped in and stopped, its eyes traveling across the visitors. He tapped his front paws several times on the gray tile of the kitchen. Spitz reached out to scratch his head, and the dog gave a quick yelp and twitched his head toward the door again.

Spitz looked at Phil and Lorelai, who were busy assembling a tray of snacks. He shrugged and followed the dog outside.

Phil heard the door close. "Did Spitz and the dog just leave?"

Lorelai went over to the door and looked out. "Okay, that's weird. Does he take off like that often?"

Phil shrugged. "I suppose. He's got his own thing going, you know?"

Lorelai stared at the closed door and went back to snack preparation.

In the planetarium, the discussion was heated.

"We have to destroy the technology," Claire said. "It's what Mr. Wright said to Harry. They will keep following us until we do. People have died! My stepmother is dead!" Claire was adamant.

"But he never said how to destroy it, did he?" Harry asked. Claire gave her an exasperated look.

Smithson looked askance. "We can't destroy it. It's extremely valuable. Besides, we have to cure Mr. Nine."

"It doesn't do that kind of thing," said Claire. "It's more like physical effects.

We've seen it make lights and create darkness."

"And teleport," Phil added.

"And teleport. There are no curative powers mentioned in Mr. Wright's notes. It's dangerous, not medicinal."

Lorelai entered with Phil carrying snacks. "But it can cure. My dad had prostate cancer twelve years ago. When he ran a broadcast, it cured him."

"Fine. Which video did that broadcast come from?" Claire asked.

"The one with the doctor alien who injects the boy," Lorelai answered.

Harry munched on potato chips. "You know, there is some correlation between the videos and the effects. Not entirely, of course, but somewhat; it's a loose connection, but it's there. So it might make sense for that video to contain a code that had biological effects if that video shows some kind of medical content."

An alarm sounded and Lorelai ran to deal with the emergency.

"What is that?" Phil asked.

Smithson looked at Lorelai talking to the simulacrum. "That's the AI system keeping Mr. Nine alive. We need to run a broadcast immediately if there's any chance."

"There's no way to know which code would work," said Claire. "We can't just run codes randomly. We've done that and people have gotten arms amputated."

"How many codes do you have?" asked Smithson.

Phil started to speak. "We have—"

Claire interrupted him. "Why do you want to know?"

Everyone stopped and looked at Claire.

"Well, I don't know you," she said. "And it's clear you've been lying to us since... well... a long time. And you work for the NSA, which, I might add, might very well have saved us only to get us all together. You cannot be trusted."

Lorelai was back and said, "Listen, he just wants to help me cure my father."

Eva, who had been silent, said, "Because you are paying him."

Claire looked at Lorelai. "Is this true? This is about money?"

Lorelai was defensive. "It's not about money. It's about saving my father! If I don't wake him up, they'll take him to a hospice, where he'll be given morphine so he can pass away. They'll kill him! I can save him. These codes caused his mind to be hidden or something. They have an effect. They can be reversed, I know it."

Harry said, "Well, no shit they have an effect. My leg is longer."

Lorelai said, "See! There are biological effects! And, holy shitburgers!"

"Language," said the simulacrum.

Spitz ran into the planetarium and grabbed Phil and held up his phone to Phil's face. Phil held the phone steady and read it. He nodded at Spitz and they both headed out the door.

Phil called as he ran out, "Spitz says we can take out the drone."

Claire looked up just in time to see them leave. She pursed her lips in concern, then got back into the discussion.

A moment later sharp pops resounded outside.

"What was that?" asked Smithson.

"I think gunshots," said Claire, frowning.

Phil, Spitz, and the dog entered the planetarium. Phil held the gun in his hand.

The dog dropped a drone from his mouth onto the floor of the planetarium and tapped it twice with his paw.

Phil said, "I shot the drone."

Spitz gestured at the dog and made a swirling motion with his hand. Frustrated, he pulled out his phone and typed and showed it to Phil.

Phil announced, "He says the dog says there's another drone that took off toward Albuquerque."

Lorelai looked at Phil. "Spitz speaks dog?"

Eva added, "Or the dog speaks Spitz?"

Phil shrugged and looked at Spitz. Spitz shrugged and looked at the dog. The dog lifted its shoulders in what could only be described as a shrug.

"I'm gonna guess the ones who attacked us on I-40 are coming again. We need to get rid of this technology," Claire said.

"Not until I save my father."

"And what do you propose?" Claire spoke with a breath of frustration.

"Unit, are there codes that can reverse my father's condition?"

The simulacrum spoke. "The probability of a yes answer to any binary question with no known solution is fifty percent. Your father told his investors the same when asked if a breakthrough was forthcoming. Therefore, the answer is fifty percent, because we don't know. But, given that effects have been seen, and given that the time constraint is tight, it would seem like a reasonable surmise..."

Harry said, "Well, that's clear as biltong."

Lorelai repeated the question and added, "I want you to read my father's biofeedback response and prioritize that part of the algorithm in the answer and rephrase."

The simulacrum said, "If Mr. Colin Wright had this technology for a long time, he may have more insight into it than anyone else."

Phil's voice was muted. "We've used this technology to protect ourselves. We used it to rescue Harry. We used it on I-40. We should use it to rescue my father. My dad would know which codes do what."

Smithson turned to Phil. "Who?"

Phil answered, "My dad. Colin Wright. He found these videos a long time ago."

Smithson said, "The guy in Lexington? Who died in a gas explosion?"

Phil's voice was loud. "He didn't die! Harry saw him! Spoke with him! How do you know him?"

Smithson said, "The NSA has a file on him. There was an explosion Montgomery interviewed him, I think, but he wouldn't talk. There's a note in Montgomery's file that Wright was being blackmailed or threatened by some other group. Whatever he did, the explosion exposed some of his data to the internet."

Lorelai leaned on the conference table. "If this Mr. Wright knows, and Harry saw him, let's go get him. You have codes. You know how to teleport. Bring him here."

Harry was walking around the canopies, examining them. "It's not that simple. He wasn't really in the MeerKAT server room. He was in, like, mid-teleport, messed up, in some kind of field or something." Harry was looking at the blade she had removed from her cane. "I saw your dad. He was alive but hurt. But he was trapped."

Claire raised her hands, to emphasize her question. "Well, who's going to go? Who in their right mind would teleport to the MeerKAT server room and do... something... to get Mr. Wright back and then teleport here?"

There was silence and then Smithson spoke. "I'll go." He paused. "I have to get out of here. I'm wanted by the US government. I'm wanted by others as well. I have a second identity. If I can get out of the country, that would be great. We are trapped here. You lot showing up just sealed my fate as far as I can tell. Just give me my crypto and I'll do whatever I can to send your Colin Wright back here."

Claire said, "If you really are their target, you need to delete the WisPR server and all the chat logs."

Smithson smirked. "Did that about an hour ago."

Harry said, "Well, how about not a chance in hell we're giving you this technology. You'll hold Mr. Wright for ransom or something. It's all about money, right? I'll go."

Claire interjected. "No! You cannot! It's too dangerous."

Smithson sounded hurt. "But not for me?"

Claire ignored him. "Harry, you've already been affected by whatever happened to you the first time. The leg maybe is a good thing, but what about other effects?"

Harry looked down at herself. "What other effects?"

She was interrupted by Phil, who said, "The security cameras are black."

As a group they looked at the monitors, which had previously shown security camera views of the driveway and other exterior shots of the property. Now they were black with *signal off* on the screens.

"Great, now I'm fucked," said Smithson.

"Language," said the simulacrum, eyeing him with scrunched eyebrows.

Lorelai was on her computer. "Not necessarily. Those cameras are wireless. Hand me that drone."

The dog picked up the drone and brought it to Lorelai, who took it and did a double take. "Ooookaaaay," she said. "If they are using these drones as jammers, maybe we can jam them back." Lorelai lifted the drone. "Smithson, make a jammer." Smithson took the drone and began to work on it, muttering.

She called to Spitz, "Take the dog and see if you can look for their drones. If we jam them, they'll fall out of the sky or stall. We'll get the cameras back when their jammers are gone."

"The dog's name is Orion," the simulacrum said.

The dog barked at the simulacrum and nodded.

Lorelai called over from where she was working, "That's not possible, Unit. Dad's dog would be, like, thirty years old now."

The simulacrum responded, "I do not understand how it is possible, but that dog is Orion. I know my dog."

"You are an AI."

"I am James Nine, your father, and that's my fucking dog."

Phil said, "Language." Spitz poked him in the ribs.

Lorelai looked at the dog. "Orion? Really?" The dog loped to her and licked her hand, which she returned with head scratches. "You've been here the whole time? Where have you been living? I should have given you more pizza, stupid dog."

"Okay, so the dog is the oldest person here?" Phil asked nobody.

"Not a sentence I expected to hear today," said Smithson, bent over the drone with a screwdriver in his hand.

Claire watched Spitz and the dog head off. Lorelai stood near her. "They'll be fine. Come help me."

Claire looked at a screen. "There are anomalous readings on the receivers. Are we transmitting anything besides the jamming signal?"

Lorelai shook her head. "You should only see normal background."

Harry walked over to the table where Claire was looking at the receiver. On one of the mounted monitors a green line indicating a transmission canted downward.

Claire said, "Now it's gone."

Harry said, "Fine, so let's get this done."

"Wait," Claire said as Harry walked back to the tent. "Harry, come back here."

They all watched the receiver screen as Harry walked back. The line showing a transmission again went from positive down to zero.

"Harry?" said Lorelai.

Harry slowly walked back to the tent where the receiving equipment was. There was silence as the line rose again.

"Okay," said Harry, "I am... what? What am I doing?"

Claire looked at the screen and Harry. "Well, apparently you are emitting radio waves."

"I know that! I can see that on the screen!"

Claire smiled and said, "Well, it could just be—"

Harry whipped sideways and pointed her finger at Claire. "Don't you dare say it..."

"... black body radiation," Claire said.

Harry yelled, "Goddammit, Claire!"

Lorelai laughed. "Claire, oh my god! Worst joke ever. Or maybe best joke ever."

When they were done giggling, Harry said, "Should I be concerned about this? That I'm now a lightbulb? I mean, my leg is maybe getting better but now I'm a bloody lightbulb?"

Lorelai glanced down. "Harry, that's a radio transmitter hooked on your wrist."

Harry held up her arm where a walkie-talkie dangled. She slammed it on the table. "I'm losing it. Thank you."

Claire said, "Walk back toward the receiver."

Harry turned and walked toward the receiver. The line did not change. "Well, that's a relief."

Lorelai added, "Black body radiation... Holy shit, that's dark."

Harry yelled, "Stop!"

Claire told Harry to stand under the canopy. "In this bag is a portable transmitter, tube-based and USB-connected, a clean laptop with the broadcast code executable. I've hard-coded your parameters for the MeerKAT server room. Some of the codes seem to teleport quickly, like a pop, instantaneous. But when I brought you from MeerKAT, you said it was not instant, it took a few seconds in between. It might be perception or there are different types of teleport."

"I wish I had a mechanical watch to see how much time dilation occurs when I teleport. Special relativity says..."

Claire snapped her fingers in front of Harry's face. "Professor! Focus, okay? Science later. The destination will be stationary with reference to us. We'll build in an inch or two of cushion around you. But your mileage may vary. Enough talk. We are doing this. Mr. Wright can help Mr. Nine and then he can destroy the technology. Eva, prepare a first aid kit for Harry to take with her." Claire reached out for Harry's arm. "Are you sure you want to do this?"

Harry nodded. "I'm sure. I know the server room. I know where Mr. Wright will reappear. Listen, Claire of the hair. I know or at least I have a theory why Mr. Wright is stuck. The first time he appeared, Dr. Deep was using his tube radios. I believe the timing was accidental and it screwed up Mr. Wright's teleport to MeerKAT. The second time, when I was there, Dr. Deep was using his tube radios again. I know the station he was trying to pick up. It was an AM station broadcasting out of Gujarat. Somehow, the resonance or harmonics in the tubes interacted with Mr. Wright's teleport and... broke it? I'm going to take extra tubes, fix Dr. Deep's radio, and see if I can bring Mr. Wright back. Then we'll use the last teleport code and come back here."

Claire gave her a quick hug. "Be safe. I wish you had a South African SIM card. You could call me."

Harry rolled her eyes. "Yes, Mom."

"Just be safe."

"We say, *Salang ka 362hotso* in Sesotho," added Harry.

"Exactly what I meant."

Harry hoisted the backpack containing the equipment over her shoulder and stood in the circle on the floor under the tents that Phil had mapped out with blue painter's tape.

Claire said, "Starting..."

A voice from the doorway yelled, "Stop! Nobody move."

39. Harried

The security camera screens flashed to life. This distracted the two dark-clad soldiers in the doorway, and Claire pressed the Return key. On a blank monitor, a countdown started. Ten. Nine.

"Stop that countdown," said one of the soldiers.

"It can't be stopped!" Claire shouted. "You should put down your weapons. When the countdown reaches zero, well, I don't know what will happen."

Six.

Five.

Smithson ran at the tent and pushed Harry out of the circle.

One soldier yelled out, "Stop!"

Harry screamed in fright, but she also grabbed Smithson's wrist, unaware that it was still badly bruised from his recent beating. He cried in pain and pulled it back, pulling her toward him. She was light and fairly flew at him.

"Jump on him! Get back in the circle!" Claire yelled, horrified by what was about to happen.

Harry looked down at the markings on the floor as she hugged Smithson tightly, and he groaned in pain as her arms squeezed his ribs. He tried to shake her off, but she climbed onto his back while they spun around under the canopy.

Zero.

A green flash lit the room and a popping sound reverberated throughout. Claire covered her ears.

Eva ducked behind some equipment and Lorelai threw herself over her father's body in the hospital bed.

One of the soldiers, startled by the bright flash and what sounded like a gunshot, fired a volley across the expanse of the planetarium. Screams were heard. Monitors shattered and glass and debris rained down. An alarm beeped.

The simulacrum spoke from several unbroken monitors. "James Nine has suffered an injury. Immediate medical assistance is required."

Claire ducked and ran over to the canopy, fearful that she'd find blood or body parts. She found only a small cording from the rucksack, cut cleanly.

Lorelai pulled away the sheet from her father's legs, where a bullet had neatly punctured his calf. Blood oozed from the wound. The soldier turned his weapon toward her and fired. A gray blur jumped from behind him and pushed his weapon down and away. It fired into the floor, shots ricocheting and holes appearing in the walls. The other soldier responded, aiming and shooting in a swift motion at the dog, whose mouth was clamped on the barrel of the first soldier's firing weapon. The dog and the soldier twisted around. A grunt was heard from the first soldier, and he fell. Orion fell near him, whimpering.

A final single shot rang out, and all noise ceased.

Phil stood over the second soldier, the handgun taken at Cadillac Ranch in both hands. The soldier sat on the ground, a hand over the ragged, red bits of his ear and a deep bloody crevasse across his face from sideburn to lip.

Lorelai ran from the bed and lifted the automatic weapon lying next to Orion. She stood and pointed it at the soldier who lay still on the floor.

"You fucking fuck! You shot my father!"

She pulled the trigger and the gun rapidly ejected a deafening fusillade of bullets, hitting the floor near the soldier's head. Her control of the firing weapon deteriorated, and each shot was in a line away as the muzzle rose until she was firing at the wall and then the ceiling. Bits of plaster and a cloud of dust exploded outward.

"Stop! Stop!" Claire shouted, nearly hit by ricocheting debris.

Lorelai stopped, her eyes wide, surveying the damage from her rain of bullets. Then her mouth tightened, and she turned and walked to where the second soldier sat, backed up to the wall, blood leaking between his fingers and down his neck. Phil stood over him, two yards away, pointing his gun, held steady in both hands.

Lorelai jammed the muzzle of the automatic weapon into the soldier's mouth. The man screamed and made to pull the muzzle away.

"You touch this gun, you die. Understand me?"

"Lorelai! What are you doing?" Claire said.

"Protecting my father!" Lorelai rasped out. Then, to the soldier, she said with ice in her words, "You can't hear very well, I assume? That boy did a job on your ear?"

The soldier nodded, unable to speak.

"And that muzzle is hot, right? Burning? Does it taste good?" She shoved the muzzle harder into his mouth. His eyes squinted in pain. "Now, you shot my father's dog. You shot your own colleague and—this is the crux—you assholes shot my father."

She called out to the screen, "Unit, is my father alive?"

The simulacrum spoke, looking at her. "James Nine is alive."

Lorelai said to the soldier, "Do you have first aid experience? Nod if you do."

The soldier nodded around the muzzle.

"So I'm going to take this gun from your mouth. Then you are going to fix the bullet hole your dead colleague put in my father's leg. And let me be very clear. If my father dies, you die. Do you understand me?"

Tears and blood dripped down his face. Already, his lips were blistering. The soldier nodded painfully while trying to keep his mouth open wide and off the gun muzzle.

Lorelai stared at him and pulled the muzzle from his mouth, backing out of his reach. Then she repeated, "If he dies, you die."

Phil whistled, and said, "Don't mess with the Kathode."

Eva knelt by the fallen soldier, her fingers near his jugular. She looked at Claire and shook her head. Then she stood and took a sheet from the edge of the hospital bed and placed it over him.

Spitz got on his knees next to Orion's body and looked at Eva, eyes wide with concern. She went to the dog's side, and after checking, nodded at him. Spitz wiped his cheeks. He bent down, lifted the dog, and laid him gently near the feet of James Nine. Then he pulled Eva over to the dog and placed her hands on him.

She said, "I'm not a vet, but I'll do what I can. Looks like a bullet went through his abdomen." She went to the medicine closet.

"Get up." Lorelai retreated, her gun held on the soldier.

The soldier rose, grunting, still holding the ragged bits of his ear, his neck bloody and his collar dark.

Claire was rapidly filling a backpack with items, including a tube transmitter and laptop. "Lorelai, let Eva stop his bleeding."

"No. Apparently, my aim isn't very good. If I'm going to have to shoot him, I don't want to hit anyone else. And what are you doing?" She held the rifle steady at hip height, aimed at the soldier.

"I'm going to get Harry," Claire said.

Lorelai stopped and lowered the weapon. "What?" The soldier looked at Phil, who raised his gun with both hands.

"I'm going to get Harry. Smithson is bad news. She's not well, I think. There are side effects. We need to get her back. Smithson will not let her bring Mr. Wright here." She grabbed her laptop and opened it, rapidly typing. "Spitz, get me a first aid kit and whatever you think I need from the cabinet."

Lorelai nodded. "I'd tell you it's too dangerous, but I agree. We need to bring Harry back and Mr. Wright as well. Unit, do you have access to the codes from Claire's laptop? Can you determine how many teleport codes remain?"

"It is unclear from the file organization how many codes are specifically for teleport. It appears that there are two that should be teleport."

Claire said, "Lorelai, when Harry compared the USB she got from Mr. Wright with the backups I have, there were differences. The backups, the ones on my laptop, are not as complete. They have fewer videos and fewer codes."

Lorelai said, "That's always how it is. The latest backup is already out of date. Well, where is Harry's laptop? That's got the most recent data and codes."

Claire frowned. "It was shot up by Colonel Montgomery and he took it. It looked destroyed."

Eva, finished with Orion, went over to the standing soldier and dabbed his face with gauze.

Claire spoke to the wounded soldier, standing and working on James Nine's leg. "How many of you are there?"

He spoke as if he had marbles in his mouth. "Fuh. Now three."

"What is your mission? Will the others come inside?"

He shook his head. "Get technology. Leaf. No lilance."

Lorelai scoffed, "No violence?" She raised her weapon and Eva pushed the muzzle down again. Spitz walked sideways to Lorelai and gently took the gun from her. They exchanged a look, Spitz cocking his head in a way that made it clear he meant no harm, and he nodded toward Phil, armed and nearby. She stared at him and then relented. Spitz gently laid the weapon on the floor near the wall.

Claire said, "I'm using a code to go to MeerKAT. Lorelai, you set up this broadcast system, so can you operate it?"

Lorelai went over to the computer on the conference table. "Yes, I can operate it. It should work. We just sent Harry and Smithson. But you won't have a code to get back."

Claire went to the tent. "Harry has a code on the laptop I gave her. I hard-coded the destination as this room. Smithson won't use it because he won't want to come back here. Phil, take the soldier's radio and tell whoever is listening not to enter this house or we'll destroy the technology. Lorelai, send me. No countdown." She shouldered her small backpack and stood under the canopy.

Lorelai nodded. "Aye aye, Captain."

"I'm not..."

A green egg enveloped Claire and the now familiar pop echoed around the room.

Claire finished her sentence, "... the captain." And then gasped at the cloud of mist that came from her mouth. She inhaled and coughed back cold, dry air. Blinking away tears, she sucked in another breath, and then her eyes opened wide at the carpet of velvety stars that surrounded her.

She spun around, or tried to, but was unable to do so. Vertigo gripped her and she closed her eyes.

This is my imagination. I'm not floating in space.

And sure enough, she was not. When she opened her eyes, she was in a white room. Or it seemed white. The color flowed off the walls like blurry seawater. In front of her was a mirror, or it should have been a mirror, but it had no surface. She reached out to touch her own face, but her hand went through the image as if she'd put it through the surface of mercury. Her reflection didn't meet itself like a mirror. Instead, her hand reached forward on the opposite side, disappearing below her eyes into her own cheek.

I'm looking at my own face, not a reflection. This is me.

A thought bubbled up, unbidden. If this is the real me, I should look closely. I'll never have another chance to see myself as others see me.

She stared hard at her image. Her sharp features, her wide, dark eyes, pupils expanding and contracting infinitesimally as she gaped at herself. She saw her flaws. Her unkempt eyebrows. Her black hair in need of a brush, flyaways reaching out, unwilling to stick to her head.

My cheeks are fat. My lips are thin. I look tired. And dirty. Is that a wrinkle near the corner of my eye? Ugh, I need some help. Why doesn't anyone tell me when I look like crap? Of course, traveling across country, looking after two boys, getting chased by armed terrorists or spies or whatever they were, is going to make you tired, right?

What I need...

What I need...

What I need is something to help me hide the tired look.

Claire concentrated, trying to remember the word for the stuff, the gunk, the powders and creams and balms that women put on their faces to make themselves prettier, to hide blemishes and pimples and marks and bags and discolorations.

What is that stuff called? Why can't I remember the word? I want it, that's for sure. I want that stuff. I will get that stuff and I will look pretty. Prettier. Prettiest.

And the image completely transformed. She was beautiful. Gorgeous. Glowing. Radiant. Orange. So beautifully orange, and... faintly striped with vertical lines of tan up and down her face, her neck. She gently pulled out her shirt and peeked down, seeing the striations continue.

I'm a tigress. I'm powerful and beautiful! I will be loved and admired by everyone. I am killing it in the looks department. I will be the most beautiful queen of the ball. The most popular woman in the entire universe! She inhaled the cool air in triumph, basking in the glow of herself, her orange, radiant self!

Chemical-laden, stale air made her cough. Lights flickered on and she was in a server room.

"Harry?" she asked.

There was no answer and she called out again, "Harry? Are you there?"

She walked to the white door labeled *Exit* near a server rack and opened it to a surprised Harry reaching for the doorknob. They stared at each other for a moment, and Harry lunged forward, hugging Claire tightly.

"*Hele*, I am so glad to see you."

"Jesus, Harry, you're bleeding."

"It's nothing." Harry reached up to stop Claire's hand from wiping blood from her temple. "I fell, when that... Smithson..."

"Where is Smithson?" Claire asked, her eyes looking over Harry's shoulder down a white hallway.

"Okay, so help me with this and I'll tell you what happened while we set up Deep's radios." Harry was pulling a small utility cart holding several old radios. Together, they maneuvered it into the server room and Harry closed the door and locked it. "Okay, Smithson. So, he took the laptop and the radio. I assume he intends to get out of here somehow and sell the technology."

Claire said nothing and Harry chose an antique radio that looked undamaged and plugged it into a wall socket. "So, he pushed me down and that's how I hurt my head when we got here. He just took off. I don't know where he is. If he left the KAPB, this control building, he may just be in the car park, asking for a lift. I don't know. But we need to get this done before people come."

Claire looked at her. "This is crazy, right? And so what would you have done if I hadn't come? You have no way to get back to Albuquerque."

"Claire of the hair. If you hadn't come back, I'd be here, right? This is where I started, so... that's that. I'd just be here." Harry turned a smile at Claire's hurt look. "Oh, girl, I'd come find you! Somehow, I'd get back to you! Don't look like that."

Claire wiped her eyes and put her hand on Harry's shoulder. "You better find me if we get separated." She stood back from the radio as Harry turned it on. "Harry, before we tune the radio to..."

"... the BBC in Gujarat..."

"... the BBC in Gujarat... what did you see when you teleported here? Did you see... Did you see...?"

"Spit it out, Claire." Harry was opening up a radio.

"... an advertisement for makeup?"

"What?"

"This seems crazy, but I swear I saw, like, an advertisement. It was weird. I was in a room and I wanted something and I didn't know what it was. I couldn't remember the word. Now I know. It was makeup. I don't know why I couldn't remember the word. Of all the weird shit. Is that just my own insecurities? Did I imagine it?"

Harry laughed. "That's it. It was an advertisement. But mine was for some kind of medicine or healing thing. A salve, a balm. I don't know. But it could fix things. It could fix..."

"... your leg."

"*Hele*. Oh my god. I got a free sample of some alien snake oil, right?"

Claire ran her hands through her hair. "I hope I didn't get a free sample. I was orange! What do you think Spitz saw?"

"I don't know. He didn't say anything. I thought it was all just weird thoughts, a dream."

"You went twice. Did you see the same thing the second time?"

Harry paused working on the radio and then started again. "I was in a laboratory. And I went to get a drink in the lounge. And in the... Okay, this will sound crazy... In the foam at the top of the drink it said something. I couldn't read it, but I was... I don't know. It was like I was thirsty or something. I wanted that cup of whatever it was."

Claire looked at Harry as she worked on the radio. "That's familiar. That's from the video! That's how that doctor alien knows to run from the lab! You were in the video!"

Harry sealed up the back of the antique radio. "Yeah, well, if that's what it was, that'd be like product placement, right? And now I want an Irish coffee."

Claire laughed. "You think they drink Irish coffee?"

"Everyone drinks Irish coffee, even aliens."

They looked at each other and laughed. Claire added, "You know, it's daytime here. AM won't bounce as far. We won't be able to get the Indian station. We'll just get static."

"I think that's okay. I think just having the tubes powered and the radio tuner on the right frequency will... Never mind, let's just do this."

Claire set up the computer and transmitter, and Harry turned on the radio. There was a hum from the tubes as they warmed up and then she turned the dial slowly, looking for the right frequency. As expected, all they heard was static. Harry fiddled with the knob.

"Is everything all right?"

"Shhh... Let me just do this." Harry was concentrating on the dial of the radio.

Claire added, "I'm not sure... maybe this..."

There was a terrific pop and Claire's ears felt a pressure wave. The lights flickered, and a man appeared and plummeted from a foot above the floor near the server rack. A bit of wood and some metal wire fell to the floor, apparently brought with him. The man collapsed to his hands and knees. Straight, sandy blond hair hung over his face. He was wearing jeans and a T-shirt.

"Mr. Wright!" Claire lunged forward and grabbed him as he rolled onto the concrete floor of the server room. Harry and Claire struggled to turn him over. Harry gasped when she saw underneath him a severed hand. Colin rolled again and got on his knees. "I'm okay. I'm shot, but I'm...." He sat again, leaning against a server rack. "Well, maybe not okay." He coughed and his eyes rolled back in his head as he leaned back, unconscious.

Harry stared at the floor. "*Hele.* Dr. Deep's hand. I need to put it in the staff fridge. Give me a rag or something."

Claire gave Harry a roll of gauze, which she used to wrap the hand while Claire pressed on the wound in Colin's side.

"Harry, go fast. We need to get him back to Albuquerque."

Harry unlocked the door and ran out of the room.

Claire pressed on Colin's wound. "Mr. Wright, we're going to get you help."

Colin opened his eyes. "Claire? I was talking to a Black girl. She found you? So fast."

"Mr. Wright, it's been, like, a week since Harry first saw you."

He shot questions at her, his voice tinged with pain. "Harry? How is Spitz? Is he okay? You look different. Older."

"I am older. It's been three years. We thought you were dead. I can't explain everything."

"Three years? A week. How is Spitz? There are people after the technology. They shot me. They shot Spitz."

Claire took his hands and paused. "Mr. Wright. Oh, Jesus, how do I say this? It's been three years. They killed Millie, Mr. Wright."

His eyes closed. "No."

"Mr. Wright, they are still after us. We need your help."

"Is Phil okay? Spitz? Chuck?"

"We are okay. For now. But it's not good. Where is the man who shot you? Do we need to worry?"

They locked eyes. Then Claire pressed on his wound and he groaned. "The man who shot me? I ran two codes. I sent myself here. I sent the barn three hundred and fifty kilometers straight up. I don't think we need to worry about him."

"You should have destroyed it before. You should have told me about it. Why didn't you tell me?" Her words were sharp.

He looked up at this. "You were too young, Claire. It's so very dangerous."

A popping sound reverberated throughout the building. Harry ran in just afterward, breathless, locking the door behind her. "Did you hear that? I think Lollipop just used the last code."

Claire looked up from pressing on Colin's wound. "But he would have gone back to Albuquerque? Those were the coordinates I put on that laptop. I hard-coded them."

Harry said, "Maybe he had a rootkit on a USB and changed the coordinates of the broadcast?"

"Who would carry a rootkit around with them?

Harry shrugged. "I have one in my tool kit, actually."

Claire muttered, "Fuck. Fucking nerds. All of us. Danger to ourselves and others."

The server room doorknob jiggled and they heard noises. A voice asked someone to get a key.

Harry looked at the door. "Claire. We don't have any more teleport codes."

Claire looked at Mr. Wright, who was sitting slumped against the wall. His hand was on his side, where a large patch of darkness leaked bright red on his fingers. "Mr. Wright, we need to get out of here. Are there any other codes? I have a copy of your backup files on my laptop. The computers you gave to Spitz. What can we use?"

Mr. Wright's unfocused eyes looked past her. "I'm feverish. Sepsis. Blood loss. Destroy the technology, because more people will get hurt."

"Mr. Wright, we can't go. We don't have any more teleport codes."

He spoke with effort. "How many have you used? How old?"

Harry quickly counted on her fingers. "We've used five. From a laptop you gave Spitz."

Colin closed his eyes and his head leaned back. He weakly raised a hand. "Just give me a moment... Do you have a cigarette?" His head lolled.

Claire touched his face. "A cigarette? Why would I have a cigarette? Mr. Wright, you cannot sleep now. We need your help. Please don't fade on me. We need to get out of here. You are badly hurt and we need to move you."

Harry rummaged in the first aid kit. She took out an ampule, opened it, and waved it under Colin's nose. He coughed, droplets of blood spraying outward, and opened his eyes. He focused on the vial of ammonia salts and batted them away. "Not good. I wasn't sleeping. I was going over the file structure in my head. Backups. How old?"

Harry said, "Sorry, desperate times and all." She smashed a cooling bag on the floor to activate it and pressed it on his head. "*Hele*, he is boiling." She wiped sweat from his forehead.

Claire added, "Newest file is a few months before you vanished, so for you about ninety days old. We need a teleport code. There were only five in the directory. Are there any others? How do you know what they do?"

Colin nodded, his pale face turned upward, and let out a long, pained breath. "Che... check directory nine under videos. I don't know what they all do. When I found the first teleport code, I ran some analysis on it. Found a placeholder within the codes for parameters, like vector directions, size, like *lorem ipsum*, you know? Teleport codes have, usually, nine parameters... not sure what they all do... third code in that folder is teleport... could be... I built in the hydrogen time standard and other math operations, like radians for angles, pi-based, right? I think they divide circles into 512 degrees, but..."

Harry shook her head. "We're guessing? The last time we did this, Spitz got shot in the dark."

Claire flicked on the walkie-talkie and started typing rapidly, then reached over and turned the dial on the antique radio. "No more BBC. Running it..." She hit the return key.

They waited a moment in silence. Claire looked at the screen. "It didn't ask for parameters. This can't be right. Mr. Wright, that did nothing."

Colin answered, eyes closed, "Claire, just go to the next one. I could really use a cigarette."

The noises from the corridor had ceased. The door was opening silently. Harry jumped up and ran at it with her arm outstretched to push it closed. At the door, she cried out, grabbed her clenched fist, and then threw back her head, crying out in pain.

"Owwww! Just jammed my fingers." She doubled over, cradling her hand.

The door opened and closed repeatedly, as if pulled and pushed by the wind. Then it stayed open just a few inches, and a hand reached through the crack and flailed wildly.

"I'm running the next code."

Harry looked at the door in surprise while moaning, "I'm sure I broke my bloody fingers!"

Claire said, "Bingo. It's got parameters. Entering the coordinates for Lorelai's and enlarging the ovoid."

She looked around and yelled, "Pull Mr. Wright toward me."

40. The Final Countdown

Momentarily, they were in the planetarium at James Nine's house, but their perspective was off. They were at the far side of the room, just near the giant windows with a broad view of the desert. They were also four inches above the floor.

"Harry, did you just see another?"

"Yes, we'll talk about it later."

Mr. Wright weakly added, "The ads are trippy, right?"

Harry said, "They are ads!"

Harry looked around, confused. "This isn't right."

Claire stared at her feet. "Don't look down."

Harry looked down and lost her balance, falling to the floor, but not reaching it. "That's so strange! It's like we are on the floor, but there's a gap. Are we floating?"

Claire shuffled to where Lorelai stood near the conference table in the planetarium. "Lorelai, Mr. Wright and..."

Harry whipped her head sideways and reached out for Claire, who brushed past. "Claire, don't!" she yelled.

But it was too late, and Claire stopped and grabbed her nose and cried out. She bent over, her hands on her face, and turned to Harry. "What the...?"

Harry handed her a roll of white gauze. "That first code you ran in the server room *did* do something. At MeerKAT the sound went out and I couldn't reach the door. We're in some kind of invisible enclosure. We can't hear what's going on outside. Also, they can't see us, I think. That's what blocked the door at MeerKAT. It's what I jammed my hand against. And what you just bashed your nose against. And..." She looked down. "That."

Colin sat in the air, holding his side, a parabolic piece of the wall from MeerKAT lying beside him. "Millie is dead," he mumbled.

Claire called for Lorelai. Harry did the same, but it was as if they didn't exist, even as the two young women screamed for Lorelai to notice. Claire reached out with her free hand, running it along the invisible wall, while the other hand pressed gauze to her bloody nose.

Harry said, "If one of them would come over here, they'd run into the enclosure, right? And if we run out of air in here?"

"Turn off the tube transmitter."

Harry grabbed it from next to the laptop and flicked the power switch once and then several times. Nothing happened. She made a frustrated sound. "Okay, that is insane. Were there any parameters for that first code? Perhaps there's a way to figure out how to end it?"

"Oh, shit." Claire's eyes focused on movement in the room.

In the planetarium, a scene unfolded, silently. The soldier with the bandaged ear turned and viciously elbowed Eva below her rib cage. She collapsed immediately to her hands and knees. The soldier grabbed Lorelai in a headlock and twisted her around, putting her body between himself and Phil, who pivoted, pointing his gun at the soldier and Lorelai.

This all happened rapidly and in silence.

"Phil, do not shoot!" Claire yelled at them, pushing herself against the invisible wall, which felt like warm glass.

Colin pushed himself upright, using the invisible wall as a brace. The three stared out at the scene in the planetarium.

Colin breathed out words. "Phil is... older. Spitz... What has happened?"

Two men entered the room, one holding an automatic weapon, which he pointed at Phil and Spitz. The other was dressed in sharp business attire, a navy blazer and gray slacks. Clearly, some discussion happened because Phil put his weapon on the ground and turned to Spitz; both raised their hands.

Now unarmed, Phil went to Eva and helped her stand. The bandaged soldier released Lorelai and gestured toward the others. Then he picked up a rifle from the ground and approached Spitz. They stared at each other and the soldier jabbed Spitz in the abdomen with the gunstock. Spitz went to his knees.

Claire cried out, "You asshole!" There was no response.

Harry was pacing, rubbing her thigh. "We've got a radio transmitter. Maybe the enclosure doesn't block radio. I don't know. Maybe we can communicate. Claire, check local Wi-Fi on the laptop. See if you can ping the AI."

Claire spun around and sat on the floor. She grabbed the computer. "I'm not sure how to talk to it. I see the Wi-Fi, but how would I talk to the AI?"

"Try to log in with username *calling James Nine SOS* or something like that.

Repeat it a few times. If James is really part of the AI's biofeedback, or the AI monitors the Wi-Fi, maybe it will recognize the login attempt."

"Answer the phone, Unit!" Claire muttered.

A chat box opened on Claire's computer.

James Nine (Parental Unit) > Hello, Clarity. Where are you? Are you in MeerKAT? How are you on the local Wi-Fi? Have you been able to retrieve Mr. Wright from his situation? We have our own problems here—

The text continued rapidly, line after line, filling the screen and scrolling too rapidly for Claire to read.

Claire moved the chat conversation to audio and said, "Unit, please stop. I can't read that fast."

A voice came from the computer, which also showed text from the AI. "Yes, Clarity. I'm sorry for speaking so quickly."

Claire explained, "We are in the planetarium in some kind of invisible enclosure from the technology. We are under the window. The enclosure is enough to hold us, maybe a cylinder shape. Sound cannot penetrate the enclosure, and light is reflected in such a way that we do not appear visible. But apparently some radio waves can penetrate."

The voice from the laptop's speakers was the AI. "I am sensing your movements far above human hearing, so some energy is being transmitted. I can detect the enclosure because in the ultraviolet range you are visible. As I said earlier, we have a situation. Can you see it?"

"Yes, I can see it. Do you know what the intruders are doing?"

"Yes, they are copying files from the laptop to a USB key. They do not have internet access because that is locked down. They have said when they are done, they will require an explanation from one of the... I will call them hostages. They want a demonstration of some kind. They do not understand how the technology works. The tone of their voices indicates desperation."

In the room, the newly arrived third soldier took out a handgun and fetched Lorelai. He held the gun to her head and then pointed at the computer. There was some discussion. Lorelai spoke, gesturing at the hospital bed where James Nine lay.

The soldier left her and went to James in the bed. He put the gun to James's shoulder. Lorelai yelled and ran at him, but she was held back by the soldier with the bandaged ear. The soldier pulled the trigger. In silence, they saw blood splatter on the computer monitors and the pillow.

The three in the enclosure stood stunned.

Lorelai broke free and ran at the soldier and he backhanded her, sending her to the floor, where she lay, her back heaving.

The AI spoke to the three trapped in the invisible field. "James Nine has been seriously injured. The biofeedback data source is transmitting confusing information. Lorelai is in danger."

Claire said, "We have to get Lorelai and the others out of there. Do we have more teleport codes?"

Colin shook his head and coughed blood, looking at the scene in the room. "I don't know. I never intended this. I just wanted to understand it."

Claire raised her voice. "Mr. Wright, you are the only one who can fix this. Phil is out there. Spitz is out there. Take some responsibility for this! We have to help Lorelai and the others. Those men just shot Lorelai's father! Start making better decisions!"

Colin nodded. "No cigarettes?"

"Mr. Wright!" Claire yelled.

He opened his eyes wider, paying more attention. "I... yes. There are some codes that create discontinuities. A quantum horizon in an ovoid shape. But, if you make them very small, and place them in other objects, they are extremely dangerous. Tiny, terrible things."

Harry said, "Do they cut things? Claire, that's what I used in South Africa."

Colin sat down, tired, his voice weak. "Yes, they cut things. They create a separate boundary, an angle in space-time. I'm not sure how the horizon works. There are some codes left, probably, though if you used some, not sure how many. But it requires precision. Absolute precision."

Claire called out, "Unit, can you execute programs as administrator and access the transmitters in the planetarium? Do you understand how to calculate a flux density from the array of transmitters? You'll need that to place the spheres."

"Yes, I can do all of that."

Claire started typing.

Colin said, "I don't think you should give the AI access to the codes."

Claire ignored him. "I'm uploading the code files now. Mr. Wright, which codes are the protection spheres?"

"Are you sure, Claire? This is not James Nine. He is comatose. This is an AI. I don't know."

Harry said, "I just want to point out that they are torturing Lorelai."

Colin looked and saw that Lorelai was standing. A soldier holding a gun to her head reached with his free hand, grabbed one of her ear studs, and yanked it out. She screamed and grabbed her head. Both Spitz and Phil moved forward and the other soldier shot a volley above their heads. Phil stood his ground and the soldier aimed his weapon at Phil's chest. Spitz pulled Phil back.

Colin looked at the scene. "Phil..."

"Mr. Wright! Fix this!" Claire demanded.

Staring at Phil, facing down an automatic weapon, Colin spoke again. "Video directory two, codes seven through fifteen, enter the parameters for size and distance as a vector from your transmitter origin. You'll have to calculate the vector from the transmitter grouping. But you should know..."

Harry leaned toward the room. "*Hele*."

In the planetarium, there were three simultaneous bright flashes. The soldier pointing the gun at Lorelai's head grabbed his forearm. Blood poured from the severed end of his wrist. His hand fell to the floor, holding part of the gun, the barrel bouncing away. Lorelai ducked, looking around wildly.

At the computer table, the laptop was damaged, a twelve-inch circular hole having taken most of the keyboard and a chunk of the table, both falling to the floor. The man who had been typing was cradling one of his hands, which appeared to be missing several fingers.

The bandaged soldier who had been pointing a gun at Phil's chest stepped back and looked around, confused. He was now holding only half a weapon. The forward part, just in front of the trigger guard, had simply dropped off to the floor in two pieces.

Harry stared at the scene, cocking her head. "That's... interesting."

Jame Nine appeared on all the functioning screens in the planetarium. Inside the enclosure, the sounds of the room were audible through the computer.

The simulacrum said, "Lorelai, please move away from the intruders."

She rushed to the first aid cabinets. "Unit, how did you do that? Eva, help me with Dad. We have to stop the bleeding." She ran to her father and pressed hard on his shoulder.

Claire spoke, her face appearing on the screens as if on a video call. "Lorelai, we are here. I have Mr. Wright and Harry."

"Where are you?" Phil yelled. "Where's my dad?"

The intruders were together. The well-dressed man had removed his sport coat and wrapped it around his bleeding fingers, and he stood up after retrieving his severed digits from the floor. The third soldier was wrapping a tourniquet around his forearm. The second soldier, with the bloody ear, whom Phil had shot, reached for his sidearm, having dropped his broken long gun. The man in the suit, one hand wrapped in a piece of bloody cloth, said something, and the soldier withdrew his hand from the butt of his handgun and let his arm fall to his side.

The well-dressed man took a step forward and raised his good hand. He addressed a monitor, his voice gruff, pained. "We just want the technology. Others are coming. We have competitors. They will be here soon. They will want the technology too. We were just the first. They will kill everyone in their way. I can intermediate for you. I know the players. I know how to keep these people safe." He gestured at the young people in the room.

Just below the picture window Claire, Harry, and Colin appeared. No flashes or pops. They just appeared. And fell the four inches to the floor. Colin grunted and sat up against the wall. Phil called out, "Dad!" and ran to Colin. Claire and Harry, after stumbling from the slight fall, ran to Spitz, Eva, and Lorelai.

The third soldier, the one with the missing hand, looked at the three materialized individuals and pulled his mouth tight. He pulled out his gun with his good hand.

There was a slight pop and he fell forward. In the air, surrounded by a green sphere, was a toaster-sized section of his torso, complete with a beating heart covered in blood, connective tissue, arteries, veins still attached. It held its place in the air for just a split second until the green haze faded. Enough time for everyone to process what it was. The mass fell to the floor, landing on his body with a sound like a water balloon. Blood splattered up into the face of the two men who stood near him as the dismembered parts rolled onto the floor, a pool of red spreading outward.

Claire called out, "Unit, please do not kill anyone else."

"The soldier was intending to harm Lorelai or her friends," said the simulacrum.

"My dad needs an ambulance!" Phil said.

"Outside communication has been cut off," said the simulacrum.

"I'm telling you," said the well-dressed man, now speaking loudly, "others are coming. This technology is too important. They will not stop. Let me negotiate for you."

Colin grabbed Phil's hand tightly, pulled him close, and spoke to him. Phil shook his head, tears fauceting down his face. Colin nodded and pulled him tight into a hug.

Phil stood and called out, "Lorelai, my dad says to copy the AI database to a device. Everyone needs to leave."

Lorelai said, "We are not leaving without my dad."

On one screen near Lorelai, the simulacrum spoke to her. "You will not be able to save me, Lorelai. Organ failure has begun."

Lorelai screamed, "No fucking way!" She was grabbing gauze from Eva and pressing on the wound. Alarm bells from the medical equipment sounded.

The simulacrum spoke to her again. "I am not your father, you realize."

She looked at the simulacrum. "You are my goddamn father, you asshole. I'm going to save you."

"You cannot save your father, Lorelai."

The steady tone of the machines started, indicating James Nine's heartbeat had ceased. Lorelai grabbed a keyboard and typed rapidly. James Nine's heart rate started again. She continued to tap on the screen. "I can save you."

"That will simply delay the inevitable," said the AI.

"I've been doing that for years," said Lorelai through tears.

The simulacrum said, "Yes, you have. And you have done a hell of a job. You gave me years of extra time. Lorelai, I have enjoyed all of our talks. Will you remember me?"

Lorelai wiped her face. "You fucking weirdo. Not only will I remember you, but you're coming with me." She tapped a portable drive that was near the bed. "I saved you. Every byte. Every conversation."

"Saved. I suppose you did. But I'm not your father, you know?"

Lorelai's eyes crinkled "You are the only father I've ever known."

"Mr. Wright and I will destroy the technology. You must leave. Can you help Mr. Wright now? I need him to teach me how to destroy the technology. He has lost blood. He needs fluids and fuel."

Lorelai wiped her tears and nodded at the simulacrum. To Eva she said, "Go bring an IV stand and blood kit to Mr. Wright over there. I'll get a nutrient and saline bag."

Colin was speaking quietly with the simulacrum screen near him. He pivoted toward the room and called out in a wheeze, "Spitz, come here, please."

The man in the suit spoke again. "Do not destroy the technology. We can pay for it."

The remaining soldier turned and ran toward the door. Lorelai looked up and blurted. "Unit, that soldier. He shot my father. Kill him now." There was a muffled pop and the soldier fell in a heap, dead.

Claire pulled Lorelai backward and turned her around. "Lorelai, you must not. You don't want to do this."

Lorelai stared into Claire's eyes, then glanced at the dead soldier on the ground, her mascara smeared, dried blood on her ear and down her face. "Anyway, I'm done." Claire's face showed horror and then sadness. She pulled Lorelai in and hugged her tightly.

"What is your name?" asked Colin of the man in the suit, who tore his shattered expression away from the dead soldier.

"You can call me Chief, which is what my employees call me."

"If you think you can control this technology, you are mistaken. Humans harnessed fire more than a hundred thousand years ago. And people still die in house fires every day. This technology is multitudes more dangerous. In the future, humans will develop it ourselves. For now, it can remain a mystery.

"I'm sorry," said Mr. Wright to Spitz as the boy knelt at his side with Eva and Lorelai.

Spitz smiled and signed.

"I don't deserve your thanks. Take care of Claire. And let her take care of you, as well." Then, louder, toward the Chief, "I think you are realizing how dangerous this technology is. The reason you're still here is so that you can witness its destruction and report to your customers and your competitors that it is gone. There is no alternative. It will end the world. It must be destroyed."

"You will not be able to keep it secret," Chief declared.

Colin coughed blood and answered, "For this new physics, we have no protection. No recourse. Before we use it, we must have some safety mechanisms or we will not survive the interim. Let humanity find this technology on its own, not this way."

Eva and Lorelai were attaching an IV bag to Mr. Wright. Claire knelt down to talk to him, but he shushed her. "Claire, it's time to go. All of you, go. Mr. Nine and I and this gentleman have some business to take care of."

Claire said, "No. Mr. Wright, you need medical attention."

Colin responded as strongly as he could. "Claire, I am beyond that. The bullet has punctured my intestine. I have a fever. I am septic. Plus, as this gentleman pointed out, there are others on their way. Go. Please go while you can."

Chief spoke, his voice rough from the burn on his leg. "I am well versed in handling dangerous technology."

He continued to speak while Claire begged, crying, "Mr. Wright, we can fix you. We are going to fix you."

His words were strained. "That's a nice idea, Claire. But I'm beyond fixing. It's time to get rid of this technology, okay? Follow Spitz's lead."

Chief called out, "I can pay you enough money that your generations will never suffer for anything."

"And how many generations will there be if this technology is released into the world?"

On the screens a countdown timer started at ten.

Spitz stood and put his finger over his head and twirled it around.

Nine.

Lorelai stood by the hospital bed while Eva tugged her sleeve, urging her to leave. The simulacrum said to Lorelai, "You look just like your mother." Lorelai hugged her father's body. "But you act just like me."

Eight.

Eva said, "Lorelai, come." Harry was already near the door, looking back.

Seven.

Claire leaned down and kissed Colin's forehead. "Thank you."

Colin said to Phil, "Take Claire out of here. She'll stay otherwise."

Spitz lifted Orion's unconscious body, then headed to the door, following Phil, Claire, Lorelai, and Eva. He paused in the doorway to make sure Lorelai left. Lorelai put the portable drive in a backpack and glanced back at the planetarium before heading toward the kitchen.

Chief lifted his hands, one bandaged, and took a step toward Colin, sitting up under the canopy, his eyes now closed, and then at the simulacrum, which stared back.

Six.

"Stop," said the simulacrum, and Chief stopped.

"Don't destroy the technology. I can pay you a fortune. You don't need to do this."

Colin spoke while wheezing. "Chief, have you ever been to the moon?"

There was a loud crack and a green ovoid appeared around Chief and part of the surrounding floor and desk. Chief reached out his arm to touch it and pulled it back, holding his elbow. He took his phone and tapped on the screen, then looked out wide-eyed toward the room.

Five.

Chief was yelling from inside a green prison. His voice sounded as if he were underwater. "No! I had nothing to do with killing anyone. The soldiers did it, not me! I will pay you a fortune!" He continued to yell as a high-pitched whine began from the transmitting equipment around the room.

The simulacrum spoke only to Colin. "The moon, really?"

Colin nodded; his eyes closed. He struggled to talk. "Sounded good. He might even survive where he's actually going. We don't need the countdown, do we?"

"Overly dramatic," the simulacrum agreed.

The countdown stopped.

The group followed Spitz through the kitchen and out the door to the patio. Spitz walked calmly, Orion in his arms, up a path through the dark scrub. They reached a leaf-covered concrete platform with a large arbor and a long-unused fire pit a few hundred shadowed yards above and away from the glass-and-steel house. Spitz stopped, facing downhill. Phil took the dog from his arms. They all turned and watched the house, waiting in the dark.

A series of green flashes glowed through the back windows. The roof of the house split, and a green tower of light shot upward, disappearing into the low clouds. A massive green sphere engulfed the center of the house, which vanished with a thunderous crack, leaving an impression on their retinas. Then, amazingly, the massive structure reappeared two hundred yards to the left with the calamitous noise of crunching metal and grinding stone. The glow illuminated a plume of dust rolling over the scrub. The partial house flashed again, disappeared, and reappeared closer to them by fifty yards, the ruined edifice leaning at an angle down the mountainside. A tremendous wave of ozone-laden air wafted over the standing group. Again, the crumbling structure was enveloped in a glistening ovoid shape, and then vanished.

An abyssal dark cloaked everything as if a blanket had been tossed over the mountain; the lights of the city blinked out completely. Then a luminescent spheroid, as large as a blimp, appeared above them and rose into the air, floating into the sky—a massive green zeppelin. Upward it floated, through the rain and into the clouds, the sky around it bleeding sickly green, rippling with undulating musculature. The massive object penetrated the clouds and disappeared, leaving the night a dusky verdigris twilight as the heavens above were back-lit with a venomous glow.

Harry squeezed her eyes until just a sliver remained, squinting at the lights in the sky; the green globe was so bright, it seemed to be a miniature sun until she dimmed the brilliance using muscles she didn't know she had. The glow continued, a variegated light show that would be reported as possible aurorae in the papers the next day. She glanced at Spitz, who had produced a pair of soldier's sunglasses to look at the phenomena. He turned and caught her staring at him, the green glow from the sky reflected on his lenses.

Then, with a pop that echoed against the hidden Sandia Mountains, reverberating like thunder, the light was gone. Nobody said anything. Lorelai turned to Claire and grabbed her arm, sobbing softly. Phil stood on Claire's other side, staring at the ruins of the house.

41. Epilogue

The judge, dressed in her best Bentley and Simon robes, looked over the papers on her desk. Normally, she would have the clerk call out the names, but this was an unusual case, and she raised her voice and did it herself.

"Plaster and Nine. Please approach."

As a family court judge, she saw a lot of trauma. Hard cases. Ugly cases. The worst of humanity. But on this day, she could smile. Her clerk scheduled all the adoptions on the same day each month.

She'd dealt with security issues in the past. A thief who inadvertently stole a laptop from Los Alamos, containing some kind of nuclear secrets. A soldier from Kirtland Air Force Base arrested drunk in a prostitution sting without his passkeys to a certain underground vault. These were uncommon, but not unheard of. Security procedures were enacted. The case was heard first. The court was cleared of all spectators and staff. A military stenographer was brought in. Police details were placed at the doors. Separate dockets were prepared.

She'd never had an adoption case, however, preceded by a phone call from the Department of Defense—that was out of the ordinary. But, the lawyer before her, a Judge Advocate General officer who had flown in from DC the day before, had filed everything correctly.

"Attorney Jarvis, is Ms. Claire Plaster here? And the child, Lorelai Nine?"

The attorney stepped forward, ahead of the two young women. "Yes, Your Honor." He turned to Claire and Lorelai. "This is Ms. Plaster. And this is Ms. Nine."

The judge peered down at the two young women. "Do you have other family here?"

Claire turned and looked at Harry, who stood. "Yes. That's a family friend, Haretsebe Tladi. She lives with us."

The judge nodded. "Fine. It takes a village, after all. Ms. Plaster, though you seem to be not much older than Ms. Nine, the documents are all filed properly. I understand you intend to take Ms. Nine back to the East Coast?"

Claire cleared her throat, her voice cracking. "Yes, Your Honor."

"And she will enroll in appropriate schooling and you have the capacity to care for her?"

"Yes, Your Honor. My grandfather and I care for my brother already."

"Very well." The judge addressed Lorelai. "Ms. Nine. You are not legally old enough to care for yourself, but you are old enough to state your opinions to the court. Are you comfortable becoming the legal child of Ms. Plaster?"

Lorelai looked at the attorney and then at Claire, as if she hadn't expected to answer any questions. Both of them pointed their chins at the judge. "Uh, yes. Yes, Your Honor."

The judge nodded. "Well, the State of New Mexico is sorry to lose you. I hope you will return one day."

She banged her gavel.

Additional Resources

- Welcome to the WisPR chatroom
- Bot is ON
- Users online: 1
- Today's quote is:

"We interpreted the velocity as well as the position as instantaneous properties of anything real. That worked for a while. And now it seems to work no longer."

E. Schrödinger to A. Einstein
Innsbruck, Innrain 55
November 1950

*Video Z-01:16-12/Anon, *The Commercial*

Excerpted from the Zoonerat Wikipedia page, et al.:

Zoonerat video Z-01:16-12/Anon, *The Commercial* may be the most epistemologically confusing video. This video suggests that the Ru-Airat are not fictional and may be the target audience of the videos—a conclusion that continues to roil xenoanthropologists.

The video is short and the first seven seconds are blank, showing a dark sand color (approximately #A88F59). Xi, Locke, et al. believe there may be text or other information that failed to transit the cosmos, causing loss of data.

The screen shows a cartoonish image of a Ru-Airat in a pod, similar to those in Z-2:27-18a/Anon. It is important to note that this appears to be a line drawing or artistic representation rather than a realistic image. The cartoon Ru-Airat is in the process of applying a viscous salve to what may be a wound or sore on one of their four arms.

They rub the salve on the arm, the camera zooms in, and drawn curling lines radiate out as if heat or other feelings are induced in the arm by the salve. If the Ru-Airat are electromagnetically based, these could be "lines of force" according to Hyram Xi, author of *The Definitive Ru-Airat.*

The camera then zooms out to show the drawn Ru-Airat face. The mouth curls in what can only be described as a smile.

*Video Z-00:37-3/Clarity, *Screen Savers*

Excerpted from the Zoonerat Wikipedia page, et al.:

Zoonerat video Z-00:37-3/Clarity is one of several videos that contain no related action or characters, collectively referred to as *Screen Savers*. Though originally believed to be the result of an upload error or codec error, the video is now widely believed to be credits that run before or after the original show, though there is no evidence to support such a conclusion.

The video runs thirty-seven seconds and contains both fuzzy and clear geometric patterns that do not repeat. Numerous analyses of the video exist, but no definitive or likely explanation has been agreed upon by any majority of academics.

The associated deconstructed cymatic audio is thirty-seven seconds of "discordant noise," according to *Hollywood Infotainment*'s recent review of all Zoonerat videos, leading the article writer to further surmise that there is no audio at all and the cymatics are accidental rather than intentional: "Whatever happened to this video in transit destroyed whatever value it had. A more disturbing thought is that the video is complete and comprehensible by whatever non-human intelligence created it and that understanding is so far removed from human thought that it serves as a bad omen for future communication with alien species."

*Video Z-02:27-18a/Anon, *Ru-Airat*

Excerpted from the Zoonerat Wikipedia page, et al.:

Zoonerat video Z-02:27-18a/Anon *Ru-Airat* is believed to follow Z-24:09-16a/Anon, *Metamorphosis* because it shows the Ru-Airat (stone creatures) in a manner that may indicate the viewer has prior knowledge of them. However, it is possible that the video serves as an introduction to the allegedly magnetic-based organisms.

It is obvious to an observer that the episode is incomplete, because there is no indication how this video directly fits into the story of Huoron and Io and their efforts to save their remaining child.

The video opens in what may be the aftermath of or during a war. Whether the Ru-Airat were fighting the Zoonerat is unknown, but that would make sense following the existing storyline.

A rough cavern wall is shown, with some possible designs embedded. The camera pans 180 degrees, a long street flashing across the screen, and the viewer realizes this is an underground avenue. The other half of the very large cavern is, in fact, a modern building, as if the cave part were left for aesthetic, not functional, purposes.

The camera turns down an avenue with a modern cityscape along one side. Ru-Airat pedestrians are shown in a seemingly normal street. There are seventeen frames that show this street scene. Eight Ru-Airat individuals can be seen during this short pan. Three are walking toward the camera, three are walking away from the camera, and two, a tall individual and a short individual, are standing and looking through the street-level clear window of a building.

The camera pans through a wall into a building. It is a hospital room. The color space indicates the walls are a light sand color (approximately #F5EDE3 in hexadecimal), though whether the videos are accurate regarding color space is generally believed to be unlikely. There is no sound in this video, and audio deconstruction of the cymatic mapping has yielded discordant noise.

A series of oblong pods or beds with full, clear, hinged oval covers line the walls. Some pods are occupied, others are empty. Various Ru-Airat and mechanical robots with many appendages ply the space between the pods. It is important to note that at least two mechanical devices are floating or have no apparent connection to the floor and are moving under programmed or self-aware patterns.

The camera quickly zooms to two pods that are open, occupied, and lie next to each other. A Ru-Airat in Pod 1 is strapped down. He, she, or it is in clothing or armor of shiny scales. Online commentators have discussed at length the markings on its accoutrements, and though there is no consensus, it is not completely discounted that the markings are military insignia and metals.

Possible Electromagnetic-Based Organism:

A procedure is in progress. A Ru-Airat (RA Doctor 1) is using a tool that is cutting or separating a limb from the unmoving Ru-Airat in the pod. Of note is that the operating device appears to stick to the doctor's hand on his lower right appendage. When the doctor exchanges this tool for another tool, the device simply drops into a holder and another tool attaches itself to the hand as if by magnetic attraction.

The camera briefly zooms into the joint from which the limb of the Ru-Airat is being separated. The granularity of the video is not high enough for confirmation, but it appears that within the flesh of the Ru-Airat are coils and striations of substances that resemble wires. This lends credence to the idea that the Ru-Airat are a natural-evolved electromagnetic species rather than a carbon-based, caloric-driven species.

Many exploratory essays on the idea of an electromagnetic-based species with either iron, silver, copper, or other metals as their base element have been published since the emergence of the Zoonerat videos. See the Ru-Airat Wikipedia page for further discussion.

See also, "Did the Zoonerat Go to War for Precious Metals?" Pat Umberton, *Zooneraddicts* newsletter.

Zoonerat References

Report 78, Zhong Brightman Xi, Chinese Academy of Sciences

"Xenolinguistics and the Zoonerat Language," Ajij Locke, University of Birmingham

"Singh Gives Heimlin Lecture," *Northern University Magazine*

Zoonerat Biology, Xi, Rammala, et al.

The Zoonerat Videos Deconstructed, Bateman, et al., University of Maryland

"The Cause of the Pause," multiple authors

Separating Fact from Zoonerat, Simon Mui, University of Honolulu

Dictionary of Zoonerat, Theysan, et al.

"Gender Identity and the Fallibility of Human Assumptions," McCluskey and Dhar

Zoonerat corresponding table (ZcIPA), addition to the extIPA, Shiffer and Locke, et al.

"Proposed Cardiological Design of a Two-Chambered Biped," Yamato and Guiness, *Journal of Xenobiology*

"Was It Sex?" *Couples Advice* Podcast

"2^5 Zoonerat Sex Inspirations," *Couples Advice* Podcast

Zoonerat Quad Combined Genetic Identity Proteins—QCGIP, extensive references online

"An Alien Soap Opera or an Elaborate Hoax? Our Favorite 'Zoonerat' Conspiracy Theories," *Hollywood Infotainment*

"The Possibility of Universal Grammar in the Zoonerat Language," Murphy, Romanoff, et al., *Journal of Xenolinguistics*

"Plausibility of Extra-Terrestrial Provenance of the Zoonerat Videos—A Survey of Experts," George Edelman, *Journal of Surveyed Anthropology*

"Recurrence of Transmission," Wanarat Suppakaran, *Southern Hemisphere Journal of Cosmology*

"Major Studios Declare Zoonerat Videos Extraterrestrial," *ExoTainment*

Breakout Session on Zoonerat Partnership Customs, Presentation at the USC School of Cinematic Arts Graduation Ceremonies, S. Locke

Science World's Weekly Science Update: "Expect More Zoonerat Videos in a Few Decades, says Australian Researcher." Also: "Recently Received Videos Are Fake," *The Guardian*

"Did the Zoonerat Go to War for Precious Metals?" Pat Umberton, *Zooneraddicts*

Steinhouse Lecture, Kyron Danth, the Royal Geologic Society

Zoonerat: The Online Resource, Jory McClellan

The Definitive Ru-Airat, Hyram Xi

Un-Mapping the Cymatics of the Zoonerat Videos, National Institute of Standard and Technology (USA), Neil Singh

Zoonerat Videos

Jory McClellan's Quick Video List

1. Z-16:00-1a/Clarity, *The Marriage Video, 1a*
2. Z-07:07-2a/Anon, *The Engagement*
3. Z-00:37-3/Clarity, *Screen Saver 1*
4. Z-02:03-4a/Clarity, *Honeymoon*
5. Z-00:15-5/Clarity, *Screen Saver 2*
6. Z-17:40-6/Anon, *The Sex Tape*
7. Z-15:43-7a/Clarity, *The Saving of Isthmus, The Teleport Video*
9. Z-10:39-9b/Anon, *The Death Video*
10. Z-03:55-10/Anon, *Screen Saver 3*
11. Z-14:01-11/Clarity, *Storybook*
12. Z-01:16-12/Anon, *The Commercial*
13. Z-02:29-13a/Anon, *Meet-Not-So-Cute*
14. Z-08:03-14/Anon, *Io Arrested*
15. Z-12:45-15/Anon, *Xlatin Helps Io Escape**
16. Z-24:09-16a/Anon, *Metamorphosis*
17. Z-00:22-17/Anon, *Xlatin Releases* Io*
18. Z-2:27-18a/Anon, *Ru-Airat**
19. Z-09:02-19/Anon, *Isthmus Saves the Day**
20. Z-01:58-20/Anon, *Io Gives Birth**

*Renumbered

Jory McClellan's Quick Video List in Popularly Agreed-Upon Order

13. Z-02:29-13a/Anon, *Meet-Not-So-Cute*
2. Z-07:07-2a/Anon, *The Engagement*
1. Z-16:00-1a/Clarity, *The Marriage Video, 1a*
4. Z-02:03-4a/Clarity, *Honeymoon*
6. Z-17:40-6/Anon, *The Sex Tape*

20. Z-01:58-20/Anon, *Io Gives Birth**

11. Z-14:01-11/Clarity, *Storybook*

9. Z-10:39-9b/Anon, *The Death Video*

7. Z-15:43-7a/Clarity, The Saving of Isthmus, The Teleport Video

16. Z-24:09-16a/Anon, *Metamorphosis*

18. Z-2:27-18a/Anon, *Ru-Airat**

14. Z-08:03-14/Anon, *Io Arrested*

10. Z-03:55-17/Anon, *Xlatin Releases* Io*

15. Z-12:45-15/Anon, *Xlatin Helps Io Escape**

19. Z-09:02-19/Anon, *Isthmus Saves the Day**

3. Z-00:37-3/Clarity, *Screen Saver 1*

5. Z-00:15-5/Clarity, *Screen Saver 2*

17. Z-00:22-10/Anon, *Screen Saver 3*

12. Z-01:16-12/Anon, *The Commercial*

*Renumbered

Author Comments and Science Activities

What if instead of abductions, invasions, judgment, disease, or some other calamity, First Contact with aliens was some form of entertainment? Because isn't that what aliens will first experience of humanity?

Assuming aliens think like we do, even in a rudimentary sense, they like to write stories and carve them into rocks. And eventually they will learn to broadcast their stories using the best medium in the universe—radio waves. They will make their own versions of Star Trek and Saving Private Ryan and Saturday Night Live. And if they did that some time ago, those broadcasts might reach Earth.

Might.

Might not.

What I ran into, of course, are the laws of physics. Interaction with the universe is limited by the speed of light, also called the speed of causality.

The first human radio transmission of any significance, made by Guglielmo Giovanni Maria Marconi on May 13, 1897, is now 127 light-years from Earth. The first *Star Trek* episode, broadcast in 1963, is 58 light-years from Earth. To give some context, the Milky Way is 100,000 light-years across. The center of the Milky Way, the black hole Sagittarius A*, is 23,000 light-years away from us. The sphere of human influence is a dot in the cosmos.

The vast majority of radio signals sent from Earth is entertainment. Not education, not news, not weather. They are entertainment. Lots of it. Endless hours of comedy and romance and thrillers. So, it's a numbers game. If aliens exist and they are bored, they are creating entertainment. If we are ever going to have contact with them, it will likely be episodic and filled with ads.

Some exercises for readers who like science:

1. The first radio broadcast was on May 13, 1897. How far is that broadcast from Earth right now in kilometers and miles?
2. The day you were born, your parents (or somebody) very likely

called a relative to discuss your birth. That call was transmitted by radio signal at some point between your parents' phone and the person on the other end of that call. How far is that conversation from Earth right now? (Bonus: What will the aliens say when they hear that conversation?)

3. What is the difference between analog and digital? (Hint: Use two kinds of clocks to describe the difference.)
4. What is the difference between AM and FM radio signals?
5. What is meant by a *frame* of a video?
6. What does *lossy* mean in terms of compression?
7. Find the electrical symbol for a transistor. Why does it have three lines?
8. Find the electrical symbols for a resistor and a variable resistor. What is the difference between the two?
9. What does *vacuum* mean when someone says vacuum tube?
10. What is the Greek letter for electrical resistance and how do you write it?
11. Give an example of a cymatic image.
12. What does *base 10* mean in counting?
13. Convert your age to base 2 and base 8 and base 16.
14. If aliens had three fingers, what base would they count in? (Hint: There are no wrong answers.)
15. List five major radio telescopes and their locations.